DIABLO®

MOON
OF THE SPIDER

DIABLO®

MOON
OF THE SPIDER

RICHARD A. KNAAK

Library of Congress Cataloging-in-Publication Data available.

ISBN: 978-1-956916-17-1

First Pocket Books printing: January 2006
First Blizzard Entertainment printing: March 2023

10 9 8 7 6 5 4 3 2 1

Cover art by Glenn Rane

Printed in China

For all those readers asking for more
of Zayl and Humbart . . .

MOON
OF THE SPIDER

⊕NE

✳

The thick, gray clouds enshrouded much of the northern side of the mountains. A chill wind cut deep into the flesh of every man in the party save the slim cowled figure in the thin, black travel cloak guiding the party. At this level, there were even traces of snow and, especially, frost. The frost was very prevalent, giving the forest of firs through which they stalked a deathlike sheen.

Two paces behind their guide, Lord Aldric Jitan drew his own thickly furred cloak tighter. From under the hood of the rich brown and white garment, the red-haired noble's narrow eyes—one deep brown and the other ice-blue—darted back and forth along the landscape, seeking. His square jaw clenched in impatience.

"How much farther, sorcerer?" he muttered, his words accompanied by dense white clouds.

"Not much farther at all, my lord," the black-clad figure calmly replied. Unlike the noble and the five burly men-at-arms, he strode along the uneven path as if on a pleasant afternoon hike. His voice was surprisingly deep for so thin and studious-sounding a figure, even deeper than Lord Jitan's. He glanced back at the broad-shouldered aristocrat—a man built much like the fighters who served him—revealing glimpses of a head with short-cropped gray hair and an angular face with matching eyes so narrow they made Aldric's seem round. The skin had a darker, slightly yellowish cast to it, almost as if the speaker suffered jaundice. "In fact, I daresay, the first hints will soon manifest themselves."

"I sense nothing."

"Your skills are not honed as mine are, my lord, but that shall be remedied soon enough, yes?"

Aldric grunted. "That's the point of all of this, isn't it, sorcerer?"

The lead figure turned his gaze forward, leaving the noble only the back of his black hood at which to gaze. "Yes, my lord."

They fell to silence again. Behind Aldric, the five servants struggled under heavy packs. In addition to foodstuffs and blankets, they carried pickaxes, huge hammers, and shovels. Each man also wore a sword at his side. As desolate as this forest seemed, there were dangers, especially from night howlers. The huge beastmen were rare to find—not that most were so foolish as to go hunting for them—but when encountered had to be slain quickly. Night howlers thrived on meat, including human flesh. Legend said that they had not always been so monstrous, but no one in the Western Kingdoms cared about such legends. It was the blood-soaked facts that mattered. The only good night howler was a dead one.

After all, as Lord Aldric Jitan could attest, the dead ones at least made for fine, warm cloaks like the one he wore.

Several more minutes passed and still the noble sensed nothing. He probed for some distance ahead and only noted the continual emptiness of the mountainous land. Even for this part of southeastern Westmarch, the region was desolate. Not at all like the lowlands, where the lush, rich soil and pleasant rainfall made this part of the Western Kingdoms the envy of all other regions of the world. Even the thick fir forest through which they trudged felt sterile, more a ghost than a living thing.

Lord Jitan grunted. And this had once been the heart of ancient Westmarch? This had once been where the vast, dominating estates of the Sons of Rakkis had loomed over the first, burgeoning kingdoms of the land? The moldering parchments and crumbling stone slabs through which Aldric had for months pored had spoken of a much warmer, much more regal land, of huge city-sized estates, each of them run by one of the five lines descended from the legendary paladin-lord.

Few today knew the origins of King Rakkis—founder and first ruler of Westmarch—and most of those, Aldric included, understood only that he had come from somewhere in the east, possibly even beyond the jungles of Kehjistan. As one who believed himself descended from that very same lord, Aldric thought this most definitely the case and the explanation for the narrowness of his own eyes.

What had happened to the last of the Rakkis line was up to conjecture, albeit by very few since the legacy was all but forgotten in modern times. Lord Jitan gathered from what little existed that, somewhere deep in the past, there had been a struggle for power between factions over an object of power. In fact, there had been more than one reference to it, and that had been what had first instigated him to search on. Yet, until the chance encounter with his foreign companion ahead, the noble had found only dead ends.

And dead ends were not something Aldric needed. The dreams were growing worse with each night. They tortured and beguiled him at the same time. They hinted of enemies seeking his weaknesses, shadowy figures who had become so very real to Aldric despite never having clear faces or intelligible voices. Each night, the whispering phantoms drew closer to overtaking him, and each night the fear in him swelled greater. Often, he woke full of sweat, certain that his screams had been heard throughout his estate.

But those dreams had also given him the first clue, the one that had led to the history of the Lords Rakkis and, finally, to this climb into the chill mountain region. Each time Aldric had nearly been taken by his faceless, horrific enemies, something had saved him. At first, it had been only an indistinct object, one that had appeared magically in his cupped palms. In progressive dreams, however, it had taken on form, gradually becoming a sphere, a huge pearl with odd yet familiar markings. At the same time, hints of the Rakkis ties to it had materialized—old, rotting banners with the House symbol still intact, dank catacombs with the snarling wolf carved into the stone, and more.

Most men would have simply thought themselves mad, but then, most men were not Lord Aldric Jitan. Even before he had determined that within him coursed the blood of the Sons of Rakkis, Aldric had known that he was of a select few. After all, he had been gifted with the touch of magic. His skills were slight, true, but in the dreams, they had grown when he had touched the gigantic pearl. That had, in fact, been the only reason his dream self had thus far survived.

And if Lord Jitan was to survive in the waking world, did it not make sense that he find what his subconscious kept steering him toward? Did not all his dreams and research mean to culminate in locating what the eastern devil called—

"The Moon of the Spider . . ."

Aldric stood as if suddenly as frozen as the trees around him. He glared ahead hopefully, but saw only more of the same bleakness.

"Sorcerer!" the noble snapped. "What by the Lords was that utterance for? There's nothing here!"

His guide did not even look back. "Your senses are not attuned enough, my lord. You cannot see what there is to be seen, but I promise that it lies just before us." One arm stretched back, the narrow, yellowed hand gesturing Aldric forward. "Step up and I will show you a taste of what you desire to wield."

Lord Jitan needed no encouragement. Driven by his demons, he battled his way up to where the slim figure awaited him. The five servants, much more encumbered, did their best to follow their master.

"Where? Where, damn it?" All that stood before him were mounds of stone and ice and the same endless forest.

The yellowed hand suddenly reached out and seized his

own, squeezing with a strength that made Aldric wince. "See . . ."

And the western aristocrat did.

Everything was as it had been before, and yet now Aldric saw distinctions that his sweeping glance had so quickly dismissed. The mounds of stone and ice had definition, if one only looked close. Definition that nature could not have created on its own.

Lord Jitan stared up the length of the mountainside and took in the full scope of what those definitions meant.

"Can you sense it now?" asked his companion, releasing his grip on the noble.

Aldric nodded. How could he miss it now? More to the point, how could he have not sensed it in the first place?

The stronghold of the last of the Sons of Rakkis . . .

Ahead lay what to the ignorant simply appeared a large, oval depression between two ridges. Of course, those ridges were much too uniform and, to Aldric's now-awakened senses, were the flanking walls of the entrance to a much larger structure rising up several stories above. The Lords Rakkis had built their massive estates into the very mountains, carving out the rock where needed, adapting where it was not. Now Aldric saw the stepped city that they had built, each level once luxurious and spanning. There were small terraced villas and gardened walkways, all draped by the culmination of centuries of weather. Higher up stood a tower from which the ruler himself would have looked down upon his realm. Aldric squinted, noting that what had appeared to be an outcropping near the top was actually the thrusting arm of a great statue that might very well have been of Rakkis himself.

The noble grinned as he drank in the truth. Buried beneath the snow, ice, and stone was an structure to rival any of which he had seen or heard, especially in Westmarch.

Behind him, the men-at-arms muttered excitedly among themselves. They no doubt thought of treasure. Aldric paid them little mind. He already knew that anything of such base value had long been stripped away in the aftermath of the Lords' downfall. The riffraff would have to be satisfied with what he so generously paid them.

But as for his own treasure quest . . .

His eyes were drawn to the depression at the base of the sprawling ruins. Marching up to it, Lord Jitan confronted the layers of earth and ice he was now certain kept him from his goal. He turned back to his servants, snapping, "Well? Drop that gear and come dig!"

They immediately set to work, rightly fearful of their lord's wrath. As the clatter of picks and shovels echoed throughout the otherwise still region, Aldric could not help feeling as if the clamor might somehow stir up the ancient rulers themselves. Curiously, he found himself more fascinated than uneasy. So little was known of them and, as likely one of their last descendants, Aldric felt their history was his. Had matters turned out differently, perhaps *he* would have now sat in that high tower, master of all Westmarch and beyond.

Master of *all* . . .

It occurred to the aristocrat then that perhaps it was even they who had reached out from the abyss of death to give him this key to his future. With it, *all* his enemies, known and otherwise, would be swept away before him. Then—

A heavyset, flaxen-haired servant wielding a pickax abruptly screamed. He and his weapon fell through a sudden collapse in the ice and rock, a darkness like a hungering mouth swallowing him in an instant. The other workers leapt back rather than risk themselves in a vain attempt to save him.

Lord Jitan reached the hole just in time to hear the fatal thud. He ignored the mishap, instead eagerly peering down into the darkness.

"A light! I need a light!" he ordered.

No sooner had he demanded it than suddenly a pale, bone-white glow appeared next to him. It emanated from an object in the hooded figure's hand. The voluminous sleeves of the cloak obscured it from Aldric's view, but all that mattered to the noble was that now he had the means by which to see what lay within the mouth.

Cracked stone steps turned on a rightward spiral for two floors. The hapless worker's broken body lay to the side of the bottom step, his pickax just at the edge of the illumination.

"Shall we descend, my lord?" asked the shrouded spell-caster.

Lord Jitan answered by immediately doing so. The figure next to him chuckled, then followed after.

The peculiar illumination wielded by Aldric's guide cast an eerie presence over the stone chamber as the party descended. In it, savage lupine creatures seemed to leap from the very walls themselves . . . more stone gargoyles following the wolf motif of the ancient lords. The heads of each were three times as large as that of a man and the huge, toothy jaws stood open as if ready to seize any who dared step near. The sleek heads stretched back to power-ful shoulders. Even a pair of wicked paws thrust out beneath each head.

The detail was so remarkable that Lord Jitan could make out the individual hairs on the heads. The sudden urge came to touch one, to see how it felt, but as he took a step closer to the nearest, a sense of foreboding filled him. With a frown, the noble immediately stepped away.

His hooded companion moved on ahead, illuminating more of the long chamber. An intake of breath—the first break in the spellcaster's ever-calm demeanor—immediately caught Aldric's complete attention.

"What is—" He got no further, for words escaped him then.

A sarcophagus.

It was tall and rounded. At least the height of a man and three times that from front to back, it had been built from a substance Aldric did not recognize. Not stone, for none that he had ever seen, not even the whitest marble, could compare with its sleek, gleaming finish. In fact, as the two drew closer, it *shimmered* in the pale light, almost as if alive.

Pearl. That was what it reminded Aldric of. Iridescent pearl. It was as if the thing before him had been created from a single, gigantic pearl.

No matter where he looked, he could see no construction seam. There was something more curious, though. Aldric Jitan studied the curvature, the curious markings that, the longer he stared at them, seemed to radiate with a light of their own.

"This is not of the Sons of Rakkis. . . . It should not be here!"

The other shook his hooded head. "No, my lord, it is not of the wolf lords. Did you expect it to be? This is Vizjerei work you see . . . and, yes, it should be exactly here."

The noble waited for further explanation, but none was forthcoming. Unable to contain himself any longer, Aldric inspected the sarcophagus more closely. As he did, he spied another marking higher up, one at the edge of the light.

"Sorcerer . . ."

His guide shifted, the light now sweeping across the symbol that Aldric wanted to see.

One of the servants gasped at the sight revealed, stumbling back in surprise. He hesitated directly in front of one of the great wolf heads.

With an ear-splitting roar, the head stretched forth, its mouth opening wide. The jaws enveloped the stunned man's head, clamping tight.

It bit down.

The headless body tumbled to the floor. Immediately, the stone wolf receded to its previous position . . . then stilled. Its jaws remained shut, but crimson drops now dotted the floor beneath.

The remaining three attendants started retreating to the steps, but a fierce look from Lord Jitan drew them forward again. Satisfied of his control over them, he gazed once more in rapt attention at the symbol draping the upper part of the elaborate sarcophagus. Despite the forces he could now feel emanating from within, Aldric did not hesitate to bring his finger up and trace along the vivid crimson outline that had so frightened his followers.

A huge circle . . . and within it, the stylized shape of a menacing, eight-limbed creature. An arachnid.

"The sign of the Moon of the Spider," the noble whispered.

"Did I not promise?" asked the other.

Lord Jitan began seeking some manner by which to open the sarcophagus, but his grasping fingers could still discover no crack, no handle. "Are we in time?"

"We are."

The more his efforts proved for naught, the more frantic Aldric's search became. He started banging his fists on the top, striking the spider emblem hard.

Finally frustrated, Aldric whirled on his servants. "Break it open! Hurry!"

With clear reluctance, they came forward with pickaxes.

"My lord—" began the hooded spellcaster.

Jitan did not listen. He pointed at the center of the arachnid. "There! Strike there!"

As one, the trio laid into the effort, striking with practiced efficiency. Once, twice, thrice, each tool bit into the top of the sarcophagus, almost always pinpointing the spider symbol perfectly.

But not one of the strikes so much as marred the surface of the structure.

The head of one pickax cracked off, flying through the chamber and clattering against a wall. At that point, Aldric ordered the three men back.

"Sorcerer?"

"I have the means, yes."

An enraged Lord Jitan turned on his guide. "Then why did you let us waste precious moments?"

Rather than point out that he had attempted to tell the noble earlier, the spellcaster suggested, "Those three would make better use of themselves at the moment lighting torches. We will need the fires' illumination in a moment."

A wave of Aldric's hand set the servants to work. Within seconds, two of them wielded blazing torches.

At that point, the outlander hid away the object he had used to first light up the tomb. Pushing back his hood, he surveyed with satisfaction the sarcophagus.

"I'm waiting!" snapped Aldric.

"Patience is essential to the Balance." One hand came up. In the palm, a tiny black crystal glittered. "As is sacrifice."

Suddenly, the crystal sprouted *tiny legs* . . . eight in all. To the astonishment of all save its master, it leapt from the palm, landing readily atop the symbol on the sarcophagus.

Where the pickaxes had made not even the least penetration, the eight limbs thrust with utmost ease into various parts of the lid surrounding the center of the crimson image.

There was a brief hiss . . . and the rounded top slid back.

Lord Aldric Jitan did not question where his companion had procured the macabre key. All that mattered was that the way was open. Leaning, he eyed the contents.

A long, robed form lay stretched within. There was something amiss about it.

"Bring the torches up!" Aldric commanded.

In the fire, the occupant was revealed. Although he had already expected it not to be the remains of one of the Lords Rakkis, the identity of the entombed figure still startled him.

"It's one of their own! A Vizjerei!"

The Vizjerei were sorcerers whose origin also lay in the east, but they were of a more worldly nature than Aldric's companion. They had ambitions and desires and in his life Lord Jitan had paid some of them for nefarious services. Not all were of such dubious nature, but to Aldric, the distinction between good and bad Vizjerei was negligible.

But why waste such effort for the burial of one of their

own in this of all places? Why make such a trek here in the first place?

Skin still covered the bones of this ancient spellcaster, as did wisps of a long, gray beard and hair. The familiar, orange-colored, wide-shouldered robes called the *turinnash*—a style hardly changed after centuries—wrapped around the emaciated body. Golden runes supposedly designed to enhance the wearer's power and protect him from harm lined the garment. A gold breastplate and belt gave some hint of past glory and riches, but such things were of no interest to the noble. At the mummy's left side lay one of the rune-etched staves generally wielded by those of the order.

And in the gnarled, gaunt hands resting atop lay the object of Lord Jitan's quest.

It was not as large as in his dreams, but it was no less spectacular. The size of an apple, maybe a bit more, but that was it. It resembled a pearl of lunar radiance—a perfectly round moon—that somehow made the sarcophagus seem crude and dull. An entire city—nay, *all* of Westmarch—could surely have been bought with it.

Had there been no more to the artifact's appearance, perhaps Aldric would have done just that, for then it would have been otherwise useless to him. As it was, though, even the clawed fingers of the dead Vizjerei could not obscure the eight ebony streaks perfectly crisscrossing the pearl. They were the reason for its name, the reason he had sought this treasure out.

They were the reason it was called the Moon of the Spider.

Lord Jitan started to reach for it, but his shadowed companion prevented his hand from rising.

"Taking from the dead is hardly the work of one of your station, my lord," he suggested to Aldric, his low tone hinting of something more than the proprieties of caste.

Brow arched, Aldric snapped his fingers at the nearest manservant. "Rolf! Retrieve that for me."

Rolf grimaced, then bowed his head. Handing his torch

to one of the others, he strode up to the sarcophagus. With a grunt, he reached two beefy hands toward his master's prize.

His fingers grazed those of the cloaked cadaver.

Rolf howled. A fiery aura spread forth from the Vizjerei's corpse to manservant and back again.

The transformation took place in less than the blink of an eye. The very life essence was sucked from Rolf as Lord Jitan might have sucked the juice from a piece of orange. The manservant's skin shriveled and his eyes sank into their sockets. His burly form melted into a wrinkled skeleton. He tried to the very end to pull free, but could not.

And as his dry corpse collapsed in a grisly heap upon the floor, the mummified Vizjerei sat up.

His skin was still dry and cracked, but there was some flesh beneath it now. The ghoulish visage shifted, yellowed teeth suddenly bared and the lids opening to reveal not eyes but a sickly yellow pus.

A guttural sound arose from the empty throat and in that same moment, Aldric sensed powerful magical forces arising.

Something surrounded by a pale glow flew from the direction of the noble's spellcaster. Aldric expected it to strike where the ghoul's heart had once been, but instead it curved upward at the last, burying itself in the decaying figure's forehead.

The cadaverous ghoul uttered a harsh gasp . . . and crumpled back into the sarcophagus, his body turning to ash at the same time.

The gray-haired man beside Aldric quietly and calmly walked up to the dust-laden remains and easily pulled free what he had tossed at the ghoul. A dagger, but one that Lord Jitan knew had not been forged from metal. It was white, but the white of ivory . . . or bone. Even with the torches near, its pale illumination was still noticeable.

"The path to your desires is now open, my lord," its wielder remarked.

Unwilling to wait any longer, Aldric Jitan dared seize

the Moon of the Spider from what fragments remained of the Vizjerei's fingers. No terrible spell seized him, no ghoul leapt up to suck his soul away.

It was *his*. At last, it was his.

"The first step," remarked his gray companion. "Now we must prepare for the rest. You do recall that, do you not, my lord?"

"I recall very well, Karybdus," Aldric murmured, using the other's name for the first time in days. He stroked the artifact as if it were a lover, tracing, as he had with the sarcophagus, the lines from which it drew its name.

Karybdus began removing his travel cloak. In the same calm, studious tone he ever used, he said, "Then, we must begin now. Time is of the essence."

And as his cloak slipped to the floor, Karybdus's own garments were better revealed. Utter black, save for a curious trio of bands across the upper chest and another that stretched down the midsection. One shoulder also bore a jutting, protective cover . . . which on close inspection an onlooker would have realized was the skull of a horned and fanged creature that could have never walked the mortal plane in life. It and the bands were all the same in color: *bone*-white.

Much of what the gray-eyed spellcaster wore resembled armor of a reptilian look, with ridges and scales. Despite that, when Karybdus moved, his garments flowed as if silk and he made no sound whatsoever. His leather boots rose above the knee and melded perfectly with the rest of his armor.

And at his waist, he carried the dagger which had so readily slain the undead Vizjerei. It still glowed, pulsating as if with a life of its own. The blade had a serpentine shape, coiling back and forth before ending in a pin-sharp point.

Upon its hilt was the one symbol to mark Karybdus's identity with any certainty, an almost invisible image seared into the handle. It was the tiny icon of a serpentine creature over whom hung a pair of weighing scales.

Though some might have readily recognized the beast as a dragon, only the rare outsider would know why the scales were set so.

The dragon was known as Trag'Oul: He Who Is the Fulcrum of the Balance. Trag'Oul was as near to a god as Karybdus had, as any of his kind had.

Trag'Oul, who watched over the followers of Rathma.

The necromancers.

TWO

The Inn of the Black Ram was a flat-roofed stone building in the lower end of Westmarch the city that saw its fair share of the suspicious and the unsavory. Paradoxically, that meant that the establishment also saw its fair share of the powerful and wealthy, both those who sought the dank environment to close questionable deals and those who simply desired a thrill. There was some of each this particular evening, the various types seated at their booths and tables and murmuring over tankards of throat-scorching ale or half-burnt mutton.

But, whatever their reason for choosing the Black Ram this foggy eve, all without exception found themselves turning for no reason that they understood toward its creaking door just as the great bells of the city struck the late hour.

He was pale of skin and had a narrow face better suited for a studious clerk than a mysterious figure shrouded in dark cloak and robes. His eyes were his most arresting feature, for they were distinctly curved and of a startling gray. From out under the hood of his cloak, a few strands of flat, black hair hung over his forehead. The stranger was of slim build, but in that way that acrobats were.

The newcomer's high leather boots made no sound on the aged planks as he strode toward an open booth. His cloak billowed as he walked and in the flickering light of the boxy brass oil lamps above, tiny silver symbols sewn into the trim of the garment glittered, disappeared, then glittered to life again. Under the cloak, several small pouches and one larger one hung from the stranger's belt.

The large pouch held some round object in it the size of a huge grapefruit.

He slid onto one of the benches in the empty booth with the same silent ease that had marked his entrance to the inn. The other occupants of the Black Ram eyed him a moment more, but when he did nothing but sit back in the shadows, most returned to their own dealings and drinks. A few of the more disagreeable souls pretended to do the same, but their gazes constantly shifted back to the pouch and its mysterious contents.

And in one corner opposite from the new figure, a young woman whose graceful beauty stood out like a beacon in the neighborhood of the Black Ram watched him most intently. With her sat two men, one a giant with the clear look of a bodyguard and the other roughly her age and with enough similarity of features to be easily identified as related to the woman. He scowled in the stranger's direction, clearly repulsed by what he saw.

The plump, blond serving woman who should have seen to the hooded figure's needs refused to step from behind the waist-high wooden counter where the ales were poured from the barrels. The proprietor, a balding, stout man of middle years, tugged on his thick lower lip, then wiped his hands and proceeded out himself.

Hands clutching his faded apron, he approached the booth. Under a heavy brow, he eyed his newest patron with far more respect than he generally gave to all but the most highborn. "G-greetin's, master! Hyram, I am! Master of the Black Ram! 'Tis an unusual honor it 'tis to have one of yours here, unusual, but not unheard of. Been one or two . . . over the years."

The seated figure nodded once. His voice was smooth, calm. "Yes, I would not imagine many have come . . . to Westmarch."

"What—what can I bring you?"

"The stew I smell will do. I would ask for water . . . but here I suspect it would be healthier to drink the ale."

Hyram grunted. "Aye."

"Then, that is all . . . unless you also have a room for the night."

The innkeeper swallowed. "Just one night?"

"Yes." Sensing Hyram's hesitation, the figure reached a gloved hand to one of the pouches at his waist. As he brought it up, it clinked with the song of good coins.

Much of the innkeeper's trepidation vanished. "Aye, for one night we can help you, Master—"

"Zayl. Just Zayl." His gray eyes shifted away from Hyram.

"I'll be gettin' your meal and drink immediately, Master Zayl," Hyram declared, ignoring the other's last statement. To the proprietor, anyone who had the money to pay well was deserving of a title, even one such as this.

Left alone again, Zayl surreptitiously surveyed the room. He had never been this far from home and, despite his demeanor, was uneasy. It had not been his intention to leave the jungles of Kehjistan for the Western Kingdoms, but he had been drawn here by forces far stronger than himself.

Would that I could be like them, he thought, *blithely ignorant of the troubles converging on us all.*

His journey had taken him to the kingdom of Westmarch and the capital city of the same name. Cautious questioning of locals—cautious because one of his calling ever risked the notice of the authorities—had garnered Zayl only hearsay. Enough to keep him enticed, but not enough to explain to him why he had felt driven to come to this particular region.

He noted the woman across the room still eyeing him whenever she thought him unaware. From the glances and murmurs that passed between her and the smaller male—a sibling, Zayl suspected—they knew him for what he was. A follower of Rathma, a devotee to the maintaining of the Balance.

A delver into the world of the dead.

Many shunned necromancers—not without good reason, sometimes—but those like Zayl who had given themselves over to the teachings of Rathma meant people no harm. Zayl's kind fought against the Darkness, against the Prime Evils, for victory by the forces of Hell would forever send the Balance completely awry. The Rathmians' methods might not always meet with the approval of the uninitiated masses, but the results were what counted. One terrible defeat could mean the end of all.

Each necromancer was taught to follow the course of the ongoing struggle on his own, choosing his path on the basis of where his senses dictated he had to go. It had come as a great shock to Zayl when he had felt himself compelled to journey west across the Twin Seas, but he had not shirked from his duty. The Balance was in too precarious a state to turn a blind eye from what needed to be done.

After all, the *Worldstone* had been destroyed . . .

His dark reverie was interrupted by the return of Hyram with his meal. The stew, a greenish-brown mass with bits of old vegetables and stringy meat in it, had a tolerable odor and taste and the ale looked fresh enough. Having expected worse, Zayl nodded his approval. He was nearly hungry enough to devour the table, though he would have never visibly revealed such weakness even to himself. Rathmians learned to fast for extended periods of time in order to purge their bodies of impurities, but Zayl had gone longer than normal. Even this questionable fare would go far in restoring him to his full faculties.

Paying the proprietor, the necromancer took off his left glove, picked up the iron spoon resting in the bowl, and began to eat. The right hand remained covered, even despite the growing warmth of the room.

As he reached for his drink, a muffled sound emanated from the large pouch. Zayl's gloved hand immediately slipped to the pouch, slapping it once. The sound cut off.

Out of the corner of his eye, he looked to see if anyone had noticed. Only the woman appeared to have noticed anything unusual, but instead of being disturbed by it, she was now speaking more animatedly with the young male.

He, in turn, shrugged and said something clearly derogatory about Zayl.

The necromancer turned his attention back to his meal and his thoughts. In truth, he could actually not be certain that the Worldstone had been destroyed, but the evidence was certainly there. Mount Arreat—where legend claimed it had been hidden—had exploded, its entire top ravaged. The destruction had been heard about even here in faraway Westmarch. More to the point, the rumors among those with the sight gave starker credence to the horrific claim. It was said that one of the Prime Evils themselves— *Baal*, Lord of Destruction—had been the cause, and if so, the mortal plane was in for far worse to come. The Worldstone had existed since time immemorial, created, so the teachings of Rathma said, to keep the mortal world protected. Now, both the powers of Light and Darkness reached out to fully claim humanity, and in their battles against one another the two cosmic factions threatened to destroy what they desired. Somehow, all that tied into Zayl's own urge to come to Westmarch. Somewhere in this vast kingdom, the repercussions of Baal's heinous deed would soon be felt.

The only trouble was, he had no idea what to do next. Arriving in Westmarch was as far as his sense of urgency had brought him. Now, Zayl felt adrift, confused.

If you cannot find the way, wait, and the way will find you. Rathma himself had supposedly said that, and from past experience Zayl had found it to be all too true a statement. Yet, despite his extensive training, he was finally growing impatient. If the Balance—and, therefore, all else—was in jeopardy, it behooved the way to find him, and *quickly.*

He smelled before he saw the man suddenly standing beside his booth. The whiskered and capped figure looked as if he had been to sea much of his life and, from the scars and missing finger, a good part of that had probably been as a privateer. The mariner leaned over the table, obscuring Zayl's view of all else, and looked the Rathmian up and down.

"A friend of mine, he says that you be a necromancer . . ."

"He is correct," Zayl quickly returned, hoping that would end the conversation there and then.

Alas, such was not to be. Bending so near that his breath came at the spellcaster in smothering waves, the westerner continued, "So these marks on your cloak . . ." He seized a portion near Zayl's shoulder and pulled it up between them. Seen close, the symbols almost danced. "They're all about death, then."

"They are about aspects of the mortality of life and that which follows after."

"Death."

"Among other things." The necromancer had no wish to draw more attention to himself, but he could see this conversation coming to no good end. What intention did the man have—

"Get your grubby fingers out of my eye!" bellowed a voice all too familiar to him.

From somewhere behind Zayl, there was a gasp and a curse. They were followed by a thud and the same voice shouting, "Damn! I can't stop myself! Zayl! Zayl, lad!"

The man who had been speaking with the necromancer suddenly grabbed for Zayl's throat.

Zayl moved faster. The heel of his left hand barreled into the villain's jaw, throwing the latter back. At the same time, the necromancer muttered a few words under his breath.

The scarred mariner looked around the room in absolute panic. He pointed at an empty corner and gibbered, "By the Twin Seas! What is that beast?" His gaze shifted left. "Another! Demons! There're demons everywhere!"

Screaming, he shoved past his partner in crime, a stocky, bearded figure holding a dagger in one hand. The second mariner's other hand was still half-clenched. Zayl quickly glanced down at his waist. While he had been distracted by the first man, the companion had cut free the large pouch without his sensing it.

Of course, that had been the worst mistake that they could have made.

The second thief belatedly noticed Zayl rising. He started to lunge, but the spellcaster muttered another word.

The blade went completely past Zayl. His attacker stumbled, then gasped. He began frantically waving both hands about.

"My eyes! I can't see! My eyes!"

The effect was a temporary one, just like the spell that had made the first brigand think that he was surrounded by demonic creatures. Zayl started to reach for the blinded villain—

"Look out!" called a female voice.

He ducked back just in time to avoid the curved edge of a sword across his midsection. A wiry figure who was clearly in league with the pair grinned as he slashed again at Zayl.

The necromancer reached to his waist and removed a small dagger. His adversary laughed, for although the spellcaster's dagger was a curious one—being serpentine of shape in the blade and carved from what appeared ivory—it hardly matched the length of the villain's sword.

But when the cutthroat attempted to get past Zayl's guard, the dagger was there, meeting the longer blade and deflecting it with ease. Twice more, the attacker lunged, only to be foiled.

Zayl then pressed. He easily came under the other's guard, his dagger cutting the brigand in the arm and the chest. The necromancer's foe began to retreat—only to stumble over the purloined pouch.

"Watch where you're steppin'!" complained a voice that seemed to come from within it.

The would-be thief collided with the floor. In desperation, he flung his sword at Zayl, then leapt away. He seized the arm of his still-blind comrade, then both men fled through the door.

Zayl had no intention of giving chase. He thrust the

dagger into his belt, then quickly retrieved the pouch. An epithet started to escape it, but a quick tap by the necromancer brought silence.

Of the other patrons, most had fled at some point in the struggle. The few who remained seated eyed him for the most part with trepidation, loathing, and not a little fear. Zayl found it of interest that the woman and her bodyguard were standing as if having been prepared to give assistance. They were, in fact, the only ones who did not now treat him as a pariah. The Rathmian recalled the warning cry and knew that it had been the noblewoman who had given it. He bowed his head slightly in her direction, noting how she appraised him even now.

Turning back to the booth, Zayl found Hyram anxiously coming over to him. The necromancer easily read the innkeeper's expression, for it was one that he had seen far too often.

"I will be leaving," Zayl informed his host before Hyram could get up the nerve to ask him to do so. "I will not be needing the room, either."

The proprietor could not hide his relief. "'Tis not me, master, but the others, they don't understand—"

Shrugging off Hyram's attempt at explanation, the black-clad figure retrieved his one glove from the table. Putting it back on, he tossed some coins to the innkeeper. "This will suffice, I think."

The stout man eyed what lay in his palm. "More than enough, master! I can't in good faith—"

"Do not trouble yourself." Zayl was not wealthy, not at all, but as this had been his first stop in the capital, he wanted to leave with some semblance of respect from the locals, even after such chaos. A lost cause, surely, but he felt that he had to try.

With the same silent stride with which he had entered, the necromancer headed out of the Black Ram. Zayl had no notion as to where he would spend the night, but, if necessary, he would do so out in the wild. He was used to doing so in the jungles of Kehjistan and so this would not be so different, albeit cooler. His training had taught him to ignore most differences in temperature, and, fortunately, the weather here was not that chill anyway.

The mists had thickened since his entrance. Zayl focused, trying to see with more than simply his eyes.

"Damned brutes . . . ," grumbled a voice at his side.

"Be quiet, Humbart."

"You weren't the one rolling helplessly over the floor . . . and that without so much as a single drink beforehand!"

Zayl tapped the pouch. "No, I had only a sword against which to contend."

"And you're welcome for my help there, lad! What would you do without me?"

The pale figure permitted himself a brief smile, but otherwise did not answer.

Then, he sensed another presence nearing him. In a whisper, he commanded, "Silence . . ."

"Are you just—" But another tap by the necromancer on the pouch finally quieted his unseen companion.

Reaching out with his heightened senses, Zayl located the newcomer behind him. With one hand near the hilt of his dagger, he continued along as if unaware.

Heavy thuds signaled the other's approaching steps. Stealth was clearly not a strong suit of the one following him.

When he felt that his pursuer had gotten close enough, Zayl spun around. In the necromancer's hand, the pale blade stood ready.

The shadowed form of a giant met his gaze. Something about it struck Zayl as familiar and when he looked closer, he recognized the man. It was the bodyguard of the noblewoman who had given Zayl warning.

The giant's hair was shorn close, stubble peppered across the dark skin of his face. He stood with the stance of a well-trained fighter, in that manner reminding the necromancer of Captain Kentril Dumon, a mercenary whose path Zayl had crossed and whom he respected highly.

The bodyguard was clad in dark blue livery with crimson edging on his sleeves and pant legs. An emblem—a red circle surrounding a blue hawk's head—had been sewn on the uniform just where the heart was located, one of those unfortunate traditions that often gave enemies a perfect point upon which to target their weapons. The broad-rimmed boots seemed a bit garish to the Rathmian, but he would not have ever been foolish enough to say so to such a mountain of a man.

"I come at the behest of the mistress," rumbled the bodyguard, showing both hands empty. He had an accent that marked him as coming from near to Lut Gholein, on the western edge of the Twin Seas and a place through which Zayl had passed on his way to the Western Kingdoms. "She would seek your counsel, Rathmian, in a matter of the soul."

"Would not a Zakarum priest be more appropriate than I?"

The giant grinned, and even in the misty dark Zayl could see his white teeth . . . his many white teeth. "The Zakarum, they would not appreciate the mistress's intent."

The fact that she asked a necromancer to come to her made that clear enough, but Zayl was not ready to simply acquiesce. "And what would she wish of one of mine?"

"She must speak with her husband. A matter of urgency."

And if the woman needed Zayl, it was because her husband was dead. An inheritance, no doubt. There were those who thought the Rathmians no better than the charlatans who read fortunes or gave séances at the fairs or on the roads. Paid performers, even if some of them had the gift.

He started to turn away, but the bodyguard would not have it. The man reached for Zayl's arm, unaware of the danger of doing so.

"She has nowhere else to turn. She said that something

drew her to the inn and when she saw you, she felt certain that you were the reason."

The necromancer hesitated. The last was likely a lie, but her suggestion that she had been drawn to the same location as him made Zayl think again of Rathma's words. Was the way being shown to him now?

He balanced the pros and cons of agreeing . . . and found the cons slightly the stronger. Yet, when Zayl opened his mouth to speak, it was to answer, "Very well. I will see her."

"Thank you . . ." The bodyguard's tone hinted of tremendous relief, something that Zayl had not expected from a hired fighter for an employer. Most would have simply accepted the response. Zayl read in this man a deep loyalty.

His large companion led the necromancer through the mist-enshrouded streets. Despite his agreement to see the noblewoman, Zayl remained cautious. This could still be a trap set by thieves or even the Zakarum.

But if a trap, it appeared an elaborate one. Some blocks from the Black Ram, Zayl and his still-unnamed companion confronted an elegant coach pulled by four muscular white horses. A dour driver in the same livery as the bodyguard nodded to the giant. Zayl noted that the house insignia was not at all obscure, a contrast to the age-long practice of aristocrats out on such ventures. The noblewoman was either very open about her deeds or very naive.

The bodyguard moved ahead to open the door of the coach. As he did, someone within leaned toward the opening. Zayl faltered slightly.

Her skin was a shade darker than his own, her full lips a deep, rich coloring that he knew was not the result of any enhancement. The hair cascaded down past her shoulders, ending below her shoulders. He had no doubt that her face and form attracted many a man, but she was clearly one who did not in any manner use her gifts for influence or gain. Certainly not with a foul necromancer, especially.

The noblewoman eyed Zayl closely, then glanced at her companion. "Thank you, Polth."

The giant bowed. "Mistress . . ."

She extended a slim hand toward the Rathmian. "Please. Enter."

"I would first know a name, my lady. A *true* name."

Before she could answer, a male voice within the coach snarled, "By the stars, Salene! I told you that this was going too far! Tell him nothing and let's be gone from this stinking area! I've known much better places to get drunk in than that flea trap we just left!"

Zayl recalled the man in the Black Ram that he had assumed was her brother. So far, there seemed little similarity in their personalities. That he had already given away her first name while insisting she tell him nothing said much.

"Hush, Sardak," she returned quietly, smiling at Zayl as if well aware of what he thought of her brash companion. "What he asks is fair if he's to assist me."

"You can't trust his kind! The Church of Zakarum says he's a desecrator of graves, a ghoul—"

Salene's smile hardened and the gaze she turned on the unseen Sardak immediately silenced him. When she looked again at Zayl, it was with honest apology. "My brother is protective of me, Rathmian, as I am of him, Master—"

She no doubt had to be more protective of the impetuous Sardak than he of her, but Zayl did not say so. He nodded, then drew closer. "I am just Zayl, my lady."

"Nothing more?"

"Among my calling, we most often forgo any other name, for we are but servants of the Balance, with ties to no House or clan."

"Well, 'just Zayl,' I am the Lady Salene Nesardo and if that is enough introduction, I'd prefer that we leave here now. What I wish to speak to you about is better done elsewhere."

She retreated into the coach, her invitation for him to sit

beside her obvious. Zayl's brow arched; few women there were who would have willingly offered that, even for the summoning of a rich husband's spirit. He had expected her to insist he sit next to the charming Sardak.

A muffled snort escaped the pouch. Polth frowned, but when the noise did not repeat itself, he relaxed again. Still holding the door, he said, "Master Zayl?"

Bowing his head slightly to the bodyguard, Zayl slipped up into the coach with the quiet ease of a shadow. Salene emitted a small gasp at his grace and swiftness and from the other seats Sardak mumbled a curse.

His vision more attuned to the night than that of most people, Zayl saw the sour expression on the brother's face. However, despite Sardak's threatening attitude, Zayl calculated that the man was little danger to him. Drink was Sardak's only weapon, which he used against himself.

In that brief moment during which her brother had captured the necromancer's attention, Lady Nesardo had fully recovered her wits. She glanced at the large pouch. "The coach is small. I can have Polth put that in the storage box in the back, if you like. You might be more comfortable then."

Quickly sliding a hand atop the bag, Zayl replied, "It stays with me."

She had obviously seen the movement of his hand, but said nothing of it. "Yes, I saw how those thieves learned that lesson, to their dismay."

Lady Nesardo said no more about the pouch, not even evincing any curiosity as to what it held. That despite having no doubt heard the voice in the inn. She would find out soon enough the truth if Zayl agreed to what she requested.

Sardak remained grimly silent throughout the ride, staring at the necromancer as if Zayl had grown fangs and a pair of horns. Zayl had expected his hostess to begin explaining her needs, but when she spoke it was only to ask him such mundane questions like how his journey across the Twin Seas had gone and what Lut Gholein was like. Salene did not ask *why* he had traveled so far, though. The noblewoman did her utmost to treat him with a respect due another of her station. As one who was generally looked upon with disdain, distrust, or fear—all feelings embodied in her brother, at the moment—Zayl found it refreshing.

Then, without warning, a black wave washed over him, overwhelming his senses.

It was too much even for his training. A gasp escaped Zayl's lips and the cloaked figure suddenly sprawled against the back of the seat.

The interior of the coach vanished. The necromancer was caught in a bottomless, black vortex. He felt bony fingers clawing at his flesh and heard the wailing of thousands of lost souls. The fingers tore relentlessly at him, resurrecting another horrible time that made the Rathmian's gloved right hand clench tight.

Suddenly, Zayl became trapped in a sticky substance that he could not see. It was everywhere, and even his slightest struggles entangled him further. The wailing grew more strident. He heard the sounds of battle and the cries of death. Magical forces sprung into play around him.

And then . . . something else approached. It reached out from beyond death, from a place far worse. Even though it was so very distant, he could sense its awful malevolence—

But at that very moment, another presence entered his struggling thoughts. Who or what it was, Zayl could not say, only that it sought to drag him forth from what assailed him. He seized the lifeline it offered, and finally managed to focus his will.

The necromancer's mind tore free of the stickiness trapping it. The clawing hands and the mournful voices receded, and with them the pain. Foiled, the dark presence sank back into the foul place from which it had emerged.

And the mortal world began to come into focus again.

The first thing that Zayl saw was Lady Salene Nesardo's shadowed face looming over him. Her expression was filled only with concern. She had one cool hand against his temple.

He realized then that *she* had been the source of his lifeline.

The noblewoman had some gift of magic herself.

"His eyes are focused again!" she muttered. Her other hand thrust toward her brother. "Give me your flask!"

"Salene—"

"The flask!"

A moment later, she brought a small silver drinking flask to Zayl's lips. The disciplines of the Rathmians did not preclude drink, but still the liquid that slipped down Zayl's throat burned like fire.

The necromancer coughed violently. Through his struggles, he heard Sardak chuckle.

"Can handle the dead, but can't handle his liquor . . ."

Salene glared at him. "Considering what you pour into your system, be thankful that I'm not having to ask him to summon *your* spirit."

"At least my spirit would be full of spirits!"

Zayl ignored their argument, clearly an ongoing one of no relevance to the stunning attack on him. He shifted back to a proper sitting position, his face betraying nothing of his thoughts. Calm he might have seemed, but inside the necromancer was still feeling the effects of the earlier strain. It had taken him completely by surprise, catching him with most of his defenses down.

From where had it originated? He had sensed nothing upon his arrival in Westmarch, nothing even at the Black Ram. How could such a powerful force be so localized?

"Are you better?" asked Salene.

"I am well."

"What happened to you?"

Instead of answering, Zayl eyed her and asked, "There is more to this than simply speaking with the shade of a loved one, is there not?"

The coach came to an abrupt halt. The Lady Nesardo quickly glanced out of the window.

"We're here," the noblewoman declared, utterly ignoring Zayl's question.

"Home sweet home," added Sardak with some mockery.

Polth appeared at his mistress's door. He swung it open, then gave the Lady Nesardo a hand down. Sardak, moving with astonishing grace for one in his inebriated condition, slipped out right after her without so much as a glance back at the necromancer.

From without the coach, Salene commanded, "Help our friend, Polth. He did not have a pleasant ride."

Without batting an eye, the bodyguard held his huge hand out to the Rathmian. "Master Zayl?"

"Thank you, but I am recovered enough." Keeping the pouch near his side, he stepped out. While he had been recouping his strength, the coach had apparently not only arrived at the gates of its destination, but had entered them. A huge brick wall with spikes atop surrounded a wide, manicured lawn. Zayl saw that the vehicle had driven up a stone path that wound from the iron gates to the front steps.

"Welcome to our humble abode," jested Salene's brother, stretching his arm toward the house.

Zayl looked up . . . and up farther yet.

In the midst of so many tall, arched buildings with jutting towers and gargoyles atop the battlements, the House of Nesardo stood unique. It loomed higher than any of its neighbors, but where their towers ended in tiled, weathered points, its did so with a pale, moonlike roundness that seemed so pristine even in the dark of night that Zayl first thought it a new addition. But a cursory study of the structure as a whole immediately put that notion to rest. There were no breaks between the sections, as was always evident with even the most intricate reconstruction. This was the house as it had originally been designed.

Zayl's gaze moved on. From the peculiar, rounded roof, the sleek walls of the tower descended to a more typical rectangular design which stretched out nearly twice as wide as the next largest domicile. The roof of the main section arched so sharply and narrowly that it gave Salene's residence the feel of a cathedral or church, a complete contrast to the top of the tower.

There were eight windows on each level and each of those windows was shaped like an octagon. Eight fluted columns also stood guard at the entrance, which consisted of a pair of massive iron doors, each with eight bracketed frames decorating the front. To reach the doors, visitors would first have to ascend an equal number of lengthy marble steps wide enough to hold several dozen people at once.

At most any other time, such an obsession with a particular number would have struck Zayl with much interest, for the teachings of Rathma included understanding the influences of all numbers on the Balance. There were numbers whose use could tilt it one way or another with ease, if manipulated by the knowing soul.

But, for the moment, Zayl did not pay that any mind, for he was struck instead by something more immediate, something most unsettling.

The building before him housed not only the Nesardo family, but also the *source* of that which had nearly taken him in the coach.

THREE

Zayl gave no hint of his discovery as he followed Salene Nesardo and her brother inside. Once more, the words of Rathma returned to him. How truly they had been spoken . . . but what yet did it all mean? How was this bound to the destruction of the Worldstone?

The halls of the Nesardo house stood high and were filled with shadows created by an array of round-bottomed oil lamps standing guard in braces on each wall. Their sheer number alone meant that there had to be more servants than the pair he had thus far seen, but none were in sight, nor did he hear any movement beyond that of his own party. Concentrating, he sensed the presence of several others around them, all moving with a wariness that the necromancer deemed caused by him.

As he proceeded through the long, oddly empty corridors, Zayl realized that everything here had been built larger than it needed to have been. Again, he felt more as if he had entered a vast temple than a home. The necromancer did not even have to reach out with his heightened senses to understand that Salene's residence was also far more ancient than he would have expected. In fact, from what he had seen of Westmarch, it had to be older than nearly every other structure in the capital.

"The House of Nesardo is one of the oldest in all of Westmarch," his hostess informed him without warning. Had she read his thoughts? Ignorant of Zayl's brief, suspicious glance, she went on, "The original structure was said to be part of the fortress first raised by the great Lord Rakkis."

The name registered with Zayl, but what he knew of the

legends surrounding the man did not set with what he sensed of this place. Whatever its present occupants might think, there was something much older here, something as old as any ruin in the jungles of Kehjistan.

"We will be most comfortable in here," Salene added a few seconds later, gesturing at a sitting room large enough to hold more Rathmians than Zayl himself had ever met.

A wide fireplace whose opening had been carved to resemble the maw of a huge wolf greeted them with a gullet of flame. The huge fire looked to have just been kindled, although again there was no servant about.

"They heard you were coming," Sardak blithely remarked, showing that he, too, seemed to be able to read Zayl's thoughts now and then. "They were just dying not to meet you."

"Please forgive my brother," the Lady Nesardo interjected, smiling warmly at the necromancer. "He is concerned for my welfare."

"And why not? That bastard thinks that he can take what is yours through deceit, and he has the influence to make the magistrates decree such lies lawful!"

Her smile faded. "Yes, that's quite possible."

Zayl decided that it was time to take the reins. He already had too many questions concerning the house itself and knew that they would never be answered if he continued to react, not act. After all, while Rathma preached that there were times to wait, he also preached that hesitation was the first step to defeat.

"You wished of me some assistance," the necromancer uttered, drawing the veiled gazes of both siblings. "Being what I am and having heard what I have, I can make some very accurate assumptions. However, before I promise my efforts, I must hear the absolute truth . . . and I will know if it is not."

The last was in some part false, but the reputation of his kind made many believe such powers to exist. It often enabled the necromancers to better determine their course of action.

"Yes . . . we delay too long." The noblewoman indicated three plush, leather-clad chairs set near the fireplace. Sardak immediately dropped down in the one nearest the flames and reached for a smoked-glass decanter set atop a crested golden tray on a small, square, oak table. Although there were three matching goblets beside the decanter, the brother started to put the edge of the container to his lips.

"Sardak! Remember yourself!"

With a grunt, he replaced the decanter. "My apologies, dear sister."

Salene nodded her satisfaction. She moved to seat herself, Polth—ever the silent shadow—holding her chair for her.

"Thank you, Polth. You may go now."

"Mistress?"

"I have the utmost faith in Master Zayl's integrity, Polth. You are dismissed."

The bodyguard bowed to her, to Sardak, and even to the necromancer. However, as his gaze came up, Zayl read in them a warning, should anything befall his employer.

When Polth had shut the doors behind him, Salene gestured at the third chair. "Please sit down, Master Zayl."

"Thank you, I prefer to stand . . . and it is just Zayl."

"Will you at least have something to drink?"

Zayl shook his head. "My only interest is in hearing your tale, Lady Nesardo."

"I will tell it, then, but if you continue to be 'just Zayl,' then you will from this point on refer to me as 'Salene,' not Lady Nesardo."

"And I," announced Sardak with a flourish and a mocking grin, "you may not refer to at all, necromancer."

Ignoring him, Zayl looked into his hostess's eyes. They were of a startling green, one that reminded him of the lush plants of the jungles. They had strength to them. She had a look about her, too, as if she could trace in part of her background an ancestry not that far-flung from his own. "You were saying, my lady?"

Her brother snickered. She pursed her lips, but did not

correct Sardak again. "This is the House of Nesardo. An old House, as I said. Unfortunately, it is a dying House, Zayl. You see before you the last survivors of the blood-line."

Sardak raised his goblet. "Here's to the overdue end of a bad thing."

Zayl frowned, something suddenly occurring to him. "You are the Lady Nesardo, but your husband was also—"

"His name was Riordan. My third cousin, once removed, but bearing the same surname, yes. A necessary match by our parents. We had never met and it combined what remained of the Nesardo finances, making them stronger." Salene shook her head. "It did not do the same, I regret, for our union. We had mutual respect, and even some affection. Still, that would have been enough, if any child had come of it."

She had barely been of age when they had married. Riordan, a bull of a man in body, was a gentle soul by nature. He sought for the good in every man, sometimes searching for it too long. More than once, he was cheated, although never by any drastic measure.

"We were wed three years and a quarter when illness took him. No one could do anything to slow it. He might as well have been struck down with a sword. Riordan was dead in two days."

With his passing, the weight of Nesardo's fortunes fell to the young widow . . . and she proved to be far more competent in managing its resources than her good-willed husband. In the three years that followed, she rebuilt what had been lost, to the point where she felt that she could at last breathe safely.

And then had come Lord Aldric Jitan.

"My husband knew him, did business with him, but once Riordan passed away, I heard nothing from Lord Jitan . . . nothing until he came to my door just a month ago, holding in his hands what he said was proof that Nesardo was now *his*."

The documentation appeared authentic, a turning over

of the estate in lieu of money borrowed from Lord Jitan for an enterprise the noble said had not proven out for Nesardo. Salene had recognized her husband's signature and seal, but the scope of what he had promised the other noble stunned her. She could not believe Riordan that naive.

In reply to her demand as to why he had waited three years to bring this dire news to her, Lord Jitan had spoken pretty words about giving the widow time to grieve, but Salene had sensed that there was something more to it. Unfortunately, she could not read him as she could others.

At this point in her story, the Lady Nesardo took the goblet her brother suddenly proffered her. Her expression had grown more strained since she'd first begun the tale, but in her Zayl noted no guile. Thus far, what he'd heard appeared to be the truth.

"How long have you known of your gift?" he asked the moment Salene finished sipping.

She did not try to avert the subject this time. Her steady gaze meeting his, Salene nodded, answering, "It began to manifest when I reached adulthood. I've kept it quelled much of the time since. It's not considered a comely trait for a woman of my station."

"It is unschooled, then."

She nodded. "Yes, although some aspects of it I understand better than others."

The necromancer recalled how she had come to his aid. "In the coach . . . you sensed what happened to me. You knew I was under attack . . . and by something involving this house."

"Yes . . . I've never seen it act against anyone, though, or else I wouldn't have risked bringing you! I almost demanded that you leave, for your own sake—"

"Which I would have refused at that point. I do not like to leave such mysteries unanswered." He considered something. "You lived in this place before your husband. Riordan Nesardo was the newcomer to it, not you."

"I was born here."

Zayl glanced at Sardak. "And you?"

"I was born here, too . . . but I didn't live here for very long. You see, my mother was a servant."

"Sardak is actually my half-brother, Master Zayl." Salene gave her sibling a loving look. "Born two years after myself. Our father had him and his mother sent off to a country estate, where he was raised. After my mother passed away, Father had Sardak brought back . . ."

"And do you also share the gift, Master Sardak?"

"I'm very lucky at cards, if that counts," the brother smirked, taking another deep swig.

"He has a trace, no more. The gift is much stronger in me." Salene met the Rathmian's gray eyes. "Although I never used any of it for gain—"

"More's the pity," Sardak interjected.

Ignoring him, she continued, "—I've always been able to sense the intents of those seeking my favor . . . until Lord Jitan, that is."

"And from him?"

"Utter emptiness. Nothing at all."

Which, to Zayl, was sufficient indication that this other noble also wielded the gift. "The magistrates will side with him on his claims, you say."

Salene put down her goblet. "He is a man. I am a woman. This is Westmarch."

"What do you hope to obtain from conversation with Riordan? The magistrates will certainly not take his testimony."

Sardak chuckled. "The Rathmian's got a sense of humor, even if he doesn't know it himself!"

"I've no other recourse. I hoped that Riordan might be able to tell me something I can use . . . that's all."

The necromancer frowned. "You were waiting for me in the Black Ram. Me, in particular."

"Not you," she murmured, gazing down at the floor. "I waited for something. I didn't know what, but I felt certain that I would find it there, though it took five anxious nights."

If you cannot find the way, wait, and the way will find you. It appeared that the words of Rathma applied not only to his loyal followers, but to others as well.

Yes, there was definitely more to this than merely a struggle over valuable property, but what it truly concerned Zayl still did not know. He saw only one course of action that might reveal matters to his satisfaction.

"You need say no more. I will do what I can to summon the shade of your husband, though I cannot promise if the results will be as you hope."

"I expected nothing more."

She was a pragmatic person, something that the necromancer could appreciate. Zayl considered all the factors involved in what he had to do and added, "With the rising of the moon tomorrow eve, we can begin."

"Tomorrow?" Sardak did not look at all pleased, which came as no surprise to Zayl. "Why not get it over with tonight?"

"Because it must *be* tomorrow night," the Rathmian returned, gray eyes boring into the noble's. Sardak slunk back into his chair.

Salene Nesardo rose. "Then you'll be our guest until then, Master Zayl." When he started to speak, she smiled and added, "I'll insist on that and I will *not* call you 'just Zayl' so long as you continue to call me other than 'Salene.' "

"As you wish . . . my lady."

Her smile turned to a frown, his response clearly not what she had anticipated. "I'll show you where you can sleep. Sardak, please don't drift off by the fire."

"Never fear, sister dear. Once burned, twice shy."

"If you'll follow me, Master Zayl?" Striding gracefully across the room, Lady Nesardo opened the door. The necromancer trailed after her, silent and ever observant of his surroundings.

In the corridor, Salene reached up to one of the oil lamps. Only then did Zayl see that each was removable. In addition, a rounded handle hidden on the backside enabled the noblewoman to carry the lamp with ease.

"Thank you for doing this," she whispered. Her eyes glittered in the light of the lamp.

"I can promise you nothing," Zayl replied, suddenly a bit uncomfortable.

"Which is more than I had before," Salene remarked, turning and leading the way. "Which is much more than I had before . . ."

Luxury was not something a Rathmian sought, and so Zayl found no comfort in his surroundings. The plush, down-filled bed, the high, polished rafters, the elegant, embroidered rug that had made the journey all the way from Lut Gholein . . . they only made him yearn for the jungles of his home.

They also resurrected dark memories.

The last time he had been offered such opulence, it had been in a far eastern kingdom called Ureh. He, Kentril Dumon, the Vizjerei sorcerer Quov Tsin, and the captain's companions had all become the guests of the realm's lord, Juris Khan. The finest the kingdom had to offer had been given to the outsiders.

There had been only one problem: Ureh had proven to be a kingdom of the damned, a place once cast into the realm of Hell whose inhabitants had returned to the mortal plane as soul-sucking monsters. Of all those there, only he and Captain Dumon had survived.

Zayl clutched his gloved right hand. *Barely* survived.

"I'm assuming from the silence that we're alone!" came the voice from the pouch. "And if we're not, then damn it all anyway, lad! I want out!"

"Be patient, Humbart." The necromancer untied the pouch from his belt and brought it over to the table beside the bed. Undoing the string atop, he reached in and removed the contents.

The empty sockets of the skull seemed to glare reprovingly at him.

"About time!" echoed a rough voice emanating from somewhere within the fleshless cranium. The skull lacked any jawbone and missed several teeth. There were cracks here and there, too, all the results of the fate that had befallen the owner. "Well, isn't this a pleasant place?"

Humbart Wessel had been a treasure hunter much like Captain Dumon and his men. He had been part of an earlier and no-less-fatal journey to reach lost Ureh—only, in Humbart's case, death had come from a high fall when he had attempted to return to the city on his own some years later. A young Zayl avidly studying the lore concerning Ureh had come across the remains and had animated the skull in search of answers. Somehow, he had never managed to get around to sending the mercenary's spirit back to the netherworld, not that Humbart appeared to be in any hurry.

They had traveled much together and, despite the skull's earthy tendencies and outspoken attitude, Humbart had more than once proven the difference between Zayl's own life and death. That included Ureh, especially.

The Rathmian set the skull square on the table, giving its owner the best view possible. Despite having no eyes, Humbart saw. He could also hear, smell, and, of course, speak. At times, the spirit grumbled that he would have traded all of these for the ability to eat and engage in mortal pleasures, but for the most part he seemed satisfied just to exist.

"Such a pleasant, pleasant place," the skull repeated. "Like the curtains. So, tell me, is the grand lady of the house as elegant as this and as pretty a thing as her voice makes her sound?"

"The matter is hardly of our concern."

Somehow, the remains managed a snort. "Spoken like one of Rathma's own! How is it you lot have managed to survive the ages with such a lack of romantic notions?"

As he had so often, Zayl let that gibe, too, pass. Instead, he stepped to the huge rug and sat down. Crossing his legs, he pushed back his hood and stared at the wall before him.

"Zayl, lad, there's a lush, sweet bed right there for the enjoyment! For my sake, use it! How often do we get this chance for such—"

"Hush, Humbart. You know that is not my way."

The skull grumbled, then made no other sound. Rathmians generally did not sleep much; they sank into a form of trance that enabled their bodies to get the rest they needed while their senses continued to explore and expand upon their abilities. It was a necessity, the necromancers ever needing to hone their skills in their effort to protect the Balance.

Zayl stared at a point on the wall, but his eyes no longer saw it. Almost immediately, the room faded into the background, replaced by a grayish haze.

It was his intention to discover more about the House of Nesardo . . . especially what its earliest history entailed. The malevolent force that had nearly struck him down in the coach was somehow bound in part to this location . . . but why?

One by one, Zayl peeled away the shields he had built to protect his mind from the earlier assault. Each step was a cautious one, for eagerness would only lead to disaster.

But instead of the malignant force against which he had earlier fought, the necromancer discovered something else—a faint but definite presence. It permeated the walls, the floors, the very timbers of House Nesardo. He probed deeper and deeper and found layers to this presence. It was everywhere, existing as the edifice itself did, a part of it as much as any nail or bit of stone. A gasp escaped his still body when at last he recognized it for what it was.

A collective of *souls*.

Their numbers were legion. Zayl had never come across so many in one place, not even in the oldest cemeteries or burial chambers of the east. More astounding, the souls before him existed in a semiconscious state, unaware of their deaths, but also unaware of the mortal world. He felt them reliving their lives over and over, like actors in a play without end. They did not mingle, yet coexisted so intimately that the necromancer knew they drew from one another.

Fascinated, Zayl observed a few. A woman clad in a voluminous ball gown covered in glittering jewels spoke gaily with the empty air. Near her, a grim-countenanced swordsman of middle years swung his blade desperately at what seemed to be three or four foes. Two toddlers—twins—played with one another. Their faces were marked with pox, a clear sign of the reason for their early departure from the mortal plane.

Curiously, they were the ones who finally noticed *him.* Although Zayl had no true form, to them he would have appeared much as he did in life. The toddlers ceased their game—one involving a ball and small stick figures—and gazed up solemnly at the necromancer.

Play . . . , the one with the ball finally said to him, the mouth remaining still. The child held the ball up for Zayl to take.

I do not know the game, he replied, his own lips moving.

This admission caused the twins to lose interest in him. They turned back to their playing, bouncing the ball between them and then choosing a stick figure from the group. A moment later, the twins faded into the background, indistinct but still visible.

Only as he studied more of the shades did Zayl see one common trait among them. They all had eyes similar, if not identical, to Salene Nesardo.

Were these the souls, then, of the many generations of her House? If so, the bloodline of Nesardo had once been far more fertile.

Fascinated, he moved on, gazing at one reenactment after another. Lovers, liars, scholars, fools, fighters, and cowards. The ill, the impractical, the impressionable. The gathered souls of Nesardo covered the spectrum of human frailties and triumphs.

Then it occurred to him that Riordan Nesardo should be among them.

The necromancer concentrated, silently repeating the man's name; doing so bettered the chance that the shade would be drawn to him. It seemed possible that Zayl might be able to elicit not only the answers Salene needed, but also a few of those *he* desired.

Riordan . . . Riordan, husband of Salene . . . come to me, Riordan . . .

Of all the souls here, Riordan's had been the most recent addition and, therefore, the easiest to to call. The pull to the mortal plane was strongest at the moment of death and weakened as the years went on. Summoning a shade from centuries past required far more effort than summoning one but weeks gone from life. Of course, from what Zayl had witnessed here so far, those rules meant nothing to the the shades of Nesardo. Many of those the Rathmian had so far studied had been dead hundreds of years, yet they seemed as freshly passed on as the most recent lord.

And where *was* Riordan? Zayl still could not sense that particular soul anywhere. He of all those here should have reacted to the necromancer's presence. Instead, some of the other specters began to notice the stranger in their midst. The woman in the extravagant gown paused to stare, her lip trembling. The swordsman staggered, shaking his hand and clutching several suddenly bloody wounds. His eyes locked upon Zayl with a mixture of denial and rage. A pair of lovers, their haunted faces revealing the telltale sign of poisoning on their lips, clutched one another in sudden fright.

And then, the dead began a horrific transformation.

Their skin quickly shriveled and decayed, crumbling off their bodies in great pieces. Rich garments blackened and tattered. Frightened eyes sank into fleshless skulls . . .

Zayl had intruded too deep. The shades were beginning to understand their deaths. They were seeing that what they were now was nothing more than a facade, that their true selves were moldering away in crypts, graves of earth . . . or worse.

The necromancer immediately retreated. As he did, he

felt the sensations of despair, fear, and anger that had arisen all around him begin to subside. Just as Zayl had hoped, by his leaving the dead alone, they had reacted like the twins, losing interest in the intrusion and slipping back into their perpetual activities.

As the misty realm faded away, Zayl took one last look to verify his suspicions. The necromancer caught a fleeting glimpse of the woman in the gown. Once more she was the focus of an invisible ball, resplendent in her costume and obviously being chatted up by gentleman admirers. The cadaverous corpse of a moment before was gone and there was no sign that she recalled his intrusion at all.

Relief coursed through Zayl as he drifted back to his body. He had come very close to upsetting something core to the secrets of House Nesardo. That could have caused a catastrophe to the Balance. There was a particular reason why those of the bloodline returned here after death, one that he was determined to unveil. More and more the Rathmian saw that his encounter with Salene had not come about completely by chance and certainly had to do with more than contacting the spirit of her husband.

And, for that matter, where *was* Riordan Nesardo? Why had he not answered a call that few dead souls could deny?

The myriad paths laid before him intrigued Zayl. Caught up in trying to puzzle them out, he paid little mind to his return to his mortal shell, an act almost as reflexive to him as breathing.

That is, until he discovered that he could *not* enter.

Something *else* had gotten to his body before him.

It clearly sought to claim his form for its own. Zayl probed, but found nothing to identify its origins. It was not one of the souls he had discovered—of that the Rathmian was certain. Curiously, he sensed some familiarity with it, but exactly what that meant escaped the necromancer.

Then, all that concerned Zayl now was claiming what was rightfully his.

Whatever intruder it was that had usurped his body, it lacked the natural ties that Zayl had. A Rathmian knew how to strengthen those bonds even in precarious situations like this. To understand death as they did, necromancers also had to understand life, and so Zayl knew well what kept a soul attached to its body.

He focused his will on those ties, strengthening them, using them to their utmost. Whether or not the intruder chose to leave, Zayl intended to enter.

What felt like a solid wall briefly obstructed his way, but it could not deny the strength of that which bound the Rathmian to his mortal form. Zayl pushed, slowly but inexorably making his way.

And as he bit by bit reentered his body, he began to become aware of his surroundings.

The first thing Zayl noticed was that Humbart was screaming. The skull's voice rang loudly throughout the room and no doubt a good portion of the building.

"Drop it, damn you, lad! What's gotten into you? Drop it, I say!"

As his mortal senses took over, the Rathmian felt tension fill his body. He realized that he was standing and that his arms were stretched before him.

In his left hand, Zayl's bone dagger was turned toward his chest.

The only thing that had prevented it from being driven in was his gloved right hand, which held the other wrist in a death grip. The two limbs struggled with such violence that the necromancer's body shook.

"Listen to me, Zayl, lad!" the skull continued. "Wake up! This isn't you!"

Someone pounded on the door. Zayl heard Salene's voice, but what she said he could not understand.

The necromancer focused his full will on forcing the left hand to drop the dagger. At first it resisted, but then one finger curled open, followed by another . . .

Without warning, Zayl recovered full use of his rebellious hand. The rest of the fingers opened and the dagger dropped onto the rug. At the same moment, the insidious invader within vanished.

Gasping, Zayl dropped to one knee, his right hand still clutching the other wrist.

"Zayl! You're awake! Praise be!"

Although unable to answer, the necromancer was by no means inactive. His mind swept the vicinity, seeking any trace of his unseen foe. Yet, despite a thorough search, Zayl discovered only one thing amiss.

Salene Nesardo stood next to him.

Zayl knew very well that he had bolted the door, the better not to be disturbed while in a trance. He had also laid three subtle spells around the entrance, ensuring that no one would enter without his permission.

But the noblewoman had done just that, which spoke volumes about her gift.

"Zayl!" Salene gasped, taking him by the shoulders. "What happened here?"

She had not witnessed the struggle, Zayl realized. All Salene likely knew was that there had been a commotion and that somehow the necromancer had been injured.

The Rathmian decided it best for her not to know the full truth, at least for now. "My own fault. I was attempting some study of the forces inundating this building and overextended myself. I was foolish."

"Overextended himself?" blurted Humbart. "That was—"

"Quiet, Humbart."

"But, I only—" the skull protested.

"Humbart!"

Salene gasped. "Who said that—?" Her gaze fixed on the skull. "It came from *you*."

Zayl finally ignored them both, instead taking up the dagger with his right hand. He stared at it, thinking.

Whatever had sought his body had desired his death and had chosen his dagger, an integral part of the Rathmian calling, as the tool. Coincidence? Perhaps, but there was something about the entire incident that made

Zayl suspect that the thing knew much concerning the necromancer . . . *too* much. The followers of Rathma kept their ways and methods most secret from outsiders.

What had he stumbled upon?

Karybdus studied his dagger, its faint glow giving it an especially ethereal look. He frowned, not disappointed, but also not pleased.

He sat on the stone floor of a chamber completely unlit save for the light from the blade. His cloak and robes were draped across the floor in such a manner that it almost looked as if he had melted into the stone.

In the darkness surrounding him, something large scuttled about.

"Calm yourself, my love," he murmured to the shadows. "It was to be expected . . . but it will be remedied." Karybdus placed the bone-white dagger in his belt and rose up with just the aid of his legs. His voice carried only detachment. "The Balance will be set proper again. It will be . . . at all necessary costs."

F⊕UR

✳

Salene insisted that Zayl rest for a day before he began the summoning, but the necromancer needed no such respite and, in fact, was more eager than ever to call up the spirit of Riordan Nesardo. Twice now, he had been assaulted by mysterious forces, but the more he meditated on that which had sought to slay him by his own hand, the more he felt the second assault separate from the first. There might be a factor that bound them together, but the latter attack had a more mortal feel to it.

Could it be this Lord Jitan? If so, then he had studied the followers of Rathma closer than most. The necromancer was very much interested in meeting this particular noble.

The skies remained dark that next day, an omen to Zayl, but one he did not mention to his hostess. He silently began his mental preparations, aware that this summoning would surely not be like most. There were wards and other defenses he would need to prepare.

Sardak slept most of the day away, but Salene came early to see if there was any way in which she could assist the necromancer. Zayl found her quite different from the usual women of her station, and even most of the men. That had to do with more than merely her gift, something the Rathmian *had* run across on occasion when dealing with other nobles. Salene Nesardo was strong of personality and will and braver than many others.

Humbart Wessel was a perfect example. Salene's initial shock did not give way to abhorrence, but rather fascination. When she returned in the morning, she greeted the skull as if he were as much a guest as Zayl . . . an act which tickled the spirit to no end. Humbart would have regaled her with story after story of their adventures—somehow with him taking the physical lead—but a glance from the necromancer cut him off. He also kept the promise that Zayl had forced out of him after the noblewoman had departed following the attack—that Salene was not to know what had really happened.

Under normal circumstances, Zayl would have needed little time before commencing, but with all he had so far experienced and the fact that Salene's husband had not answered him during the necromancer's excursion into the netherworld, the Rathmian wanted all factors in his favor.

"The hour after midnight," he finally informed Salene and her just-waking brother. "Before the place of burial."

"That would be below the house. In the crypt."

Zayl had assumed that House Nesardo had such a place and suspected that it was the nexus to which the souls he had discovered had been drawn. "Good, then—"

From somewhere without, a great bell rung once, twice, three times. It had a finality to it that caught the necromancer's interest immediately.

"The bells," muttered Salene, eyes narrowing sadly. She glanced at Sardak, who was, for once, somber. "King Cornelius is finally dead."

"Took long enough," Sardak replied. "When I die, I want it to be quick, not lingering for weeks like that."

Some fragments of conversation that Zayl had heard when departing the ship that had brought him to Westmarch came back. He knew that the king of the land had been ill, but not to what extent. A new sense of urgency struck the Rathmian. This death was too timely for his tastes.

"Has the king an heir?" he asked.

"Three sons originally, one dead as a youth." Lady Nesardo pursed her lips. "His heir and namesake died from a spider bite while out in the countryside some months back. Now, it's to be Justinian. The fourth of that name."

"Justinian the Wide-Eyed, some of us call him," Sardak

added, not looking at all pleased. "As naive a boy as ever lived, and he's as old as I."

"He had no idea he would be king, Sardak. Everyone expected it to be Cornelius the Younger."

"Which will not help Westmarch at the moment, sister."

A wise old ruler dead of sickness. A promising heir poisoned by accident. An untried, unready successor . . .

"A spider?" Zayl suddenly muttered. "A poisonous spider? Are they common here?"

"Actually, very rare, but—"

Salene got no further, for just then a white-haired female servant appeared. Wringing her hands and trying not to look at the necromancer, the servant announced, "Mistress, General Torion is at the door!"

"General Torion?" The noblewoman looked perplexed.

"Perhaps he comes to spirit you off to Entsteig, dear sister. Should I pack your things?"

"Hush, Sardak! Fiona, please tell the good general that I really haven't the time—"

"Surely you do, at least this day," boomed a voice from behind the servant.

Fiona let out a squeak and rushed away. In her place there came the epitome of the polished, capable soldier that stories spoke about but whom Zayl had never actually met in life. General Torion had flowing brown hair brushed back over his shoulders and a trim beard with a hint of gray in it. His aquiline face sported a small scar below his left eye, one of a brilliant blue pair. He stood a head taller than Zayl and was likely a third again as broad in the shoulders. He was not a giant like Polth, but the catlike ease with which the veteran officer moved made Zayl suspect that the bodyguard would have been on the losing end of any battle between the two.

The Nesardos' visitor was clad in a red uniform with a golden breastplate, and in the crook of his left arm he carried a plumed, open-faced helm. High boots and a sheathed sword with a rounded guard made up the rest of his ensemble.

"Torion!" declared Salene, recovering. "To what do we owe this honor?"

The commander had first smiled upon seeing her, but now his aspect turned much darker. "You heard the bells. The old man actually passed away last night, but we've spent all this time preparing. Justinian's going to need the support of the majority of the nobility from the outset, and all agreed that your word for him would go a long way toward his getting that. We don't want a repeat of the Cartolus Insurrection."

"What happened then?" Zayl asked.

For the first time, Torion—like the necromancer, he seemed to have no other name—appeared to register the black-cloaked figure. The general started to draw his sword. "By the Church! What is this dog doing here? Salene, has he taken control of your mind?"

Sardak immediately stepped out of any possible path that the man might take in charging Zayl. Salene, on the other hand, stepped directly between the officer and his intended target. "Torion! You forget yourself, general!"

His reaction was immediate. He released the sword and grimaced as if slapped in the face. The Rathmian had no trouble understanding why.

Torion was deeply in love with Salene.

"Salene," began the soldier. "Do you know what this *thing* is? Do you know what depravities he commits in the graveyards and tombs of—"

"*Torion.*"

He quieted, but continued to glare daggers at the necromancer.

The Rathmian's hostess indicated him and said, "This is Zayl. He is here at my behest. I think you know why."

"That trouble with Lord Jitan? Salene, if you would just grant me the honor I've asked more than once—"

"Fourteen times, by my count," offered Sardak.

For a brief moment, the general's anger focused on the brother instead of Zayl. Then, "As I was saying, if you'd just grant that, this would no longer trouble you—"

"Torion, Nesardo is my family, my legacy." She said no more, clearly having explained her feelings often enough.

Eyes again on the necromancer, Torion abruptly snarled, "If any evil befalls her and I can trace it to you, dog, I'll have your head!"

In response, Zayl only nodded.

Before the encounter could become violent again, the noblewoman said, "Give the council my word of my support for Justinian. I believe him to be good for Westmarch. He lacks confidence mostly, Torion, and I think you can help him there."

"It's good of you to say so." He clutched tight the helmet, his face showing a different concern. "Salene, come see me if you need any help . . . and be wary around this grave robber."

"Torion—"

Recalling himself, the general clicked his heels, bowing to her at the same time. He gave Sardak a cursory nod and utterly ignored Zayl as he departed.

"That man has a taste for the dramatic entrance," Salene's brother concluded with some mirth. "I swear he timed it so as to arrive just after the stroke of the bell! I wonder if he had to wait outside for a while beforehand."

"Torion is a good man, Sardak."

"I doubt our friend here would think so. I was certain that he was going to cut out your heart, friend Zayl. Tell me, could you have put it back in afterward? I'm just curious—"

"Sardak!"

He made a fair imitation of the officer's grand bow. "I think I've overstayed my own welcome. If you need me, sister dear, you know where to find me."

Salene did not look pleased. "Yes, the Hangman's Noose. With that rabble. Be back before the time Zayl told us. If you're not coming with the crypt, I'd at least like you near."

"Have I ever failed you?"

The noblewoman kept her expression constant. "I'll refrain from answering that."

With another chuckle, Sardak moved closer and kissed his sibling on the cheek. With a mocking nod to Zayl, he left the pair alone.

"I'm so very sorry about both of them." Salene shook her head. "If you'd rather forget tonight and leave Westmarch, I'd understand perfectly."

"I will be staying."

She brightened. "Thank you . . ."

"It is not merely because of your request," he told her bluntly. "There are matters that I myself am curious about."

"Of course. I should have remembered that those of your calling are not normally found this far west in the first place unless it's on some important matter."

"No, we are not." Zayl found himself wishing that such was not the case. It would have been good if he could have found another of Rathma's servants. He would have liked to have conferred with someone else fluent in such matters in order to assure himself that he had not missed anything.

But it was too late to concern himself about that. The hour was fast approaching and he had much more to do.

"Can I be of any help to you at all, Zayl?"

There was one way, but he had been loath to ask. It was the first thing that might make her begin to regret having asked a necromancer for aid. Yet, it had to be done.

"If I may be so bold . . . I will need some of your blood, my lady."

"My *blood*?" For just the briefest of moments, her eyes reflected what he had feared. Then, Salene pulled herself together again. "Of course." She stretched forth one smooth hand, turning it so the wrist was up. "Take what you need."

"Only a drop or two," the Rathmian clarified, impressed by her willingness to trust him even in this. "You are kin to Riordan, however distant. Your blood will help call him. I would have perhaps asked your brother—"

"Better that you didn't. I'm willing, Master Zayl. Take it."

"There is no need to stand. I would prefer if you would

sit, my lady. Please." To emphasize his desire for her to be relaxed, the necromancer held the nearest chair for her.

"You are a gentleman," she replied with a smile, seating herself. "Thank you."

An unfamiliar emotion coursed through Zayl. He quickly immersed himself in the task at hand, taking from his belt the dagger and from a small pouch next to it a tiny, smoke-colored glass vial. Removing the glove from his left hand, the Rathmian began muttering to himself and tracing a pattern before his hostess.

Fascination filled Salene's face. She said nothing, made no move. When Zayl brought the point of the dagger to her palm, the noblewoman purposely held her breath, which further steadied her hand for the act.

Zayl pricked her palm.

Blood pooled over the opening, but only for a moment. Defying the natural laws, it started coursing up the side of the blade, coloring it crimson.

When Zayl saw that he had what he needed, he pulled the dagger up. Then, drawing another pattern over Salene's palm, he sealed the wound.

"You healed it . . . ," she whispered, touching the spot and finding no trace of the jab. "I didn't think—"

"We are servants of the Balance. If we are to understand death and its repercussions, then we must know something about life and its healing processes. There are limits, though."

As he talked, he maneuvered the tip of the blade over the minute bottle. Muttering under his breath, the necromancer released the blood. Zayl watched in satisfaction as every single drop fell into the container. When he was finished, the dagger was spotless.

Laying the tool to the side, the hooded figure stoppered the bottle. He looked up at Salene . . . and hesitated. Framed by her rich, red hair, the perfection of her features caught him by surprise.

"Why do you do that?" the noblewoman asked.

At first he thought that she meant his staring. Her eyes,

however, looked not at him . . . but rather at his right hand.

"Why do you never take your glove off that one?" Salene pressed. "Always your left hand, but never your right. Never both."

She was observant . . . *too* observant. "A matter of form among those of my calling," he lied. Zayl slipped on his other glove, then put the bottle in the pouch. "If you will forgive me, my lady, I will need to continue the rest of my work in private."

Salene nodded, but her eyes lingered on the right hand. The necromancer shifted so as to remove it from her sight and then, with a courteous bow, left her sitting alone.

But not very alone. Polth stood just outside the room, the giant bodyguard eyeing Zayl speculatively. He had clearly been nearby all the time, although even the Rathmian had not noticed him.

"She trusts you, Master Zayl. You should know: That is much coming from her."

"I will endeavor to do what I can, Polth, but I promise nothing."

"Except that you'll not cause her harm." Polth's expression warned the necromancer of the danger he'd risk should he fail in that regard.

Zayl nodded once, then started past the bodyguard, only to have Polth's thick arm bar the way.

"One thing more, Rathmian. It would be good to stay inside. Friends I have who say the Zakarum are asking about black-dressed strangers with the look of grave robbers. They speak the words 'heretic' and 'desecrator,' and fire is mentioned in regard to both."

The news did not surprise Zayl. The Church ever found whatever excuse it could to hunt down the Rathmians. Still, he accepted Polth's warning gratefully. The bodyguard could have just as easily kept such news to himself and then, once Zayl had done his work, allowed the necromancer to walk into the hands of the inquisitors.

"I will remember, Polth."

"I'll be with the mistress this evening, too," the giant added. "Just to make certain."

"Of course."

Polth finally let him pass, but as Zayl headed toward his quarters, he sensed the man's gaze follow him long after he had stepped out of sight.

"Where've you been?" snapped Aldric. "I've gotten *nowhere* with this thing!"

Lord Jitan angrily waved the Moon of the Spider about as if it were little more than a trinket he had picked up in the market square. For all the wonder that he sensed within it, it might as well have been a painted rock. Everything he had done had come to naught. Not an iota of power had the noble wrested from the artifact.

"There were matters to attend to, my lord," replied Karybdus solemnly. "Besides, the night in question is not yet upon us. You must be patient."

"But you promised that even before that I'd be able to draw from the forces contained in this thing! So far, I've received nothing!"

"You are unschooled in the arts, Lord Jitan, and so seek to take with the equivalent of a hammer what can be yours with a simple twist of the key . . ."

"Spare me your poetic words, sorcerer! Show me!"

Karybdus looked about the chamber. Six men-at-arms stood guard in what had once been the library of the House of Jitan. High wooden shelves lining three of the walls bespoke a wide collection of tomes and parchments, but the shelves were now empty, even dust-laden. In the course of his obsession, the aristocrat had thrown out any writing that had not aided him, the result of which had been the loss of several rare works on other subjects. Karybdus ever hid his frustration with Aldric for this heinous act, aware that his overall goals would only be met by giving his host what he wished.

For all his imposing appearance, Lord Jitan sat dwarfed by the huge oak table filling much of the library. The polished, rectangular piece of furniture had four legs shaped like those of a dragon, down to taloned paws clutching spheres. Parchments lay scattered over the table, the wasted efforts of Aldric's magical spells.

Karybdus had known that his host would fail, but had deigned not to mention that fact. Everything had to work as the Rathmian planned, else his attempt to reorient the Balance would go awry and the world would slip further into calamity.

But it was now time to show Lord Aldric Jitan a taste of what he sought. Karybdus studied the six men standing so attentively. His senses probed deep, analyzing their psyches. Yes, they would do nicely. They contained the necessary ferocity within. It only needed to be called forth.

"It is very simple, my lord." Karybdus signaled for the guard by the door to shut it, then strode toward the noble. "Set the artifact squarely in your palms." The necromancer came around the table, stopping just behind Aldric. He leaned forward in order to whisper in Lord Jitan's ear. "The men here have served you well. They can serve you better through the Moon of the Spider . . ."

The noble listened as Karybdus explained what he needed to do. At first, Aldric looked unsettled, but his expression quickly shifted to one of eager anticipation.

The Rathmian stepped back the moment that he finished. Aldric gazed up at his loyal followers, summoning them around the table with but a glance. Long in the service of the Lord Jitan, they silently obeyed. None of them were aware of what had taken place in the ruins.

Aldric focused on the arachnid pattern, his thoughts mentally caressing each limb and outlining the body. As he stared, the shape seemed to move of its own accord. The legs stretched languidly, as if the spider within stirred to waking. Two bright, red flashes—eyes—looked back at the noble, who grinned.

Without warning, the spider abandoned its position. Yet, in its wake, the shadowy form left a copy of itself. No sooner had the first moved away than the *second* followed suit. It also left in its wake a duplicate . . . and that, too, moved on.

Aldric gradually realized that, with the exception of Karybdus, none of those around him saw this astonishing magic. He almost said something, but the necromancer was suddenly there at his ear again.

"The Blessing of Astrogha is yours to bestow, my lord . . ."

The spiders now stood poised atop both the sphere and Lord Jitan's hands. Curiously, Aldric felt no repulsion from their touch. He gazed at the shadowy arachnids, then focused.

Each spider leapt up into the air toward one of his followers.

Only at the last did the men appear to notice the creatures, far too late for any of them to do anything but scream as the arachnids, growing larger as they flew, landed atop their heads.

With rasping hisses, the blood-eyed spiders sank their legs into the skulls of their victims.

The six stricken guards teetered back, some clutching in vain at the horrors on them, others simply trying to escape. None, however, made it farther than a few steps before falling to their hands and knees.

Animalistic howls erupted from their lips. A transformation seized hold of each of Aldric's chosen. Their backs began to arch and thicken. Legs grew wiry and feet all but disappeared. Their arms stretched and narrowed and their hands became splayed paws, but paws still able to grasp and ending in sharp nails designed for scoring flesh. In their frenzy, they began rending their garments, ripping off cloth and armor with equal ease and flinging everything about the chamber with wild abandon. Nothing, however, came within range of either Lord Jitan or Karybdus, the necromancer discreetly deflecting all.

Then, from their chests, the two lower ribs on each side burst free. The mutated men howled anew as blood and ichor spilled on the floor. But the wounds quickly healed and the twisting ribs, now covered in flesh of their own, began sprouting thin, misshapen claws designed for both walking and climbing. The new limbs grew and grew until they were as long as the others, their claws finally slapping hard against the stone floor.

At the same time, a coarse black fur sprouted over each man's face and form. Features contorted, stretching and reshaping. The ears and noses shriveled away and, as Aldric Jitan continued to watch in fascination, the eyes split apart over and over, clustering together like grapes in two macabre groups. Although the eyes—*all* the eyes— remained fairly human in appearance, save that both the whites and pupils were now all blood-red, they glared without any compassion or sanity.

As one, the six transformed figures hissed, revealing sharp, yellowed fangs dripping with venom.

And atop the head of each new horror, a spider continued to cling tight. *Their* red eyes focused on Aldric and the six things that had once been men suddenly quieted. As one, they turned to the smiling noble . . . and knelt.

They were spiders, huge spiders . . . but they still remained men of a sort. Spiders, men . . . and something primal that the noble could not identify . . . not that he truly cared. "Incredible . . ."

"They have become the Children of Astrogha, who once numbered thousands," explained the necromancer as if reciting to a class on history. "Mortals blessed with his favor, his likeness."

The Children of Astrogha bobbed up and down on their four back limbs. The other four appendages constantly opened and closed, as if in eagerness to do Aldric's bidding.

"Your enemies are doomed, my lord," Karybdus murmured close. "The Children serve unquestioningly the master of the sphere. You should know, to wield this much of the Moon's power even before the coming of the Convergence is a sure sign of your right to the legacy it holds. All that you dream, all that you would claim, will be yours, mark me."

"All of it . . . ," agreed Aldric, eyeing those who had once served him loyally as men and now would do so as both less and more.

"And with that in mind," Karybdus continued, "there is a task at hand. One of your enemies has made himself known, and he strikes at the heart of your hopes and desires . . ."

Aldric leapt to his feet, mouth curled in fury. "What do you mean?"

The Rathmian's expression remained impassive. "He is in the House of Nesardo, with the Lady Salene."

Immediately, Lord Jitan's baleful gaze turned to the monsters that had once been men.

Karybdus nodded. "Exactly as I was thinking, my lord . . ."

FIVE

As evening neared, a violent storm swept over the city, the worst of it finally centering over House Nesardo. There, the tempest appeared to stall, as if a plant setting down roots. It raged and raged, with no sign of lessening.

There always seem to be storms, Zayl thought as thunder once again racked the building. *Yet, rain is no more evil than the sun or moon. It is only that those who work dark deeds who prefer to cloak their evil with it.*

He took the thought to heart as he readied himself for his spellwork. Zayl had the sample of blood from Salene and the tools he would need for drawing up the pattern. She, in turn, promised to bring with her three items of close personal value to the late Riordan.

All they needed to do now was to descend into the crypt.

With Humbart in the pouch, the Rathmian returned to the main corridor downstairs. Salene already awaited him there. Polth, a lit lamp in one hand, stood protectively behind her. The Lady Nesardo wore reasonable attire for journeying below the earth, a riding outfit with green pants and leather boots, besides a similar-colored cotton blouse, over which was buttoned a black leather vest. A matching belt with a small, sheathed dagger completed her ensemble.

The noblewoman smiled anxiously as the tall, slim figure approached.

"I've brought the articles you mentioned." She held up a sack that clinked, indicating that at least two of the pieces were, in some part, made of metal.

"Then, if you will lead the way . . ."

Lifting another of the lamps from the nearest wall, Salene complied. Polth left her to take up a position at the rear. For the bodyguard to choose such a place was a clear sign that, in the crypt of Nesardo, Polth considered Zayl the only questionable factor.

The necromancer did not find it odd that the family would have its crypt beneath its home, for the practice was not unknown in Lut Gholein or the eastern half of the world. The powerful and wealthy seemed especially covetous of their dead, as if their mortal shells were of any more value than those of the lowest beggars in the streets.

Yet, there was something more to House Nesardo's crypt, something that made the necromancer eager to see it. As Salene guided them through the house, he sensed again the collective of souls beneath his feet and the unidentifiable energies that seemed to either coalesce around them or that were, perhaps, the reason for their being there at all.

The trio descended a series of stone steps that took them beneath ground level. They passed empty, dust-laden chambers whose brutal history Zayl could sense from the stark emotional impressions still lingering.

Salene suddenly hesitated. Turning to the necromancer, she said, "My family is not without its black deeds, Master Zayl."

He nodded, the only answer that his hostess required. As one with the gift, Salene had likely felt the emanations from these chambers throughout most of her life and so suspected that he now did, also.

At the end of the corridor, they descended once more. The Rathmian tensed, aware that they were very near their destination.

Moments later, they confronted a thick iron door. Salene held her lamp close, revealing an eight-sided starburst pattern set in the center. Polth stepped up to the front and, after handing his lamp to Zayl, tugged tight on the rounded handle.

The bodyguard pulled the ancient door open, a grating squeal accompanying its movement.

A torrent of whispering voices rushed up to meet Zayl. They spoke not to him, though, nor to any living thing. They were the voices of the very dead he had confronted earlier, the voices of Nesardo's past reliving their former lives, over and over . . .

As Polth retrieved his lamp, Zayl noted Salene watching him intently. "Sometimes," she murmured, "sometimes I think I hear my ancestors when I come down here . . ."

Lady Nesardo turned and entered. With Polth close at his back, the necromancer did the same.

And as he first beheld the crypt, Zayl realized that his visit among the dead earlier had given him only a mere indication of their final resting place.

Although the shadows hid the full enormity, the edifice clearly ran the length of the house and beyond. Zayl did a quick estimation and decided that it covered most of the family grounds. The ceiling was as high as that of many cathedrals. He and his companions actually stood at the top of yet another set of steps which led down to the meticulously built stone floor. To each side, vaults at least ten high held the remains of Salene's bloodline. White, polished stone markers covered each space, the name and dates of the individual carved on them. The vaults continued on into the darkness, not one space in the immediate vicinity empty.

"We will have to walk a little farther," whispered Salene, stepping down. "Riordan's place is midway through this chamber."

"Are there other levels?"

"Three. One bears the bodies of loyal servants. The deepest is actually not from my family. It was an earlier crypt. The first Nesardos built this upon it."

The Rathmian's brow wrinkled. "Where would one—"

She shook her head. "You can't descend to it. The entrance caved in some centuries past during a quake. I know of it only because Riordan was always fascinated with our family history and uncovered the knowledge in his research."

More than ever, Zayl wished to commune with the late Lord Nesardo's shade. There was much that Riordan might be able to explain beyond Salene's current needs.

A layer of gray ash covered the floor. Vague footprints preceded the three. One pair matched Salene's in size and shape. So deep underground, the dust came, but came slowly. From the number of prints and their pattern of movement, he knew them to have been created during Riordan's burial procession some years back. Glancing at his hostess, Zayl saw her unconsciously retracing her steps. He wondered if she now relived that tragic moment.

Deep below the surface they might be, but that did not mean the crypt was devoid of life. Scavenger beetles, some as large as Zayl's palm, scattered out of sight as the lamps illuminated the way. Millipedes burrowed into cracks in vaults. Most astounding of all, though, where the shroud-like webs draping so many parts of the crypt. Several were large enough to cover a man and in them could be seen tombs of another kind: the wrapped, shriveled bodies of the spiders' victims. Most were other insects, but a few were small rats, no doubt sickly ones to have fallen prey to the much tinier arachnids.

"When Riordan died, I had an army of workers clear this crypt of such vermin," said Salene with a disgusted survey of the webs. "I can't believe that it's gotten this bad again. Where do they come from?"

Zayl did not reply, for he was instead caught up in the ever-increasing intensity of the psychic emanations. Each vault's inhabitant existed in the same dreamlike state, their spirits active when they should have either rested or gone on. The whispers had reached such a level that he was at times tempted to cover his ears.

They had gone only a few steps more when the noble-woman suddenly paused. A look in her eyes was all the information the necromancer needed, but a glance up at the marble plate just above her head verified that they had indeed come upon the mortal remains of Riordan Nesardo.

"If you would prefer a moment to yourself, my lady—"

"No. I've had enough such moments since his death. I cared for my husband, Master Zayl, even loved him in a certain way, and likely always will. But now I think it's best to continue with what we must, then leave him in peace."

But the cowled spellcaster was not so certain that it would be as easy as Salene thought. From Riordan's vault, Zayl suddenly realized that he sensed *nothing*. This was the only vault where no spirit was active. Why that, when all the others could not rest?

Such questions would, he hoped, be answered very soon. "I shall work here, then." He returned, reaching into his cloak and removing a piece of white chalk from a pouch. "If I may have some room, please . . ."

As Salene and Polth stepped back, Zayl knelt. He placed his own lamp next to him, then began drawing a five-sided pattern. In the corner of each, he drew the five elements as Rathma preached them—earth, air, fire, water, and time— in the center the outline of a serpentine form, and under it a downward arch. This was a simplified version of the symbol representing Trag'Oul, one commonly used for spellcasting. As the fulcrum of the Balance, the dragon was bound to all the elements and they to him. Although the symbol was simplified, the overall pattern was far more complex than Zayl had often utilized in the past. Myriad symbols soon decorated each of its borders. The necromancer suspected that all of them would be necessary if he hoped to achieve results.

When the pattern was finally complete, he reached into the large pouch and removed Humbart.

"What a depressing place!" the skull growled. "I wouldn't be caught dead here . . . if I had any choice in the matter, that is."

From Salene's direction came a brief chuckle, while from Polth there emerged only a grunt. His having expected the shade of Riordan Nesardo to possibly appear at some point, a talking skull evidently seemed far less astounding to the bodyguard.

"Quiet, Humbart," the necromancer murmured. He placed the fleshless head in the center, over the mark of Trag'Oul. There were times when uses arose for the skull, and this was one of them. As a soul midway between the afterworld and the mortal plane, Humbart Wessel offered a link like no other. He was yet another precaution Zayl had put in place to better his chances of reaching Salene's departed mate.

"Don't know why I'm doing this," Humbart continued to grumble. "Them souls are all so flighty, so full of their misery and loss. If I had a stomach, it'd empty from all their whining . . ." That said, the spirit stilled.

The Rathmian retrieved the tiny vial of blood donated by Salene, then, with the tip of his dagger, drew the contents up onto the blade. He took the weapon and outlined a circle around the skull and the mark.

Looking up at the noblewoman, Zayl said, "The items, please."

Salene handed him the sack. The necromancer reached in and removed the pieces one at a time. The first was a ceremonial dagger with the Nesardo symbol etched into the hilt—a hilt that looked to be pure gold. The edge of the weapon was blunt, the item for show, not for use.

The second piece Zayl removed was a blue, silken scarf such as the Rathmian had seen adorning the throats of a couple of returning nobles aboard ship. Imported from across the Twin Seas, such an item marked Riordan's high status in Westmarch.

Setting the scarf and dagger outside the circle of blood, Zayl located the last piece in the sack: a medallion with a golden chain. The necromancer frowned as he gazed upon it. The chain was of recent forging, but the medallion was much, much more ancient. More ancient than House Nesardo, in fact.

The metallic piece had almost been worn smooth by time, but he made out a shape—a head—with eight limbs sprouting from it. Zayl frowned, trying to recall anything in his teachings that matched such an image. When nothing did, he reluctantly added the final item to its proper place outside the circle.

"I will begin the summoning now," he informed Salene. "It would be best if you were next to me so that your near proximity can enhance our hopes of success."

Without hesitation, she complied. Her sudden closeness momentarily distracted Zayl, who was more used to performing summonings without another nearby. He sensed her power pulsate with each breath she took, the gift so naturally a part of her that the woman likely did not know the potential she carried.

Polth suddenly stirred. Zayl assumed that he was somehow the cause for the bodyguard's reaction, but Polth, hand on his weapon, instead peered into the darkness farther in.

"What is it, Polth?" Salene asked.

"Nothing, mistress. One of the vermin, I suppose."

The necromancer held the ivory dagger over the center and began to murmur. He felt energies swirl around him, gathering for the spell. The whispers of the ghosts halted as they felt the intrusion into their plane begin.

Riordan . . . , Zayl silently called. *Riordan Nesardo, husband of Salene . . . Riordan, Lord of House Nesardo . . .*

Several previous lords of the manor briefly stirred, then returned to their dream states when they realized it was not they whom the necromancer sought. Zayl had learned from the earlier incident to focus more, so as not to re-create the havoc he had caused those souls.

The crypt had always been cool, but now a stiff chill filled it. Salene abruptly shivered and Polth let out a low curse. To the Rathmian, however, the sudden shift in temperature was a promising sign. It meant that his spell was indeed reaching into the spirit world.

Riordan . . . Riordan Nesardo . . . come to us . . . come in the hour of your bride's need . . . A reluctant soul was often more willing to respond if a loved one was so involved.

Zayl felt a sudden stirring. He manipulated the dagger over the pattern, uttering words passed down by Rathma to his followers, words in a language known only to the faithful.

But nothing further happened. The necromancer sensed that something wanted to come, but that other forces held it back.

Without glancing at Salene, Zayl said, "My lady, if you would place one hand on the hilt of the dagger, I would ask then that you softly call your husband's name."

She obeyed without question, clearly trusting in his knowledge and skills. Zayl adjusted his grip so that she could properly touch the hilt, then focused his spellwork to coincide with her summons.

"Riordan?" the noblewoman whispered to the silent crypt. "Riordan . . . can you hear me? It's Salene. Please, Riordan . . . I need to speak with you . . ."

Now the presence stirred anew, pressing closer, but something still held it back. The necromancer had a vague impression of a winged form—

He grabbed for Salene. "Down!"

"Something's coming, lad!" roared Humbart. "I think it might be a—"

A flesh-rending howl filled the crypt, echoing over and over again. Rats, insects, and arachnids scattered in primal terror.

From the webs and dust formed a monstrous thing with wide wings both fiery and yet dry and decayed. Its body was a cadaverous corpse with not even enough flesh left to cover its bones. There was some semblance of a face—a man's, so it seemed—with wisps of hair and even some beard remaining. But there were no eyes left, only black pits, and the howling skeletal mouth was distended beyond mortal limits.

The arms, too, stretched far beyond anything human and, like a bat's limbs, were part of the wings. The remaining fingers were twisted talons clearly capable of shredding.

Even as it coalesced, the ghastly shade soared down

upon them. Zayl had barely thrown Salene to the floor before the fiendish shadow passed directly over them. Had they still been kneeling, it would have gone *through* their bodies.

"What is it?" blurted the noblewoman. "Is that—is that *Riordan*?"

"No . . . it is a *wraith*, a damned soul!" And what it was doing here now was of especial interest to the Rathmian. Unfortunately, before he could consider the reasons, he first had to survive the encounter. "Polth! Take her!"

He need not have even spoken. The bodyguard had already leaned down to seize his mistress. Polth lifted Salene to her feet as if she weighed nothing. He then kept one protective arm around her while with the other he brandished his weapon.

But a sword was no match for a wraith. Rolling to his feet, the necromancer brought up his dagger. Not at all to his surprise, the monstrous spirit fixated on him. Wraiths ever thirsted for what they no longer had, and spellcasters offered them a double bounty. Both Zayl's life force and his magic presented a bounty. They would not slake the horror's thirst—nothing mortal could—but that would not keep the wraith from draining him of everything regardless.

And then it would go after Salene, who also had the gift.

Eyes on the shrieking ghoul, Zayl commanded, "Take her upstairs! It will not follow out of the crypt! Go!"

"No! I won't leave you alone!" The Lady Nesardo struggled to escape Polth's ursine grip.

"Mistress, you *must* come!" The giant began dragging her toward the distant steps.

With a chilling scream, the wraith flew down at Zayl. Although its origins had once been human, it no longer had a lower torso. Instead, a savage, bony tail whipped back and forth—acting almost like a scorpion's sting. The sinister shade was not in any way corporeal, but if any part passed through the Rathmian, it would be as if a hundred blades had been thrust into his heart.

And that agony would pale in comparison to what he would suffer when the wraith began to suck him dry.

Muttering quickly, Zayl held the dagger up. From the nearest vaults, a torrent of bones burst through the marble. They tumbled in front of the necromancer, forming in an instant a wall whose brilliant illumination matched that of the dagger. Zayl disliked disturbing the bones of Salene's kin, but had no choice.

The wraith veered off just before it would have touched the bone barrier. It shrieked angrily, seeking a way around Zayl's spell.

That would not take long, either. In truth, such a defense would hold little against the monster, but the necromancer sought only a delay so that he could prepare a better defense. At least with the focus on him, Salene was safe.

But then, from the shadows, he sensed the movements of others.

Risking himself, he glanced toward the darkened steps. "Get her out of here, Polth! Quickly! There—"

Finally having determined that the bones were no menace to it, the wraith chose that moment to plunge. As it flowed through the barrier, the bones quivered . . . and the entire structure collapsed in a heap.

Zayl brought up the dagger again, but too late. He turned the ghoulish creature aside, but one wing passed through his torso.

It was as if someone had stolen a piece of his soul. Crying out, the Rathmian dropped to one knee. It was all he could do to keep a grip on the dagger.

"Zayl, lad! There's a foul beast atop the vaults! A big, hairy bastard of a spider thing with fangs and claws! By my lost soul, there's another!"

Low, sibilant hisses, coming from all sides—even from overhead—now filled the crypt.

Several monstrous forms dropped through the thick webs above.

Salene screamed.

Through pain-racked eyes, Zayl saw the darkened figures of her and Polth suddenly surrounded by at least four hunching shapes that would have been nearly as tall as the bodyguard if standing straight. They seemed some hellish cross between men and giant, black arachnids. Polth held them at bay with his sword, but the creatures, moving about on the back four of their macabre limbs, paced around the pair in clear preparation for a group attack. One opened wide its lipless maw, hissing and revealing a pair of huge fangs such as the necromancer had seen on jungle spiders of the most virulent toxicity.

But concern for Salene and Polth faded into the back of his mind as Zayl sensed the wraith returning for him. He rolled out of the way just as the specter dropped into the area where he had been kneeling.

"Come and try that on me!" snapped Humbart. "I'll take you on with no hands to tie behind my back!"

The wraith moaned at the skull and with a vicious beat of its ethereal wing somehow sent Humbart rolling. He swore as he collided with one wall of vaults.

But his distraction did what it was supposed to. Given the chance to recover enough, Zayl cast another spell.

A spear of bone formed in the air before the Rathmian. With a single word more, Zayl sent it flying at the wraith.

The Talon of Trag'Oul was a weapon both physical and mystical. That the wraith had no mortal substance made no difference.

The Talon's target turned just as the spear reached it. The wraith sought to twist out of the way, but moved too slow.

Zayl's missile tore through its side.

A shriek more horrifying than any previous escaped the specter. Still screaming, it turned and vanished into the deeper section of the crypt.

Gasping from his efforts, the necromancer looked to Salene and Polth. Their grotesque attackers had finally worked up their strategy. One leapt up onto the vaults, then to the ceiling, where it dropped down toward the bodyguard. Polth instinctively shifted to meet it. The moment he reacted, two others—the foremost crawling across the opposing vaults—charged Salene.

But she was evidently not the helpless figure that they thought her. The crimson-haired noblewoman gestured toward the one leaping at her from the vaults—and a bolt of ice struck the hellish arachnid square in the chest. Hurtled back at the wall, it hit with a bone-cracking thud, then crumpled in a heap on the floor. Frost covered its entire body and sprinkled the air around the corpse.

Salene gaped at what she had done.

The second horror tried to use her shock to its advantage. Fangs dripping and claws out, it lunged for her throat.

There was a flash of icy blue light, and in its brief illumination what appeared to be a shield of some sort came between Salene and the fangs.

Howling, the monster pulled back a paw completely frozen solid. Again, Salene seemed startled at what was clearly her own handiwork.

Polth had managed to avoid the first creature's plunge at him. With expert swordplay, he drove it back, then, seeing a moment, turned and ran the one with the ruined paw through.

But then another leapt out of the shadows, bowling the giant over from behind. Two more of the demonic arachnids joined their comrade in assaulting the bodyguard.

Without hesitation, Zayl threw his dagger. The glowing blade flew unerringly at his target, sinking into the back of one of the creatures. Hissing sharply, the man/spider spun in a circle, grasping frantically for the deeply buried weapon.

The fact that it *was* still buried there startled the Rathmian utterly. By rights, the dagger should have returned to him once its grisly task had been done. By blood and sacrifice, it had been bound to his conscious will years ago. If he desired it to come to him, it did . . . but not now.

Only then did Zayl understand that he had played right into someone's hand.

The sixth beast fell out of the dark webs above him, hissing lustily as it landed upon the spellcaster. The heavy weight crushed Zayl into the floor, nearly knocking him unconscious. He felt clawed hands tear at his back, rending his garments with ease and leaving bloody gashes in his flesh. Burning venom dripped onto the back of his neck.

But Zayl was not easily subdued. He slammed his elbow into his adversary's midsection and heard a satisfactory grunt of pain. Some of the weight vanished, enough so that the Rathmian could turn on his back and better face his foe.

The monstrosity snapped at him with yellowed fangs as long as Zayl's fingers. Its breath stank of the grave. Yet, the eyes were the most unsettling aspect of all, for Zayl could have sworn that they carried in them a human trait.

Then, the Rathmian's gaze shifted upward and he saw an odd growth atop the head of the fiend. After a moment, the necromancer realized that it was a *separate* creature . . . a smaller spider, but one still larger than his hand. It stared in his direction with baleful red orbs, its own smaller fangs twitching evilly.

The revelation almost undid Zayl, for his astonishment gave the larger fiend the chance to tighten his grip. The fangs drew near the necromancer's throat and—

Suddenly a heavy fist struck the monster in the side of the head. The beast tumbled back. Polth filled Zayl's view. The bodyguard's uniform was ripped to shreds and he had scars everywhere, but he wore a triumphant grin.

"My thanks, Master Zayl," Polth rumbled. "The one you took from me, it was enough. The other two, they fled, having learned their folly!"

Sure enough, other than the Rathmian's foe, the only creatures left were the dead ones. Even as Polth helped Zayl rise, the final creature scurried back up into the shadows.

The necromancer frowned. He was forced to acknowledge that he could not magically sense the creatures. They were a complete blank to his abilities. Small wonder that he had been caught off guard by the one dropping from above.

Another concern took over. Zayl tried to look past the imposing bodyguard. "Salene! Is she—"

"Untouched she is—but unharmed . . . I can't say."

Zayl saw why. Salene Nesardo stood where he had last noted her, both arms wrapped tight around herself. She stared at the beast she had slain, and Zayl knew right then that this was the first life that his hostess had ever taken. That it was some monstrous creature seeking her own death did not matter.

"We must get her upstairs and into bed," the necromancer suggested. "The surroundings will help ease her thoughts. You go to her. I will be with you shortly."

"Aye."

Humbart's skull lay eye sockets up. A low mutter flowed from the late mercenary's fleshless head, much of it having to do with wishes for a good sword arm and a pair of legs. Aware that if his companion could grumble so he was undamaged, Zayl went first for his dagger, still tight in the back of its victim. As he stumbled along, he crossed what was left of the spell pattern.

Wait please wait please wait please listen please listen please!

The frantic intensity of the voice suddenly inside Zayl's head made him clutch his skull in renewed pain. He concentrated, drawing up mental shields that made the cry more tolerable.

He seeks the moon seeks the moon seeks the moon he has it but it is not the moon but it is the moon and if the moon is held to the moon then the spider will come again . . .

Zayl tried his best to make sense of the rambling words. He knew immediately their source. Riordan Nesardo had finally responded, albeit neither in the manner expected nor on the subject for which his shade had been sought. But his frenetic tone indicated that this was a warning that needed to be told more than anything else, and that was what mattered now.

What do you mean? the necromancer thought. *What of the spider? What of the moon?*

A vague, misty form drew together near the vault where Salene's husband had been buried. *Spider moon spider moon spider moon moon spider moon spider moon of the spider moon of the spider the time comes the spider comes Astrogha comes . . .*

"Astrogha?" Zayl blurted. Something about the name struck a chord. "Moon of the Spider?"

"Zayl!"

Riordan's presence vanished from his head, as did the shadow on the vault. Zayl heard Polth's swearing voice and realized that the one who had called the necromancer's name had been Salene.

"Look out, lad!" added Humbart. "It's back—"

Strong hands grabbed the Rathmian, tossing him far. Zayl landed atop the very beast toward which he had been heading. His face slid against the hilt of his dagger. He instinctively seized the mystical weapon, tugging it free and spinning around to see what was happening.

The shriek that filled the crypt was answer enough even before Zayl finished turning. The wraith had returned, seeking to feast upon the distracted spellcaster.

But Polth had thrown Zayl out of its imminent path. The bodyguard stood defiantly, his sword again out just as the wailing specter fell upon him.

Yet, where the Rathmian might have had some defense, the fighter did not. The wraith coursed through him without pause, its taloned wings seeming to grasp at Polth's chest as it did.

The giant screamed. His body shook and his skin shriveled. The sword fell from his crumbling fingers. Polth's desiccated flesh turned to ash and even before he fell, there was little left of him but a skeleton.

The wraith continued on, its hunger unabated. Salene stood directly before it, the noblewoman so horrified by the death of her loyal servant that she stood frozen.

Zayl held the dagger before him, point down. He spouted out the words to the spell as quickly as he could.

Polth had perished for him; he would not let the same fate befall Salene.

The pale illumination spread from the dagger to the wraith, enveloping the winged fiend as if in one of the spiders' webs. The wraith shrieked as it still sought Salene, who stood barely a yard from its vile reach.

Standing, the necromancer cried, "Ulth i Rathma syn!"

The light pulled back into the blade . . . and with it came the thrashing specter. The creature howled and flapped as hard as it could, but it was unable to escape the pull. Zayl shuddered with effort, for the spell he used drew from his own soul. Yet, if he let up in the least, the Rathmian knew full well, the wraith would have both the noblewoman and him.

His spell was a variation of the life-tap that a necromancer could use to revitalize himself with the essence of a foe. It was ever a dangerous spell, for in taking in the life of another, one risked taking on the victim's attributes. There were legends of Rathmians who had literally become their vanquished enemies, necromancers who had then turned to the side of Hell until hunted down by their brethren.

But what Zayl attempted now had even greater risks. He had combined the life tap with a mastery spell generally used on the recently deceased. Utilized against a common shade, there would have been little risk, but here Zayl sought control against one of the most malevolent of the undead. Worse was the fact that though what he absorbed now weakened his adversary, it also sickened the Rathmian. Zayl took not life into him, but the undeath that was the wraith's essence. The coldness that filled the human was one that even a servant of the Balance could not long tolerate and live.

Passing above Polth's ravaged corpse, the shrieking wraith neared the blade. Zayl gritted his teeth. He had one last spell in mind, but he wanted the specter contained as much as possible before he attempted it or else all the necromancer would accomplish was slaying the noblewoman and himself.

Closer . . . closer . . .

There!

Zayl focused on the bodyguard's remains.

Polth's corpse exploded, the anguish of his death a most powerful force. Zayl steered that force at the wraith.

Amplified by the necromancer's magic, the death energies overwhelmed the specter, burning it away. The wraith managed one final, angry shriek—and vanished without a trace.

Zayl tried to unbind himself from the wraith's destruction, but his effort was not entirely successful. The deathly energies enveloped him . . .

The last thing he heard was Salene's cry.

SIX

✳

Salene Nesardo had not known what to make of the pale, dark-haired figure when she had first decided to have Polth approach him in the Black Ram. It felt right to seek the necromancer's skills, despite a childhood in which the Zakarum Church had played a significant role. Perhaps her choice had also been in part due to her gift—or *curse,* as she sometimes thought it—or perhaps when she had looked into his gray eyes, the noblewoman had recognized the man within. Rumor and legend made the necromancers vile, disturbed scavengers of the grave, spellcasters in league with evil, but that had not been what Salene had seen inside Zayl. She had, in point of fact, seen something akin to what she noted in her own mirror: a silent determination to do what had to be done, no matter what the consequence to one's self.

And now, Zayl had nearly died because of her.

He lay in the bed she had set aside for him, the first time he had made use of it. Fearful to leave him alone in the crypt while she ran for help, Salene had dragged him up the steps as best she could. Only when he had been safely out had she gone for Sardak. With her brother's aid, they had brought him back to the room.

Salene's hands still shook. She witnessed Polth's death over and over in her mind. He had served her loyally even before her marriage to Riordan and had not hesitated to protect the necromancer. That last had surprised her, but perhaps Polth had believed Zayl the best chance for her survival. It shamed her that there was nothing of the man left to bury—the Rathmian's last spell had destroyed what little the wraith had not—but she knew that Polth had never been one for ceremony. He would have liked Zayl's using him as the weapon that had destroyed his slayer.

An unusually subdued Sardak had offered to summon servants to help her, but Salene knew that none of them would come near the necromancer. Fortunately, she had never been as delicate as some of her counterparts, and in fact knew something of aiding the injured from having had to help her brother after some of his more elaborate drinking bouts.

And if her own skills proved too limited, she evidently had the aid of the late Humbart Wessel upon which to call.

"Gently there, gently there," admonished the skull as she peeled away what remained of Zayl's cloak and shirt. "You brought some good strong whiskey for those wounds, I hope."

"It's right next to you." The mercenary's skull—brought back at the same time as Zayl—sat atop its usual place, the flask of whiskey to its left side.

"Make sure you drench each of those beasts' slashes with it. I hope it's got some good bite in it, not like some of those fancy liquors bluebloods drink . . . beggin' your pardon, my lady."

"My brother drinks it. It should kill any infection."

Humbart chuckled hollowly. "Wish I could taste it, I do!"

As she used a knife to cut away the strips of material, Salene noted that at least Zayl breathed steadily. That said, his already-pale skin was practically pure white, save for some blueness around his lips. That frightened her.

The noblewoman took a moist cloth from a ceramic bowl she had brought with her and began wiping clean the wounds. Sweat matted the hair on Zayl's chest and his body felt like an inferno despite the snowy look.

When she was satisfied that she had wiped off the wounds as much as possible, Salene retrieved the whiskey. There were herbs that she knew could have also helped, but it was too late to send out a servant to find someone who sold them.

With extreme caution, the noblewoman poured a few drops on the first wound.

Zayl flinched slightly. Salene waited for more of a reaction, but none followed.

"Have no fear, lass," Humbart assured her. "Zayl's got a strong pain threshold. That's all I'd be expecting from him even now."

Breathing easier, she applied more whiskey. Each time, the necromancer reacted in the same mild manner.

"That should be enough," Salene murmured a few minutes later. As she stoppered the flask, she realized for the first time that she had never bothered to remove the long glove from Zayl's right hand; he had taken off the left one at some point during the summoning. Wanting him to feel as comfortable as possible, the Lady Nesardo began tugging on the garment.

"There's no need for that!" the skull suddenly piped up, the tone bordering on frantic. "He's perfectly fine with the glove on! It's a Rathmian thing, you know! Just leave it—damn!"

A brief scream escaped Salene.

She stumbled back in horror at what lay beneath. It twitched as if in response to her scream, further heightening her shock.

"Salene!" Sardak banged on the door with his fist. "Salene, what's going on?" He shoved the door open, pushing her to the side at the same time.

"'Tis nothing, lass!" insisted Humbart. "Nothing at all! You—"

"Fire and brimstone!" snapped her brother. "What did I tell you about his kind?"

Salene continued to stare, her horror now mixed with morbid fascination. She heard neither Sardak's nor the skull's words. All that mattered was the grisly sight before her.

Zayl's right hand was fleshless.

Only a few well-placed strands of sinew seemed to hold the bones together. Otherwise, no skin, not a single patch, draped the horrific appendage. The entire hand was the same from the tip of the longest finger to the wrist. Only there did bone and flesh come together, and even then it was at first in a charred stump that continued for two or three inches into the forearm.

Sardak seized hold of her. "Come with me, Salene! Leave this monster to his own devices—"

"Here now! Zayl's as good a man as any you'll find!"

The noblewoman shook her head, her thoughts gradually clearing. "No . . . no, Sardak. He saved my life, and tried to save Polth's!"

"Salene—"

She gently guided her brother back to the door. "Thank you for your concern, Sardak, but I'm all right. You return to your room. If I need you, I'll come for you."

Her brother tousled his hair. All the drink had burnt out of him. He eyed the skeletal hand with continued disgust, but finally nodded. "You'll do what you think best, sister dear. You always do." Sardak met her gaze. "But know that I'll be listening for you. The slightest damned sound out of the ordinary and I'll be back—with a sword ready!"

He closed the door behind him, leaving Salene alone with Zayl and the skull. Salene tentatively approached the still form on the bed.

"Did it . . . is it from what happened in the crypt?"

Humbart's voice was entirely subdued. "I'd like to say that was the case just so you'd think more kindly of him, but, no, lass—my lady—it wasn't. That happened a while back."

"Tell me."

"'Twas cursed ones who took it, slavering damned souls from a lost city called Ureh. The lad and a bunch of treasure hunters had found the place—actually, he and I were trying to keep them from entering. We already knew that there was something bad about the city, but never expected what we found! It was a ruin then, but it came to life while we were all there. All beautiful and peaceful, we thought—until everyone started disappearing and the city's ruler

turned out to be bound to one of the Prime Evils themselves! Zayl was one of two to survive, but it cost him his
hand, ripped off by those fiends."

"Then how—"

The skull snorted. "Most folk would've been left without anything to do, but he's a clever one, that lad. After he
and the good Captain Dumon—the other survivor—got
themselves healed by some others of Zayl's kind, the boy
got a notion in his head. He went back to where he'd lost
the hand and somehow managed to find what was left.
Took him three days and three nights, but damned if Zayl
didn't fuse it back on with fire and spellwork. Hell, in
some ways it's better than new! Paid a heavy price for it,
though, a heavy price."

As she listened, some of Salene's horror drained away,
replaced more and more by fascination. Would she not
have done the same in his place if she had wielded his
power? What other choice would there have been? A *hook*,
as Salene had seen upon many a mariner? A simple stump?
Among the nobility, there were those who had lost a limb
and had replaced it with metal reproductions which they
clothed as the necromancer had. The Lady Nesardo had no
doubt that many of them would have paid well for work
such as Zayl had performed, even likely have shown it off,
despite the doctrines of the Zakarum about such magic.

She leaned forward and gently removed the rest of the
glove. Only now did Salene see that the inside was thickly
padded so that it could mimic a hand of flesh and blood.
The noblewoman recalled how Zayl had used that hand
more than once with no seeming difficulty.

Her fingers poised over the skeletal appendage. Biting
her lip, Salene touched the back of Zayl's hand. To her surprise, it felt warm and smooth. She touched one of the
joints, then quietly gasped when the bony fingers
twitched.

Murmuring, the Rathmian shifted. Salene stepped back,
not wanting to disturb his recovery.

"He'll recover just fine, my lady," Humbart assured her

again. "You might want to get some rest yourself. I'll keep an eyehole on him, don't you worry."

"I should stay, though. I can't leave it all to you—"

The skull snorted. "And what else do I have to do, lass? I don't sleep, least not the way the living does. Won't bother me to stay awake all night . . ." A surprisingly soft tone touched the spirit's voice. "I won't let anything happen to him. You've got my promise on that."

Despite the skull's immobility, Salene believed him. In his own way, Humbart Wessel could be trusted to see to Zayl as much as poor Polth had always seen to her.

"Call out immediately if there's a change," she insisted.

"I'll do that."

"Thank you . . . Humbart."

Salene almost could have sworn that the skull's eyeholes shifted. "No . . . thank *you*, lass."

The Lady Nesardo slipped out of the room, her thoughts deeply concerned with Zayl. She kept wondering what else she could do to aid his recovery—

Salene suddenly collided with a figure in the hall. She instinctively backed away, then saw that it was only her brother.

"Sardak! You frightened me! What are you doing out here? I thought you'd be in bed!"

His expression was not pleasant to behold. "I didn't get very far, sister. Couldn't just forget what I saw in there."

"Really, Sardak! It's nothing—"

He grabbed her by the shoulders so tightly that Salene grunted with pain. Sardak loosened his grip, but did not release her. "He's got to go, Salene! You can't keep a thing like that in this house! He's a danger to you, to all of us! Look what happened to Polth, damn it—and he was a paid fighter!"

"Polth died trying to save both Zayl and me, if that's what you mean, but only after Zayl nearly did the same! You weren't there! Something monstrous happened down in the crypt, Sardak!"

He grimaced. "Yes, I know, I know. But, still, Salene—"

"He stays. I owe him that. I'm sorry if you feel this a disagreeable situation, but—"

"But you *are* the mistress of Nesardo and I am merely a lowly bastard . . ." When she made to protest his words, Sardak bowed his head. "Uncalled for, I know. You've given me every chance and made this as much my home as yours, Salene. Forgive my words."

Salene touched his cheek. "I understand your concern. Let's forget this happened."

Her brother glanced at Zayl's door. "I'll follow your will on this, sister dear, but if he does anything that even remotely endangers you, he *will* answer to me."

And with that, Sardak kissed her on the cheek and headed off to his room. Watching him, Salene had no doubt that he would follow through with such a promise. In that way, Sardak was much like Polth. They were both very loyal to those for whom they cared. They also made for deadly enemies to those who crossed them.

The noblewoman hoped that the latter would never be the case for Zayl.

Zayl dreamed of spiders. Many spiders. Large ones. Small ones. He was tangled in webs, spun in cocoons. The spiders surrounded him . . .

Through his tortured dreams, a face drifted above. A face with gray, cropped hair and certain features reminiscent of his own. The face watched his struggles with clinical interest and gave no indication of any intention to help the necromancer.

And so, Zayl continued to fight alone . . .

The storm raged unabated through the morning and afternoon, letting up only slightly as the night again neared. Salene spent her waking hours mainly in watching over the Rathmian's prone form. She found it disturbing that he had not yet stirred and, although Humbart did not say it, Salene knew that the skull was concerned also.

Sweat bathed Zayl, and his brow was furrowed as if in

deep thought. Curiously, the noblewoman sensed some magical fluctuation around his body, as if something was going on of which she had no understanding. Uncertain as to what else to do, she dabbed his lips with a clean, moist towel and tried to keep him as comfortable as possible.

Sardak brought her meals, the servants refusing to step beyond the doorway. The younger Nesardo said nothing as he handed her the tray, but his eyes ever watched the necromancer warily.

Salene ate her evening meal in silence, neither she nor Humbart able to summon any words of encouragement for one another. The skull still insisted that Zayl would be all right, but his words had a hollow ring to them that had nothing to do with his fleshless state.

Then, barely minutes after Salene had finished her meal, an anxious servant knocked on the door, muttering, "Mistress, there be someone to see you in the drawing room."

"In this foul weather?" the noblewoman responded, rising. "Who?"

There was no answer from the hallway, and when Salene opened the door it was to find that the servant had fled. Grimacing, she shut the door behind her, then descended to the ground floor. As she did, another servant carrying an empty tray emerged from the drawing room. He bowed when he saw her.

"He has been given wine, my lady, and now sits by the fire."

"Who? Who is it, Barnaby?"

The hawk-nosed servant looked startled at her lack of knowledge. "Why, the Lord Jitan, of course!"

Jitan? "Thank you, Barnaby. You may go."

He bowed, then scurried away. Salene struggled to maintain her calm in the face of this unexpected, unwarranted, and certainly undesired visit by the man seeking to take from her the legacy of Nesardo. Only when she was confident of her demeanor did the noblewoman finally glide into the chamber.

"My Lord Jitan!" Salene called. "To what do I owe the honor of your visit on this of all nights?"

Wine goblet in one hand, Aldric Jitan rose from the chair as if he and not the woman before him was the host. The noble might have cut a dashing figure, but there was something about his mismatched eyes and his mouth that ever put Salene off. The former constantly shifted gaze, almost as if Jitan suspected enemies hiding in the shadows of the room. The latter, meanwhile, curled upward in what she thought a rather *hungry* turn, reminding her of a famished wolf.

"My dear, dear Salene," he returned, raising the goblet. "I drink to your flawless beauty."

Even under the best of circumstances, she would have found nothing to appreciate in such flowery talk from him. Still, the Lady Nesardo curtsied politely.

Despite the foul weather, Aldric's clothes and hair were both dry and impeccable, which meant that his servants had shielded him all the way to the door. Salene surreptitiously looked for his cloak, but did not see it. It was a pity; had it been at hand, it would have given her the opportunity to further shorten what looked to be a very uncomfortable encounter.

"I came to see if I could make peace between us, dear Salene," Lord Jitan finally answered. He took another sip, then stepped closer. Suddenly, his eyes did not dart about anymore, but focused sharply on her own. Salene felt herself drawn to those eyes despite her loathing for the man. "We have been at odds for no good reason."

"You seek to take the roof from over my head, leave me destitute on the streets."

"Hardly that!" Aldric leaned closer, his eyes all the noblewoman could now see. "My hand is forced! I deal with nearly every major family in Westmarch! Many of my transactions involve great sums of money or vast properties! The reason that I've maintained the reputation I have is because everyone knows that I mean what I say. If I promise someone profit for joining in my ventures, they understand that they *will* profit. Yet, at the same time, if the deals I make include assurances against the other party's defaulting—a necessary precaution, especially against those who would seek to cheat—I must then follow through, no matter what the reason for its happening."

Despite not wishing to, Salene discovered she had some newfound sympathy for Aldric's position. It was too often the case that aristocrats in declining financial states made poor deals, then attempted not to pay back their creditors. If they had the influence of others to back them up, as was often the case, those who had taken their word in good faith ended up with nothing.

"But Riordan was a man of his word and careful to agree to only what he could do . . ."

"That he was." The mismatched eyes gleamed. Lord Jitan stood almost close enough to kiss Salene, and uncharacteristically, she did not pull away in revulsion. "But he never got the chance to fulfill his part of the deal—which he most certainly would have if not for his untimely death—and so the collateral that was agreed upon by the two of us falls, by law, to me." He shrugged. "If I don't take it, my dear, I will be cheated by every other person with whom I do business and I'll be ruined within a year. Then, I'll be the one with no roof over my head. You wouldn't want that, would you?"

She could not tear her eyes away from his. "No, I wouldn't. I wouldn't . . ."

"Then, you should consider my proposal, Salene. As Lady Jitan, you'll retain the legacy of your family and also have all my own line offers. A transaction of mutual benefit." He touched her chin as if to kiss her. "Mutual."

Without warning, Zayl's face suddenly materialized in her thoughts. Salene jerked away from Aldric. His smile momentarily transformed into a snarl, which was then replaced by a much less agreeable version of the former.

For some reason, Salene felt an urgent need to return to the necromancer's quarters. Lord Jitan, noting her sudden anxiety, asked, "Are you ill? Can I be of any service?"

"No . . . thank you, no. I'm sorry, Aldric, but I must again decline your offer."

His smile grew even more strained. "Think what you're saying, Salene . . . I *will* do what I must."

No longer did his unsettling eyes hold her. The noblewoman became defiant. "That may yet not be the case. I've not exhausted all courses of action. I'm still investigating my husband's financial dealings . . ."

"But what—" He shut his mouth and, without warning, suddenly looked up in the general direction of Zayl's quarters. Aldric's face grew stony. He suddenly bowed. "Very well. If this is to go no further tonight, then I'll bid you good evening . . . and pray that for your sake you see reason very soon."

Thrusting down the goblet, Lord Jitan strode out. Salene made no attempt to see him to the door, which he could easily find from the drawing room. She listened tensely and was rewarded seconds later by the sound of the door slamming hard. The harsh clatter of hooves and the rattle of coach wheels accented the noble's furious departure.

Finally satisfied that Aldric Jitan would not suddenly return, Salene rushed toward the stairs. A startled servant ducked out of her way as the Lady Nesardo all but leapt up the steps.

At the top, Sardak, hair unkempt, confronted her. He had a concerned look on his face which proved to have nothing to do with the necromancer. "I just heard from Barnaby that Jitan was here! What the devil did he want this time?"

"The same as always. He encouraged me to marry him to put an end to the matter."

"So popular, my sister is! Torion's going to be very jealous! He did ask first—"

She had no time for this. "Enough, Sardak. After Jitan, I can do without your flippant remarks!"

He seized her arm as she plunged past him. "I'm sorry! Next time, have Barnaby summon me immediately. I don't want you alone with that bastard!"

Salene almost told him that she could handle Aldric Jitan quite easily, thank you very much—but then recalled how she had come so close to acquiescing to his demands. He had even nearly *kissed* her.

"I'll remember," she answered softly. With a smile, the noblewoman added, "Thank you for worrying."

"It's what I do best . . . besides drinking." He noted the direction in which his sister had been turning. "Back to him?"

"Yes." The urgency continued to push her. "I have to go."

"Better that one than Jitan for company, anyway," muttered Sardak reluctantly. "You *will* call me when you need me, right?"

"Yes, Sardak, I will. I promise."

Only then did he release her. Salene immediately hurried on, hoping that she was not already too late.

But when she swung open the door, it was to find everything as it had been before. Zayl lay motionless on the bed, still sweating despite the cool air of the chamber.

Yet, the concern would not leave her. "What's happened, Humbart?"

"Happened?" Despite a lack of features, the skull somehow wore a quizzical expression. "Nothing at all, occasionally punctuated by moments of absolute stillness."

"But I was certain—" Going over to the bed, Salene touched Zayl's forehead.

Instantly, her anxiety grew a hundredfold. She felt a threatening force, a crushing one, centered on the necromancer. Where it originated from, though, the noblewoman had no idea.

"Zayl . . . ," she whispered without thinking. "Zayl . . ."

He turned his head toward her and suddenly moaned.

"He moved!" Humbart blurted. "By Mount Arreat, he moved! Finally!"

The tips of her fingers where she touched his skin felt warm, but not uncomfortably so. His breathing seemed more regular than before and when Salene moved to wipe the sweat from his brow, it did not immediately grow damp again.

Her hopes rose. "I think he's—"

Zayl's eyes suddenly opened wide.

"Karybdus . . . ," he blurted.

No sooner had the necromancer spoken than his eyes shut again and his head tipped to the side. Salene gasped, fearing that he had died, but when she looked closely, the noblewoman saw that Zayl merely slept . . . and slept peacefully.

"Karybdus?" growled the skull. "Now what the bloody blazes does that mean?"

Karybdus sheathed his ivory dagger, his expression, as ever, one of indifference, despite the outcome of recent events.

"Thrice now," he said. In the darkness, the thing to whom he spoke scuttled about in what could best be termed anger. "Thrice now. There will not be a fourth time."

The Rathmian's gaze turned toward the ceiling, and though there was no apparent reason for it, his expression briefly reflected satisfaction.

"Rest easy, little one. Things still go according to the needs of the Balance. We know the impediment to success. We know now that his name is Zayl." Karybdus stretched out his arm and something large, black, and many-legged leapt upon it. The necromancer scratched its body lovingly. "Zayl . . . of course, it *would* be him."

SEVEN

General Torion was a man of action. Inaction drove him mad, and so thus was his mood this night. There were still two more days before good Cornelius would be laid to rest. That did not suit Torion at all. The king was dead and needed to be buried so that his successor could take his rightful place on the throne, thereby solidifying his claim. The longer the last took, the more the talk would increase that perhaps another should lay claim to Westmarch.

There were too many willing to do that, too. Salene Nesardo's agreement to back Justinian would help bring some of the other Houses around, but the list of trouble-makers was still far too long for the commander's tastes. He found himself wishing for a simpler time, when those who served the throne could take more direct measures. More absolute ones.

Accompanied by a personal guard of six men, he rode toward the palace, a gray stone edifice with pointed tow-ers, jutting buttresses, and gargoyles on every rooftop. The palace was built like a fortress, with high, stark walls lined with spikes and a deep moat with smooth, unclimbable sides. The lowest windows were three levels up and barred with iron.

If a fortress was indeed what first came to mind, that was because that was how the palace had begun. Before there had been a city, there had been the palace. It had started as the first refuge of the new land, chosen as the base from which Westmarch would grow. Torion was no student of history save where it concerned war. He knew of the Sons of Rakkis only because of their legacy of power, and admired this, their creation. They had also created the first of the outer walls of the city, which later architects had copied and embellished upon. The capital was a strong-hold in itself, an extension of the palace in a sense.

Of course, any stronghold, no matter how well-built, could fall from within. The throne had to be secured.

Would that the lad had more steel in his back, like his father, the general thought, not for the first time. *No one would question his ability to rule.*

Citizens wrapped in furs and thick cloth coats bowed their heads as he passed along the cobblestone street. Torion acknowledged them with an occasional nod. Shop owners and craftsmen peered out of their establishments to eye the man known as the Sword of the Realm. Some likely wondered why Torion did not himself seek to take the throne from the weak heir. The general sniffed disdain-fully at such talk, though. His duty was all that mattered to him. Not for Torion the unwieldy and oppressive weight of rule. Justinian was welcome to it.

At the wall surrounding the palace, wary-eyed guards in red uniforms, gray steel breastplates, and ridged helms stood at attention, their pikes held high, sheathed swords hanging ready at their side. Overhead, the royal banners fluttered madly, the lunging black bear in the middle of each seeming to be dancing a mad jig.

The guards gave way quickly, Torion the one man not needing to identify himself to them. Through the wrought-iron gates he and his party rode. The wind howled, but the commander did not notice it, his mind concentrating on more important matters. Indeed, he paid no mind to the rest of the journey to the palace steps, nor even to the trek up to the huge, iron doors with the glaring wolf heads . . . the symbols of the original masters. Only then did he pause, mostly to admire the power inherent in those images. The Sons of Rakkis might have died out as a ruling dynasty, but their legacy was everywhere, including in the blood of many of Westmarch's people.

The tall, gray hall through which he trod was lit by

torches and both walls were lined with Torion's most trusted men. The lupine images continued uninterrupted, one snarling animal after another. However, a predecessor of Justinian's had at least attempted to prove who now ruled by hanging huge, elaborate—and to the general, *gaudy*—tapestries from the ceiling with his own line's emblem. The giant bears dangled overhead, but to Torion, they seemed more frightened then frightening. It almost appeared that they stayed so high up so as to be safely out of reach of the ancient wolves' jaws.

General Torion made an abrupt right turn that took him away from the direction of the throne room. Justinian could never be found there; the new monarch preferred the comfort of his own quarters, where he had lived since a baby. His insistent refusal to sit upon the actual throne only worsened political tensions.

"General!" a voice suddenly called from behind. "My lord general!"

Torion immediately recognized the nasal tone: Edmun Fairweather, the new king's aide, a high-strung, wheedling man who had far too much of Justinian's attention.

"What is it, Edmun?" the general said, turning.

A thin figure clad in black vest and pants, Justinian's man had a faint avian look to him. His pate was bald save for a ring of brown running from one ear back to the other.

"His majesty . . . his majesty you will not find there."

"Oh? Is he down in the kitchens?" Torion's new lord considered himself a bit of a chef, and when it had seemed he would never be ruler, he had spent much of his time toying with recipes. It was another trait that had lessened him greatly in the eyes of so many of the nobility.

"No, my lord general! His majesty awaits you in the throne room!"

The general grunted in surprise. This was a first. Justinian had stayed away from that chamber as if merely entering it would give him plague. Torion tried not to get his hopes up. It was one thing for Cornelius's heir to build up his nerve enough to go there, another to actually look as if he belonged.

"Lead on, then."

Edmun spun around on one heel, guiding them back to the throne room, where four sentries at the doorway stood at attention. Edmun snapped his reedy fingers and two opened the doors. The general's personal guard took up positions in the hall. Their presence in the royal chamber would have been considered a slight to the king, and Justinian could not afford even the least lack of respect at this juncture.

But as he stepped inside, Torion's brow arched at the sight he beheld. He went down on one knee without even realizing it, so caught up was he by the man before him.

Justinian IV—Justinian the Wide-Eyed, as so many called him behind his back—gazed down solemnly from the throne at the commander of Westmarch's armies. Gone was the fearful, childlike figure. What sat before Torion had all the presence of the late, beloved Cornelius. The slim, sandy-haired youth would have been handsome if not for the pockmarks an early bout with disease had left on each cheek. He had the aquiline features of his father, but his eyes were definitely those of the long-lamented Queen Nellia, dead shortly after his birth. Those eyes generally had a weak, watery quality to them that had never been seen in the mother, but this day Torion's gaze met a pair of rich, brown orbs that utterly snared his attention.

"My Lord General Torion," Justinian greeted him, his usually-hesitant voice now matching his eyes in strength. "Always a pleasure. Please rise."

He sounds exactly like his father . . . , the commander secretly marveled as he obeyed the command. *Exactly like good Cornelius when he was fit.*

The white sleeping robes that Torion had so often found the heir wearing no matter what the time of day had vanished. Instead, the new king was clad in the regal outfit tailors had worked day and night to fashion the moment it became clear that his father would not recover. It was highly reminiscent of the general's own uniform, but with round, ornate epaulets of gold and silver and an intricate crest on the golden breastplate. The bear rearing to the left looked nowhere as fearful as those on the tapestries lining the walls and well reflected its present wearer. Golden stripes bordered the sleeves and legs. High, military-cut boots of black leather finished the magnificent effect. Torion, who knew how others reacted when he himself stepped into a room, now experienced that feeling toward Justinian for the first time since King Cornelius had knighted the general some two decades past.

"Your majesty—" Torion finally began, realizing that for once he was the one stumbling for words. "It is my pleasure to be in the presence of my liege."

Justinian opened his mouth, then seemed to hesitate. For a brief moment, he glanced to his side, his expression hinting of his usual, uncertain self. Then, just as suddenly, the confident young monarch returned. Rising smoothly, Justinian stepped down to take the hand of his most loyal servant.

"I know you've been worried about me, general. I appreciate the support you've given despite that worry."

Again, Torion felt as if he stood in the presence of his previous master. "A change in command's always a time of some uncertainty, but my trust and loyalty have never wavered, your majesty."

"Good, stalwart Torion," the king said with a sudden grin—a grin that was again so reminiscent of Cornelius. Justinian startled him further by slapping the veteran officer on the back. Only now was it obvious that they were of a similar height. The young ruler's usual habit of hunching his shoulders from a lack of confidence had vanished. This Justinian stood as tall and as proud as any of his line.

The general fought back a grin of his own. If what he saw was a permanent transformation, then those eager to use their blood claims to take the throne from its rightful owner would soon have a harsh surprise awaiting them.

"May I say how well those garments fit you, your

majesty," he declared, much more at ease than during his ride.

"They do, don't they? Who would've thought it?"

Pulling away, Justinian suddenly raised his arms up and laughed at the ceiling. Torion's brow arched again and he glanced at Edmun, who judiciously found something of interest on his sleeve.

The king quickly lowered his arms. A brief glimmer of uncertainty passed across his expression. "Excuse me, general! Just a little—uh—anxiousness. Not all the butterflies have left my stomach."

Considering what he had thought he would have to work with, Torion readily accepted the answer. Instead of a weak, untried boy, the commander found himself in the presence of a man more capable than any of the pretenders. A few idiosyncrasies were to be expected. Every monarch had them. It was in the blood.

"How strong is our support, Torion?"

Despite having already witnessed Justinian's marvelous conversion for several minutes, the direct question caught the commander off guard. "Beg pardon, your majesty?"

"Who can we trust to stand with me, general? Who already stands firm?"

Torion's well-organized mind took over. He immediately rattled off several names, concluding with the one he trusted most. "And, of course, there's the Lady Nesardo."

Justinian eyed him. "Nesardo is with us? You're certain?"

"She gave her support without hesitation . . . and if I may say so, should you appear as you do now before several of those who waver, the tide will turn decidedly in your favor."

Again, the sandy-haired monarch glanced to his side. This time, Torion simply waited. If this was the only affectation the new Justinian had, Westmarch was very fortunate.

"You have the right of it, general," the king finally returned. With another grin identical to his father's, he added, "Prepare an audience at first chance, Edmun! Invite all those old Torion here thinks should come!"

"Yes, your majesty," his aide said with a grand bow.

"I think a show of strength is also in order, don't you, general?"

He continued to catch Torion off guard. "Your majesty?"

"The military might of Westmarch must be made to be seen loyal without question to me. Can you arrange that?"

Torion considered. "Much of the realm's marshaled forces are levies belonging to the various lords, who lend them to the crown as a sign of their trust. Several of those I would not wish near your presence at this time . . . if you know what I mean."

"What can you deliver to me?"

"In addition to those I know are loyal, I can summon forces from the edge of Khanduras, I suppose." Khanduras, to the northeast, was a region from which brigands often entered Westmarch. Khanduras itself was very jealous of its neighbor's natural wealth and Torion suspected that its coffers received a share of the bandits' ill-gotten gains. Unfortunately, the last had never been proven.

"Some might find that risky. Not sound judgment for a king," pointed out Justinian.

"Your wisdom impresses me, your majesty."

The king frowned, then looked to the side once more. A moment later, the steel returned to his gaze. "Of course! How silly of me! The City Guard is part of your personal force, isn't it?"

Torion was not certain he liked where he thought this was heading. "Aye, but—"

Cornelius's son clapped his hands together. "It's perfect, don't you see? Well, we certainly don't need to worry about an invasion here, and any of the nobles who've been considering taking my place would hardly go up against them! We'll use them to show the strength of our claim!"

Some of Torion's newfound hope dwindled away. He considered the walls of the city an essential part of the realm's defense, no matter how far away Khanduras and Ensteig might be. A strong capital gave confidence to the rest of the land.

But Justinian had made up his mind. Before General Torion could suggest anything else, the king declared, "Let it be done! I think we can strip the most men from the walls facing the mountains and the forest! Not much out there to worry about except a few wolves, am I right, general?"

"Very likely," muttered the commander. He did a quick calculation. Yes, if it had to be done, those walls would be the best to empty. Still, Torion would also need to reorganize the watches, and that would take some time, as would putting together the overall display. "It'll take some doing, but it'll be done."

"Splendid!" Justinian patted him on the shoulder again, once more emulating the late Cornelius to perfection. "I leave you to see to it, then."

Torion felt all turned around. He had not come here expecting any of this to happen. "Yes. As you wish, your majesty." The officer recalled the reason that *he* had come. "King Justinian, if I may—"

"Yes, you may go . . . with my thanks and my blessing."

Justinian turned to speak with Edmun. Seeing that the audience was over, General Torion bowed and exited the chamber. His mind raced as he weighed the good and ill coming from this change in Cornelius's son. The general's personal guard fell in line around him, but he barely noticed.

The walls should be left well-defended. It's always been so, he thought. Yet, there were too many questionable factors concerning the levies, and for what Justinian desired Torion would have to gather quite a force. There was no choice but to temporarily strip the city walls.

But that matter aside, the commander left the halls with much-renewed hopes. Justinian had just showed more backbone than he had in all the years Torion had known him. With the general's capable guidance, surely that backbone could be strengthened further yet. Many a king had started out uncertain and untried, only to rise above himself and become legend.

This is a good thing, General Torion insisted to himself as he stepped out into the foul weather again. *This will preserve the kingdom. This will preserve Westmarch.*

And in the end, that was what mattered most.

A servant brought King Justinian IV a goblet of rose-colored wine as Edmun droned on about the upcoming gathering of nobles. The young monarch took a single sip.

"Enough."

Edmun paused in mid-word. "Your majesty?"

"Please leave me, Edmun. Take the rest with you."

The aide bowed so low that Justinian thought he would scrape the floor with his prodigious nose. "As you desire, your majesty."

Straightening, the black-clad figure snapped his fingers at the guards.

The lord of Westmarch watched all of them slowly file out. Their backs to the king, Edmun and the others did not see his eyes abruptly grow round with anxiety and his mouth twist down in deep distress. The hand holding the goblet shook so much that droplets rained upon his pristine garments.

When at last the doors closed and he was left alone, a gasp escaped his taut lips. Justinian let the goblet fall from his grasp, ignoring the clatter and the spreading stain on the stone floor. Moving like a caged animal, he stepped to the center of the throne room and looked around.

"Ah!" His gaze fixed on empty space in one far corner. With trepidation, the king reached one trembling hand toward the shadows there.

"Father!" Justinian gasped. "Did I do *well*, Father?"

In the dark of the storm, a single light flickered in the sky. Those few who might have seen it likely would have imagined that somehow the clouds had parted just long enough for this one star to shine through.

But had they now witnessed it drop toward the ground, they would have instead called it a portent, an *omen*.

In both cases, such onlookers would have been entirely wrong . . . and entirely correct.

But the light did not simply plummet, as most such astonishing sights did. Its descent was swift, yet focused.

And just above the city, it paused.

A guard on the outer walls happened to glance in its direction, perhaps somehow sensing a difference in the world. His eyes immediately glazed, then turned away. He went about his duties, the unearthly vision plucked from his memories.

The light continued down, dropping into Westmarch. As it did, its unnatural brilliance faded, blending into the gray realm below.

Just above the House of Nesardo, it faded from mortal sight.

EIGHT

The three hooded figures stood in judgment as a kneeling Zayl carefully drew the pattern in the soft earth. The harsh cries of the nocturnal denizens of Kehjistan's jungle echoed now and then, eerie calls accenting the unsettling nature of the Rathmian's task.

With his dagger, Zayl drew two arcs over a circle with a slash across it. Each image flared red the moment it was finished, then faded to a faint green. The young spellcaster's breathing grew rapid as his work progressed.

"It is almost complete," he announced to the elders.

"What does Rathma teach us of touching the Balance so?" asked the middle of the three, a gaunt, gray-tressed female with twin black stars tattooed on each cheek.

Zayl answered without hesitation. "That the least imbalance in either direction can cause great catastrophe."

The woman pursed her thin lips. "That is the rote answer, what every acolyte is told in the beginning so that they do not see the skills they learn as something to use as they please. You are far advanced beyond that point, Zayl, son of Icharion."

"Look deeper into yourself and your work," suggested a bald male whose face was nearly as fleshless as the bones with which the necromancers performed their mysterious work.

"Concentrate," murmured the third, whose visage could not even be seen under the voluminous hood. His voice had a curious echo to it, as if he spoke from deep within some cavern. "Think in terms of yourself, for that is where every spell and every consequence comes from."

"Conclude the pattern," added the cadaverous man.

Zayl added a wavy line—representing water—to his design.

He leaned back, studying each detail and finding nothing amiss. At the same time, another compartment in his mind analyzed the question. So, it had something to do with the pattern upon which he worked. The questions of the elders were ever tied to the moment, for the moment was always the most important aspect of time. The moment shaped the future, decided the course the Rathmians needed to take to keep the Balance as it should be.

He studied the symbols—the broken sun, the water, the arcs that represented lives, the jagged marks that were fire. For some reason, they struck a chord deep within Zayl, one that stirred an emotion long buried.

Then, he saw both the pattern's meaning and the answer they desired. "No . . ."

"What does Rathma teach us, Zayl?" the woman insisted.

"Do not make me do this . . ."

"The lesson must be learned for you to take your place among us," reverberated the faceless figure. "Strike the pattern, young one. Let loose the spell."

The skeletal instructor raised one bony hand toward their student. "But first . . . you must answer the question."

Zayl's hand shook. He almost reached down with his empty one to wipe away the abomination he had drawn. But then, his teachings took over. He focused on the pattern, trying to see it clinically, not emotionally. They would expect him to do no less.

"Rathma teaches us that to use the Balance so"—he involuntarily swallowed—"will destroy our own focus, and, therefore, our souls. And if that should happen, we become the very threat that we seek to keep at bay."

"A near enough answer," proclaimed the woman. "Complete the spell, Zayl."

Gritting his teeth, the student plunged the dagger into the center, burying the sacred blade to its hilt in the soft ground.

Utter silence filled the jungle . . . and then new howls tore through the air. They were not the cries of animals, but rather originated from another place, a place given opening into the mortal plane by Zayl's pattern.

Ethereal wisps of energy burst from the center, rising up and swirling around the caster. Zayl's hair and cloak rose as if electri-

fied. Even the garments of the skeletal man and tattooed woman reacted, although their shadowed companion appeared untouched in even the slightest way.

Zayl watched the wisps wrap around him. His expression he managed to keep in check, but his eyes revealed a trace of deep, dark emotion.

Many of the wisps rose up into the jungle canopy, where they darted about. The howls turned to moans that sent shivers through Zayl's body.

And then . . . two of the wisps returned to the student, spiraling about him before finally floating back over the pattern.

"Look at them," commanded the hood.

Zayl would have preferred to keep his gaze anywhere else, but he obeyed. Even had the elder not ordered him, his own guilt would have made him look.

As he focused on the wisps, they briefly took on forms. Shadowed, barely glimpsed forms . . .

A man. A woman. Both with some distinct resemblance to him.

Zayl reached out to them, beseeching. "I did not mean for it to happen! I—"

The hooded form stretched an iron boot toward the pattern, obliterating the outer edge of Zayl's design.

The howling and moaning ceased. The wisps vanished in an instant . . . the two before the young necromancer the last to fade.

Falling forward, Zayl cried, "No! Come back! Please—"

"Please!"

He jolted up, the vision still burnt into his memory. His body quivering, Zayl desperately looked around for the two.

But he was not back in the jungles of Kehjistan, not back at the moment when the gifts of Rathma had finally been become his in full.

Not back at the moment that his secret desire had been forever crushed by those who had been his mentors.

No, these were the quarters Zayl had been given by Salene Nesardo. He was across the Twin Seas, in

Westmarch. The memories came flooding back . . . the inn, the thieves, the emanations from House Nesardo, the struggle against the crypt fiend.

But—there was a gap afterward. Something had been wrenched from his mind. Zayl put his hands to his head as he tried to focus—

And immediately he felt the cold touch of the right appendage.

"No . . ." The necromancer stared at the hand and its accusing fingers, its hellish aspect. What he had done to make it so went against Rathma's teachings, but at the time, Zayl had not cared. It had been a necessary matter to him.

But Salene had seen it, and knowing that she had twisted his gut in a manner the necromancer had not experienced since . . . since his folly had slain the two most important people in his early life.

Mouth set, he looked over his shoulder. The skull of Humbart Wessel sat silent, but Zayl was not fooled.

"You cannot sleep, Humbart. Pretending otherwise is beneath you."

"Nothing's beneath me, lad, save this piece o' furniture!"

The Rathmian slid off the bed. His muscles ached, but he ignored the inconvenience. "Spare me your witticisms. What happened in the crypts?"

"What didn't?" The skull quickly told him the details, adding the flourishes the undead mercenary's stories generally contained. Zayl bit back further retorts as he listened, his analytical mind piecing together the facts between Humbart's exaggerations.

Polth's death he already knew of, and although the children of Rathma were supposed to be above mourning—for was not death simply another state?—Zayl regretted the bodyguard's sacrifice. Salene had one less protector, something the noblewoman could ill afford. She was entangled in a matter that stretched beyond the mortal plane and even beyond the realm of the dead. There was a foulness to this that disturbed the necromancer, a foulness he felt was tied in part to the destruction of the Worldstone.

The dark ones will be stirring, a jungle spirit had told him during a summoning he had made prior to sailing. *Even the lost ones . . .*

"She took your . . . handiwork well, lad," Humbart belatedly added. "After the initial shock, of course. When I told her how you lost it—"

"You did *what*?"

"Easy, lad, easy! She's a strong one, that girl is! Could be one of your kind, at least in terms of will! Understood right off what you were trying to do in Ureh and why you felt you had to fix that limb as best you could."

The words did nothing to assuage Zayl. "And you told her what I—"

The skull's brow ridge almost seemed to wrinkle. "Of course not! Some things should remain better unknown, or forgotten!"

"Yes . . ." Zayl's head suddenly throbbed so much that he had to sit back. He breathed cautiously, letting his measured inhalations calm him. The throbbing subsided. "Did anything amiss happen while I was unconscious?"

"The lady had a visitor. I gather it was this Lord Jitan."

That perked the necromancer's interest. "Indeed? I wish I could have met him."

Humbart snorted. "He certainly left her in an ill mood, I could tell that."

Zayl would speak with Salene about the sinister noble when the next chance arose. For now, though, he had to recoup his strength and try to fill in the empty spaces in his memory.

"So," interjected the skull. "Who's this Karybdus character?"

"Karybdus?" The Rathmian eyed his undead companion. "What do you mean?"

"You were struggling even while out, lad. The only thing that seemed to finally bring you back was the lady.

She's got a gift on par with yours, I think, if only she'd know how to use it properly."

Salene had done well enough at first down in the crypt. Still, instinct went only so far. What the noblewoman needed was proper training by a sorcerer. Not Zayl, of course, but someone whose area of expertise was more *acceptable.*

He returned to the subject at hand. "And this is when I mentioned . . . Karybdus?"

"Somewhere about there. So, who is he?"

Frowning, Zayl responded, "I have no idea."

"And are you usually in the habit of mouthin' names you don't know? I've not noticed that since our partnership began, boy."

"I am not." The necromancer pondered the name again, rolling it over his tongue and tossing it about in his thoughts. Karybdus. It had a familiar ring, and yet nothing came to mind.

The holes in his memory . . .

"I said nothing more."

"Wish I could tell you otherwise."

Zayl filed away the name for later investigation. Perhaps Karybdus was a demon. Certainly that would explain much.

And yet . . .

Rising, he headed for the door.

"Where do you plan on going?"

"I need to return to the Nesardo crypt."

"Not like that, you shouldn't," pointed out Humbart.

The necromancer paused to gaze down at himself. He wore only his pants, the one item the modest Salene had left him. And those were torn. His boots stood at the side of the bed, forgotten by him in his haste. It showed Zayl's chaotic state of mind that he stood barefoot and all but unclothed, yet still ready to reenter the treacherous realm below. He had not even thought to take his dagger with him.

"I think you'd better sit down for a while still, lad."

"I have no—" There was a tentative knock at the door. Without thinking, Zayl said, "Enter."

The door swung open, and Salene stepped in. She took one look at Zayl and gasped.

The necromancer instinctively brought up his hands, belatedly realizing that he now presented his hostess with another good look at the right one.

Pulling it behind his back, he muttered, "Excuse my state, my lady."

Salene had already turned away. "I thought I heard your voice, but I expected you to be in the bed. It was careless of me! I was just so relieved to know that you were conscious!"

Looking around, the Rathmian located the remains of his cloak. He draped it over his form, and despite its ragged condition, it helped ease his thoughts. "I was inconsiderate. You may look this way again."

As she turned, he noticed a blush on her cheeks. Not accustomed to such reactions from women, the necromancer glanced at the bundle in her hands. "Clothing?"

"Your measure is near enough to Sardak that I dared have some garments ordered. Simple ones, but akin to what you wore. The cloak lacks the markings of your calling, but—"

He took the clothing from her. "But they will all do splendidly. I am in your debt."

Her expression grew utterly serious. "Not in the least. Not after . . . all that."

"I am sorry about Polth. I know that he meant much to you, as you did to him. Such loyalty is not bought with coin."

"Polth's father served my father." Salene bowed her head. "As did his father before him. The Nesardo curse appears to be on his family as well, for he was the last of his line."

Zayl considered. "If you would like, I could—"

His unfinished offer was quickly cut off by her gaze. "No. No more of that. Let Polth rest. Let my husband rest.

It was more than a wasted effort . . . it was a costly one."

"But not entirely without some knowledge learned. Tell me, does the name 'Karybdus' mean anything to you?"

"No . . . but it seemed as if it did for you, Master Zayl. You uttered it with some recognition."

He nodded ruefully. "Yes, but that recognition seems to have escaped me in waking."

She looked sympathetic. "With some more recuperation, perhaps."

"Perhaps . . ."

"We can talk about this in a few minutes," Salene insisted. "You must be famished."

The unfamiliar rumble of hunger *had* made itself noticed, but Zayl considered such a mundane necessity the least of his concerns. Still, it would allow him to dress and give his hostess a moment's respite. "Some broth will do."

"You'll eat more than that if *I* have a hand in it." She turned away. "I'll see to it immediately."

"Lady Salene." When the noblewoman looked back, Zayl continued, "You had a visit from Lord Jitan, I understand."

"Yes." Her expression indicated her deep distaste for the man.

"Should you find yourself in his company again, it would be best if you did not for any reason mention this Karybdus to him."

"You think he would know who he is?"

The necromancer silently cursed, realizing that he had just put a notion in Salene's head. "Please do *not* mention the name."

She turned from him again. "I doubt I'll be seeing Lord Jitan anytime soon, at least if I can help it. I'll be back with something for you to eat."

She closed the door behind her. Humbart chuckled darkly.

Zayl glared at him. "What jest so amuses you?"

"'Tis clear that Rathma teaches much, but obviously little when it comes to dealing with a woman . . . or maybe it's just yourself."

"She will listen. She is sensible."

The fleshless head said nothing.

Beset by an unfamiliar sense of frustration, Zayl focused on dressing. Salene had found garments remarkably similar to his own, even the cloak. It lacked many of the inner pockets with which his previous one had been adorned, but the necromancer could add those when he had time.

One thing, however, could not wait. Unlike his previous cloak, this new one had not been made ready.

Spreading it across the bed, Zayl went to one of his pouches and removed a crimson candle. He gently centered the squat piece on the cloak, then, locating his tinderbox, lit the wick.

The moment it ignited, the oil lamps illuminating his room muted. Shadow fell upon the chamber. The flame from the candle rose strong, but its color was as red as blood and only served to add to the ominous aspect of the spell.

Zayl stretched forth his skeletal hand and touched the tip of the flame.

What sounded like a brief, angry whisper emanated from the candle. A small wisp of smoke rose above the bed. It writhed for several seconds, then slowly formed a murky mouth.

"*Zayl . . . ,*" it rasped. As it spoke, there appeared brief glimpses of long, vicious teeth, also made of smoke.

"I have a demand of you, X'y'Laq."

The smoky maw grinned. "*A request. A wish.*"

"A *demand.* You know what I hold over you."

The spirit chuckled. "*The candle grows shorter. Soon, it will not light.*"

Zayl shrugged off this reminder. "I will worry about that when the time comes."

"*You should be worried about it always, human . . .*"

From seemingly nowhere, the Rathmian's left hand suddenly revealed his pale dagger. Zayl held it near the wick.

"Until then, remember what I can do because of the binding."

The arrogance went out of the spirit's voice. *"You have summoned me. What do you need?"*

"As you did before with my previous cloak, do so with this one, but add to it the Scale of Trag'Oul . . . which you conveniently forgot the last time."

The smoky mouth drifted downward, hovering inches above the cloak. *"You did not specify. You must specify. Those are the rules . . ."*

The dark-haired spellcaster waved off the excuse. "You knew what I wanted . . . but, yes, I should have been specific. The Scale of Trag'Oul here." Zayl touched part of the hem. "The rest—*all* of the rest—just as they were on the other cloak. No deviations, no missing marks. Exact duplication."

"You are learning well, Zayl human. May others of your ilk not be so swift to understanding." The mouth grew broader. *"I am ever hungry."*

"Do as I commanded. Now. I'll waste no more of the wick on you." To emphasize his point, Zayl touched the edge of the flame with the dagger's tip.

What could best be described as a gasp escaped the entity. The mouth floated closer to the cloak. For a moment, nothing happened, but then suddenly the mouth inhaled sharply.

"No mistakes or lapses," reminded Zayl.

X'y'Laq made no reply. Instead, the demonic mouth exhaled.

Small symbols composed of smoke issued forth, scattering over the cloak. Zayl's practiced eye quickly surveyed each rune, noting shapes and nuances. On another level, he sensed each rune's individual magic.

But the count was off. "All of them, X'y'Laq."

"I merely paused to catch my breath," the mouth quickly assured him. It exhaled again and two more tiny symbols fluttered out to join the rest.

Zayl looked them over one more time, finally nodding.

No sooner had he done so than the symbols dropped upon the hem and other specific places on the cloak, even those located underneath.

Zayl touched the garment, and the first of the runes crystallized. It flared a bright silver, then seemed to vanish from sight.

One after another, the rest of the symbols did the same. Zayl watched until he was certain that the last of them had become a part of the cloak, then at last pulled the dagger away from the wick.

"Rightly done."

"*Would I fail you?*"

There was a knock on the door.

"Salene . . . ," Humbart somehow managed to hiss.

The mouth rose up, turning toward the door at the same time. "*A female? Do invite her in. I want to see if she is soft and tender to the—*"

The necromancer's right hand caught the wick between two fingers and doused the flame.

With a snarl, X'y'Laq's murky maw dissipated.

"A moment, please," called the Rathmian. He seized the padded glove from where Salene had placed it. She had already seen the macabre appendage, but for some inexplicable reason Zayl believed that she would forget about it if, from this point forward, he kept it hidden. "Enter."

However, it was not Salene who stepped inside, but rather Sardak. Sardak, looking very sober and very distrustful.

"The servant told me you were awake. Who were you talking to just now?" He peered past Zayl.

"That would be me!" piped up the skull.

Sardak barely batted an eye. Like his sister, he readily adapted to the bizarre. In some ways, perhaps the brother was even more comfortable with such than Salene. Drink could produce unsettling and horrific companions. "No, this voice sounded different . . . envious and with an insatiable appetite . . . for more than just food."

"Was there something you required?" asked the necromancer.

Sardak shut the door. "Just a short, friendly talk before my darling sibling returns with your meal. I don't like you or your kind, *Master* Zayl. You pry into things that no one should. The past is often better left to rest—"

"Agreed. Those of my order only do what must be done to preserve the Balance."

Sardak gave him a mocking smile. "I've no idea what that means and I don't really give a damn about it. What I do give a damn about, though, is Salene. That's why I wanted to see you before she came back up."

"Then, would it not be best to simply get to the point?"

"The point," remarked Salene's brother, casually stepping up to where Humbart lay, "is that there're worse things than you hovering around her. My head's finally clear enough to reach that conclusion . . . and one of those things rang a bell with me once I could think. A name mentioned once by a fellow drunkard. Salene'll tell you I've got an awful good memory when I've not been dipping into the wine, ale, and all else. It's actually one of the reasons I do drink. My memory's too damned good. I can't forget *anything*."

Zayl had met the likes of Sardak before and understood what some of those memories dealt with. However, such was not his concern at the moment. He had a suspicion he knew what name Sardak had heard. "This other man. He mentioned the name Karybdus?"

Salene's sibling leaned down to peer into Humbart's eyeholes. To his credit, the skull kept silent. "Exactly the one! Just in passing, but with a rueful sort of tone. I can especially recall that name because it's so damned unusual and ominous. Sounds like a chasm opening up under one's feet, ready to swallow everything and everyone."

Oddly, his description stirred just such a sensation in the Rathmian. "And what else did he say?"

Sardak suddenly took hold of Humbart and turned him to face the wall. The skull let out an inarticulate protest, which made Sardak chuckle.

But as he faced Zayl again, the man's expression lost all humor. "Nothing else, damn it. That was all. My friend, he looked guilty for having even muttered the name once. I never heard it again. Never drank with him again, for that matter."

And so, once again, Zayl was at a dead end. No, not entirely. If Sardak's companion had brought up the name, then the odds were that it belonged to a man, not a demon. Still, in the necromancer's experience, that made the situation no less threatening. The evil of men often outweighed that of the most cunning of demons. It was one reason why Hell so often eagerly enlisted their aid.

"I thank you for telling me this."

"Didn't do it for your hide. Did it for her and no other reason." Sardak looked resentful, though Zayl had given him no reason to be.

"You love her deeply."

"She's my *family*! All of it. She's been not only my sister, but my mother and, yes, even my father at times! I'd die for her and kill anyone I thought was trying to kill her!"

Zayl nodded. "I believe you."

Sardak returned to the door. He exhaled deeply, then muttered, "Anyway, I thought that telling you I heard the name might help in some way. I don't like you, but she trusts you, and she's the better judge of character."

He had also come to vent at Zayl, not to mention warn him against betraying Salene. Nonetheless, the necromancer offered, "She trusts *you*, too."

For the first time, he caught Sardak off guard. "Yes . . . I suppose she does."

Zayl considered all that he had been told. One possible, albeit remote hope came to mind. "Your fellow drinker. Perhaps I could find him, learn more from him. Do you know *his* name or where he might be found?"

"Oh, I know where he can most definitely be found, but you won't be able to get there. They'd never let one of your kind in. That would cause all sorts of wonderful chaos!"

The younger Nesardo snickered. "Almost be worth it . . . not that it could ever come about."

Zayl had sudden visions of himself trying to enter the Zakarum Church itself. Surely Sardak's companion had been some worker or low-level acolyte for the brother to have such a reaction. "He is among the clergy, then?"

"Good grief, no, although that would be humorous, too! No, *Master* Zayl, Edmun's in an even more stifling place! He's personal aide to our new, beloved *king*."

NINE

It was a tradition among the Western Kingdoms that when a king died and his heir prepared to assume the throne, the great nobles of that realm gathered in the capital to pay homage to both and show support for the latter. The converging of so much political and military might was also supposed to be a sign of stability to the general populace.

Some journeyed by winding caravans pulled by great, thick-coated horses or mules. Others came in single carriages, and not a few rode in with a detail of well-armed and wary mercenaries surrounding them. A hundred banners fluttered past the gates, something that made wealthy citizens and peasants alike marvel, for many of them had been born just before or during old Cornelius's reign and so had never witnessed such a gathering.

But those who began arriving in the city were of mixed intentions. Many came to praise the dead monarch, but also considered burying his successor with him. Others who came to offer their loyalty to Justinian IV did so halfheartedly.

Still, for whatever reasons they came, the point was that they *did.*

At least, that was the point to Aldric Jitan.

The noble watched from the balcony of his hillside villa as the latest arrivals announced their appearance with trumpeting and much waving of their banners. Lord Jitan sniffed in disdain.

"The red, orange, and blue pennant of Baron

Charlemore," he muttered. "One of the last, as usual. Display worthy of a peacock." Aldric glanced over his shoulder into the darkened room. "There'll be maybe seven or eight more, but that's pretty much the lot. Are you any closer?"

From within the darkness there came a brief glitter of pale, emerald light. In that moment of illumination, Karybdus was revealed. The steely-eyed Rathmian leaned over a table upon which charts of the stars lay. The intermittent flashes of light originated from a small, sharp crystal shaped like a carnivore's tooth. Dangling from a silver chain, the crystal swung back and forth over the charts. On occasion, it would pause over some alignment, at which point would come the momentary glitter.

"Patience is a virtue," reminded Karybdus. "Especially for a ruler-to-be."

"But I can taste it even more now," murmured Aldric, glancing once again at the baron's arrival. "You said it would take place while they were all assembled here."

"And so it shall. All the signs remain constant. The Moon of the Spider is nearly upon us."

"About damned time! And what about that interfering fool? What about the other necromancer? You said he would be no trouble by this point!"

Another brief flash revealed Karybdus's expression momentarily shifting to resentment. "He is a resourceful one, but he enters the game ignorant of the rules and the players, not to mention the consequences."

Lord Jitan set one powerful hand on the hilt of his sword. "If we can't use the sphere on him at this juncture and your own traps've failed, then maybe good steel would do the trick!"

"If necessary." The stone glittered one last time, then vanished from sight as the necromancer's fingers enveloped it. A breath later, he appeared beside the noble. "It would be an ironic ending for him."

"What's that mean? You speak like you know him well, sorcerer."

Karybdus shook his head slightly. "No, but his reputation—for one so young—is one of which I am aware. If he were not misguided, his feats might even be considered admirable."

"And he knows of you, too?"

"He did, but that knowledge I have managed to block from his mind." The armored necromancer straightened and, with a hint of pride, added, "He is, after all, only Zayl, while I am who I am."

Aldric gave a noncommittal grunt. "This Zayl's still managing to be trouble, despite who you are."

"No more. We can proceed as planned." Karybdus started back into the darkness, but the noble suddenly put a hand on his shoulder. Lord Jitan could not see the necromancer's countenance from his angle, or else he might have thought twice about touching Karybdus so.

"Remind me again just what *you* get out of all this, sorcerer. I know what I get—and well-deserved it is—but I'd like to hear that again, too, just to humor myself."

When Karybdus looked back, his expression was that of the scholar once more, analytical and unemotional. His words came in a flat tone, as might have been used by one giving a lecture to students. "We who follow Rathma serve the Balance. The Balance is the All. Without it, the world would tip into anarchy, chaos. We strive to keep that from happening by bringing order." He nodded toward Aldric. "You are a vessel of our work. Westmarch is in a time of flux. An iron hand is needed. You are needed to keep the Western Kingdoms from collapsing."

The tall noble smiled, susceptible like so many of his caste to flattery even when it was obviously such.

"When you are ruler, there will be demands upon you that some would call vile, even evil. They will not understand the necessity of what you need to do. Sacrifices will have to be made, sacrifices that will, in the long run, benefit humanity. There will come a time when the name of Aldric will have after it such titles as 'the Great,' 'the Far Seer,' and 'Champion of Mankind.' " Karybdus indicated himself. "As for me, my reward will be that I have served the Balance and my fellow man as best I could and kept back the tide of chaos by aiding in your ascension to the throne . . . which will not be long in coming now."

"No . . . it won't," agreed Aldric, gazing toward the ceiling. He saw his coronation. The adoring crowds would be cheering. The horns would be blaring. He looked further ahead and imagined himself at the head of a vast army— the Moon of the Spider held high in his gauntleted hand— charging down first on the forces of Khanduras, then Ensteig and, when those were his, the barbaric northern regions. Then, Aldric would turn his sights on legendary Lut Gholein.

There would be order in the world . . . *his* order.

And when he was certain that he no longer needed Karybdus, he would slit the necromancer's throat. Aldric knew that the spellcaster was not telling him everything. Karybdus had ulterior motives in mind. The noble was certain of that. After all, *he* had them.

"Oh, I forgot to mention. I have made another discovery, my lord. It will, I am pleased to say, speed up our task."

Breaking free of his reverie, Aldric eagerly looked at his companion. "What?"

Karybdus pocketed the small green crystal. "We do not need the House of Nesardo after all."

"But—"

The black-clad figure disappeared into the darkness. A frustrated Aldric Jitan followed after him. Despite his mismatched eyes quickly adapting to the lack of light, the noble could make out no sign of Karybdus.

"The pit beneath would have been a prime location from where to do our work, but my search has revealed an even better place that lies without the city walls," came the Rathmian's voice from farther ahead.

"Better than the original temple?" Aldric tried to think where he could draw forth the powers he sought to harness more reliably than in the place where the priests had raised up the monument to their lord. Tried and failed. "What is it?"

A pale, ivory glow suddenly erupted in front of him. With a gasp, Lord Jitan backed up.

Karybdus's face appeared above the glow . . . a glow radiating from the Moon of the Spider. The arachnid design on the sphere seemed to pulsate in time with the noble's rapid breathing.

"The place where this was created. The place where last stood the Children of Astrogha after the slaughter of the faithful at the temple."

"But I thought that was the ruins where we found it!"

The necromancer held the artifact closer, snaring Aldric's gaze. Karybdus's voice echoed in his head. "What we found was where the Vizjerei hid the Moon, hoping that it would never be found. They lacked the power to destroy it or that for which it had been created. No, the location which I have uncovered is far more relevant than either previous. It is a focus into a realm beyond . . ."

"A realm beyond . . ." Lord Jitan tore his gaze away. "Then, we've no more need of that—"

"Oh, yes, we have much need of her," cut in the necromancer. "The blood. Remember. The blood."

"Yes, I'd forgotten that. She has to die for it, doesn't she?"

The pale spellcaster handed the Moon of the Spider to Aldric. As the noble lovingly held it in his palms, Karybdus answered, "Most assuredly, my lord. Most assuredly."

Aldric caressed the artifact, his fingers stroking the arachnid as if it were a favored pet. "It wasn't a problem for me before, sorcerer. I've not changed my mind now."

"Splendid." Karybdus backed out of the light. "Then, there is nothing to worry about."

"Except this other Rathmian."

From the darkness came another sound, that of a large creature padding along the floor—or maybe the wall; Aldric could not say which. From Karybdus's direction came an odd sound, the necromancer cooing as if to an infant.

Then, "No, my lord. Zayl will not be a problem any-more. I have decided that the king will take care of him for us."

"That miserable—oh, you mean, Cornelius . . ."

Again came the cooing sound, followed by the long hiss with which the noble was by now quite familiar but that ever unsettled him. "Yes, good Cornelius will deal with the blasphemer in Westmarch's midst."

Zayl secluded himself in his chambers, drawing upon his training to regather his wits and strengthen his body. For hours, he sat motionless upon the floor next to his bed, reaching out to the innate forces inundating House Nesardo and learning from them.

But when he determined that he could do no more where he was, the Rathmian decided that, despite the good Polth's early warnings, it was time to step out into the city.

Salene and even Sardak tried to talk him out of such a plan, warning that the Zakarum would look for the slight-est excuse to toss him behind bars and try him for a heretic. Humbart, too, attempted to deter his friend, perhaps in great part because Zayl intended to go out on his own.

"You're looking for one man in a huge city, lad! One man! How many taverns of ill repute do you think there are? One? Two? More than likely a hundred, as I recall!"

But all argued to no avail. Salene finally planted her hands on her hips and declared, "Then, if you plan to be so foolish, I will go with you so that someone knows where to lead you!"

"If that's the case, sister dear," interjected Sardak, "it should be me. Who knows the haunts better?"

Zayl cut both of them off. "My lady, you are already clearly a target of some force. Out among the populace, it would be impossible to keep you from harm, and, in the chaos, perhaps your brother or myself as well. You will remain here and I will set in place protections known only to those of my calling. As for you, Master Sardak, since the most important thing in your life is your sister, it would behoove you to stay here sober, not go from inn to inn, likely to fall prey to an ale or two . . . or three or four."

That Sardak did not take offense was certain indication that the Rathmian had appraised him correctly. As for Salene, she still fumed, but Zayl had put into her head the potential threat to anyone seen with her. While the necromancer knew that she was willing to risk herself, endangering others was not Salene's way. He hated manipulating her so, but it was for her own good.

"Please be careful, then," the noblewoman said . . . and to his surprise, brushed her fingers against his cheek.

With a brusque nod, Zayl quickly left the pair. Although his expression did not show it, Salene's touch remained part of his attention for several minutes after. The necromancer was not used to such contact with outsiders, and would be happy when this matter came to a conclusion. Then, providing that he survived it, he could return to the comfort of the jungles of Kehjistan . . .

The servants were only too happy to hasten his departure, the lanky Barnaby quickly opening the door for him. Two men in livery and cloaks dared the incessant storm to swing the outer gates aside, then, just as eagerly slammed them shut once Zayl was beyond.

And so, peering from under his hood, the Rathmian got his first good glimpse of Westmarch.

The Black Ram proved a feeble shadow of a structure in comparison to the row upon row of buildings stretching forth for as far as the eye could see. The first were, of course, great homes and estates like that of Nesardo, but Zayl, moving with the patience and determination of a swift jungle cat on the hunt, very soon entered one of the commercial districts. There, stone fronts marked elegant shops selling merchandise of all sorts, including items that the Rathmian recognized from his homeland. One or two especially caught his eye, clearly looted from sites he knew to be sacred.

Inns of a more genteel nature also lined the cobblestone streets. Some of them had smartly clad guards with swords or other weapons, men whose job it was to keep the riffraff away. Music drifted out from the inns, some of it attractive to the necromancer's trained ear, some so discordant that he wondered if deaf imps played it to torture some victim for the Prime Evils.

Then, the Rathmian came upon a church of the Zakarum.

Twin towers—one on each end—thrust up high above the rest of the nearby structures. They pierced the sky sharply, as if seeking to impale angels upon their tips. The roofs were of scaled tile, giving the great church—a cathedral, truly—a passing resemblance to some hunched-up dragon. The walls of both the towers and the main building were lined with intricate, stained glass windows likely twice as tall as Zayl. Each image was taken from the writings of the Church and to the Rathmian all had a dire look to them. There were fiery angels with gleaming swords, misshapen creatures fleeing a glowing priest, and world-sized beasts devouring unbelievers. It seemed that the Zakarum hierarchy had decided that the faithful always needed to be reminded of what happened to those who did not adhere to the faith exactly as preached.

Four guards in the blood-red armor and capes of the Zakarum stood at attention by the massive wooden doorway. Soldiers of the Faith, they were called. Zealous in their duties, in their belief. They generally acted only as protectors of the most high in the Church.

One visored guard peered his way, the man's eyes and face completely obscured. Zayl kept his expression calm as he walked past, aware that he had been marked by the figure as someone much out of the ordinary and, therefore, of possible threat.

But no guard shouted out and at last the necromancer left the sight of the church. Only then did Zayl glance back. When he saw that no one was in sight, he allowed himself a brief exhalation, then continued on his trek.

Zayl had ignored the first inns, they being unlike those Sardak claimed this Edmun would likely frequent. Now, however, less glorious establishments rose ahead, and in these the spellcaster took an immediate interest. He looked at the nearest two, then chose the one on his left, that one being the noisiest and most disreputable-looking.

Barely an eye glanced his way as he entered, surely a hint of the depths to which those before the necromancer had fallen. Even those who did not know Zayl's calling could generally sense how different he was from most travelers.

Music, laughter, and argument assailed his ears, which one the most strident, he could not say. Zayl strode among the patrons, surreptitiously eyeing them in search of one who resembled this "king's man." It would have been much easier with Sardak beside him, but while Zayl was gone from the estate, he preferred that the half-brother remain with Salene.

Still, it soon enough became apparent that no one here could possibly be King Justinian's personal aide. The Rathmian turned around and—after narrowly avoiding a drunken merchant—stepped out once more into the rain. Pulling his cloak tight, he proceeded on to the next tavern.

But that, too, proved a waste of his efforts, as did the next two he entered. Zayl understood the difficulty of his task, yet, once again he counted on Rathma's claim that the way would come to him. Some clue as to finding the elusive Edmun would soon reveal itself, of that the black-clad figure was certain.

Zayl had not told Salene of another, just as pressing reason he wanted to go out alone. Away from Nesardo, the necromancer would be free of the interfering forces of the house and thus perhaps be better able to sense his mysterious adversary, this Karybdus, without having to rely on the questionable Edmun at all. Should that happen, Zayl intended to immediately close in on the other's location— again, a very good reason for keeping Salene far, far away.

He suddenly collided with a sturdy form clad in the hard leather of a mercenary. Startled as much by his lapse of concentration as he was by the actual collision,

Zayl glanced up into the tall figure's half-obscured face.

"*Captain Dumon?*" the necromancer blurted.

But a scant moment later, he realized that it was not his fellow survivor from Ureh. There was quite a resemblance, but also enough differences to mark this other fighter as someone else.

"You should keep an eye on your path at all times," returned the Rathmian's unexpected companion. His voice was unusually cultured for one of his calling.

"My humblest apologies . . ."

The mercenary grinned. "I'd make you buy me a tankard at Garrett's Crossing just for the inconvenience, if I had the time. Best drink in the city at Garrett's. Everyone goes there."

Zayl started to reply, but, with a friendly nod, the large man moved on. The necromancer paused to watch him for a moment, then went on his own way.

He came across a cluster of inns of various quality and paused. Zayl was aware that his hunt for Edmun was like looking for the proverbial needle. Unfortunately, his other quest, the one in which he had had more hope, was also proving fruitless. Despite a continuous mental probe, there was no hint of any other spellcaster, Vizjerei or otherwise.

Of course, he could always just go to the palace itself and ask for the elusive Edmun. Zayl smiled ruefully at the thought of such a move. The guards would take one look at him and either cast him in the dungeons or send him fleeing from Westmarch.

The wind picked up again. Zayl clutched his cloak tight, keeping the hood close. The wooden sign over one doorway swung wildly, each movement accompanied by the squeak of metal. A particularly loud squeak made Zayl briefly glance up—

And then glance again.

Garrett's Crossing.

Zayl abruptly glanced over his shoulder, certain that someone stood behind him but finding only drenched air. He looked back at the sign.

Expression set, the necromancer pushed open the door and went inside.

Garrett's Crossing was an establishment well above the Black Ram in quality, but certainly not on the level of one of the elaborate inns that Zayl had seen earlier. The patrons clearly had coin to spend, but not so lavishly. Still, there was music playing and much good-tempered laughter. The tavern area was well-filled, which meant that even a dour-looking figure such as Zayl caused little notice as he wended his way between tables.

But his gaze caught no sign of the elusive Edmun and he began to silently berate himself for having believed that he would find the man here. The Rathmian started to turn to the door—

And at that moment, from a back hall, a man who matched Sardak's description of the king's aide stepped out. He looked flushed, clearly the result of drink . . . and something more. A moment later, that something more slipped past Edmun in search of her next client.

Edmun adjusted his clothing. Zayl took the opportunity to move in on him.

The other looked up as the necromancer neared . . . and let out a howl of dismay. He pointed a condemning finger at Zayl.

Now the entire room noticed the Rathmian.

Edmun whirled away. Zayl moved to follow.

But from every direction, crimson-armored figures wielding gleaming swords suddenly burst into the tavern. They pushed aside patrons without care, even shoving over tables full of drink and gambling.

Zayl's quarry darted past one pair unmolested. The Zakarum closed ranks and converged on the necromancer. Behind them, Zayl saw a robed figure guiding the efforts, his expression one of zealous devotion to his cause . . . a cause that, for the moment, centered on capturing the Rathmian.

Zayl quickly drew a symbol resembling a sleeping eye in the air, accompanying his gesture with several muttered words.

To his senses alone, small, black spheres formed in the air above the charging men. The spheres immediately plunged down, covering the heads of the men.

The charge faltered. Armored figures suddenly collided with one another or crashed into tables and startled patrons. The cohesive line splintered, Zakarum's holy warriors now staggering blindly in a dozen different directions. Even their robed leader flailed around angrily.

The blindness would not last long, though. Ducking down, Zayl slipped past a lumbering guard, then into the densely packed crowd watching. Not unexpectedly, the latter parted for him without hesitation, no one wishing to touch a necromancer.

Out into the rain he ran, but not to escape. Instead, Zayl twisted around the corner of the building and headed toward the exit he believed Edmun had used.

Sure enough, the door in question swung haphazardly in the wind. As for Edmun himself, there was no sign, but the Rathmian could sense his trace. Now that he had found his quarry, the necromancer would not rest until he had a chance to question the king's man.

Turning a corner, the Rathmian caught sight of the drenched figure in question leading a horse out of some stables. Zayl focused, intending to repeat the spell he had used on the Zakarum.

But as he started to gesture, a party of armored riders suddenly swarmed between him and Edmun. Zayl's initial thoughts were that another band of Zakarum had come upon him, but while the garments of these men were red, it was not the blood color of the Church.

He attempted to turn the focus of his spell upon them . . . and only then realized that others came at him from behind.

Heavy, armored bodies brought the Rathmian crashing to the ground. Zayl heard a voice shouting orders and then a mailed fist struck him hard in the temple.

He felt nothing from that point on.

TEN

The more and more she thought about it, the more Salene regretted being talked out of journeying into the city with Zayl in search of Justinian's man. Zayl hardly knew Westmarch and he had already been attacked more than once because of her, which the noblewoman still greatly regretted. She was not one to let others fight her battles for her, not even those like Polth, who had been paid to do so.

And so, Salene determined that she would go out and find the necromancer before something terrible happened.

It was not difficult to slip past Sardak. For all his care for her, her half-brother trusted her too much. When she retired for the evening, Sardak accepted her kiss on the cheek and wished her well. He then went to his chambers—near hers—and promised that he would come the moment she called him.

But the noblewoman waited only long enough for the house to quiet, then, clad in an outfit similar to what she had worn to the crypts, wrapped a cloak about her and snuck out of her room. In order to even better avoid Sardak's hearing her, she took a route that brought her past Zayl's chambers. It required a longer trek, but at least no one would be wise to her departure.

Or so she thought.

"Bundled up well for a stroll through the halls," rang out a voice from behind the necromancer's door.

Salene tried to ignore the unseen speaker, but then he began humming loudly and off-key. Desperate, the Lady Nesardo slipped into the room to quiet him.

"No more, Humbart! Sardak will hear you!"

"And why should he not?" returned the skull only slightly more quietly. "You're not to be going out there and you know it, lass!"

"Zayl is risking himself for my life in a city he knows nothing about in search of a man he would recognize only from my brother's dubious description! I cannot fathom how I let him journey out there on his own!"

"You'd be surprised how resourceful the lad can be. If this Edmun's beyond the palace gates, he'll locate him." Then hesitation crept into the skull's voice. "Still, it *is* a big city . . ."

"And I know it far better."

"But you shouldn't go out alone, either, my lady."

She remained defiant. "I'll not risk Sardak out there for my decision."

"It wasn't him I was thinkin' of." Somehow, the fleshless head jostled. "Pick me up and we can be on our way . . ."

"You?"

"Lass, I searched for gold and hunted men for most of my mortal life! And I know Zayl better than anyone! You want to find him, and find him fast . . . you'll need me."

He made sense . . . and that worried Salene. "I don't know . . ."

"If you're fearful about carrying me around in the crook of your arm for all to see, just grab that sack next to me. 'Tis what Zayl uses when we're travelin'. All I ask is that you take me out now and then so I can get my bearings."

Not certain what else to do, she complied. As she opened the sack, the noblewoman asked, "You're certain you can lead me to him?"

"He and I are bound together by more than magic, my lady—gently there!" The last referred to her attempt to put the jawless skull in the pouch without losing her grip on him.

Once Humbart was settled within—and arranged right side up—Salene carefully shut the bag and tied it to her belt. The skull was surprisingly light against her hip. "Are you all right there?"

"As good as I can be . . ."

Salene grimaced. She had talked to the skull as if he were alive, which he was not. However human Humbart Wessel acted, he no longer *was*.

It proved easy for Salene, familiar with the routine of her own home, to slip past the few servants on night duty. Before long, she and Humbart reached the darkened stables. Accustomed to being self-reliant, the Lady Nesardo had little trouble saddling a mount. She did not run into another soul until reaching the outer gates, where only a single guard stood duty.

"You really want to go out in this, my lady?" questioned the armed man. He had served her ten years and so did not even think to actually suggest that she turn around and go back to the house. The Lady Nesardo did what the Lady Nesardo chose. That was all there was to it.

"Yes, Dolf. Consider this like the year my mother died."

"Aah." Expression set, the guard opened the way for her. As she rode through, he muttered, "A better outcome for this venture, I hope, my lady. Rest assured, no one'll know, especially your brother."

When they had ridden some distance from the Nesardo estate, Humbart suddenly asked, "Now what did you both mean back there?"

"When my mother grew ill, Dolf recalls me riding out each night, supposedly in search of someone who could heal her."

"And that wasn't the case?"

Salene shook her head, in her mind revisiting that dark time. "No, at least not later. First I sought the aid of a Vizjerei, hoping that he could teach me how to save her. That failed."

The skull hesitated, then: "Where there's a first, there's a second . . . What was it?"

"It was the first time I went in search of a necromancer." The skull could not see the tears beginning to mix with the rain dotting her face. "Then, I thought that if I couldn't have her alive, I'd have her raised from the dead, to stay with me always."

Again, Humbart hesitated. "You didn't find one, did you, lass?"

"No . . . and for her sake, I'm glad I didn't . . ."

The skull wisely did not comment.

The rain lessened slightly as they left the vicinity of House Nesardo, something that did not get past Salene. Even before Zayl had pointed it out, she had known that her home was the nexus of ancient powers. That had not bothered the noblewoman so much in the past, but now something was focusing those same powers against her.

Zayl had insisted on going on foot, something she had not understood but that now surely gave her some advantage. As swift and catlike as the necromancer could be, he would still need far more time to cover any area than Salene.

Under the hood of her travel cloak, the noblewoman peered out at the first establishments coming up ahead. She sincerely doubted that she would be so fortunate as to discover either the Rathmian or his whereabouts on her first foray, but, at the same time, Salene dared not pass any place by.

"Best to get started," she muttered, but as Salene began to dismount, from the pouch came a whisper.

"The lad's not been here for some time. Move on."

She paused, asking in the same quiet voice, "How do you know?"

"We're bound to one another, as I said," came the curt reply. "Ask no more. Just take my word: I know he's not around here. Move on."

Salene remounted. Whenever she would come to an inn or a tavern, she would put a gentle hand on the pouch. The skull would then respond with a single word—always, much to her dismay, "no."

This allowed them to proceed faster, but at the same time it disturbed her to discover how deep Zayl had already gotten into the city.

Her concern grew tenfold as they passed the great cathedral of the Zakarum. The wary guards looked not at all bothered by the harsh elements, concerned only with watching for the heretics they believed everywhere. The necromancer surely would have caught their eye, even if for his appearance alone.

"Slowly . . . ," Humbart suddenly muttered. "It's not been long since he was near."

Her pulse raced. This close to the Zakarum, that could not be a good thing.

"Hold up here," continued her companion in the same low tone. "Best check the nearest establishments. His trace is strong."

She pulled in front of an inn and tavern called Garrett's Crossing. Tying up her horse, she adjusted the pouch in which the skull lay, then started toward the entrance.

But just as she reached for the door, a large figure stepping out all but barreled into her. The man—a professional fighter from his general appearance—seized her by the arms just in time to prevent her from falling backward into the wet stone street.

"Here now, little one! You've got to watch yourself better!" He all but picked her up and set her down next to her mount. "I could've hurt you!"

"No harm's done," she returned, attempting to get past him. "If you'll excuse me, I'm looking for a friend of mine."

Somehow, the giant figure managed to keep in front. Although his features were half-obscured by his hood, there was something about him that reminded her of good, lamented Polth.

It softened her attitude toward him, even when he again kept her from entering. "That's no place there for the likes of you, my lady. They're still clearing things up from the trouble."

Trouble? Salene heard a slight sound from the pouch and quickly tapped it as she had seen Zayl once do. Humbart immediately quieted. "What do you mean? What happened?"

Her new companion rubbed his chin. Leaning down in

an almost conspiratory manner, he replied, "Seems there was a dark one, one of those sorcerers who raise the dead, in there. He was looking for someone, too, they say. But what he didn't know was that the Zakarum were looking for *him* at the same time."

It was all the noblewoman could do to keep from gasping. She prayed that the darkness and the foul weather kept her expression from this talkative stranger. "So the Church captured him?"

"The necromancer? Nay, he showed them how blind the Zakarum could be all right—literally—then slipped out after the man he'd been hunting."

The exhalation of relief escaped Salene before she could stop it, but, fortunately, the man did not notice. "Quite a lot of excitement," she finally managed to say. "Yes, you're correct. I won't look for my friend in there."

"Aye. If I may say so, my lady, any friend of yours is more likely to be a guest of the great General Torion than a patron of a squalid place like this." The leather-clad man nodded. "You'll pardon me, but I've got to be going. A good evenin' to you, my lady . . ."

With that, he finally stepped out of her way and descended into the storm-soaked street.

Salene hesitated by the entrance, but not because she any longer wanted to go inside. Something the man had said struck her.

More likely to be a guest of the great General Torion . . .

For some reason, the more Salene thought about it, the more she believed such an outcome a very reasonable possibility. Torion controlled the city guards, and such an incident would have quickly drawn them. If the Church did not have Zayl—as her brief companion had clearly indicated—then, unless he was still roaming Westmarch, it was likely that one of his kind would have been brought directly to the general.

A part of her argued that there were many flaws in her conclusion, but that part was drowned out. Filled with a sudden determination, the noblewoman untied her horse and mounted. Torion's sanctum—which served as both his headquarters and home—lay some distance away, but she had come this far already. Zayl deserved whatever help she could offer. Torion would listen to her . . .

As she urged the horse forward, a muffled voice growled, "Are we alone?"

"Yes, Humbart."

"Are you all right, Lady Salene?"

She detected a concern in his words that had nothing to do with her search for the necromancer. "Of course!"

A pause. Then, "Where're we riding to now?"

"General Torion's, naturally."

"And would you mind telling me why?"

His line of questioning made no sense to her. "Because, if the Zakarum didn't capture Zayl, then it stands to reason that the city guards likely did."

Again, there was a pause, one so long that at first Salene thought she had answered the skull's queries. "What's that about the Zakarum Church?"

Perturbed by his lack of understanding, she slowed the animal. After gazing around to see if anyone else was near enough to hear through the wind and rain, she said, "You heard everything he said about what happened in the tavern, didn't you?"

"The tavern?" After a moment, Humbart added, "I didn't hear a damned thing about any tavern, Lady Salene. Neither that nor anything at all about the Zakarum or General Torion, unless it came from your lips! It was a strange, one-sided conversation I heard, nothing more!"

Salene reined the horse to a complete stop. Shaking off some of the rain dripping down her hood, she brought the pouch close. Humbart's fleshless countenance pressed against the material. "A man came out of the tavern! He talked about Zayl's nearly being captured by the Church! You must've heard all of it!"

Even in the gloom, she could almost make out the eyeholes of the skull staring back through the fabric . . . and staring back, Salene imagined, in concern.

"You talked to no one that I could hear, sorry to say, my lady! All I heard was you talking to yourself . . ."

He had to be speaking nonsense. The man had been there, had even, in his own way, suggested Torion's quarters as a possible place to find the necromancer.

Torion . . .

Letting the pouch settle back at her side, Salene urged the horse on again.

"Where're you off to now, blast it?"

"The same place I was before," she replied, steeling herself against any argument by the skull. "I'm going to see if Zayl is with Torion. That's all that matters."

The storm chose that moment to unleash a long rumble of thunder, drowning out any possible comment from Humbart.

Not that Salene would have listened, anyway.

"What am I to do with you, necromancer?"

It was not a question Zayl enjoyed hearing upon first waking up. Nor was the voice—a voice that he recognized—one which he welcomed.

The side of his head still pounded. Despite a tremendous urge to sleep until the pounding ceased, Zayl opened his eyes.

Sure enough, General Torion gazed down balefully upon him.

The Rathmian started to rise, only then realizing that he was chained to a wall.

"The officer in charge of the men who brought you in heard about your little display in the tavern. You're damned lucky that he didn't just gut you when no one was looking."

Zayl managed to push himself up to a sitting position. As his head cleared, he became more aware of his surroundings . . . or lack thereof. He was a guest of one of Westmarch's cells, a deeply buried one from what he sensed. The floor was dirt and straw, the latter much-used. The walls were ancient stone, so ancient that the necromancer could sense touches of magic Torion likely did not know existed. There were also haunted memories here, just as there had been under House Nesardo. Some spirits still lingered or were perhaps even imprisoned in this place.

A dampness clung to the chamber. Moss covered the corners. The door was a thick iron plate with a bar that could be slid into a slot on the wall outside. A small grate toward the top of the door represented the only access to the world beyond the cell. The only light came from a square oil lamp that his captor held close.

"I ask you again: What *am* I going to do with you?"

"Release me?"

The corners of the general's mouth rose ever so slightly. "The necromancer has a sense of humor. Will wonders never cease." His expression darkened again. "Or perhaps you really think I can do that."

"I have done nothing. I was the one attacked."

"Not according to his majesty's personal aide, Edmun Fairweather, and he has Justinian's ear. Oh, and the Zakarum have their righteous bone to pick with you—but that should be no surprise to a necromancer, I suppose."

Zayl met the commander's steady gaze with one just as strong. "And what crime do they claim against me?"

"Blasphemy, naturally. Also casting evil spells upon guardians of the faith . . . and, no, self defense means nothing to them. They don't like your kind, necromancer, and neither do I."

"I see."

Zayl's flat reply seemed to stir something up within General Torion. "But I consider myself a fair man even to those I dislike. I've found no accountable crime, so I'll do what I can to get you out of here. Be grateful my men happened along. If the Zakarum had gotten you, nothing could have freed you from them. They are their own law within their walls. Your present surroundings would have been a lot hotter. The Church believes in cleansing *everything* with fire."

Turning from the prisoner, Torion knocked on the door.

A moment later, a harried guard opened it for him. The general would have left without another word, but a matter of concern occurred to the Rathmian.

"General Torion! Salene must not be drawn in by the Zakarum or—"

He was stopped dead by the other man's dire expression. "Don't you tell me about any danger to the Lady Nesardo! You're the one who's risked her life simply by being in her company! You want to keep her safe? Don't mention her name again! Better yet, forget you ever met her, necromancer!" After a pause, he added, "Oh, and don't think *we've* forgotten your skills. This section was designed for your ilk. Your spells won't work here. Go ahead and try; they all do. It'll give you something to do while I try to save your miserable hide."

With that, the tall soldier barged out of the cell. The anxious guard peeked inside at Zayl, then slammed the door shut. Zayl heard the bar slide into place . . . and then there was only a silent darkness.

They had taken his dagger and pouches, and if what Torion had said was true, they had removed the danger of his magic, too. Despite that, Zayl had every intention of trying to escape and believed that he had a very good chance. Necromancers were rare in the Western Kingdoms. If the cells had been warded against Vizjerei and their kind, it was possible that *he* might yet find his skills available.

It was certainly well worth the try. To depend upon the efforts of the general or the good mercy of the Zakarum was likely suicide. Even if it meant becoming a fugitive in Westmarch, Zayl felt it his best option. Besides, he had the very distinct suspicion that time was rapidly running out for everyone, especially Salene.

Muttering under his breath, Zayl called upon his dagger. No matter where it was, it would do its best to come to him. He focused on the piece, imagining its every facet to perfection. His blood fueled it; it was as much a part of his body as his hand or heart.

And almost immediately, Zayl sensed its presence. The ritual blade was not that far from him, but something held it back. Perhaps he had underestimated the spellwork of which the general had spoken. The Rathmian concentrated harder, beads of sweat forming on his brow despite the chill of his surroundings.

Then, to his surprise, a murmuring reached his ears, a murmuring that at first he took as coming from the hall outside. Only after listening longer did the necromancer notice that, in fact, the murmuring originated from the very *shadows* of his chamber.

Something was in the cell *with* him.

As he stared into those shadows, Zayl intensified his efforts to summon the dagger. The murmuring grew. It came from every direction. The words were unintelligible, but the malevolence in their tone was unmistakable. There was a sense of incredible age . . .

There was also a dread familiarity to it, and it took the Rathmian a moment to recognize the growing presence as the same ancient force he had encountered at Salene's home.

He began tugging hard at his chains, well aware how futile his efforts were.

The shadows took on the reddish touch of freshly spilled blood. Chanting arose, such as might be heard before a ritual sacrifice. Images came unbidden to the necromancer—twisted men and women wearing odd black headpieces and clad in cowled robes upon whose chest was the mark of a sinister arachnid. They wielded blades with serrated edges and before them writhed row upon row of helpless, brutalized victims.

Then, Zayl realized that what he had taken for head-pieces were, in fact, the same sort of spiders that had controlled the creatures in the crypt.

He shook his head hard, trying to focus only on the dagger. The chanting filled his ears. To combat it and the foul visions, Zayl raised his own voice higher, repeating over and over the summoning spell.

Without warning, the cell door swung open and the guard who had peered in earlier stepped before him. One hand holding a lamp and the other resting on the pommel of his sheathed weapon, he leaned over the prisoner.

"Here now!" he growled. "Stop your babbling or I'll cut your tongue out! Quiet, I say!"

Zayl did quiet, but only because he now stared in horror at what the lamp revealed of the surrounding walls.

A moistness dripped over the stone—the blood, he somehow knew, of those sacrificed in the visions. It spilled onto the floor and quickly spread toward the captive and his unsuspecting jailer.

"Get out of here!" urged the Rathmian. "Hurry, before it's too late!"

"What's gotten into you?" With the lamp, the guard followed his gaze. "'Fraid of a few spiderwebs or rats?"

He looked directly at the ever-growing bloodbath but clearly did not see anything. The guard even went so far as to take a step toward the far wall, inadvertently stepping into the edge of the macabre pool.

Satisfied that there was nothing, the man turned to face Zayl again.

As he did, out of the wall behind him oozed a pair of skeletal, ichor-bathed arms. Though they could not reach the guard, the twisted fingers grasped eagerly, hungrily . . .

Another pair of arms began emerging to the side of the first. Then another . . .

"For the sake of your life and your soul," Zayl went on, unmindful of the other man's darkening expression, "leave now!"

Brow furrowed, the guard peered over his shoulder and apparently still saw nothing.

But for Zayl, the walls now held a hundred or more pairs of clutching, grasping hands, and adding to the horror were fleshless, angry heads that to his higher senses screamed with the condemnation of those forever damned by their sacrifice to the twisted priests' master.

The guard suddenly slapped Zayl across the face.

"Don't try your stunts on me, sorcerer! You'd best pray to whatever deity you serve, because when the Church takes you, they'll—"

The monstrous, clawed hands could finally reach the unsuspecting soldier. As the man gaped in surprise and dawning horror, more than a dozen seized his arms, legs, throat, and torso.

And with one easy effort, ripped the hapless guard apart.

The skeletal hands flung gore-soaked body parts everywhere. The lantern crashed to the floor, falling on its side but still staying lit.

What was worse to Zayl than the physical carnage, however, was what he could see happening beyond the mortal plane. The guard's soul—a wispy thing with some vague resemblance to the man—was still held prisoner by several hands. They mercilessly dragged the wide-eyed shade toward the wall, then threw it against the screaming skulls.

Like a swarm of the carnivorous river fish Zayl had once come across back in Kehjistan, the heads closed on the helpless soul, voraciously devouring it.

And when there was nothing left, they turned their monstrous attention back to the chained necromancer.

The pool of blood now reached Zayl, but instead of flowing around him, it climbed up his boots and clothing, pouring over the Rathmian as if intending to encase him. Zayl felt his legs stiffen. He kicked at the foul liquid, but it adhered to his body like tar. Worse, it was colder than ice, chilling him all the way to the bone.

Zayl could have called for help, but he knew that to do so would only condemn anyone foolish enough to come to a fate akin to that of the unfortunate guard. The Rathmian watched helplessly as the monstrous hands converged on him and the blood continued its surge over his body . . .

But when the skeletal appendages seized Zayl, they did not rend him to pieces. Instead, two tore his chains from the wall, removing the last thing preventing them from dragging him toward the mouths.

The skulls' jaws opened wide and eager. The screams of the ancient dead and the chanting of their torturers filled his ears . . .

Zayl threw all his will into calling the blade.

It flew through the open door and landed in his grip even as he was dragged forward. Without hesitation, he twisted his hand around, severing the fleshless fingers holding his arm. As they fell away, the cloaked spellcaster cut at the foul crimson coating over the lower half of his body.

The chanting reached a crescendo, the cries becoming mere backdrop. A wave of icy wind made Zayl shiver. He looked up at the wall.

Another hungry skull formed, but this a gargantuan one that reached from the floor to the ceiling. It crowded out the others. When it opened its huge maw, Zayl saw that it was filled with webs upon which emaciated corpses lay. Each one looked as if it had been sucked dry.

Only then did the necromancer note that this skull had *eight* eyeholes.

Zayl muttered a spell. The dagger gleamed. He touched the blade against the fiendish hands, which released him as if burned by the weapon's touch.

Hopeful, Zayl brought the dagger to the blood. The tide flowed backward, clearing from his torso and legs.

Eyeing the open door, the Rathmian rolled to the side—

From out of the grotesque maw shot a thick, white spray.

The spray covered Zayl from head to foot. It stuck to him as even the blood had not. The Rathmian struggled to cut his way free, but his very blade stuck.

In desperation, Zayl shouted, "Zi i Odyssian mentus—"

The huge skull inhaled, drawing in the web . . . and with it the necromancer.

A moment later, Zayl vanished into the black maw.

ELEVEN

Zayl plummeted through a vortex of maddening sounds. Screams, cries, laughter—they assailed his ears until he prayed that he would go deaf.

He continued to clutch the dagger tightly, well aware that it was all that stood between him and a fate far worse than any he could imagine. The ritual blade flared bright, but its comfort was minimal in this monstrous realm.

Then, without warning, the webbing vanished. The necromancer tumbled free—

And collided a moment later with a hard surface.

Zayl lay there stunned for a time, unable to do anything to defend himself. With each moment that passed, he expected to be torn apart, yet nothing happened.

Finally, with great effort, the Rathmian pushed himself to his feet.

Only then did he see that his garments had changed. He wore the robes of the men and women he had seen in the vision, the priests with the spider emblem on their chest and the unsettling headpieces.

Holy one, you must hurry . . . , rasped a voice from the grave. Strong hands seized the startled necromancer's arms, guiding him over to what he now saw was a long stone walkway. *The moon is in ascension. The sacrifice must be made and only you are permitted to do it.*

"What?" Zayl glanced at the speaker, barely managing to bite back an exclamation when he saw him.

The man's face was a decaying horror upon which countless tiny arachnids made their homes. Where webs did not cover the rotting green flesh, other spiders lunched on what remained of the muscle and sinew, sucking on it with vampiric gusto. One eye was turned in and dried, the other had long ago been devoured by the creatures.

Long strands of mite-ridden hair draped down the back of the skull. The robe was tattered and soiled and where it clung to the torso, gaunt ribs showed through the material. The hand that held Zayl's arm was no better and everywhere upon the ghoulish priest the spiders crawled and crawled and crawled . . .

Atop his head, what Zayl had once assumed a headpiece stared back at him with baleful inhuman orbs.

A parasitic spider.

The necromancer instinctively pulled away, only to bump against another priest. This one was no better. In fact, his lower jaw hung to the side, the muscle on the left the only thing still holding it. He still had both eyes, but they were dry and yellow.

They have all been made ready for you, the second one said in a voice identical to the first. *They are impatient to be sent to the arms of Astrogha!*

Astrogha? The shade of Riordan Nesardo had spoken of an Astrogha. And had there been something about a moon then, too? Zayl tried to think, but the chanting returned, filling his head and crushing his thoughts. Zayl gripped the blade tighter, hoping to at least keep the voices within from driving him further to the edge.

The first priest suddenly reached for the dagger. *You'll not need that, holy one. Tokaric has the proper blade. Let me relieve you of that burden.*

"No!" Zayl could suddenly not recall why he wanted to keep his dagger, but he would not let it go.

As you wish for now, holy one. The macabre figure attempted as best he could a placating smile.

We are nearly there, holy one, added the second, his jaw swinging with each word.

The necromancer forced his gaze forward . . . and beheld an endless array of stone altars running on and on until eternity. Each was octagonal in shape and upon each was chained screaming, writhing forms.

All of whom, Zayl saw, had been flayed alive.

They cry from eagerness . . . , said the first.

Praise Astrogha! uttered the second reverently.

But the Rathmian shook his head. "This is wrong. This is an unbalancing of the All!"

They seemed not to hear his protest. With strength that their cadaverous conditions belied, the priests all but dragged Zayl toward the first of the altars. There, two more decaying figures in the spider robes met them with deep bows.

The moon is nigh upon us, said the taller of the pair, a thing so decrepit that only the voice hinted that it had once been female.

Astrogha is ascendant, added her companion, whose more rotund stomach squirmed under the festering garment. Several arachnids of various sizes and ferocious appearance scrambled in and out of the tears in the robe.

The first of the victims screamed wordlessly.

The female cadaver softly stroked the victim's skinned head. *Let us not leave him waiting any longer, holy one. He yearns to be a part of Astrogha's glory.*

"Yes . . . of course . . ." Zayl slowly raised the ivory dagger.

Not that blade! she immediately interjected, catching his wrist. In her withered hand, she held up another dagger. It was utterly black and had etched on its hilt a wicked, eight-legged pattern.

At the same time, the first priest again attempted to peel Zayl's fingers from the ivory blade. His efforts proved for naught, however, and at last the ghoulish group was satisfied when the disoriented necromancer instead took the black weapon in his free hand.

Over the heart, urged the heavy priest. *Two swift slices and the organ comes out still beating . . .*

"The heart," Zayl muttered. His eyes swept over the agonized figure. The upper layers of skin had clearly been flayed with great expertise, enabling the victim to live through it. The Rathmian suspected a potion of some sort had been administered to the man before his torture so that shock would not kill him, either.

With the decaying priests to guide his hand, Zayl prepared to cut into the chest cavity. Two swift slices. They would have to be deep ones if he wanted to reach in and immediately grab the heart.

He glanced at his own weapon. It would really be best to be rid of the other dagger. It had nothing to do with Astrogha's sacrifices and would only make tearing the vital organ out that much more troublesome.

But before he could hand it to one of his companions, the priest with only a partial jaw gazed up and declared, *The Moon of the Spider is upon us! Astrogha is with us!*

Zayl looked up.

The moon was a perfect sphere, round and gleaming. At first, it was completely pale, but then over the upper edge shadows crept. They flowed down in one river after another until there were eight. Then, as the first of them reached midway down, a larger, round patch of blackness followed.

And in seconds, the gargantuan form of an arachnid filled much of the moon. Zayl stared at it, stunned by how real the shadow seemed.

You must strike now! insisted the female, whispering in his ear.

Strike now! urged the first priest.

Strike now!

Strike now!

The robed figures flanking the other altars took up the new chant. *Strike now . . . strike now . . .*

Strike now and the blessing of Astrogha will be upon you! the flayed victim suddenly declared, lidless eyes burning into the necromancer's own. *You will be the vessel of my glorious renewal! You will be a god among mortals!*

Zayl's hand faltered. He shook his head and when one of the decaying priests sought to help him finish, the Rathmian suddenly tore away.

"No! By Rathma, by Odyssian, by Theroni—I command you to be gone!"

The ghoulish figures moved toward him. *Now, holy one,* began the very first. *You have a duty to fulfill. A destiny. Give me the white blade and all will be understood and accepted by you.*

"I will give you a blade, certainly." Zayl shifted his grip on the black dagger, then threw it at the demonic speaker.

The sinister weapon sank not into the priest's chest—for what heart would remain after so long?—but rather the *head,* where the necromancer knew that the force animating this corpse linked to it.

The dagger buried itself in the skull. The priest's hands jerked to the spot, where they feebly tugged at the hilt.

The ghoul collapsed in a ghastly pile of rotting meat, bones, and cloth.

The female figure lunged toward Zayl, the others right behind her. *You must complete the sacrifices!*

Zayl held his own dagger before them, repeating the names and adding to them. "By Rathma, by Odyssian, by Theroni, by the Jalak, by Mumryth of the Wing, by Trag'Oul, I cast you all away! I deny this place, this monstrous realm!"

The rest of the undead priests converged on Zayl, a swarm whose form became more horrific as they neared. They reached for him with claws and hungering mouths. To the necromancer, it was the nightmare of Ureh relived . . . only this time they would tear off more than just his hand.

Muttering under his breath, Zayl summoned the Den'Trag, the Teeth of Trag'Oul. The air before him filled with gleaming projectiles that immediately shot forth at the monstrous horde. The first of the ranks, including the original priests, fell, pincushioned by the powerful spikes. The bodies twisted and turned, then melted, fading away to nothing but tiny red puddles.

But still legions poured toward him. Although he knew the effort would prove fruitless, Zayl glanced behind him in the hopes of finding some escape.

And there, but a few yards distant, a white hole beckoned.

Aware that it might be a trick, Zayl nonetheless ran. He could not stay and fight indefinitely. His escape from the hypnotic spell cast over him had been a fortunate turn, but against such numbers, he would surely succumb.

As the cloaked spellcaster neared it, the hole suddenly flared. Zayl covered his eyes and held out his dagger, certain that he had stepped into yet another trap.

Instead, from behind him he heard a tremendous moan. Daring to look back, the Rathmian saw the first ranks of the demonic priests turn to dust in mid-stride.

Whispering an oath to Trag'Oul, Zayl threw himself into the hole. Behind him, he heard the outraged hiss of something far more malevolent than the throng of undead. Something struck his back and he felt his momentum almost slow to a halt.

At that moment, the hole closed—

And in the next instant, a deluge of rain poured down on the startled necromancer. He fell to the ground with a heavy thud, every bone quivering.

Thunder briefly deafened him. Stiff and weak, Zayl lay there for several minutes. Had the undead horde fallen upon him then, he could have done nothing to stop them from ripping him apart.

Gradually, though, his breathing became regular and the agony coursing through his body subsided to something tolerable. Blinking clear his eyes, the necromancer finally surveyed his surroundings.

A thick, shrouded forest of pines and oaks greeted his gaze. A steady rain beat down on him. Despite Zayl's exceptional vision, he could not see very far or very much. It was night, which made him suspect that he had not been long out of his cell, and the forest looked like one he would have expected to find in Westmarch.

But where was the city? In every direction, the Rathmian saw only more shadowed trees.

Slowly it registered to him that he still held his dagger in his left hand. Holding up the mystical blade, Zayl muttered a short spell.

The blade flared bright for a moment, then dimmed slightly.

Zayl turned in a circle, muttering as he moved. A third of the way around, the dagger suddenly flared again.

So, he was at least in the vicinity of the city. How far, though, the necromancer could not say. He suspected that he was in for a long walk.

The rain continued to pour. A mist began to take shape, adding to the murkiness of the forest. Zayl adjusted his cloak and hood, then started off.

The nightmare through which he had just suffered remained burned in both his mind and body. He had come very close to being lost to the foul entity that had invaded the cell. Worse, Zayl had the growing belief that it had sought not just his soul, but his body as well.

But why? Who—or what—was Astrogha? His symbol was the spider. Zayl knew that he should have recognized one or both, but that knowledge, like the identity of the mysterious Karybdus, had likely been blocked from his consciousness.

The other necromancer and this Astrogha clearly had to be linked. Was Karybdus a Vizjerei who sought some legacy of Astrogha's ancient rule? Clearly, the events in the vision were a twisted version of something that had happened long ago. The priests had once been living, breathing men and women completely devoted to their foul master. It would not be the first time that an avaricious Vizjerei had delved into lost and forbidden realms in his lust for power.

The ground dipped as he headed toward Westmarch. Zayl considered what he knew of the land and guessed that he was not far from the mountains that he had seen when first arriving. Likely if it had not been so dark and misty, he would have been able to make them out between the treetops. If so, it meant that the weary spellcaster had been correct when he had guessed that his return would take some doing.

And what then? They would discover him gone and the guard brutally slain. There would be no doubt in anyone's mind—even Salene's—that he had been the butcher responsible. Every man and woman would do their part to hunt him down.

Salene. Zayl found himself more disturbed by her belief in his evil than by everything else, yet he doubted that he could ever make her see the truth. He himself would have found it impossible.

Perhaps it would have been best to abandon all matters concerning Westmarch, but the necromancer could not. Even if he had not already become so embroiled in them, it was clear that something ominous stretched over much of the land. If he simply abandoned his efforts, it would be as if he himself had worked to upset the Balance and sent the world into the talons of the Prime Evils.

His boots sank in the torrent-soaked ground. Zayl's progress slowed, but his determination grew. He had sworn an oath to the spirits of Rathma and Trag'Oul. He had given over his life to his calling, forsaking all other paths. The way of Rathma had allowed him in some small manner to redeem himself for his own transgressions . . .

How Zayl wished again that another of his kind might be found here, especially one of the elders who had instructed him. But Falaya, gaunt Horus, and the faceless Nil were on the other side of the Twin Seas . . . assuming that the eternal struggle had not taken them since last he and they had met. Likely there were a handful of younger Rathmians here and there in the Western Kingdoms, but if there had been any others nearby, Zayl surely would have sensed them and they him.

It is up to you alone, he chided himself. *Is that not the way you always desired it? You alone . . . all alone?*

A harsh, animalistic roar suddenly cut through the thunder and rain. Something huge crashed through the misty forest.

Bringing up the dagger, Zayl summoned more light. He had a brief glimpse of a towering figure with eyes of red and fur of a thick white-brown. It moved like a man, yet also like a beast.

Then . . . it was gone into the forest once more.

But the necromancer was not lulled by its vanishing. He spun around, using the dagger and his heightened senses to search for the creature.

What *was* it? No bear; it was far too manlike. There were traits that Zayl could recall from the momentary glimpse that reminded him of something else, something from his teachings . . .

The leaves behind him rustled ever so slightly.

Zayl rolled away just as a giant shape lunged at where he had been. The necromancer attempted to cut at it as it went past, but the creature proved quite agile for its size and twisted out of range.

The beast did not hesitate, bounding into the forest again and vanishing as if it had never been.

Breathing heavily, the Rathmian waited. When several seconds passed and the huge figure did not return, he cautiously rose. But by no manner of the imagination did he believe himself safe. With the two attacks, the beast had taken his measure. When next it returned, it would take *him.*

Drawing three symbols in the air, Zayl pointed the blade at where he had last seen his elusive adversary. Unfortunately, the dagger's glow—now supposedly focused on the beast—revealed nothing.

He waited. Nothing happened. Finally, the necromancer was forced to move on. He knew that the rain and thunder would make it difficult to hear anything unless it was right upon him, which by then would be too late. Each footstep took an eternity as Zayl's anticipation of some sort of attack grew.

It is only an animal, he told himself. *You are a man. You can outthink it.*

But Rathma had taught that in nature everything worked to maintain the Balance. Therefore, where humans had gained the upper hand in intelligence and tools, the beasts of the forest had grown more silent, more swift. More deadly.

There were several spells which he could use against it, but only if he saw the creature before it took him. In many ways, he faced a far more dangerous enemy than a Vizjerei or the undead priests.

A crackle of lightning illuminated the region. The necromancer made good use of the momentary light, eyes registering everything made visible. Yet still there was no hint of his adversary.

Had it abandoned him for simpler prey? Zayl had his doubts, but if it still pursued, then why had it not attacked again?

He stumbled along for several minutes more, wary of every shadow and movement. The ground dipped more steeply, the incline such that the soaked spellcaster had to hold on to underbrush with his right hand as he made his way down to more even land.

A trickle of water caught his attention. Squinting, Zayl barely made out a stream running across his path. With great caution, he put one foot into the water, then another—

From out of nowhere, a great fist caught him across the face.

The necromancer slipped into the stream, his dagger flying. Again, he heard the bloodcurdling cry of earlier and the sound of splashing. With a rush of water pouring across his backside, Zayl looked up.

The outline of a brutish giant filled his gaze.

Zayl's left hand instinctively shot to the side. The dagger flew from where it had fallen, landing neatly in his palm.

He brought it up and fed the full force of his will into its illumination.

The area erupted with light as if a dozen bolts from the sky had struck simultaneously. The beast let loose a startled roar and instinctively covered its eyes.

And for the first time, Zayl beheld the night howler.

It was indeed built like a man, but disproportionately,

for although its legs were thick, hairy trunks and its lower torso was twice as wide as Zayl's, they were dwarfed in comparison to the barrel chest and the colossal shoulders, which surely spread six feet across. The shoulders had to be so gargantuan, for the brutish arms attached to them would have served any army as a good pair of battering rams. Each fist was wide enough to take Zayl's head whole and clearly had the strength with which to crush his skull without difficulty. It was a wonder that the Rathmian was alive, much less conscious. The runes he had forced from X'y'Laq had clearly worked.

As for the night howler's head, it was a squat, heavy thing that, at first glance, seemed to have slipped off. It stood not on the end of a neck that was in turn perched atop shoulders—as a man's would have been —but hung low over the chest, essentially making the creature look hunchbacked. It had a thick brow ridge and tall, pointed ears, but there was some human shape to the head, and the eyes would have seemed so, too, if not for the fiery red madness in them.

The giant roared again, revealing the sharp teeth of a carnivore . . . and one who supposedly favored human flesh. From the legends that Zayl had read, that had not always been the case. These beasts had once been men. The taint of the Prime Evils had touched even their pure souls, reducing them to these marauders. While they caused havoc among humans, the true pain was that it was inevitable that the night howlers and their like would become the first losses in the struggle for the Balance. Men would and had already began to hunt them down, their lush coats a bonus since they were sought after by the wealthy.

Zayl regretted the fall of the men who had been turned into these creatures, but not enough to give up his own life as a feast to this creature. As the giant recovered, the necromancer turned his blade downward, then cast.

A pale blue shimmer momentarily surrounded the night howler, raising its fur. The beast let out a grunt, but, after seeing that nothing else happened, reached for Zayl.

And, at that point, a lightning bolt struck the monster head-on.

The force of the bolt tossed the screaming creature like a tiny toy across the area. The giant collided with a tree, which snapped under the impact, the upper portion of it landing several yards to Zayl's right.

Legs shaking, the necromancer straightened. He eyed the darkened form lying amidst the wreckage of the tree stump. The smell of singed fur touched Zayl's nostrils.

The night howler did not move.

"Rathma be praised . . . ," Zayl murmured. With both his strength and his concentration on the wane, he had doubted his ability to do anything should his last spell have failed. He had made the monster a virtual magnet to the harsh effects of both elemental magic and the very elements themselves, hoping most of all that the storm would react immediately. To his good fortune, it had.

Clutching a nearby trunk, Zayl turned from the still form. How much farther he could manage he did not know, but he had to keep going. Somehow, he would reach Westmarch. There was no choice.

From behind him, there came a long, deep grunt and the shifting of rubble.

Zayl looked over his shoulder and beheld the night howler rising like a dark phoenix from its ashes. It shook its head as it stood, and although the Rathmian could not see the eyes, he felt them fix on his.

Gritting his teeth, the necromancer propped himself up against the tree. He raised the dagger, but at first his mind was too unfocused for him to cast a spell.

The furred giant weaved uncertainly. Zayl marveled that it even lived, much less could stand and walk. If lightning could not stop the beast, what force *could*?

The creature stumbled, then fell to one knee. It paused there, its heavy breathing yet another sign that the lightning had indeed done it great damage. The necromancer grew calmer; now more than a dozen spells came to mind that would rid him of his monstrous foe.

However, the night howler then did a strange thing, an act so extraordinarily different from what Zayl would have expected of it that the spellcaster lowered his dagger and stared.

The forest denizen looked at him . . . and stretched out both hands in what was clearly a *beseeching* gesture.

The night howler—the fearsome creature who had just sought his blood and flesh—now wanted his *help*.

TWELVE

"This isn't a wise idea," muttered Humbart from the pouch.

Salene tapped the sack. "Hush! The guards will hear you."

She stepped up to the two men at attention near the doors to Torion's office. They were the fourth such set that she had confronted since arriving. The time the noblewoman had been forced to expend at each juncture had driven her to the point of fury. Somehow, Salene was certain that the general's and Zayl's paths had crossed again, just as the nameless mercenary had suggested. If so, every moment counted, for surely Torion would not treat the necromancer well.

"I am the Lady Salene Nesardo," she declared imperiously. "Kindly inform General Torion that I would have a word with him. Now, please."

Both men clearly recognized her. The senior guard bowed his head, saying, "I will relate your message to the general's adjutant."

A minute later, a young, dark-haired officer with a long nose and pointed chin stepped out. He gave Salene a gracious bow. "My Lady Nesardo! This is an unexpected pleasure!"

"Thank you, Alec. Please lead me to Torion, if you will. I must speak with him urgently."

The adjutant's expression soured. "My lady, now would not be a good time. There are matters about at the moment that have demanded his immediate attention and I can't say when that might change. You see—"

Salene knew that if she let him, Alec would go on and on with his explanation. It was the method by which he deterred inopportune visitors, for most eventually tired of the barrage of words and agreed to come back at the general's convenience, not theirs. She had witnessed him use it on others, but never before on her, a favorite of his commander.

Steeling herself, the noblewoman cut into his reply. "I understand how busy Torion is, but I think that he'll want to see me, Alec. I can promise you that."

"But, Lady Nesardo—" the adjutant began, clearly aware that here was one person who would not so easily be swayed.

They were both saved from further sparring by none other than General Torion himself. The veteran officer, the collar of his uniform undone and his sweeping hair somewhat disarrayed, came not from his office, but from the hall down which Salene had only minutes before walked.

"Pardon, my lady," rumbled Torion, sweeping past Salene without realizing who she was. "Captain Mattheus! I need you to—" He blinked, then glanced over his shoulder at her. "My Lady Nesardo!"

The noblewoman kept her expression masked. "General . . ."

"Well, that deals with one matter I had for you, captain. As for the other, I want you to send word to the Guard commander on duty. Have him send a force to House Nesardo. Better yet, *you* lead the force yourself—"

"Torion!" Salene's eyes went wide. "What do you mean to do? Soldiers in *my* home?"

Ignoring her outburst, the general continued, "The men are to treat the home with the utmost respect, but also are commanded to search every room. I want it verified that he is not hiding there." As an afterthought, he pointed at the two sentries. "Take these two with you. I'd like to speak to the Lady Nesardo alone."

Alec Mattheus gave Torion a crisp salute. "Yes, sir! Come along, you pair!"

As the trio marched off, Salene's longtime suitor finally focused his full attention on her. "I was going to send an escort to your house, too. One for you, specifically."

"Me? Why?"

His voice softened slightly. "To make sure that you were not there during the search. I am trying to protect you! Salene, I warned you about that grave desecrator! Now he's added murder of the most heinous sort to his deeds! I've not seen such butchery even on the field of battle! The guard was an innocent!"

Her fears heightened. He could only be talking about something concerning Zayl. "Torion! What's happened?"

"Your friend the necromancer was brought in by the City Guard just barely before the Zakarum's elite got ahold of him. There was a claim that he was trying to cast a spell over the crowd at a tavern, then used his powers on the Church's faithful. How much of that was true, I didn't care at the time—"

"So you had him arrested and thrown in a cell?"

He looked offended. "Would you have preferred him to be purified by the Church? In retrospect, I wish I'd let them have him! I tried my best for him because of you, Salene, and a good man's been slaughtered because of it— not to mention that somehow that damned sorcerer's escaped from the inescapable! Salene, the guard was literally torn to *pieces*!"

Dismayed by that but still secretly relieved that the necromancer was not a prisoner, Salene thrust a finger at the soldier's armored chest. "Zayl is no murderer, Torion! He's only done what he could for me, and nearly died because of it! He's a good man, one I trust—"

"He's beguiled you! I warned you of him! The Zakarum are already asking about you, you know. If I can give them Zayl, then I think they'll turn a blind eye to you." He shook his head. "Just when I thought that matters were changing for the better, with the king finally acting like a man . . ."

Ignoring his change of subject, the red-haired woman turned away. If Zayl was not here, then it stood to reason that he would return to her home . . . which meant that she somehow had to go there, too, before the men Torion had just dispatched arrived.

A heavy hand tightened on her arm. "I wouldn't suggest going right now, Salene. I must insist, in fact—"

But the veteran commander got no further, for Salene, reacting instinctively, put her own hand on his—and General Torion froze in mid-speech.

"Torion?" She peered up into the man's eyes. They stared blankly at Salene, neither shifting nor blinking.

A shiver ran through her. Peeling his fingers from her, she backed up. The general remained as he had been, his one arm stretched out, his fingers clutching empty air.

The noblewoman touched the hand again. It felt warm. She leaned close to his chest, but could not detect any breathing.

"Oh, Torion! What have I done to you?"

"What's the matter, lass?"

At first Salene thought that the general had somehow managed to speak, but then she recalled Humbart in the pouch. "It—it's Torion! He stands as if a statue!"

The hidden skull unleashed a low-spoken but very effusive epithet, then added, "Thought something went awry! Heard him send the others away, so I took a chance to speak! Does he look pale, pasty?"

"No . . . he just looks like Torion . . . only completely still! I can't detect any breathing—I've killed him!"

"Not so! Not so!" interjected Humbart quickly. "Seen the like before. Probably just temporarily frozen in place. 'Tis like he's sleeping . . . really deep."

Such sleep, Salene had seen only with the dead. She shook her head. "No! I've slain him!"

"Nay! You've got the gift of sorcery—we've seen that already—and it's coming to the forefront! He's only asleep! Likely it'll wear off soon!"

She hoped and prayed that he was telling the truth. "Is there . . . is there anything I can do?"

The skull gave a grunt. "I can't tell you what to do in

that respect, my lady, but me, I'd be chasing after Zayl, I would. The lad's my friend."

Salene did not hesitate. With a last sorrowful glance at Torion, she hurried away. Fortunately, the only guards she came across were those who had already allowed her to pass by. Unaware of what had just happened, they bowed their heads to the noblewoman but did not slow her departure.

Retrieving her mount, Salene turned back to House Nesardo. The weather remained foul, but she barely noticed it, so intent was she upon reaching home before Captain Mattheus and the searchers. Her one hope was that it took the adjutant a little bit of time to arrange his departure for House Nesardo. Still, every second counted.

It seemed an eternity before she reached the gates, but, to her relief, there was no sign of the soldiers. Her own guard saluted her, then quickly let her through.

"There will be a party of soldiers arriving shortly," she informed him.

"My lady?" Although his tone was that of a question, his eyes betrayed his suspicion as to whom they sought.

"Delay them as long as you can without causing harm to yourself . . . please."

It was a credit to the loyalty that she stirred in her servants that the man immediately nodded. "You can depend on me, my lady."

With a nod of thanks, Salene rode on to the house itself. She left the horse near the front, then leapt up the steps. The pouch carrying Humbart bounced madly at her side.

The door swung open as she reached for it. Salene jerked back out of surprise, then felt the pouch containing the skull slipping loose. She caught the sack just as the strings holding it to her belt came completely undone, then glanced up at the figure in the doorway.

"I was wondering where you'd gotten to," remarked a surly Sardak.

"I—"

"Yes, yes, I know. Zayl. You slipped out even though I

was listening for you! By the time I knew what had happened, you were gone into the night! I almost followed after, but I was afraid we'd miss each other—"

Holding the pouch in one hand, she pushed past him. "I've no time for this! They could be here at any moment! Where is he? In his room?"

"Who? The necromancer? I've not seen a sign of him and I've been in the sitting room, at this point waiting for either one of you."

Zayl was not here? Salene tried to think. She had been so certain that he would come here. To her.

Then, the noblewoman recalled the tragic scene that Torion had described. Although she was certain that Zayl had not been responsible, clearly *something* had taken place—and the necromancer would have been caught in the heart of it.

At that moment, both siblings heard shouts from the gates. Sardak swung the door shut. "Friends of yours?"

"Captain Mattheus and a squad of guards. They're here to search for Zayl."

"Well, he's not here, but they'll search anyway. What do you suggest we do, sister? Just let them go ahead? Seems reasonable."

She suddenly thought of Torion. If the adjutant met her here, he would wonder why she had so quickly returned—and also how she had managed to slip free of his commanding officer in the first place. "It might be best if I wasn't found here, Sardak. Don't ask me why . . ."

His brow arched. "And to think I always considered *myself* the reckless one. How you've changed, Salene . . ." He frowned. "But you can't very well hide from them. Torion's lapdog is nothing if not efficient. He'll peek in every nook and cranny, that one will."

Her mind raced. There was only one place she could imagine him not entering. "Then, I'll hide in the crypts."

Humbart started a muffled protest, but a stunned Sardak cut him off. "You're not serious! After what you described? Better to face the captain! What could you have possibly done that would make you even consider that place?"

"I can't tell you!" She started toward the back of the house, Sardak following. "Besides, I'm not going to go all the way down. Just to the stairs. There are some alcoves. I can wait there."

"He might go down there, Salene."

"No. It would be considered sacrilege. It's one thing to search the house and even the ancient dungeons, but another to disturb the rest of the ancestors of one of the oldest houses in Westmarch. He'll have to go back to the general for permission . . . and that will buy us some time to think."

Sardak shook his head. "I am just dying to know what terrible thing you've done."

"Later, Sardak . . ."

He guided her to the entrance, but the noblewoman stopped him from coming any farther. "I leave it to you to deal with them," Salene murmured. "Please, for me, don't—"

"Don't fail? Fear not, I won't let you down."

"That was not what I was going to say." Salene touched his cheek. "I know you'll do just fine. You always do. What I don't want you to do is risk yourself unnecessarily."

"But that's what I do best," he replied with a grin. Then his grin faded some as a sound from the front of the house reached them. "Best you go now. I'll deal right with them. You won't have to worry."

With a last grateful glance, the noblewoman descended. The painful memories buried in the old cells stirred as she entered the area, but, as Salene had done since childhood, she forced them from her attention.

At last, Salene reached the crypt door. There, she paused, struck by the sudden recollection that she had left her horse in front of the house.

Salene cursed herself for a fool, but the situation could not be helped. It was too late to go back, she told herself, and besides, Alec Mattheus might not even recognize her mount. Perhaps Sardak would be able to salvage the matter simply by saying that it was his.

Perhaps . . .

It was all too much. Salene knew that she should just go back and face the captain. Before long, Torion would be discovered and all would recall who had been the last to see him. At least if the general's men took her into custody, she would not have to fear an inquisition by the Church.

But then Sardak would be left to fend for himself . . . and there would be no hope at all of saving Zayl.

If he was even still *alive.*

The door to the crypt proved impossible to open with only one hand. Salene put Humbart's pouch on the floor and began struggling with the handle. The skull remained silent, clearly aware that even the slightest sound might be heard by the men in the house.

As she pulled, she thought again of Zayl. Had the same monstrous force that had attacked them below succeeded in taking him from the cell? If so, it seemed—as even the habitually reckless Sardak had pointed out—folly to now enter the ancient chamber.

But there truly was nowhere else to hide that Torion's adjutant would not search. The very thorough Captain Mattheus would journey all the way down into the old dungeons—but he would not go farther, not even if he suspected that there was someone in the crypts. That definitely required a higher authority.

Or so she kept hoping.

To her dismay, voices suddenly could be heard above. Eyes fixed on the corridor behind her, Salene gave the door another harsh tug.

With a creak, it opened just enough for her to slip inside.

The voices grew louder, more strident. They seemed to be nearing her. As quickly as she could, the anxious noblewoman entered, then pulled. With a much too loud groan, the door shut behind her.

The instant it did, Salene was struck by an uneasy sense that she was not alone in the crypt. She stared down the darkened steps, certain that she saw movement.

A voice *just* outside made her start. How had the soldiers

gotten to the crypt so quickly? Salene stepped away from the entrance, surprised that the search had already drawn so close. Had they *forced* the truth out of Sardak? Surely the captain would not go that far!

Not certain what else to do, Salene descended several steps to one of the alcoves that she had mentioned to her brother. Falling back into it, the Lady Nesardo waited for the soldiers to either enter, despite the sacred restrictions, or to continue on elsewhere.

The sense that she was not alone swept over her again. Salene shivered, caught between desire not to be discovered and her memories of her last visit here.

If I only had light, Salene thought as she pressed herself flat against the stone. *Just a little light. Something Alec's men wouldn't notice if they're near the door—*

A small blue glow formed before her.

Salene let out a short gasp. Fearing that she had been heard, the noblewoman waited for the door to swing open and soldiers to come rushing inside.

But the door remained shut. As she waited, Salene continued to stare at the astounding glow. For some reason, it comforted more than frightened her. Salene gave it some thought and finally realized that *she* was the cause of it. She had asked for a light, and it had formed.

Fascinated, the noblewoman reached out to it. It was slightly warm to the touch, but in a pleasant way. Curiously, at the same time, her general sense of unease concerning the crypts was fading away.

Salene glanced at the door. The voice had ceased. She exhaled, her pulse finally slowly to something akin to normal—

Suddenly a movement at the bottom of the steps caught her attention.

She stared. At the very edge of the glow, Salene made out the silhouette of a hulking figure. A hulking figure she would have known anywhere.

"*Polth?*" Salene took a step down, the glow matching her movement.

The silhouette seemed to ripple . . . then shifted deeper into the crypt.

Fascination and fear intermingled. Momentarily forgetting Captain Mattheus's searchers, the noblewoman slowly wended her way down. Yet, no matter how far or how quickly she descended, the shadowy form ever remained just at the edge of her vision. Despite that, Salene was absolutely certain that it was her former bodyguard whom she saw.

But Polth is dead! a part of the Lady Nesardo reminded herself. Nonetheless, Salene continued all the way to the base of the stairs.

The glow matched her step by step. She could now see the first few vaults, but no longer any sign of the elusive shade. A small spider scuttled out of the light and Salene suddenly recalled with vividness the attack by the demonic creatures.

Good sense returned. She backed up the last step. Better to wait in the alcove or, if she could, even leave the crypt entirely. She had made a mistake in coming here.

Her hand slipped to her side, and only then did the Lady Nesardo discover yet another terrible mistake. She had left the pouch with Humbart outside. In fact, the more Salene thought of the voice she had heard, the more it seemed that it had been the dead mercenary calling to her. He had probably tried to alert her to her carelessness, but was too late. The door had muffled his voice enough for her not to recognize it.

Berating herself, Salene started up. If one of the soldiers did come out back to search the grounds and in the process discovered the pouch and its unsettling contents, even ancient custom and privilege might not be enough to keep Captain Mattheus from daring to enter the crypt.

But as she took another step, a voice echoed in her head. *Mistress . . .*

Salene hesitated. Biting her lip, she glanced over her shoulder.

Mistress . . .

The noblewoman stepped down. She saw nothing ahead of her, yet the voice seemed real enough.

Mistress . . .

She looked to her left.

And there, half-lost in the shadows, dead Polth stared down at her. Despite his terrible demise, he now looked whole, albeit pale and somehow hollow.

Reaching out tentatively, Salene whispered, "Dear Polth . . . is it you?"

His head tipped forward, and although his lips remained set, she heard his voice again. *I live . . . to serve you, mistress . . .*

There was no mockery in his tone despite the irony of what he had said. His eyes held a sadness, yet also a defiance.

"Polth, dear Polth . . ." She started toward him, but the light followed and, as it did, the bodyguard's form rippled and retreated. Polth seemed to exist neither in the dark nor the light, but only at the edge of both. Salene immediately halted. "What—why are you here?"

I live . . . to serve you, mistress . . . , he repeated. One arm rose, pointing deeper into the darkness. *The truth . . . there . . .*

"What—what are you talking about?"

There . . . mistress . . . the truth . . . about Nesardo . . . and Jitan . . .

Jitan! For this apparition of her loyal servant to mention the name of Aldric Jitan now meant that Polth had indeed discovered something most foul.

Aware of what both Sardak and Zayl would think of her foolhardiness, Salene Nesardo followed the specter's arm. The light continued to match her like a twin, unveiling more of the crypt as it went.

She expected Polth to vanish, but instead, the figure continuously rippled wherever the edge of the light happened to be. No matter how many steps Salene took, the dead bodyguard was always the same distance at her left side. Despite what he now was, the noblewoman found herself taking a peculiar comfort from his presence.

To her surprise, the bodies of the creatures who had attacked them still lay where they had fallen. Rats nibbling on the rotting carcasses looked up as the light fell upon them, but most did not retreat from their feasting. Salene eyed the corpses with more curiosity than revulsion. For some reason, she had expected them all to have vanished, as if they had only been nightmares. That they had not done so emphasized the danger she had faced, yet put a mortal touch to it. These creatures had died as men could die.

As had Polth . . .

Even as she thought the last, Salene walked past the spot where Polth had perished. Fortunately, there was nothing left to be seen. The Rathmian's spell had been very thorough.

Full of feeling, she looked at the shade. "Polth, can you ever forgive—"

He silenced her with a shake of his head, then pointed ahead. The message was clear: Polth wanted her to continue on, no matter what. His own death meant less to him.

She journeyed past Riordan's vault and those of her parents. Soon, the names she could make out became ones only vaguely known to her, if at all. The style of markings grew archaic and cracks in the stone were common.

At last, she came to the end of the vast crypt . . . and another set of ancient steps.

"There?" she asked, indicating the path down to the next level.

In reply, Polth pointed at the steps. His ability to speak seemed very limited. A tear came unbidden to Salene; she had heard tales of ghosts doing great things for those for whom they cared, but never had she thought she'd experience it firsthand.

"I pray that you can go to your rest after this," the Lady Nesardo muttered to her companion.

Polth only continued to point down.

With her ever-present light to illuminate the path ahead, Salene descended. A thick, moist air met her as she went from one level to the next. The noblewoman coughed, but did not stop.

This level was not unknown to her. Servants who had shown deep loyalty and devotion to the Nesardo House were entombed here. While these vaults were not as elaborate as the ones of the family itself, they still represented an honor to those granted final rest here. Only a select few of each generation were allowed such a fate, and Salene had expected Polth to be one of them. Unfortunately, there existed nothing of him to put in the vault.

But the specter seemed unmindful of the honor he would miss. When the noblewoman looked his way once more, all the giant did was point insistently down the vast hall.

Moss covered many of the older vaults. Several no longer had legible name plates. As she wended her way through the crypt, Salene started to wonder if the honor would have been worthy of her bodyguard. Clearly, even before she had inherited House Nesardo, this level had been in need of cleaning and rebuilding.

Then, the light floating ahead of her fell upon a sight that gave Salene pause and made her wonder at the worth of her entire trek.

Rubble filled the rest of the chamber. The collapse was centuries old, but no less daunting. Mixed among the rock and earth were bits of carved stone and even fragments of bone. A slab that she finally identified as part of an upper floor jutted out of the top of the collapse.

She knew the tale, of course. It had taken the Nesardos years to rebuild this part of their estate after the collapse from the tremor. They had concerned themselves most with the house above and the two levels of the crypt important to them. No one, it seemed, had been eager to dig out the older level. It had been said that some had even called the collapse a blessing.

But what was the purpose behind leading her here? Did Polth think that she could float through solid rock?

Salene thought then of the magic she wielded. Did she

dare use it here and now? She glanced at Polth, but the shade merely stood there, as if waiting.

There seemed no other choice but to attempt a spell, yet the would-be sorceress had no idea just how. All of her previous spells had come unconsciously, the results of reactions to potential or immediate threats.

She stared at the vast mound of rubble. Perhaps if she tried something small at first, such as moving just a few small stones. Then, if that worked, a spell on a larger scale . . .

Steeling herself, Salene moved closer.

No . . .

The ghost's warning came too late. The rubble under her feet gave way . . . and a pit opened up beneath her. Salene desperately grabbed for some hold, but everything she touched fell in with her.

Screaming, the noblewoman vanished into the darkness below.

THIRTEEN

Zayl sat warily across from the wolf creature, trying to decipher its thinking. The necromancer and the beast had not moved since first the latter had unexpectedly reached out not to tear the man apart, but to plead for his aid.

The practical side of Zayl—generally the far more dominant side—insisted that he leave the night howler to its fate. After all, it was a cursed monster, a creature who craved human flesh. It had become a thing of the Prime Evils, nothing more. It was beyond redemption.

But a side with which the Rathmian was less familiar, an emotional side only recently stirred from a long slumber, pointed out that this beast was not acting at all as it should be. It reminded Zayl more of the ancient legends of the creature, when the monsters and their cousins had been regular people, living in the forest and mountains.

And so, after staring for more than an hour at his former pursuer, the necromancer rose to his feet and strode toward the injured giant.

Meaty hands that could have torn him into bloody gobbets of flesh stayed lowered as he came within reach. Zayl bent down and touched one of those hands, which then cautiously turned palm up. The Rathmian murmured under his breath.

In response, the night howler grunted several times. Zayl could not understand what the beast sought to say, but the tone seemed one offering peace and trust.

In darkness, there is light, even as in light, there is darkness. So Rathma preached. Zayl hoped that his ancient lord had been correct in that assumption.

He turned to the night howler's leg, the cause of the creature's distress. Sure enough, it was broken from the force of the explosion. Only the brute strength of the beast had enabled it to even rise at first.

But that was not enough to explain the change in the furred giant's persona. Somehow, the forces that Zayl had summoned had struck deep at the core of the creature's heart and soul, wrenching from them the vile taint of the Prime Evils. It was the only explanation that made sense.

The necromancer started to reach for the shattered leg, then took one last look into the beast's eyes. His brow arched. Even in the dark, he could see the astonishing transformation in them. Gone were the blood-redness and insane fury; here now was a pair of orbs so very touching in their nearly-human grief.

Those eyes decided it for him. The Rathmian touched his dagger to the area in question while his free hand drew symbols just above the leg.

The night howler let out a grunt. Its paw slid near the leg. Zayl glanced toward the huge hand, but did not falter. All that mattered was his spell.

The beast withdrew its paw, leaving the necro-mancer to his task.

A faint moonlight glow spread across the ruined limb. As it did, the leg straightened and the tears in the skin sealed themselves. The scars tightened, then completely faded. Even the fur returned.

When he was done, Zayl let out a long gasp. It had not taken him much time, but the effort had been monumental. Still, the results pleased him.

There was a loud grunt in his ear. The cloaked figure was suddenly lifted bodily into the air.

Twice, the giant touched his moist black nose against Zayl's. That done, the night howler grunted in a longer, more elaborate fashion before setting its much smaller companion on the ground again.

"You are welcome," Zayl said, not knowing how else to respond.

The giant figure grunted, seemingly better at understanding the human than the human did it.

He expected the monster to rush off into the forest, but the giant instead let out another series of growls, all the while gesturing behind Zayl. The necromancer at first thought that perhaps another threat lurked in that direction, but gradually came to understand that the giant was pointed toward *Westmarch.*

"Yes, I must go there." The rain had let up—some, anyway—and although even Zayl's training could not entirely keep his exhaustion and pain at bay, he had to continue on. However, as he started off, the night howler fell in line behind him.

The Rathmian peered back. "There is no need to come with me."

The beast's response was another series of growls and grunts, some quite elegant despite being unintelligible. Their meaning was clear. The creature would not leave Zayl to fend for himself.

"You owe me nothing. You may return to the forest."

His giant companion appeared undaunted.

Zayl frowned, then, resigning himself to the inevitable, he turned from the night howler and continued his trek. Behind him came the almost silent padding of thick feet. Compared with the creature's footsteps, his own resounded like thunder.

It took all of Zayl's reserves to make the journey, but with the night howler at his heels, the necromancer felt his confidence return. When at last he sighted the distant walls of the city, he exhaled deeply, not at all concerned at the moment about the fact that the inhabitants likely wanted his head as much as the demons of Ureh had.

"Trag'Oul be praised." Zayl looked over his shoulder for his furred companion. "The—"

But, without warning, the night howler had disappeared.

The necromancer cautiously surveyed the dark forest. There was no sign that the legendary beast had even been with him. Zayl marveled at both the creature's cunning and its ability to move in silence. He had been fortunate indeed to have escaped its initial attack.

With the capital in view, the beast had rightly assumed that any obligation it had had to him had ended now. Zayl made the sign of the Balance, and wished the forest dweller a safe return to its den. The Rathmian had made of this creature an outcast among its own kind, for they were still tainted by the power of the Prime Evils. Zayl had not given his former adversary any true blessing; the lone night howler would ever have to be at odds with the others.

Yet, the beast had been grateful to be rid of the evil within, and the necromancer now reassured himself that, under the same circumstances, *he* would have felt the same.

A slight lightening of the heavens was the only sign of the shift from night to day. The weather continued its foul course, driven, the necromancer sensed, by those powers gathering in and around the city. Powers possibly manipulated by the Lord Jitan and—and—

And then, staring at Westmarch, the name "Karybdus" suddenly came to mind.

Only . . . this time, Zayl *remembered* . . .
Remembered . . . and gaped in horror at the knowledge once again flowing free through his mind.

Salene pushed herself uncertainly to her feet. She had fallen a tremendous distance, far deeper than the third level to which she had assumed she was descending. By her own reckoning—which, at this point, she knew was questionable—the noblewoman had dropped the equivalent of three or four *additional* levels.

Had it not been for her unpredictable abilities, Salene was certain that she would have perished. The rocks upon which she now lay were jagged, sharp. That she had only a few bruises was a miracle in itself.

Stone and rubble lay scattered in every direction. The blue glow still floated near her, but its scope was limited and so her first glimpse of her surroundings beyond the area of the fall revealed little.

Peering around, Salene saw no sign of Polth. Despite what had happened, she felt certain that there had been no treachery intended on his part. His shade had expected that the same reflexes that had saved her from the creatures in the crypt would protect her now.

Salene wished that she had such confidence in herself.

She stumbled forward, the glow accompanying her. For the first time, Salene became frustrated by its meager illumination. If it had been brighter, perhaps she would have seen that the area upon which she had been treading had been unstable. Certainly *that* would have saved her much trouble.

Eyes fixing on the magical light, Salene concentrated. She wanted more. She wanted a light capable of illuminating whatever lay ahead so that she would not fall prey again.

The glow obliged, swelling several times its previous size and radiating a light so bright that at first the Lady Nesardo had to shield her gaze in order to avoid being blinded.

And when she dared look again, the sight before her caused the noblewoman to stumble back in shock.

The small passage in which she stood ended only two yards ahead. Had she taken a single step more, Salene would have discovered that fact without the amplification of her light spell.

But even then, she would not have beheld as much as a tenth of what lay beyond.

The chamber stretched downward and around, forming a vast bowl. More amazing, filling that bowl was a huge amphitheater of stone benches in which hundreds could have sat without any crowding whatsoever. Despite its obvious age, the overall structure was all but intact. Other than dust, the only signs of the onslaught of time were cracks here and there in the benches and one section where the roof above had collapsed, crushing two rows to her right.

Yet, as astounding as such a sight was, it paled against that which Salene made out at the far end of the ancient structure.

The spider hung from a web of gold that covered the cavern wall. Its humongous body was composed of a black jade that glittered evilly in the glow. Each segmented leg was arched downward and ended in ruby talons.

The head was at least as large as Salene herself and upon it was clustered eight sets of eight huge diamonds. The noblewoman averted her own eyes from the crystalline orbs, for there was something in their facets that made it seem that the spider stared back at her with great hunger.

Finishing the image were a pair of golden fangs tipped with more crimson rubies.

Vivid memories of the creatures in the crypt arose. Salene quickly looked around, but although there was no sign of any of the horrors, she wanted nothing more than to return to her home. Better to face the good Captain Mattheus than remain here any longer.

Yet, instead of doing just that, the Lady Nesardo took a step down *toward* the amphitheater. She could not explain her actions even to herself. Her mind screamed for her to turn and run, but, somehow, the huge arachnid drew her closer despite her disgust and fear of it.

Her foot touched the first stone.

A whispering issued forth from all around Salene, but she saw no trace of its source. The noblewoman took another step . . . and the whispers grew a shade louder. There was a rhythm to them, almost like singing, or *chanting*.

Drawn by the spider as if caught in its silk, Salene continued to descend. The chanting intensified, seeming to her to resound throughout the amphitheater. She now saw—or was she imagining?—robed figures of men and women seated upon the benches ahead of her, their expressions ones of rapture, their eyes staring unblinking at the overwhelming arachnid. The ghostly throng beat their hands together in sync with their chanting.

Midway down, what they said finally became clear. It was not a phrase, as first Salene's subconscious had registered it. Rather, it was one word . . . a name.

Astrogha . . . , they chanted. *Astrogha . . . Astrogha . . .*

"Astrogha," she whispered with them. There was something so familiar about the name, as if she had known it as well as her own, then had, for some inexplicable reason, forgotten it.

Astrogha . . . , the specters continued, seeming to urge her on. *Astrogha . . .*

Salene neared the bottom, the gargantuan spider god now almost hovering over her. Ahead lay an altar, faded crimson streaks lining the surface like veins.

Suddenly, on the altar lay the shade of a young woman with wide, drugged eyes. Behind her stood an emaciated priest upon whose robe was a silhouette of the spider god.

Astrogha . . . Astrogha, he called. *We offer our gift to open the way for your coming . . .*

From his voluminous garment he drew a wicked blade. The crowd's chanting reached a crescendo—

A cry filled the amphitheater.

Half-caught between the past and the present, Salene Nesardo turned at the sound.

Men in armor—men as ghostly as the robed figures upon whom they fell—poured into the gathering. Swords slashed and arrows downed those who stood to block the newcomers' path. No quarter was given.

The Sons of Rakkis are upon us! came a frantic shout. *The Sons of Rakkis are upon us!*

Finish the ceremony! This from the direction of the priest. As Salene glanced there, she saw that there were now two others, a woman and a portly man. It was the latter speaking. *Finish the ceremony before their damned Vizjerei show up!*

But the figure with the knife shook his head. *No! The moon is already slipping past! The moment is lost!* He handed something to the woman that Salene could not make out. Something round. *Take it! It must be passed on until his time comes again . . .*

But where? asked the woman.

Anywhere! To the far edge of the world if need be! growled the dagger wielder. In the amphitheater, warriors who had died centuries past put again to death those whose bones were also long dust. *So long as those who come after us remember when it must be returned . . . and where!*

But what about the blood? the other man insisted, pointing at the young woman chained before them. *Where do we find another of her blood? It is as key as the timing and the moon!*

The lead priest smiled grimly. *Rakkis himself in his eagerness to create a dynasty has provided us with the potential for many!* He, too, indicated the drugged woman. *As with her, there will be those with the proper blood! Now go! Hurry! I sense the Vizjerei even now!*

The woman nodded. With her burden and the portly figure beside her, she turned . . . and faded into history.

A monstrous expression smearing his face, the dagger wielder loomed over his intended victim. The moment might have passed for the young woman's sacrifice to be of use to his "god," but that would not stop the priest from slaying her for his own desires.

The bolt that suddenly blossomed in his throat, however, *did.*

The dagger fell. The priest let out a groan and toppled over the girl, who finally stirred. She let out a moan, then, her eyes focusing for the first time . . . looked directly at Salene.

With the Lady Nesardo's own eyes.

The amphitheater went still.

With a groan, Salene fell to one knee. The cries of the dying faded from her ears.

It took the noblewoman more than a minute to readjust to her surroundings. Slowly, she rose and looked about. The entire edifice was as she had first seen it. Dust, cracked benches, and little more. The bodies of the slaughtered cultists did not litter the walkways, nor were there any more armored men charging in through what Salene now saw was a rubble-filled passage. All that was in the far past, where it belonged.

Her gaze returned to the altar. The woman with Salene's eyes was no longer there, as much a lost memory as all the rest. Still shaken, Salene nonetheless summoned the courage to touch one of the faded red streaks. She knew it now for the dried blood of previous sacrifices.

"Horrible . . . ," Salene muttered. "Horrible."

"Sometimes, some horror is necessary for the ultimate good."

She spun about and found herself facing a cowled and armored figure. His black garments and pale, somewhat gaunt face reminded her a bit of Zayl.

"You see the dead nearly as well as we," the shrouded man commented clinically. "Perhaps, because of what you carry within, in some ways you see them even better."

"Who—who are you? You look like—like—" Salene hesitated to go any further.

"Like *Zayl*?" He gave her the ghost of a smile. "That is because I am as he is, a follower of blessed Rathma . . . a necromancer, if you will." The black-clad figure bowed slightly. "You may call me Karybdus."

Salene went pale. She spun away from Karybdus—and all but ran face-first into a monstrous shape dangling from the giant, jeweled arachnid.

A spider. A living spider as large as an infant. It spat in her direction, its savage mandibles working as if the creature was tempted to take a bite of her face. Coarse black fur covered its hideous, bulbous body. Eight malevolent green orbs clustered together just above the mandibles, all of them fixed upon the stunned noblewoman.

Salene backed away . . . and collided with the armored form of the necromancer.

Karybdus seized her wrists, keeping her pressed against his body. With his short-cropped gray hair and scholarly face, he reminded her of some of the instructors who had tutored her in her youth. That made his every word, so casually spoken, all the more horrific.

"Now, now, my Lady Nesardo. You mustn't be afraid of my little one here. Skaro does only what I ask of him, and he knows that you must not come to harm . . . yet."

"Let me go!"

"Truly, as Rathma says, the Balance will guide you if you are patient. I come here to retrieve a small, but significant item for our task—a dagger—and I find you waiting as if eager to already be upon the altar stone."

Gritting her teeth, Salene tried to summon up her power. If there was ever a time it was needed, it was now.

The glow she had created became a blinding sunburst. Grunting, Karybdus used one hand to shield his gaze.

Salene tore out of his weakened grip, racing in the only direction presently open to her. That it took her farther from the entrance through which she had fallen did not matter. All that did was that she get as far away from the necromancer as she could.

Behind her, Karybdus muttered something.

The earth beneath her feet rumbled. Salene let out an exclamation as fissures cracked open all around her.

Bones, ancient bones, flew up out of the fissures. There were femurs and skulls, ribs and shoulder blades. Whole pieces and fragments swirled around her as if she were caught in a tornado.

She tried to break through, but the whirling mass moved with her. Salene would slap something away only to have it flow right back to her.

Then, several pieces dropped to the ground. Atop them fell others, the bones quickly stacking up and creating square formations.

A wall of human remains arose in front of the noblewoman. Salene turned, but the same thing happened. She glanced behind her and saw that she was also barred there.

A cage of bone now stretched well above her. The last few pieces created a top, ensuring that Salene would not even be able to climb to freedom.

She slammed her fist against the cage, and although a flash of blue energy accented her strike, nothing happened save that Salene's hand suddenly began to throb with pain.

Calm, measured footsteps warned her of Karybdus's approach. The Lady Nesardo turned to face him. Her captor seemed not the least irritated by her escape attempt. If anything, he appeared very satisfied.

"The blood does flow true in you. I sensed it from the first. It will open the way."

"What are you talking about? Why are you doing this?"

He shushed her as one might a raucous child. "Please be aware that I do this all for the good of the Balance, and, therefore, the good of the world."

From over his cloaked shoulder, the monstrous arachnid appeared. The repulsive creature crawled along Karybdus's arm, nestling in the crook.

Karybdus gazed down at the spider, his expression finally showing emotion. He murmured to the beast as if it were a baby, scratching its back at the same time.

When his attention returned to Salene, the emotion vanished. "I must beg your forgiveness for what I am about to do. It is a variation of what we call the 'life-tap.' It is necessary so that you attempt no further foolishness."

Before the imprisoned woman could react, his free hand darted through a gap in the bone prison. The gloved fingers touched her just above the breastbone.

An incredible weakness coursed through Salene. She felt as if every bit of strength drained away from her . . . and into the necromancer. The noblewoman pulled from him, but it was already too late. She felt her consciousness slip away.

And as Salene Nesardo collapsed, she heard Karybdus, not the least inflection in his voice, say, "I am so sorry, really I am."

F⊕URTEEN

General Torion gasped.

Strong hands caught the commander as he slumped. The familiar voice of Captain Alec Mattheus boomed, "General! Are you all right? Can you hear me?"

"I can, so stop blasting in my ear!" Torion felt what was left of his leg strength going. "A chair! Quickly!"

The ever-efficient adjutant already had one waiting for him. A good thing, too, as the commander followed his last words by crumpling into it.

As Torion caught his breath, Captain Mattheus knelt down beside him with a goblet of his superior's favorite wine. The general gratefully accepted the drink, downing most of it in the first gulp.

His aide leaned close. "General . . . what happened?"

After a moment of brooding, Torion responded, "The necromancer. He was responsible for this!"

"He was here? But nobody reported anyone other than the Lady Nesardo coming or going—"

"And do you think it was *her*? Would you like to make that claim to me right here and now?"

"No, sir!" Captain Mattheus frowned. "I've just returned from her home. The search is going on, general, but from what I already saw, it's pretty unlikely that this Zayl is there . . . unless he's in the crypts."

Torion's brow wrinkled. "And you came back for permission to search them?"

"Being as it's House Nesardo and how thoroughly we might have to look . . . yes, sir."

Taking another sip, the veteran officer mulled over the

request. Finally, he muttered, "No, I don't think that's necessary. As I said, this was the necromancer's work. Clearly he came here and stole away Lady Nesardo, so he's not going to be found in the house." His voice grew firmer and there was a dark glint in his eye. "Here's what you do, Alec. I want all patrols on watch for him in the city. You can't miss him in that outfit, but I'll write up a more detailed description of his features that you can pass around. He may be in the company of the lady—was her brother at the estate?"

Captain Mattheus made a face. "Yes, sir. That one was there. Hard to believe that the two are related . . ."

"Never mind that. Sardak was at the house. So he likely won't be found with the necromancer. Still, order the men to avoid any harm to the Lady Nesardo or anyone else traveling with the blaggard if they can help it. I want no possible innocents injured. Understood?"

The adjutant nodded. "I'll see that she stays safe, sir. You've my promise."

"Good man." Torion felt his strength returning. "Help me to my desk."

After the captain had done so, the commander gathered parchment and quill. Quickly, he wrote down what he recalled of Zayl's appearance. Torion considered himself a man with an excellent memory, and the details he wrote down gave proof of that.

"Here. This'll help." As the younger soldier read the description, Torion added, "Find him before the Church can get a hand on him, will you?"

"I'll bring him right back here, sir."

The commander grunted. "If he should die trying to fight off your attempt to rescue him, Alec, I'll understand that it couldn't be helped."

His expression unchanging, the adjutant looked over the description one more time. "I'd best get on this right away."

"Do that." With grim satisfaction, Torion watched his subordinate depart. Captain Mattheus would deal with the grave robber. No blame or suspicion would fall on Salene. Things would be as they should be and, eventually, she would see that *he* was the man for her—

A guard came bursting into his office. "General, sir! He's here!"

At first Torion had the thought that the necromancer had been mad enough to turn himself in, but he knew that Zayl was not so great a fool. Rising, the commander demanded, "Who? Who?"

"King Justinian! By himself! No guards, no advance warning!"

Torion's eyes widened. Although the change he had witnessed in his new monarch was a promising one, this action bordered not so much on courage and confidence as on suicide. True, in the old days King Cornelius had often ridden alone through the city, even stopping to visit the general, but it was far too early for the son to be doing the same. Until the prepared show of force made it clear just how strong Justinian's position was and how capable he had suddenly become, he was in constant danger of assassination by those with blood claims to the throne.

However, that was a concern for another moment. What was important was that the king was *here*. "Where is he at now? Prepare an honor guard! I want—"

"But there's no need for all that pomp," a voice smoothly interjected.

General Torion stiffened to attention. "Your majesty! This is an unexpected and—and—"

"And totally bothersome intrusion. I know, I know." Justinian raised a hand to stop the veteran officer's protest. The new king was clad in a riding outfit designed in the same style as his previous outfit, save that the pants flared at the hips and a golden travel cloak protected him from the elements. To Torion, he made a splendid-looking target for any who would have wished him ill. "Please, don't say otherwise. I suspect that what you really wish to say to me is that I'm being foolhardy coming out alone like this."

"Your majesty, I would never speak so to you!"

This comment made the new ruler of Westmarch all but beam. "Not lately anyway, eh? Calm yourself, Torion. You're going to have to expect a few *more* radical changes from me! After all, if I am to remain king past the official coronation—or even up to it, if you know what I mean—then I'm going to have to start acting more like my father did."

If he acts any more like his father, thought Torion, *he will* be *Cornelius!* Not entirely a terrible thing, either, so long as the boy survived the year.

Trying to regain his mental balance, the general asked, "To what do I owe this great honor, your—"

"Please, from you, no more 'your majesty.' You will call me Justinian. My father insisted on a first-name basis with you, as I recall."

And it had taken Torion several years before he had grown comfortable with that command, but he did not say such to the man before him. "Aye, he did do that."

Justinian grinned. "Then, I could ask you to do no less. I trust you as much as he did."

Torion bowed his head in gratitude.

The king glanced at the dumbstruck guard. "Torion, there is something I came to speak with you about. Could we do so with privacy, you think?"

He even sounds like Cornelius. "Yes, your—yes, Justinian." To the soldier, Torion commanded, "Send the guards stationed outside my doors away, then return to your post. No one is to come anywhere near here unless I call for them. Is that understood?"

"Yes, sir!"

"Dismissed, then . . . and close things behind you."

When they were securely alone, Torion belatedly realized that he had never offered his august visitor a seat. Slipping from behind his desk, he proffered his own. "Please, Justinian. I insist."

"I don't plan on being very long, but thank you." Again with that grin that reminded the veteran soldier of his old master, Justinian planted himself in the plush, high-backed leather chair that Torion had personally paid to have made. "Very nice . . . it's good to be commander of the royal forces, I see."

"Your lamented father was very generous to me. If you feel he has been too much so, I—"

"Good grief, no! I couldn't think of any man more worthy of your position! I know that your loyalty, your obedience to me is utterly without question, and I consider that paramount during this troubled time . . . "

Again, Torion bowed his head. "You're too kind."

Justinian suddenly glanced to the side, just as he had done in the throne room. Less disturbed by it now, the commander waited. Sure enough, a moment later, the young monarch's gaze returned to him. "Let me get to the point, Torion. I've heard word of a stranger in our realm. A dangerous *foreigner* from across the Twin Seas . . ." The general tried his best not to show his surprise at the king's knowledge, but clearly failed, for Justinian grinned wider and added, "I see you know of whom I speak."

"There has been word—"

"And an altercation . . . and something drastic that took place in your own cells, from what I heard."

Torion no longer attempted to hide his surprise. "The throne is well-informed."

Justinian's eyes—his well-focused and now no longer watery eyes—bore into Torion's. "Isn't that exactly how my father worked? As much as he trusted in you, he always had other sources of information."

"That's true, your majesty. Yes, there's a *necromancer* in the city. A pale, dark-haired knave known only as Zayl. He was captured in an altercation involving the Zakarum—"

"Who had already petitioned me about gaining custody of this Zayl when the tragic escape took place, as I understand it. The petition caught me by surprise, Torion."

The general adjusted his collar. "I was about to inform you when the chaos broke out. To be honest—Justinian— Zayl escaped one of the nullified cells set up by your father for just his type."

"No, not quite." The young king glanced to the side,

then, pursing his lips, explained, "He's a necromancer. They're different from the Vizjerei. There would've needed to be some other spells on the cell. That was a glaring oversight." He waved his hand at the officer. "But that's neither here nor there. I certainly don't blame you."

"Nevertheless, the fault reaches to me."

"Forget that. If you feel you've failed me, you can remedy it by catching him again. Then, this time, I want this Zayl brought directly to me."

General Torion gaped. All the sense that he had thought Justinian had suddenly gained seemed to have vanished in an instant. "That would hardly be wise! With his dark powers—"

Justinian patted his chest, where something under his shirt jingled. Only then did his companion notice that the new ruler of Westmarch wore a black chain around his neck. "Don't fear. I am protected."

"What—" Torion began, only to be cut off again by Justinian.

"And how have the preparations gone?" the king asked without warning. "Everything should be done by now, I imagine. The men pulled from the walls, et cetera."

"It's all accomplished. I had the last contingent withdrawn this morning."

"They're all getting their rest? They'll be fit for when I need them?"

The veteran commander nodded. "As per your instructions. They'll be at their sharpest come the display. I'll stake my life on that."

"Let us hope that it doesn't come to that." Frowning slightly, Justinian rose. "That leaves just the necromancer. See that he's caught, Torion. It's vital to everything. Absolutely everything."

"He's trouble, surely, but hardly that."

The heir's eyes snared his again. "Just see that you bring him to me."

Under that startling gaze, Torion could do nothing but nod once more.

Justinian's mood became jovial again. Coming around the desk, he slapped the officer on the back. "Good old Torion! I know I can count on you! I've always counted on you! Farewell!"

General Torion quickly opened the door for his monarch. After Justinian had gone, he simply stood there, trying to assimilate everything that had just happened.

In the end, though, it all came down to the fact that Justinian was his king now and Justinian wanted Zayl brought to him. So long as Torion could keep Salene out of the situation, that was fine with him. Of course, if Captain Mattheus did have to kill the Rathmian during the course of the capture, the general would make his apologies to his monarch. Justinian would surely understand.

And if Zayl *was* brought back alive, Torion would be the first to volunteer to act as executioner. He gripped the hilt of his sword, imagining the necromancer's head rolling free.

Salene would eventually understand . . .

Karybdus.

As Zayl planted himself against a wall—the better to escape the searching glance of a guard above—his mind still reeled from the immense implications presented by his recovered memories.

Karybdus. Legendary even among the reclusive Rathmians. His deeds were used as examples of the ultimate dedication to the Balance, of the strict adherence to Trag'Oul and the teachings of Rathma himself.

He was the one who had nearly slain Zayl?

It was too much to believe, yet, the truth was there. Zayl had touched the other's thoughts just as Karybdus surely had his. They had never met, not to the younger Rathmian's knowledge, but he had sensed that Karybdus had recognized him as well. Some of Zayl's feats had been spoken of by his fellow Rathmians, he knew, yet to think that the greatest of their order was aware of who he was—

Stop that! Zayl bitterly commanded himself. His admiration for everything that Karybdus had accomplished in the past had nearly made him forget the terrible threat such an adversary posed. Who knew better how Zayl worked than another necromancer? Karybdus as an ally would have been a tremendous relief; Karybdus as a foe . . . Such a scenario meant that Zayl's chances of surviving were nearly nonexistent.

He crept around a corner, eyeing the street that would bring him within view of House Nesardo. Even with guards keeping watch on it, the Rathmian doubted that he would have any trouble gaining entrance without them realizing it. Zayl had to find out how Salene fared. Only after assuring himself of her safety could Zayl concentrate on dealing with one whose skills and knowledge were a thousandfold greater than his own.

But what could have caused Karybdus to be involved in something that went so much against the teachings of the sect? In the course of his life, the older necromancer had battled tyrants, spellcasters, and demons foul in his quest to maintain the Balance. It was Karybdus who had perfected many of the spells Zayl and others were taught. Where, because of their calling, Rathmians often perished before their time, Karybdus was known to be over a *hundred*, his stamina and life fueled by a drive to see the world in ultimate balance. There were many, Zayl included, who believed that Karybdus had all but reached the perfection of Rathma himself.

There had to be some dire explanation for this monstrous travesty, and Zayl could think of only one. Karybdus had faced many foes wielding terrible powers. Several of the tales concerning those struggles had spoken of his utilizing the life-tap in manners of which other necromancers could barely even conceive.

But there was always a dread danger to using the spell so often. As with the crypt fiend that Zayl had faced, Karybdus had risked taking in some aspect of each of his multitude of adversaries. Perhaps no single one had affected him, but the accumulation of such evil had evidently finally taken its toll. Eventually and without his knowing it, Karybdus had become the very menace that he had been fighting.

This revelation shook Zayl as he peered through the rain at Salene's estate. It meant that each Rathmian had to take more care than they realized; few had the tremendous will power that Karybdus was said to have. Simply fighting the crypt fiend might have been enough to turn Zayl, had he taken in just a little more . . .

He momentarily pushed aside all such horrific notions as he watched a soldier pass within a few yards of the estate. The armored figure looked as if he was simply on watch, but his pace was too slow and measured.

The shadows were a Rathmian's friend—at least, most of the time. Necromancers knew how to mask themselves in shadows seemingly too pale or narrow for any creature to hide within. The Rathmian now blended into the darkness; even had the soldier looked his way, Zayl would have been impossible to see.

By the time the armored figure was halfway back to his original position, the hooded spellcaster already stood within the grounds of Nesardo. He paused behind a tree to watch two of Salene's own guards make their rounds. While they were loyal to her, he suspected that it would not be a good thing if they saw him. It was very likely they would think that the better part of protecting their mistress would be to remove the threat at her side.

Once the path was clear, Zayl moved on to the house. There were lights in some of the windows above, where she and her brother had their quarters. Zayl studied the windows for a moment, deciphering which ones belonged to Salene's quarters . . . then vanished back into the shadows once more.

Sardak poured himself a drink from his private stock, and although his hand did not shake, he was as anxious as could be. He had the feeling that this night, already

fraught with troubles, would become only more compli-
cated as it went on.

"*Sardak Nesardo . . .*"

His hand flinched and the glass in it cracked audibly. He
looked to the shadows . . . and his surprise gave way to bit-
terness at the figure materializing like a nightmare from
their midst.

"So! The necromancer! Might've known that you'd be
skulking in corners like that! Very nice trick! Can you do it
at the festival next month? Should go over quite well!"

"Spare me further jests, Sardak," Zayl retorted, his level
tone belied by a slight darkening of his expression. "I have
been to my quarters, then to your sister's—"

"Now *that* is ungentlemanly." Sardak took a silk cloth
from his pocket and wrapped it around the cuts in his
palm. "No bits in the flesh, thank you very much." He
peered at the necromancer. "You want to know where my
sister is? My precious sister? My sister who's risked herself
just for you?"

"Sardak—"

Salene's brother took a wild swing at Zayl. The latter
easily shifted just out of reach.

"She went to the crypts, damn it! She didn't want to be
found by the good Captain Mattheus—he works for Torion
and he's got a nose like a bloodhound! She went down
there mostly for you and hasn't come up yet!"

"The crypts?" Zayl did not bother to hide his consternation. "And after she was gone for too long, you did not go
after her?"

"You think I didn't want to? Right now, stationed by the
entrance to the lower levels, are a pair of Captain
Mattheus's men. He set them there, then went back to get
permission to search below. Even the Zakarum frown on
such desecration, but for you I'm sure everyone would
make an exception."

Zayl turned toward the door. "Come with me, if you
wish."

"Come with *you*? Where?"

"To the crypts, of course. To your sister."

Despite himself, Sardak started to follow. "But the guards at the entrance—"

Zayl glanced back at him. Sardak shut his mouth. His eyes narrowed in determination.

"Give me time to grab my sword. That's all I ask."

The necromancer nodded.

The two soldiers left by Captain Mattheus were able men whom the adjutant trusted with his life. They performed their duty with the same precision he did and, although they did not know it, both were being groomed for promotion.

But to Zayl, they were merely a momentary impediment. The spell which he cast was a variation of the blindness that had overcome the Zakarum. In this case, however, the men were not aware that their vision was impaired—nor, for that matter, that their hearing was as well.

Thus it was that Zayl and Sardak—the latter holding an unlit torch—walked directly up to the duo, who grimly stood guard even as the necromancer and his companion came within a hair's breadth of them. When Zayl opened the way, the sentries did not even flinch.

Only after they had shut the doors behind, lit the torch, and gone down the corridor did Sardak finally blurt, "Damn, but I want to learn *that* spell! Could've saved myself a couple of bad scrapes in the past! Can you teach me?"

"Yes, but you will first have to take an oath to Rathma, give up drinking to excess, and—"

"Never mind!" Salene's brother responded, snorting. "You lost me forever at the drinking part. I'll just suffer along as usual . . . "

They wended their way through the old dungeons, where Zayl was again assailed by the tortured memories left by their former occupants. This time, he immediately shut them out.

"Damn, but I hate those voices," murmured his companion.

This surprised Zayl. "I did not know that you heard them so clearly."

"I don't tell Salene everything; why should I tell you?"

Sardak was clearly more magically sensitive than he had let on. Almost as much so as Salene. Zayl would have liked to have asked him more, but at that moment, a low, almost inaudible sound reached his trained ears. Unlike before, it was not the murmur or wail of a long-dead prisoner.

It was humming . . . and the Rathmian recognized the tune.

"Humbart?" he called.

The humming ceased and from the corridor ahead came, "Zayl! Lad! Praise be!"

Turning the corner, they faced the true doorway to the crypts. It was shut tight, but below it lay a large, dark pouch containing an object the size of a melon—or a head.

Zayl plucked the pouch from the floor, then opened it.

The skull's empty eye sockets stared at him with what seemed glee.

"Thought I'd be lost down here forever, I did," the hollow voice declared. "Expected the guards to come looking for you and her, but they never did! Of course, if they had and found me, likely the damned fools would've thought I belonged down in the crypt and put me back there! Ha! Can you imagine those old bones being any good company?"

"Quiet, Humbart! What about Salene? What happened?"

"Girl was terribly distracted, lad. The lady put me down, then went inside without me! I tried callin' to her, but she either didn't hear me or paid me no mind! 'Course, after she froze that Torion fellow, she was probably—"

Zayl gave Sardak a glare. "She did *what*?"

Her brother gave no response. The skull, however, was all too glad to explain. The necromancer listened, both heartened and dismayed by what he learned.

Salene's powers were now truly manifesting themselves, but her lack of training had endangered her. Still, from what he had heard, he suspected that Torion's condition was at least only a temporary one. When he said so to the others, Humbart gave a knowing sound and Sardak exhaled in relief.

"There's somethin' else," the skull muttered. "I thought I heard her talking to someone. Someone she knew."

"In the crypts?" growled Sardak. "Damn!"

Zayl wasted no more time. He slipped the fleshless head back into the pouch, which he secured to his belt.

"Mind you don't leave me like she did!" came Humbart's muffled order.

Sardak tugged the entrance open with an effort worthy of the late Polth. The party swiftly descended to the first level.

"Thought it would stink more here." Salene's sibling eyed the nearest names. "All the properly born ones. If it wasn't for Salene, I wouldn't even be considered worthy of the servants' level." His mouth tightened. "If I find it's Lord Jitan who's got her, I'll poke out both of his mismatched eyes and feed 'em to a night howler!"

The necromancer frowned, but Sardak did not notice. Lord Jitan and Karybdus were clearly bound together, although how, he did not yet know. Zayl had not bothered to mention the return of his memories. He intended that both Sardak and Salene be nowhere near when he confronted his counterpart. From Sardak, he wanted only assistance in getting the noblewoman as far away from danger as possible. Sardak stood no chance against the other necromancer.

Of course, Zayl's odds against Karybdus were not so good, either.

Sardak let out an epithet. Waving the torch, he asked, "Are those the things that attacked her before?"

"Yes." The corpses of the spider beasts lay quietly rotting or not so quietly being devoured by rats and the like. Zayl scanned the area, but felt nothing.

No . . . there *was* another presence. Faint, but familiar.

Even as he sensed it, it grew much stronger, as if drawn back to life by his presence . . .

The shade of Polth materialized before them.

Rathmian . . . came a voice in Zayl's head.

The necromancer did not answer at first, surreptitiously making certain that what he saw and sensed was indeed what he thought. Necromancers could make a shade say or do what they desired. Only when he was certain that this was Polth and only Polth did Zayl answer.

"Why do you remain here, bodyguard? Your duty in life is done. You should move on as all do."

Failed . . . failed in life . . . and in death . . .

"What's he mean by that?"

The question came from Sardak, and the fact that it did startled Zayl again. Determined to discuss the limits of Sardak's abilities with him when they had the opportunity, Zayl remained focused on the spirit. "You refer to Salene? Is she . . . no more?"

To both his and Sardak's relief, Polth shook his head. Instead, the shade pointed down. *Sent her there . . . for the truth . . . Didn't know . . . didn't know he was there! Didn't know . . . I failed her . . .*

The specter all but faded, so distraught was he by what had happened to his lady. Zayl mulled over his words, determining as best he could what Polth meant.

"Is she in the servants' crypt?" Sardak grabbed Zayl's sleeve. "Come on, damn you! She might be injured!"

When the necromancer did not move, the brother ran on without him. Zayl caught Polth shaking his head. Zayl frowned. If Salene was not down in the next level, then where—

The ancient crypt below that . . . or deeper yet?

He sought to ask the shade, but the dead bodyguard, his time spent, had vanished. The Rathmian sped after Sardak, hoping that the brother would not go rushing into disaster.

Sardak was already below by the time Zayl reached the steps leading down. The necromancer doubled his pace, hurrying to where the light of the torch flickered.

There, he discovered his companion staring at a hole in what was clearly an ancient rockfall. Zayl leaned down, praying to Trag'Oul that it was not yet Salene's time to move on to the next plane.

"She's not dead," whispered Sardak. "I'd feel it; I know I would. Does it go all the way down to the old level?"

"Farther. Much farther." Zayl shifted position. He lowered his feet into the hole.

"What're you doing?"

The necromancer met Sardak's worried gaze—worried over his sister, not Zayl. "Go back up. I must do this alone from here. It is even more desperate than I imagined."

"I'm not going to abandon her!"

"Listen to me. There are ancient forces beneath the Nesardo estate. This was once another place, a place of blood sacrifice. I sense this, and I believe you do, too."

Sardak gritted his teeth. "What of it? Nothing matters more to me than Salene. Either jump in or get the hell out of my way so I can!"

"Sardak—"

Without warning, Zayl's companion struck him with the back of his hand. It was not enough to injure the necromancer or even stun him, but it put Zayl off balance for a moment.

That was all the time Sardak needed to leap down into the hole. Zayl stretched a desperate hand toward Salene's sibling, but too late. He heard Sardak's dwindling grunts and curses, then silence.

The Rathmian gripped his ivory dagger tight. "Be ready, Humbart."

"How?" grumbled the skull.

Zayl dropped into the hole.

He tumbled madly down the gap, bouncing harshly against the jagged, uneven walls. Several times, the necromancer would have suffered bruises and injuries if not for his cloak. The Scale of Trag'Oul shielded him against such. He wondered how Sardak, who had no such protection, fared, and cursed the man for his foolishness.

Then, just when it seemed that the fall would last forever, Zayl was tossed into open air. He barely managed to
twist his body in order to land without striking his head.
X'y'Laq might have obeyed him to the letter when it came
to the protective runes, but the demon was clever enough
to have still left some fault.

Strong hands gripped him by the shoulder. Sardak
pulled him to his feet. Other than a bruise on his right
cheek and a small cut on one hand, Salene's brother looked
untouched.

"How's your head?" demanded Sardak quickly.
"Clear?"

"Yes, and you seem none the worse—"

Sardak cut him off. "I've always been lucky in certain
matters, you know that! Can you cast spells?"

Zayl frowned. "I can, but why?"

The necromancer's companion pointed past him.
"Because I think that mob might be more than my sword
can handle."

Zayl glanced over his shoulder . . . and beheld a shadowy band of robed figures converging slowly but surely
upon them. There was that in their movements that made
the Rathmian frown. He held up the dagger and summoned from it more light.

And in that light, Zayl beheld the faces of the dead.

"Gad!" blurted Sardak. "Even more disgusting bunch
than I thought!"

There were dozens within view and more shapes in the
distance. That there remained any flesh upon them was a
sign of the power that they had served . . . and the other
power that had resurrected them now.

Karybdus.

Zayl could sense that the other Rathmian had been
here . . . which meant that he likely already had Salene in
his clutches. He had also evidently expected that Zayl
would follow and, like a puppet on strings, the latter had.

"Any suggestions, spellcaster?"

In response, Zayl cast the spell for the Teeth of Trag'Oul.

The sharp projectiles immediately formed in midair, then shot toward their intended targets with horrific accuracy.

But just before they would have impaled the foremost of the desiccated ghouls . . . they vanished again.

"By the Cursed Eyes of Barabas!"

"Not what you expected, was it?" growled Sardak, clutching his sword so tight his knuckles lacked any color.

Zayl *should* have expected that Karybdus would put in place countermeasures for his spells. Again, the younger necromancer had proven himself the fool.

And as the undead encroached, Zayl noted another dire sign. What remained of their tattered garments marked them all as of the same, for each one wore a robe upon which could still be made out the symbol of the spider—a symbol enhanced by the glittering giant the necromancer's light revealed hanging from above. Even though made only of jewels and crystals, it seemed very, very much alive.

The monstrous horde suddenly stopped. The foremost figure reached out a gnarled, bony hand.

We have waited for your return, master . . . come, join us . . . join us . . .

It was the voice of one of the decaying priests from Zayl's dream . . . and he and the rest of the dead were beckoning to the necromancer.

FIFTEEN

"Do you know this lot?" blurted an anxious Sardak.

"Only from my nightmares." Zayl held the dagger before him, momentarily keeping the undead worshippers at bay. "Keep behind me."

"I wasn't planning on going anywhere else."

From the pouch, Humbart piped up, "What's going on out there, lad?"

It was Sardak who answered, "You really don't want to know."

The skull went silent.

The priest gave Zayl a grisly smile. *But come, master! Your loyal acolytes await you!*

To emphasize this fact, all but he went down on one knee. As they did, they began chanting a single word over and over.

Astrogha . . .

Sardak leaned near the necromancer. "What do they mean by that? What's an 'Astrogha'?"

Zayl indicated the immense spider image. "*That*, I believe."

"So, why do they chant it to you?"

The Rathmian shook his head. "I have some notion, but I would rather not say."

"If it means my sister's life, damn you—"

The ghoulish figure before them reached into his torn robe. From a ruined mass of innards and bone he pulled forth the wicked dagger that the necromancer had held in the dream. *Master, if you would but complete the sacrifice, you will finally be made whole . . .*

"I am very much whole, thank you. It is time for you to go back to the grave." Zayl held his own blade forward. "All of you, go back to the grave!"

Again came the macabre smile. *But we cannot . . . not without you . . .*

"I don't like the sound of that, spellcaster."

His own opinion mirroring Sardak's, Zayl quickly muttered, "Touch the tip of your sword against that of my dagger."

"Eh? Why?"

"Do it and do it quickly, for the sake of your sister, if not your own life!"

Sardak obeyed, so eagerly that he nearly severed the Rathmian's index finger in the process. The moment that the two blades touched, the glow about the ivory dagger spread over the tip of the sword, then engulfed the rest of Sardak's weapon.

Salene's brother eyed his altered sword. "I'll be damned!"

"If we do not survive this, that's very likely."

The members of the undead horde were already back on their feet. The priest frowned as best as his ruined face allowed. *Master, you are the chosen one . . . you cannot deny your true destiny . . . and we will not let you.*

Zayl would have liked to ask him just exactly what that destiny entailed, but the priest suddenly lurched forward . . . and with him came the rest of the terrifying throng.

"Damn and double damn!" growled Sardak.

The clawing hands of the ghouls reached for them, reviving once more the necromancer's memories of lost Ureh. Zayl's expression hardened.

"Not again . . . ," he muttered under his breath. "*Never* again!"

The Rathmian thrust.

Karybdus could shield the creatures against many a spell, but nothing he could cast could protect them from the dagger's might. Blessed by the dragon, it was the first and last defense of any necromancer. Thus it was that when the priest met him, it was to find the ivory dagger cutting through his robe and slashing against his ribs.

With an inhuman gasp, the ghoulish cleric grabbed at the cut area, then pulled back into the mob. Other undead eagerly took his place, ignorant of what had happened. Zayl was only too happy to show them, cutting through the decrepit throats of one pair and jamming the blade's point between the ribs of another.

Against the strong magic of the weapon, the ghouls died as men would have died. They collapsed, then were trampled by those behind them.

Zayl had expected to have to defend Sardak, but his companion proved astonishingly skilled with the sword. Sardak thrust time and time again, severing heads and limbs and cutting down as many if not more of their monstrous foes than the Rathmian.

But still the ranks appeared undepleted. All already bore the marks of violent death and Zayl could only suppose that they had perished at the hands of enemies of their "god." Karybdus had used their lust for vengeance to raise them up. That he had managed to raise so many said much about the limits—or lack thereof—of his abilities.

But . . . if Karybdus had raised them up, why did they insist then on calling Zayl "master"?

The question vanished from his thoughts as the undead swarmed the pair. Zayl cut again and again and though the ghouls gave way, he still saw no end in sight.

"They just keep coming!" shouted Sardak, beheading yet another fleshless nightmare. When the hands of the headless corpse continued to grasp at him, he sliced both off at the wrists. Salene's brother then kicked the weaving torso back into its fellows.

"Keep fighting! Do not falter!" Zayl racked his brains for something that would take the attention of the horde from Sardack and him.

His gaze alighted on the huge spider statue hanging from the ceiling.

"Rathma, guide my hand . . ." He brought his dagger around in a great arc, momentarily driving back Karybdus's hellish minions.

Eyes fixed again on the arachnid—and especially the uppermost part—the necromancer conjured.

The Den'Trag—the Teeth of Trag'Oul—formed again, but this time Zayl did not send them against the undead. Instead, the shower of missiles flew up at the spider.

Several clattered hard against the jeweled figure, but Zayl was unperturbed by this. The body had not been his target.

Karybdus had protected the undead from most of a necromancer's spells, but he had not thought to spread that protection throughout the temple. The ancient chains fashioned to look like webbing had withstood centuries of nature, but against the mystical Teeth, they had no protec-tion whatsoever. The barrage ate away at the links, ripping through until at last the heavy weight of the idol proved too much.

With a snapping of chains and a tremendous groan, the right side of the jeweled arachnid broke free. The huge idol swung like a great pendulum—

The reaction by the undead astounded even Zayl. First, they froze where they were as if suddenly no longer ani-mated. Then, as the spider crashed into the wall of the cav-ern, the ghouls began to *wail*.

Seizing a startled Sardak by the arm, Zayl cried, "Now!Now!"

Vast chunks of stone and earth rained down on both the horde and what Zayl assumed had once been their secret temple. Row upon row of benches were crushed. Several score of undead were buried under the onslaught, but many more still moved untouched.

Yet, all they continued to do was wail their grief at the idol's destruction.

As for the jeweled spider, the collision proved too much. The hindmost leg was the first to break, the giant segment crashing down upon the center of the temple. A stone altar whose bloody past the necromancer could readily sense cracked into a hundred pieces.

A second leg snapped in twain, one part tumbling into the crying throng, the other flying past Zayl and Sardak and striking another wall of the cavern. That, in turn, sent more rock and earth collapsing.

A tremor shook the area. Salene's brother shouted, "The whole damned chamber's falling apart, spellcaster!"

"We must run through the temple! I believe it to be the way out!"

Sardak snorted. "You 'believe'?"

Suddenly, a figure caught Salene's brother across the face, sending him sprawling. The Rathmian whirled and found himself facing the priest.

Desecrator! the ghoul declared. *Blasphemer! You cannot be his vessel! You are not worthy of such an honor! I will not permit it!*

He drew the sacrificial knife and lunged. Zayl's right hand caught the priest's bony wrist. The two combatants' countenances came within inches of one another. The revenant emitted a musky, dry odor, one with which the necromancer was long familiar and therefore untouched.

"Where is she?" demanded Zayl. "Is she with Karybdus? Where has your master taken the woman?"

My lord is Astrogha! I have no other!

The Rathmian tried again. "Karybdus, I said! Where is the other necromancer?"

At the making of the Moon . . . , the priest proudly informed him. *Already ensuring my lord's return! The vessel chosen for my lord's return will not be so great an offering, but it will serve him better than you!*

The undead inhaled, something unnecessary for one in his decayed state. Zayl tore himself away.

From out of the mouth erupted hundreds of black spiders. The first few who landed on Zayl immediately bit into the cloak draped over him.

But all who did quickly turned a pasty white and crumbled to ash. Still, that in no manner deterred their successors, who sought to chew their way through. The cloak sizzled where they bit, a sign of the creatures' potent venom.

The grotesque priest inhaled for a second time—then let out a startled gurgle. A few limp spiders spilled from his lipless maw. He stared down at his ruined chest and the shimmering point protruding from it.

Sardak pulled his sword free, the enchantment granted it by Zayl still strong.

"That's for Salene . . . ," he snarled.

The ghoul dropped to his knees. His head fell to one side, snapping off. The arms collapsed, then the rest of the torso joined them, leaving but a jumble of bones, dried flesh, and bits of cloth.

Zayl gave Sardak a look of thanks. He shook off the last of the spiders, which had all perished the moment that the priest had.

The two men raced down the rows of stone benches and past several wailing ghouls. None of the others made so much as a feeble attempt to stop the duo. The only ones the two were forced to fight were those that they could not go around. Most perished swiftly to either a slash from Zayl's dagger or a thrust by Sardak. Around them, the chaos grew as more pieces cracked by the collapsing idol fell loose.

But if the undead were, at the moment, of no concern, something else was. No matter where they looked, neither man could find the way out.

"It has to be here," insisted Zayl. "All logic demands it be so."

Sardak tapped the tip of his blade against solid rock. "But it's all real! Maybe that's why all those lunatics perished here! They had no blasted escape route!"

The Rathmian could not believe that. The high priests, at least, would have had a path to freedom, even if they had not had the opportunity to use it.

Of course! He had been thinking in terms of the cultists, but they were merely the dead raised up by a spell. It was *Karybdus* who had plotted all this and, therefore, *he* who had made certain that Zayl, should he have survived the horde, would not see the truth.

Or see the way out, rather. As Zayl had done to the guards in the house, so had Karybdus done to him. Zayl could only marvel at the other Rathmian's skill. He had laid down some variation of the blindness spell, one which both men had blundered into without realizing it.

"Step back, Sardak."

As his companion obeyed, Zayl raised the dagger. Under his breath, he muttered the counterspell to the blindness.

Behind him, Sardak abruptly said, "Spellcaster . . . they've stopped wailing."

Which meant, Zayl understood, that the undead were regrouping. They would surely be upon the two in moments . . .

There! The necromancer sensed the spellwork. "This way, Sardak! Quickly!"

"You're going to run right into that—I'll be damned!"

The last referred to Zayl, who, to his comrade's view, had simply vanished through the rock.

A breath later, the necromancer found himself in an ancient tunnel. Determining that there was no immediate threat, he looked back for Salene's sibling.

Thankfully, Sardak materialized. He paused to touch his chest, as if surprised to find himself in one piece. "Neat trick, that."

"The work of the one we seek. Karybdus."

"*He's* got Salene? Not Jitan?"

"I would venture that they could be found together." Zayl watched the wall through which they had come. There was no sign of the pursuing ghouls. As he had hoped, they, too, could not see the truth.

"Do we just leave that lot in there? What if they decide to go to the surface?"

A rumble shook the tunnel, one that the hooded spell-caster sensed was centered in the chamber that they had just departed. "There is little fear of that. The cavern continues to collapse. It will bury many of them again. Besides, I suspect they were raised simply because of me and, now that I am passed them, they may already be returning to their graves."

"Thank the heavens for that."

Curiously, as Sardak said the last, Zayl felt a peculiar sensation. He looked behind himself, but the tunnel was still empty.

"Something the matter?"

Zayl did not bother to ask the other if he had seen anything. The necromancer marked it down to his growing anxiety concerning Salene. So many precious minutes wasted . . .

But *had* they been? What had he heard about the Moon of the Spider? From the dream and other fragments, its true nature was perplexing, but at least part of it had to do with a certain stage of night. Certainly, the grisly priests had spoken of it so.

And, as far as Zayl recalled, night was still several hours away.

"I think we are not yet too late!" he immediately informed Sardak. "But we must still hurry!"

"Hurry to where?"

"That, I do not yet know, but I have a notion as to how to discover the answer!"

A muffled voice arose from the pouch. Zayl paused to open it and remove the skull of Humbart Wessel.

"Glad that's over with," muttered the hollow voice. "And glad I am not to have had to witness it all!"

"Was there something you wanted, Humbart? Quickly now!"

"Only that you've got a better chance of finding her if you use me, remember?"

"Use him?" Sardak looked dubious. "What are you going to do, set him on the ground and let him sniff it like a hound?"

The skull chuckled. "Somethin' like that, lad."

Zayl was not so eager. "Are you certain, Humbart?

When last I used the spell, it almost cost you your animation. There are other methods—"

"That take too long or might not be specific enough! Listen now! I'll not let that fine lady be gutted for the sake of some would-be spider god if I can help it! What kind of man do you take me for?"

"Dead?" suggested the third in their party.

"Do it, Zayl. I'll hold myself together."

The Rathmian no longer argued. "The decision is yours."

He knelt down in the tunnel, then placed the skull facing the path ahead. Zayl raised the dagger above the remains of Humbart and with it drew the symbol of an eye . . . a dragon's eye.

"Let us see the way, Rathma," Zayl muttered, "for it is necessary to the Balance."

With that, Zayl plunged the blade down.

Sardak gasped as the necromancer's dagger sank deep into the top of the skull seemingly without impediment. The dagger flared bright as it entered, the glow enveloping the fleshless head.

The spell was not one Zayl had learned from his masters, but one which he had devised himself through necessity. Thus it was that he hoped it would see past any magical veil his counterpart had cast.

The skull began to shake, as if something within fought to free itself. From the empty eye sockets, a green illumination stretched several yards ahead of the party.

And in that illumination, forms flickered in and out of existence. Two forms: a figure cloaked in black . . . and the Lady Nesardo.

"Salene!" Sardak seized the nearest image, only to have his fingers slip through his sibling's arm.

Zayl studied the noblewoman first, ascertaining her condition. The brief images indicated that Salene was in a trance. Pale of face, she walked with her arms dangling at the sides and stared without blinking at the path ahead. The necromancer frowned at this foul use of the knowledge granted by Rathma and Trag'Oul, and his gaze angrily shifted to her captor.

He had only heard descriptions of his legendary counterpart, but there could be no doubt that this was Karybdus. The short, gray hair, the wise, studious visage, and the bone and metal armor the other Rathmian had himself fashioned for epic battle against the black-hearted Vizjerei called Armin Ra.

The closest images vanished, to be replaced a few yards beyond by others of the pair. They looked much the same as the previous, with Karybdus striding along unconcerned while Salene obediently trailed behind him.

Picking up the skull, Zayl removed the dagger. Despite the separation, however, Humbart still glowed and the light from his eye sockets continued to display a progression of images.

"Come," the spellcaster said.

Sardak walked purposefully beside Zayl as the latter held the skull before them. Every few seconds, an image of Salene and Karybdus appeared. However unnerving the brief glimpses were, they also comforted both men. There was no change; the noblewoman and her captor simply wended their way along through the tunnel.

"I thought your kind was supposed to be misunderstood," grumbled Salene's brother, glaring at Karybdus. "Not evil at all—isn't that what you indicated to my sister?"

"Karybdus's actions do not follow the teachings of Rathma as I know them. His behavior is an aberration. I must conclude that he has fallen victim to the darkness against which he had dedicated himself."

"He's a 'victim'?"

The Rathmian nodded firmly. "It must be so."

Sardak's responding grunt was clear indication that he was not convinced.

They journeyed through the passage for what Zayl calculated was more than an hour. Both he and Sardak were aware that they now had to be beyond the city walls, but still no end seemed in sight.

Then, at last, Zayl felt a slight breeze on his face. "We are coming to some entrance into the open."

Sardak readied his sword.

They emerged into the forest through an opening covered by centuries of brambles and earth. From the outside, it was all but invisible, and Zayl sensed that it had been further protected by ancient wards, which Karybdus had evidently nullified.

Looking around, Sardak asked, "Do we have time to go get help?"

"I fear not. See?"

The newest vision showed Karybdus picking up his pace. Salene followed suit.

"Fine with me, then."

Zayl put a hand on Sardak's shoulder. "I offer you this chance to return home."

"You could use my help, couldn't you?"

"Yes. Someone must steal Salene away while Karybdus is occupied."

The other man started off. "Then, let's waste no more time, shall we?"

The way was slick from the almost constant rain and both men stumbled several times. Once, Zayl, despite his quick reflexes, nearly lost the skull, managing to catch Humbart only at the last moment.

Then, in the midst of the thick forest and with no warning whatsoever, the images simply *ceased.*

"What the blazes?" Sardak spun around. "Where's the next one? There's got to be a next one!"

The skull still glowed, yet, no matter where the Rathmian focused it, no image of Salene formed.

But, just as he was about to give up, one of Karybdus finally did.

Sardak saw it at the same time that the necromancer did and asked the question coursing through Zayl's own mind. "Is he looking directly at *us*?"

"Run!" was all the necromancer risked replying.

From the forest and even the treetops, horrific figures

scrambled down. The creatures from the crypt, but far, far more than before. Zayl estimated a dozen to start and, from the rustling of the foliage, knew that the numbers were much higher.

Like cats on the prowl, they bounded after the two. Sardak had taken Zayl's warning immediately to heart, and was already several paces ahead of the slower Rathmian.

Their pursuers leapt among the branches, raced across the ground on any number of limbs, and jumped from tree trunk to tree trunk in pursuit. Virulent hisses accompanied their hunt and more than once a bush or some bit of ground near one of the men sizzled with poison expertly spat.

"Thought you'd killed most of these, spellcaster!"

"There are always more unfortunates to be sacrificed for someone's ambitions!" Zayl had little doubt but that these were Lord Jitan's men, either loyal servants or mercenaries. He recalled the sinister spiders adhered to the heads of the previous creatures and did not doubt that if he looked close, he would find the same with those behind them.

One dropped down on the necromancer, claws seeking to rip through the protective cloak. Zayl rewarded the monstrosity with a thrust to the misshapen head, driving his dagger through both his attacker and the parasite atop. A foul, sickly green fluid gushed from the wound but, fortunately, touched only the Rathmian's garments.

No sooner had he rid himself of one, however, than an identical fiend fell upon him, throwing the necromancer to the ground. For a moment, the horrific amalgamation of human and arachnid features was all Zayl could see. The sharp fangs continuously dribbled and one spot of venom dropped on the Rathmian's cheek, burning him.

Aware that Karybdus's magic now likely protected them in the same manner as it did the ghouls, Zayl restored to a more mundane defense, jamming the fingers of his right hand directly in what served as his attacker's throat.

For many, such an action would have brought little

result, but Rathmians were trained in several forms of unarmed combat. They also knew the living body better than most, having studied its intricate workings through the use of cadavers.

His fingers jammed deep. The arachnid let out a gagging sound and only a quick turn of the head prevented Zayl from being doused with venom.

His attacker rolled away, two of its appendages clutching at the ruined throat. Zayl saved it any further suffering by stabbing it in the back of the neck.

From his side came several colorful curses as Sardak warned off another beast with his blade. The arachnids scattered back, but only for a moment.

"Ready to run again, spellcaster?"

But before Zayl could answer, an animalistic cry echoed through the forest. The men and their hunters had only a single breath in which to react to the eerie sound—and then a giant form came crashing into the nearest of the horrors.

With ease, the shadowy figure hefted two of its startled foes and smashed them together with such force that the cracking of their bones resounded in Zayl's ears. As the bodies went limp, the giant tossed them toward another pair turning to meet the new threat.

One failed to avoid the oncoming missiles and was thrown with them some distance away. The second twisted around the attack, then leapt at the newcomer. At the same time, two more dropped from the trees.

But if they thought that they had their adversary where they wanted it, the beasts were sadly mistaken. One meaty fist swatted the first as if it were a fly. The two who landed upon the giant might as well have been feathers for all the effect of their drop. With an almost human snort of derision, the giant tore first one, then the other, free of its hide. As they hissed and spat at it—their poison singeing the thick fur, but doing little more—their foe simply turned them on their heads and crushed them into the ground.

This seeming invincibility sent the others scurrying back

to the trees. As they fled, the giant let out a defiant howl before turning its baleful gaze at the two humans.

"A night howler!" Sardak crouched. "I think we were better off with the spider demons!"

But Zayl believed otherwise. He took a step toward the panting behemoth, who roared viciously at his approach.

The necromancer stretched forth his left hand . . . and the wolf creature quieted. It mimicked Zayl's action, the two touching fingertips.

Somehow, despite the vast breadth of the wild forest, the monster that Zayl had healed had *found* him again.

SIXTEEN

Aldric Jitan would not have taken the jagged hillside before him as a nexus of power and the birthplace of the precious artifact he carried in one arm. He would not have even taken it for a building long covered by the ravages of time. The ambitious noble would have simply taken it for yet another of the far-too-many lumps of earth dotting what he soon hoped to call *his* kingdom.

But it hardly mattered what Jitan thought of it, for his cowled companion recognized it immediately as their ultimate destination, and that was enough to satisfy the noble. Here, another birth would very soon take place, the birth of his eventual domination over the rest of the world.

He, Karybdus, and the girl were the only ones there . . . the only ones still *human*, that is. Several of Astrogha's children squatted around the vicinity, either watching for intruders or awaiting new commands. Lord Jitan had felt no remorse about turning nearly all of his followers into the creatures, for as a result they served him even better than before.

Pulling his night howler fur cloak tighter, he leaned close to Salene. The Lady Nesardo was a fair piece to look at, Aldric had to admit. Much of his hatred for her had come from her defiance toward his desires. Now that she no longer acted as an obstacle, her beauty enticed him. He reached out his free hand—

"Such desires would not be recommended at this juncture," announced Karybdus, appearing at his side as if by a spell. "Your full concentration must be upon the incantation I have taught you. You recall it all?"

"I remember every bit of nonsense," he returned. "Even if I don't know what much of it means."

The pale necromancer cocked his head. "Do you desire a language lesson or the certainty of never having any more nightmares . . . not to mention the beginning of your triumphant reign." Karybdus touched a gloved hand to Lord Jitan's temple. "Think. Have there been *any* more nightmares?"

There had not. Since Aldric had attained the artifact, his sleep had instead been filled with lusty visions of his rule. Of what need was the Lady Nesardo, when Aldric could have for himself a hundred of the most desirable maidens in the realm? It was a shame not to taste her first, but if that was the price to pay for ultimate power, then, so be it. When it had been thought that he would need to marry her in order to gain both her house and what lay beneath it, the noble had never much considered bedding her, anyway. She had been the intended sacrifice from the beginning, nothing more.

No, all he really needed from Salene Nesardo was her heart and her blood.

"So," the noble asked, his anticipation rising. "Where might the entrance be?"

"There." Karybdus pointed at a particularly ugly side of the hill.

Even to Aldric's mismatched eyes, it was clear that tons of rock and earth covered the area in question. "It'll take this bunch *weeks* to move all that! We're better off with the temple!"

The Rathmian shook his head. "You are forgetting what you hold, my lord."

"You mean *this* can remove all that?"

"All you need do is command it to."

"Tell me how, then!" demanded an eager Lord Jitan.

"Raise it over your head as if a crown. Focus your gaze on where I point. Will the way to open for you." Karybdus allowed himself the ghost of a smile. "And it shall."

"That's all?" Striding to a better position, Aldric did as

told. He held the Moon of the Spider as high as he could and eyed the hill.

"Do you see that crescent-shaped outcropping, my lord? Let that be where your gaze fixes. Do you have it now? Good. Command the artifact. You know what you wish."

The noble concentrated. As he did, he heard whispering, whispering that became a chant, a chant with which he was already familiar.

Astrogha . . . Astrogha . . .

But to his mind, it became something else. It became *his* name. *Aldric . . . Aldric . . .*

And as he imagined the invisible chanters proclaiming his glory, the arachnid pattern on the artifact began to twitch. Its foremost appendages moved until they touched where the fingertips of the noble held the sphere.

The hillside rumbled.

Open for me, Aldric Jitan silently commanded. *Open for me!*

There was a crack like thunder . . . and a fissure split the hill in two. Tons of stone tumbled to the base. Those of his transformed servants nearest to the hill scattered lest they crushed by the abrupt rockfall.

The entire hillside collapsed. Mounds of rubble lay just beyond the pair.

"It is done," Karybdus informed him. "Let but the dust settle for a minute or two."

Aldric lowered the artifact. His pulse pounded. Adrenaline coursed through his body. "Fantastic!"

The necromancer stood near his ear. "But only a small portion of the gifts of Astrogha. Imagine, my lord, what you will be able to do when the spider god's full, wondrous power is part of you."

"How much longer? Damn it, man! I can't keep waiting!"

Looking up at the heavens, Karybdus advised, "The first phase will begin in just a little over two hours. It would be best if we made our preparations."

As he spoke, the dust finally dissipated . . . and the two beheld the birthplace of the sphere.

Twin statues stood within the fissure, spider-headed

warriors with eight human arms, each of which wielded a different weapon. The ominous sentinels stood twice the height of a man and were carved so lifelike that even after the obvious centuries of burial, they looked ready to spring to the defense of what lay hidden within.

"Shall we enter, my lord?" Karybdus politely asked.

But Aldric was already walking toward the ancient structure. Again, the Moon of the Spider lay nestled in his arm, his other hand stroking the pearl-smooth surface as if the back of a beloved child or pet. With his monstrous servants forming an honor guard, he and the necromancer went past the dour guardians and into what was immediately recognizable as a far more vast edifice than the hill indicated.

As with the temple, it extended well beneath the surface. The steps down which the group marched were of an iridescent substance very much like that composing the artifact. Each time Aldric set down a boot on one, shapes seemed to move within the step, eight-legged shadows akin to the one on the sphere.

Neither man carried a torch, yet the path before them remained as lit as if they stood outside. There was no discernible source of the illumination; it simply came into existence as needed. To Aldric, it was but another hint of the tremendous forces which would soon be his to command.

Then, before them appeared that which truly marked this lost place as the destination they sought: a wide, oval altar upon which the arachnid symbol had been carved.

But there was something else, something that made Karybdus uncharacteristically hiss in angry surprise.

Three skeletons lay at the base of the altar, three mummified figures whose garments looked vaguely familiar to the noble.

"Those corpses . . . they look like that thing in the tomb." Aldric squinted. "Same damned flowery robes and such. What was it you called them? Vazjero?"

"*Vizjerei*," the necromancer all but spat. "As I have told

you, the most base of spellcasters, corrupt and ruinous men all." Karybdus drew his dagger. "And they should *not* be in this ancient place. This is the only entry point, according to all my research."

"Well, they had the Moon once, didn't they? They probably opened up the way just as we did."

Karybdus paused, as if calculating something. At last, his expression neutral again, he nodded. "As you say. That must be what they did."

Something else, though, came to Lord Jitan's mind. "Are they *exactly* like the ones in the tomb?"

He did not have to explain to Karybdus. The Rathmian was already drawing patterns in the air with his dagger. At the same time, he uttered words the like of which Aldric had never heard.

There was a squealing sound, as if the air had been sucked from the chamber. First one, then the second, and finally the third mummified corpse shriveled into itself. Dried bones twisted, tightening within. The bodies curled up until all that remained were small bundles that in no manner resembled anything even remotely human.

Karybdus made a clenching motion . . . and each pile crumbled to dust.

"Now, you need not worry, my lord."

Utterly at ease again, Aldric nodded and moved on to the altar. Behind him, Karybdus's steely eyes surveyed the area once more, then the necromancer followed.

Salene, expression still blank, trailed the Rathmian.

"You are a fount of wonders, spellcaster," murmured Sardak, his eyes wide. "Taming a *night howler,* of all things! What a yarn I could make of that in the taverns!"

"I did not tame it," Zayl returned, fingertips still touching those of the fabled beast. "Perhaps you might say that I *released* it from a curse."

"How absolutely poetic! They should write a fairy tale about it."

From the crook of the necromancer's arm, Humbart's

hollow voice suddenly piped up, "'Tis not the first time he's done such a marvel! When you travel with this lad, you come across all sorts of interesting things . . ."

"I prefer to keep my adventures to the taverns, thank you. This is far too much excitement . . ."

As fascinated as his companions were by this encounter, what interested Zayl far more was the overwhelming "coincidence" of the creature finding him again. They were far from where he had last encountered the furred giant. More to the point, there had been no reason for the night howler to even be *looking* for him, much less coming to his aid at such an opportune time.

As a devotee of Rathma and a servant of the Balance, Zayl did not believe in pure coincidence.

Sardak asked the question that was likely on all their minds. "So . . . now what do we do with it?"

"'Tis a 'he,' you blessed fool! Don't call him an 'it'! 'Tis rude!"

The skull was indeed correct, and Zayl was surprised that he himself had not previously noticed.

Sardak was not impressed by Humbart's knowledge. "Well, I say again, now what do we—"

The rest of his question was cut off by the night howler himself, who, with a series of grunts, pointed, then started off in that direction.

"We are to follow," the necromancer declared.

"Follow that? What about Salene?"

"I suspect that we will find her at the end of the night howler's trail."

The other human kept his weapon aimed at the giant. "It better not be the beast's larder we find . . ."

As they moved on, Zayl's thoughts shifted from the creature's propitious arrival to Karybdus's trap. The other necromancer seemed prepared for him at every turn. Karybdus had not only expected Zayl to follow, but had known by what method and where best to arrange his attacks.

Yet, conflicting desires seemed evident in the traps. Both

the malevolent force that had pulled Zayl from the cell and the legion of undead had clearly sought to make him a part of whatever they were. Karybdus, though, had made it quite clear that he preferred Zayl removed from the equation entirely, one way or another.

"There's something goin' on up ahead," remarked Humbart from his arm. "I can sense it—can't you, lad?"

"Yes."

The night howler added a few grunts of his own, then pointed up a hillside. Zayl and Sardak followed him there.

And from their vantage point, they saw the entrance to what had to be where Karybdus had taken Salene. Zayl eyed the stone sentinels with foreboding, then surveyed the rest of the entrance. Around the opening, several of the grotesque man-spiders scurried across the rock face and the trees of the forest, all obviously keeping watch for intruders.

"Are we too late after all?" Sardak asked, his sword hand shaking.

Zayl looked to the sky. "I believe not. The day is only giving way to the night. I think that they must wait for the moon to be in a certain position. Still, the time is surely growing short."

The other human started forward. "Then, let's get going!"

It was the night howler who pulled him back, the huge paws lifting Sardak up with surprising gentleness for a creature previously so bloodthirsty. He set the struggling swordsman down next to Zayl, then gave Sardak what could only be described as an admonishment.

"Try not to be so foolhardy," added the necromancer. "We must wait for a better moment, when their concentration cannot be turned to us without detriment."

"But they must know that we're coming anyway! Surely those monstrosities we fought returned to report their failure! Why wait? Best we go in with weapons ready! They won't be expecting the audacity!"

He was desperate to save his sister, and Zayl could

hardly blame him. "We will find another way. Of that I promise you, Sardak."

"But *what*?"

At that point, the night howler grunted, pointing to an area on the opposite side of where Salene was being held.

"Not quite certain," muttered Humbart. "But I think he's got an answer for us . . ."

He was not the only one, either, for as the creature began leading them in that direction, Zayl thought very carefully about the ways of the Rathmians . . . and how even Karybdus might think him in one place when he was in another.

Karybdus stiffened. He looked over his shoulder at the entrance, gaze narrowing.

Lord Jitan caught the action. "Something?"

"The trap was sprung, but the prey escaped."

"Which means that this Zayl is on his way? How did he escape so many? Is he bringing a military force from the city?"

"No, he would not work that way. I cannot ascertain what actually happened. There seems a confusion spread across the minds of the survivors."

"A necromancer spell. You told me about it. Surely you can break it."

Karybdus frowned. "It is not a spell, just . . . a general confusion." The gray-haired Rathmian sniffed. "And absolutely nothing to concern yourself with, my lord. We shall expect Zayl to come, and when he does, he will be dealt with."

"Like he was supposed to be in Westmarch?" asked Aldric, looking up from his inspection of the altar. "By Cornelius? By those dead cultists?"

The necromancer did not look perturbed by yet another attack on his abilities by Aldric. "Cornelius still has his part to play. It was because of him and our erstwhile Edmun that the trap was sprung by the Zakarum. That the Church failed to act swiftly enough when they knew that there was a Rathmian among them is a failing of theirs.

They were warned that he would be dangerous. Cornelius also has made certain that General Torion has focused *all* his attention on Zayl." Karybdus cocked his head. "All in all, I would say that Cornelius has actually done very well for us, my lord."

"As you put it, I suppose so. You've got a labyrinthine mind, sorcerer. I'd hate to play chess with you. I wouldn't know whether I was winning or losing." The noble glanced at Salene. "So, is it time *yet*?"

In response, Karybdus snapped his fingers. Salene immediately walked over to the altar and, as if settling down in her bed for the night, calmly and readily lay back on the stone structure.

Sheathing his dagger, Karybdus withdrew from his belt one of the cult blades. It had been this that he had been searching for when the Lady Nesardo had made her timely appearance. Karybdus had seen it as a sign that his work for the Balance was destined to succeed.

Several of the noble's transformed servants scuttled into positions surrounding the altar and the ritual's participants. They looked as eager as Aldric.

"The power will soon be yours, my lord," the necromancer intoned. "Power and a legion of followers at your beck and call. All in one fell swoop."

From within the Rathmian's cloak emerged his eight-legged familiar. The huge arachnid climbed up to Karybdus's shoulder, perching there.

Aldric raised up the Moon of the Spider expectantly. As he lifted it above his head, the artifact began to glow.

"There, my lord. You see? It is the beginning of the first phase."

"Gut her already, then!"

"Patience. There are words to be spoken first." Moving to the opposite side of the altar, Karybdus held the sacrificial dagger over Salene's prone form. He glanced up once at the artifact, then, seemingly satisfied with what he saw, started muttering. The only word that his companion would have recognized was the name . . . *Astrogha.*

From the transformed servants, there arose a low but steady hiss, a chant by the Children of Astrogha. The parasitic spiders atop the head of each seemed to watch the necromancer's work with growing anticipation in their inhuman orbs.

Karybdus brought the dagger down.

The cut he made on Salene's throat was a tiny one, superficial at best. It drew only a few drops of blood, but the Rathmian seemed quite satisfied. He made certain that the tip of the blade was bathed properly, then stretched his arm toward Aldric.

The noble lowered the Moon of the Spider just long enough to let the bloody tip touch the center of the arachnid pattern. The legs of the image twitched.

"It is pure," declared Karybdus. "It is the blood of Astrogha."

Bathed in the awful illumination of the artifact, Lord Aldric Jitan's face was terrible to behold. His lust for what the necromancer had promised him erased all vestiges of humanity from his aspect.

"Get it done with, then," he all but hissed.

But Karybdus instead looked to the side, to the shadows. His own countenance was a mask, revealing nothing about his true emotions. "*He* is here."

"Who? That damned Zayl *again*?" Aldric looked to several of the creatures, who immediately broke ranks and, with many an angry hiss, headed for the entrance.

"He is closing. He has no choice but to use the path by which we came, but he will not simply walk in. There will be spells he will set into play . . ." The armored necromancer reached out with his heightened senses. Like a bird of prey sighting fresh meat, Karybdus fixed on one point near the right side of the entrance. "In fact, I must commend him. He is here already."

"I see nothing."

"But you will." Karybdus made a gesture in the air.

A needle-sharp lance of bone—the Talon of Trag'Oul—materialized before him. It shot forth in the direction in which the Rathmian had been gazing.

As the Talon reached the entrance, there was a rippling in the air. Outlined in it was a cloaked and hooded form.

A cloaked and hooded form through whose chest the Talon now buried itself.

Lord Jitan grinned. "Ha!"

Three of the remaining servants rushed forward to see if the target somehow still lived. Sacrificial dagger in hand, Karybdus stepped from the altar. "Most curious. He is certainly dead, but I still sense his living presence . . ."

The noble also moved closer to the still body. "He must be dead! No one could survive—"

A harsh cry filled the chamber, echoing from every direction. Aldric, Karybdus, and the servants spun around, seeking the source.

A huge chunk of marble came crashing down on several of Lord Jitan's followers.

Karybdus let out a curse and brought up his own cloak just as the dead body suddenly shriveled and a pungent cloud burst from the putrefying remains. The cloud tripled in size in mere seconds, enveloping several of the creatures who had been closing in on the corpse.

The nearest of them hissed, then let out a hacking sound. It managed to turn from what remained of the corpse . . . then fell limply to the floor. Two more had only time to register the first's death before they, too, collapsed from the poisonous vapors.

At the same time, Zayl and Sardak charged out from one of the shadowed corners of the chamber, appearing so suddenly that they seemed to have walked through the very stone. A cloakless Zayl reached out and from the crumpled figure that Karybdus had assumed him something arose under the voluminous garment. As it flew up, it carried with it the cloak, revealing that what had been thought human had been, in fact, another of Aldric's mutated men. A dagger wound in the back revealed that the creature had been dead long before the Talon had impaled it.

Sardak drove his blade through another monster, then stepped up by his sister's side. "Salene! Salene! Wake up!"

Lord Jitan turned at the call. "You! Leave her be, you tavern rat! She's ours!"

Swearing, Sardak lunged at the noble. Although he held a powerful artifact in his hands, Aldric reacted instinctively, diving away from the thrust.

Turning back to his sister, Sardak slapped Salene hard. She moaned and turned her head toward him, but otherwise did not respond.

Like a shrouded specter, Zayl's cloak, held aloft by his dagger, returned to the necromancer. He pulled the black garment free, then tossed it over his shoulders. As if alive, the cloak dressed itself over him even as the dagger returned to his hand. Zayl had used the blade, tied to his life, to distract his foe. He had known that the other Rathmian would sense that life force and assume, logically, that since there was no other entrance, it *had* to be Zayl.

Of course, neither Karybdus nor Lord Jitan had known about the secret priest tunnel in the back, one with which the night howler was apparently very familiar. It had enabled the rescuers to sneak in so close.

There were many questions Zayl had concerning the night howler and his fortuitous actions, but, for now, they had to wait. Not just Salene's but their own lives were still very much in danger.

Sure enough, even as he thought that, he saw Karybdus—the hem of his cloak still over his nose and mouth—draw a circle, then add two slashes across it. Zayl felt his strength failing and immediately countered with the same symbol, while adding a third slash perpendicular to the others and dividing the circle perfectly. His strength immediately returned.

A shadow abruptly loomed over Zayl's foe. Karybdus glanced up, then threw himself as far as he could from where he had been standing. Another chunk of marble crushed in the floor, barely missing him.

Even as the missile landed, the night howler fell upon the Children of Astrogha, pummeling one to jelly with a single blow. Two others leapt atop him, biting down hard, but their vicious fangs could not pierce the thick hide and their poison simply stained the fur.

Zayl joined Sardak. "Take her from here! Quick!"

"I can't wake her! She'll have to be carried!"

"Let me see." The necromancer leaned close. Such a spell was not among those taught to novices, but over the years Zayl, like Karybdus, had learned several on his own. Rathmians accepted any spellwork that aided the Balance provided it did not cause the caster to become corrupted.

He put his right hand—still gloved—over her face. An intake of breath from Sardak was a grim reminder that what lay within the glove would not soon be forgotten.

Zayl quickly muttered words of a spell that, in its original incarnation, had been designed to summon a shade from its eternal slumber. He had long ago modified that spell so that now it performed a more simple awakening— stirring to consciousness those under enchantments.

The only trouble was, it did not always work.

But this time, Trag'Oul was with him. Salene moaned, then her eyes fluttered open.

She promptly screamed. "Look out!"

Aldric Jitan, the Moon of the Spider blazing in his hands, glared like an angry deity at the trio.

Sardak threw himself at the treacherous noble before Jitan could unleash whatever vicious spell he planned. The point of his sword buried deep in his foe's shoulder, causing the other to howl and nearly drop the sinister artifact.

But in protecting Zayl and Salene, Sardak left himself open. Distracted by his target, he did not see the attacker to his side. The eight-limbed horror seized Salene's brother and tore him from the ground before Zayl could react.

The fangs sank into Sardak's throat.

"Sardak!" Salene cried, raising a hand to her brother. "Oh, Sardak, no!"

From her outstretched palm erupted a bolt of fire. It soared across the chamber, striking Sardak's fiendish assailant with such force that it ripped the creature from the floor. Sardak himself was untouched by the force flung by his sister. As the fiery mass that had once been one of Jitan's servants collided with a far wall, Sardak clutched at his throat and stumbled back a few steps.

Salene pulled from Zayl's grip. On unsteady legs, she ran to her brother, catching him just as he was about to collapse.

The necromancer tried to follow her, but suddenly two of the dead monstrosities pushed themselves up and closed on him. Glancing past them, Zayl saw Karybdus, his expression detached, holding his dagger and gesturing not only at the risen pair, but others slain by the intruders.

Cursing, Zayl thrust for the head of the first undead. As the blade sank deep, the creature shuddered, then went limp.

At which point, the second undead twitched . . . and promptly *exploded.*

With a cry, Zayl flew back against the altar, striking with such force that every bone shook. Head throbbing, vision unfocused, he could do nothing but lay where he was. In the confusion that was his mind, it slowly registered to him that once more Karybdus had proven the wilier one, raising the dead, then unleashing the violent energies of a slain corpse. In truth, the two-pronged attack was a sinister variation on Zayl's own spell, expertly played.

Through blurred eyes, the necromancer surveyed the scene. The rescue had now very much gone awry. Sardak lay dying in Salene's arms, she oblivious to a grim Karybdus's approach. The night howler was now aswarm with Lord Jitan's fiendish creatures, so much so that they had at last brought the beast to his knees. Zayl himself was still unable to rise or do anything to aid his companions.

Jitan started toward Salene, but Karybdus pointed at the night howler, commanding, "Deal with that thing! I will make the woman ready!"

The noble grinned. Clutching the Moon of the Spider tight, Aldric pointed it at the furred giant.

But as he did, a brilliant light suddenly flashed in front

of him. Lord Jitan let out a growl and used the artifact to shield his eyes.

At the same time, the night howler somehow found the strength to stand. With an ear-shattering roar, he threw his attackers from him as if they were nothing. One that man-aged to cling on he tore off by the neck, then tossed with all his might to the floor. A single slam of his fist left his final foe a lifeless pile.

The forest dweller's ferocious gaze fixed on Zayl's rival, whose attention was on Salene. Hefting the crushed body, he aimed at the armored figure.

But, as if warned by some sixth sense, Karybdus turned and saw the corpse flying toward him. Once again, he threw himself to safety.

As he did, the night howler ran to Zayl. One meaty hand picked up the helpless necromancer.

"No . . . ," gasped Zayl. "Not me . . . the others . . ."

Seeming to obey, the giant ran to Salene and her brother, However, with one arm already filled, he could take only the noblewoman.

"Sardak!" she cried. "I can't leave him!"

Her protest went unheeded by her rescuer. With two humans in hand, the night howler raced for the front entrance.

"After them!" Zayl heard Karybdus shout. "Send the creatures after them, my lord!"

There was an angry bark from Aldric Jitan, then a series of eager hisses marking the charge of his servants. Zayl tried to call to the night howler, but his words came out as little more than a croak.

They left the temple for the dark sanctuary of the forest. Behind them, the Children of Astrogha gave chase. Aware that he could do nothing else at the moment, Zayl finally surrendered to the night howler's will. He heard Salene sobbing for her brother, and regret filled him. Sardak had proven a brave, capable man, one who had thought nothing of sacrificing himself for a half-sibling born to privileges that had been denied him in his youth.

The Rathmian's head suddenly jerked up. A *half-sibling*.

At least partly of the same blood.

Of the same blood . . .

Aldric Jitan let out a string of colorful epithets that impressed even the well-traveled Karybdus. The gray-haired necromancer let the noble unburden himself before finally interrupting.

"Calm yourself, my lord. The situation is not so dire as you think."

The mismatched eyes burned. "Not dire? That Zayl's got more lives than the proverbial cat! How can you be so calm? He's made you the fool more than once."

"Learning is never foolish. From Zayl I have learned much, and for that I honor him. He is more resourceful than even his reputation indicated."

"Resourceful?" Aldric let out a harsh bark. "Always with the understatements! That was a *night howler*, my friend! A night howler! Where in blazes did he get one of those animals?"

Karybdus nodded. "As I said, resourceful. Even innovative, although not enough." The Rathmian permitted himself a brief frown. "As to the night howler, if I may say so, you had a perfect opportunity to remove the creature as an impediment. What happened?"

"It was that damned light! Didn't you see it? I swear, it was as bright as the sun!"

"A bright light?" Pursing his lips, the necromancer commented, "Surely another trick of Zayl's, or even the woman's. She has in her a vast reservoir of untapped power. It would be interesting to study her."

"It would be more interesting to have her here for the sacrifice! The point of convergence has passed us by!" The noble almost looked ready to use the Moon of the Spider on Karybdus. "My moment's been taken from me!" His expression turned anxious. "I'll start *dreaming* again, too . . . "

Karybdus put up a gloved hand to calm him. "All is not lost, my lord. We have enough to begin. All can go on as planned."

"But how?"

The Rathmian gestured at two of the remaining servants, then pointed at a crumpled form not all that far from the altar.

Sardak.

"I was quick to act the moment I saw that he was bitten. The blood is still warm in his body, and my spellwork keeps any more from spilling out of the wounds."

Aldric eyed Sardak's corpse as he might some vermin discovered in his food. "That bastard? What good is he to us other than one less piece of trash to deal with? The man's a wastrel and a drunkard . . ." Lord Jitan rubbed the wound he had received from that very same wastrel. "I'd say toss his remains outside, but we'd probably attract more night howlers . . ."

"Such a valuable commodity I would not waste on them." As the creatures lifted up Sardak, Karybdus added, "Not when it can allow us to achieve our goals. He is her half-brother. The blood she carries, he also does, in part."

Now at last, his companion understood. A look of child-like glee spread across the arrogant noble's face. "He can be the sacrifice? Even dead?"

"He is actually at the *edge* of death." The Rathmian waited until the body had been set upon the altar, then drew the sacrificial dagger. "And that is all we need." The armored spellcaster looked to Aldric. "If you will take your proper place, my lord?"

Grinning more widely, Lord Jitan obeyed.

SEVENTEEN

Still held tight in the night howler's grip, Zayl's view of the mist-enshrouded forest was a nightmarish and often out-of-perspective series of images. Black forms scuttled and scurried among and in the trees behind them, a hissing pack whose sole purpose now was slaying the giant and the necromancer . . . and even possibly Salene.

The noblewoman had grown silent, either exhausted by the escape or simply grieving for her brother. Whether or not she could hear him, Zayl had no intention of speaking to her about Sardak. That might lead him to blurt out his deep fear, that Sardak had inadvertently given Karybdus and Lord Jitan exactly what they wanted. For the sake of not just Sardak's soul but everyone else's as well, Zayl had to hope that Salene's brother had perished from the poison in his attacker's fangs before Karybdus could do anything.

Only the fleshless head of Humbart Wessel, firmly packed in the pouch at Zayl's side, had dared any initial comment, and his had consisted of "What the devil are we doing? Is there an earthquake? What's happening?"

However, after several minutes of not receiving an answer, even Humbart had finally quieted.

The night howler seemed not at all wearied by carrying two full-grown humans—and a skull—but neither did their pursuers appear daunted by how swiftly the forest dweller ran despite his burdens. They kept pace, but could not catch up. Zayl's hopes grew as a few began to lag behind . . .

Then, without warning, two fell upon the night howler from *ahead.* Salene screamed and even Zayl let out a gasp as both were thrown free. The necromancer landed just shy of a tree trunk, his catlike reflexes enabling him to recover almost instantly. He pushed himself up and searched for Salene. Instead, the Rathmian was greeted by the unsettling sight of the night howler struggling with a creature on each arm and one on his chest, and turning to face the rest of the hunters.

Drawing an arched symbol in the air with his dagger, Zayl focused on the two at the head of the approaching pack. The pair suddenly stopped, glanced back at their cohorts ... and with the same zealousness with which they had hunted the trio, *turned* on their fellows.

Under Zayl's spell, the two creatures tore into the nearest possible targets, ripping at chests, biting at throats. The combatants rolled into some of those behind, further adding to the chaos of the moment.

Taking advantage of the momentary respite, Zayl rushed toward where he believed Salene had landed.

At first, he did not see her and thus feared that some other servant of Jitan—perhaps one of the creatures who had leapt on the unsuspecting night howler—had already taken her, but the rustling of branches to his right finally alerted Zayl to her whereabouts.

Unfortunately, they also revealed that the noblewoman was running *back* in the direction of her brother.

Moving stealthily, the necromancer followed. Farther back, the roar of the night howler mixed with the savage hisses of the hunters. Zayl wished that he could have done more for the forest dweller, but he had to stop Salene from her evident madness. If Sardak *had* perished before Karybdus could make use of him, then the villains *would* still need the Lady Nesardo.

Salene ran wildly, in her frenzied state obviously not entirely certain of her path. Zayl followed as if born to this very forest, easing around the trees and nimbly avoiding branches and upturned roots.

The Rathmian soon closed the gap. Salene did not seem to hear him. Zayl, on the other hand, heard every gasping, frantic breath . . . and now and then the muttering of her half-brother's name. Salene was driven by Sardak. She would not stop trying to reach him until there either was no strength left in her body or Zayl managed to catch her.

He reached out, trying to grab at her cloak—

A nightmarish form rose out of the forest ahead of her. The creature seized a startled Salene in a four-arm grip. The fangs went for her throat—

And a second later, the horror squealed. A fire seemed to blossom from its back. Quivering uncontrollably, it released the noblewoman and tumbled back onto the ground.

The fire died even as the creature did. Salene, the glow in her hand already fading, briefly stared at the ruined form . . . then rushed on.

But the struggle had taken long enough to enable Zayl to catch up. His right hand closed on her arm. "My Lady Nes—"

She looked over her shoulder, her expression terrible to behold. Salene instinctively put her own hand—again glowing—on his gloved one.

The glove burst into flames.

Had it been his left hand, Zayl would have suffered cruelly. As it was, he was forced to release her, then quickly peel the fiery garment off.

The sight of his fleshless appendage finally made Salene falter. She stared at the hand, the burning glove, and then into Zayl's eyes.

"I didn't mean—I—"

"There is no need for apologies," he interjected in a low tone. "Now come with me! Quickly!"

Using his gloved hand, he tried to lead her toward Westmarch, but Salene slipped out of his grip.

"No! Sardak needs me! He needs me!"

Gritting his teeth, the Rathmian responded, "Sardak is dead, and he gave his life trying to save yours, my lady! Do not let his—" The word "sacrifice" almost escaped Zayl's lips, but at the last moment he caught it. "—courage be for nothing! We must head for Westmarch!"

"We dare not go there! Torion—"

"Will not let harm come to you. He will protect you any way he can, my lady."

She put her hands on her hips in defiance. "And what about you?"

"I will make do. Now—"

Salene turned away. "No! There must be somewhere else!" She glanced back again, the strain of events clearly showing. "Besides, I can *feel* him! He needs me!"

Feel him? Was her relationship with Sardak so close that she could sense if he was alive or dead? Sardak had hinted something of the same earlier. That renewed Zayl's concern that Karybdus might be able to use the dying brother in place of his original sacrifice.

But Zayl could take no chances. For her sake and much more, Salene *had* to come with him.

With her gaze once more turned from him, Zayl brought up the dagger.

"Forgive me for this, Salene," he whispered.

He touched her on the back of the head with the hilt. Salene let out a slight gasp and fell forward. Leaping, the necromancer just managed to grab her.

"What did you do?" asked a voice from his side. Humbart, aware of the danger of distracting his friend, had stayed silent throughout the entire struggle, but now finally thought it safe to speak up. "I can't see it, but I know you've done something to the lass!"

"Quiet, Humbart. I have no choice."

The skull grumbled, but otherwise said nothing.

When he turned her face to his, her eyes were open. Zayl waited until he was certain that they would not blink, then whispered, "You will come with me, Salene Nesardo. You will return to the city. Even if I should fall to harm, you will do your utmost to return to Westmarch and give warning to General Torion."

Torion would listen to her. More to the point, he would, as Zayl had earlier said, protect Salene from danger. There was no greater shield than love.

He released his hold on her. Salene straightened. Her eyes continued to stare unblinking, but she turned toward the unseen city. Zayl nodded, then started in that direction. Salene moved when he did, her actions exact copies of his own. Aware that Karybdus had also enchanted her so, he felt much guilt even though there had truly been *no* other choice.

Silence suddenly reigned in the forest, whether a sign for good or ill, the hooded spellcaster could not say. The night howler had become as dedicated and respected a companion as Captain Kentril Dumon had been in Ureh. The forest dweller had risked his life more than once for Zayl and, because of Zayl, for Salene and Sardak as well.

It made him more determined than ever to reach the capital, no matter what the risk to himself.

He did not at all contemplate returning by means of the passage leading to the depths below House Nesardo. Assuming that the cavern still existed in some part, there was the danger that the undead followers of Astrogha still haunted it. While Zayl believed that the magic that had resurrected them had faded, he did not want to chance Salene's life that way.

No, it would have to be through the front gate, if only for her sake.

A howl filled the silence. It was followed by another and another and another . . .

"Now what's that?"

"Quiet, I said, Humbart! I—"

Only then did Zayl notice, though the day had faded away, a light shining down from the sky.

The Rathmian looked up and beheld the moon . . . but a moon such as even he had never witnessed. It was round and full at a time when it should not have been and seemed so very much closer than was right.

And over the upper edge, a peculiar, almost menacing shadow had begun to spread.

A shadow with eight limbs trailing down.

"Odyssian's Wedge!" snapped the necromancer. He

picked up his pace, nearly running. Salene, caught up in his spell, obediently matched him.

"So this isn't good, whatever it is," complained Humbart. "Wish I had two more legs to lend you . . ."

Zayl did not answer him. The wolves continued to howl and others of their ilk joined them. Zayl also heard owls and other nighttime birds calling. The creatures of the forest sensed the unnatural change in the moon.

His gaze shifted back and forth, even up as he hurried along, but he saw no sign of pursuit. It was possible that the night howler had slain them all—no doubt himself perishing in the process—or that the surviving creatures had lost the scent and now chased a false trail. Those were the choices for which Zayl held out hope.

The third and final choice was the one that he most feared. It was possible that Jitan's servants had returned to their master because Zayl and Salene were no longer of primary significance to either the ambitious noble or Karybdus. If Sardak's blood was indeed sufficient to their vile task . . . then, in running from them, Zayl had ensured their triumph.

He stopped dead in his tracks. Salene imitated him.

The necromancer took a step in the direction of the ruins and Karybdus. Immediately, the noblewoman followed.

This would not do. Thrusting his maimed hand at her, Zayl commanded, "Salene, hear me! You will go on without me! The spell upon you—"

A branch snapped. The necromancer spun, expecting either the demonic hunters or, perhaps, by some miracle, the night howler.

Instead, he heard the snort of a horse.

Armored riders suddenly charged in from all sides, all with weapons drawn and pointed in the general direction of the Rathmian. They rode in a tight circle around him, somehow always keeping him in their sights.

But one rider came much too close to the still Salene. Fearful that she would be injured or cut, Zayl started to pull her near.

"Get your filthy demon hand off her, necromancer! And drop that dagger!"

As the other soldiers reined to a halt, an officer with a plumed helm rode up. Zayl had never seen the man before, but the latter's contempt for the Rathmian somehow bordered on the personal.

"Fate is surely with me!" he crowed. "The elusive Zayl, at last! I finally came to the conclusion that you were no longer in the city, which was why I volunteered to lead this hunting party myself! Still, I never thought my luck would be so good!" The officer drew his sword and looked ready to behead the necromancer. "Now, we can be rid of your evil doings!"

"Listen to me!" Zayl protested. "The kingdom is in danger! You must—"

"Silence, cur!" shouted one of the other soldiers. He made a wild swing at the necromancer, who was forced to jump back or be cut.

Salene imitated his action.

The patrol leader swore. "How dare you play her like that? Remove whatever enchantment you have upon her, sorcerer, if you even hope for any mercy!"

Rather doubting that he would be granted mercy under any circumstances, Zayl nonetheless willingly obeyed. Whatever his own fate, he would do what he could to save Salene.

A simple gesture with his hand was all that was needed. The noblewoman coughed. Blinking, she slowly registered the presence of not just the necromancer, but the armed party as well. Her gaze focused specifically on the lead rider.

"Alec?"

"Captain Mattheus, please, my lady." He touched the front brim of his helmet in respect to her. "And may I say that I am pleased that you look unharmed by this wretch."

"Who—Zayl?"

"My lady," interjected the hooded spellcaster. "It is essential that you go with these men to General Torion and tell him what we have witnessed—"

"Be still, you!" growled the soldier who had swung at Zayl earlier. This time, the flat of his blade caught the Rathmian on the shoulder. With a grunt, Zayl stumbled a few steps forward before regaining his balance.

Salene grew livid. "Stop that!" she roared, chastising the soldier. The man looked nonplussed. Turning to the captain, Salene added, "Alec—Captain Mattheus—Zayl is my friend and just saved my life!"

"He is a heretic and a danger to the kingdom—"

"A heretic, is he? And are you now a warrior of the Zakarum Church? And what danger is he, pray tell? It's only because of him and Sardak—" Salene faltered. "Poor Sardak . . ." She stiffened. "If it's a villain you seek tonight, Captain Mattheus, then you should look for Lord Aldric Jitan! He meant to have me sacrificed tonight!"

As Zayl expected, the officer looked dubious. "You are telling me that Lord Aldric Jitan, a senior-ranking member of the Council of Nobles, intended to have you *sacrificed*, my lady? To what, if I may ask?"

"A spider demon of some sort! It—"

He cut her off. "Clearly you are still under some enchantment of this foul one! Either that, or your mind, distraught by the trials it's gone through, has mixed this man up with the Lord Jitan!"

"He will not listen to reason," Zayl told Salene. "It might be best if you—"

"Reason?" scoffed the leader. "I've heard nothing remotely resembling reason!" Surprisingly, Captain Mattheus sheathed his sword. "It is obvious to me that this situation is more delicate than I'd desire. We'll have to take both of you back to the general, where he'll get all this nonsense out of your head—if you'll pardon me for saying so, Lady Nesardo!" Before she could protest, he went on, "As for you, necromancer, you've bought yourself a reprieve . . . a *temporary* one at best. Brennard! Bind that cur's wrists behind him! Yorik! Your horse for the lady! Double up with Samuel. His horse is the largest and strongest beast!"

"Aye!" shouted the men in question. Brennard, a

bearded veteran with a scar across his nose, walked up to Zayl as if the latter were Diablo himself.

"Hold your mitts behind you," he gruffly ordered.

The necromancer obeyed. Brennard swore when he got a closer look at Zayl's right hand.

"Captain! It's rotted away to the bone! There's little else but that and some sinew!"

"Well? What did you expect from one of his kind? It's still a hand! And don't you worry, if he tries anything, his reprieve's up! You understand that, *Master* Zayl?"

At that moment, another howl echoed through the night. Some of the soldiers looked around anxiously.

"Damned beasts are actin' up again," muttered Yorik, who had dismounted.

"Just a bunch of hounds calling to the moon," their leader interjected. "If there's anything unnatural about it, the cause stands before you."

Zayl paid him no mind, the Rathmian more interested in the moon itself. It was all he could do to keep his concern masked. The limbs of the sinister shadow now spread nearly to the bottom.

So, the Moon of the Spider was both an artifact and a phase of the lunar orb. Jitan had one already and now the second had nearly come into phase. Zayl could only guess what would happen when the true moon resembled the representation.

He knew that, at the very least, it would spell catastrophe for the city.

"Eyes where I can see them," the captain insisted. He and the rest of the soldiers appeared oblivious to the unsettling sight above.

Zayl could not go back to the city after all. There evidently was no more time. He had to return, and return quickly, to where Karybdus and the noble worked their dire deeds.

He twisted slightly, causing the pouch at his side to jostle.

Captain Mattheus instantly focused on the bag. "Brennard, see what's in there."

Brennard looked none too pleased, but he moved to obey. However, as his fingers touched the pouch, an angry voice shouted, "Just who do you think you're manhandlin' there?"

Brennard leapt back. Several of the horses snorted, and more than one stirred nervously.

"Do *I* go layin' my mitts on *you*?" continued Humbart. "Do I? I should say not! Of course, the fact I don't *have* any shouldn't matter—"

The horses began to shy. Yorik fought to control his.

Zayl threw himself toward the unmounted Yorik, colliding with the distracted man. Although much wider and heavier than the slim Rathmian, Yorik tumbled back.

With a single, smooth motion, Zayl leapt onto the saddle. He reached his skeletal hand out and his dagger flew up from the ground and into his hand. A gaping Brennard watched the scene unfold without so much as moving a muscle.

The only one to react, in fact, was Captain Mattheus. He drew his sword and started after Zayl. "Samuel! You're in charge of the Lady Nesardo! Take her back with the rest of the men! You six! After me! I want that cur!"

Salene reached for the necromancer. "Zayl! Take me with you!"

He shook his head. "You must warn General Torion! Tell him something terrible will happen tonight! He must guard the walls with flame! Warn him to watch for spiders!"

"Zayl—" If she said anything else, he could no longer hear her.

The horse he had stolen was an excellent runner—as the Rathmian had suspected—but so too were those of the men chasing him. Zayl cursed that part of the Balance that seemed to insist upon his being pursued by one foe after another. Captain Mattheus and his men were a special thorn in his side, for they pursued him out of ignorance. He strove to save their lives, yet they saw *him* as the monster, not the elegantly clad and nobly born Lord Jitan.

Karybdus must laugh at my antics, Zayl thought bitterly. *I have been as merely a flea to him.*

The wolves continued to howl. Zayl glanced again at the moon, the shadow upon which more and more resembled a gargantuan arachnid seeking to devour it. The Rathmian feared that he was already too late.

Captain Mattheus and his band silently raced after him, swords at the ready. The soldiers spread out among the trees, each trying to follow a path that would enable him to catch up to his quarry. General Torion would no doubt decorate the man who brought him Zayl's head.

Deeper and deeper into the forest the necromancer rode, never quite able to lose his pursuers. Paradoxically, it was not so much for his own self that he desired to do so. There was yet the risk that Lord Jitan's grotesque servants might also be hunting for him, and Zayl feared that the unsuspecting captain might ride right into them. Yet, there was nothing he could say or do that would make the soldiers turn back. Nothing, that is, except turn himself over to their "mercy."

With *that* in mind, Zayl urged his mount to greater swiftness. He glanced again at the moon, saw that the shadow had all but engulfed it, then focused on the dark landscape.

A frown crossed his features. Only now did he notice the utter quiet of his surroundings. The wolves—indeed *all* the animals—had ceased their anxious calling.

Unable to resist, the Rathmian looked up yet again at the shadowed moon.

But as he did, something ahead made his horse shy. The trained animal suddenly reared. It was all Zayl could do to even hold on. His steed kicked wildly at the darkness, then jerked around.

The necromancer tumbled off.

With a frightened whinny, the horse headed back in the direction of the capital. Zayl, meanwhile, rolled several yards away, finally pausing next to a thick bush.

Even as he struggled to his feet, he heard the clatter of

other hooves and a shout from Captain Mattheus. The patrol was nearly upon him.

Scrambling forward, Zayl slipped around the nearest tree. He planted himself against the trunk, relying on his black garments and, especially, the cloak to allow him to blend into the landscape.

A rider went past. Not the captain, but a wary-eyed soldier almost as huge as the night howler. The man slowed his horse just past where the necromancer hid. He glanced over his shoulder, staring straight at his quarry.

But *not* seeing him. So long as Zayl stood still, he had a very good chance of being missed.

At last, the soldier looked away. Eyes searching the path ahead, he urged his mount to a slow but steady pace. The two gradually disappeared into the woods.

As Zayl left the protection of the tree, from his side came Humbart's low tone. "What's happening, lad? Damn, I hate being bound up in here . . ."

"Hush, Humbart! We are back farther into the forest. I will let you know if anything happens." After a pause, Zayl added, "And thank you for your timely interruption."

"Weren't nothin'. Now be careful. There's something not right around here . . ."

The skull was not referring to the moon, but rather an uneasy sensation that Zayl now also felt. Something was in the vicinity and converging on his very location. It did not feel like the servants of Lord Jitan and yet . . .

"Halt! Stand where you are!"

Captain Mattheus and another man rode into sight. Zayl cursed; whatever he had sensed had distracted him from his other predicament.

He turned to run . . . only to find another rider coming up from that direction. The necromancer raised his dagger, but before he could cast any spell, he was struck hard in the back.

He landed face-first. Before Zayl could rise, an armored boot pushed him back into the dirt.

The clink of metal warned him of another's approach. Seconds later, he heard Captain Mattheus growl, "Finally! Let's be done with this! Roll him over! Make it look like he fought back and had to be slain!"

"Aye, captain." The soldier who had knocked the Rathmian down threw him on his back. The face of Captain Mattheus leered at him from his left.

"Scum! The general will be quite happy to hear about your death."

Zayl attempted to call his dagger to him, but some force kept it from coming. He glanced in the direction it had fallen and saw one of the officer's boots atop it.

"We'll have none of that," Torion's subordinate muttered. To the soldier, he added, "Finish it! Now!"

The other man held a sharp sword over Zayl's chest. The soldier raised his arms as high as he could, preparing to bury the point deep in the necromancer's heart.

Zayl attempted to cast a spell, but both his breath and his mind proved insufficient for the task. Hopes fading, he readied himself for the journey to the next stage of existence. The necromancer prayed that Rathma and Trag'Oul would deem his efforts in this one worthy.

Then, Captain Mattheus looked beyond his captive, growling, "What is that?"

The next instant, one of the soldiers shrieked. A horse whinnied. Something scurried past Zayl's head, too small to be one of Jitan's transformed servants, but radiating a presence akin to them.

"Get it off of me!" cried another unseen soldier.

Someone swore. There was the scuffling of hooves—as if one of the mounted men attempted to ride off—followed by a horse's grunt and another human scream.

The soldier standing over Zayl hesitated. He looked in the same direction as his captain.

The necromancer caught the soldier's legs with his feet, sending the soldier falling back.

Captain Mattheus reacted. Forgetting whatever it was that was attacking his party, he lunged at Zayl. The tip of his sword buried deep into the soil where the pale spell-caster's throat had just been.

Two more dark forms scuttled past the rising necro-mancer. Zayl caught just enough of a glimpse to under-stand the vile threat to them all. A quick glance at the moon—and the shadow completely enveloping it—was enough to verify his worst fears.

A cry broke out from the man he had tripped. As Zayl turned, he witnessed a horrible sight. All but covering the hapless trooper's face was a black, furred form with eight legs, inhuman orbs, and savage fangs.

The same sort of parasitic spider he had seen atop the mutated servants.

Despite the soldier's best efforts, he could not peel the arachnid free. Captain Mattheus, however, suddenly moved in and stabbed the creature through the torso. Unfortunately, he also slew the soldier in the process.

"Damn! Damn!" The enraged officer whirled on Zayl. "Call them off, sorcerer! Call them off and I'll spare your life! This is your last chance!"

"They are not mine to command, captain! They serve the Lord Jitan . . . at least for now."

But Torion's man clearly did not believe him. Alec Mattheus slashed at Zayl even as those under his com-mand struggled in vain for their lives. Soldiers knelt or even lay on the ground, desperately pulling at the viselike grips of the monsters atop their heads. Most of the horses had run off, but two lay frozen, their heads also covered by the parasites.

Then, one of the soldiers first attacked abruptly stilled. He looked unchanged, which surprised Zayl, who had expected a transformation akin to that of the noble's fol-lowers. Instead, the man, a spider's limbs horribly buried in his skull, slowly rose and turned to where the Rathmian and the officer stood.

"You would be wise to run, captain," urged Zayl. "Run for Westmarch with all the strength you have in you! Run as if the Prime Evils are behind you, for you would not be far from the truth!"

But Captain Mattheus proved an obstinate man. "Don't try to frighten me, sorcerer! A blade through your black heart will stop your spell and free my men!"

Again, the necromancer dodged his blade. The soldier prepared another lunge—and a spider leapt onto his shoulder. The captain tried to brush it off, but he might as well have been trying to remove his own arm.

Another jumped onto his back.

"Away, damn you!" he shouted. In his attempt to deal with the one behind him, he knocked off his helmet.

Zayl realized the fatal mistake. "Captain! The helmet! Put it back on before—"

Instead of listening, Captain Mattheus slashed at him.

The spider on his shoulder leapt up onto his head.

The officer screamed as its taloned limbs instantly burrowed through flesh and bone. He made one feeble attempt to tear the creature free, then dropped to his knees.

Well aware that it was too late to save the man, Zayl tried to flee. He shook off two arachnids trying to cling to his cloak, but managed only a step before a new danger confronted him.

The soldiers, each with a parasite guiding him, now blocked his path. The eyes of the men stared blankly at the Rathmian. Each soldier held his weapon ready.

Summoning his dagger, Zayl thrust the gleaming weapon toward the possessed figures. As he hoped, they pulled back from the illumination.

But from behind him, a powerful hand struck his arm, causing his grip on the dagger to falter. The light dimmed.

Zayl was seized from behind. He heard Captain Mattheus's voice in his ear.

"Don't bother to struggle, sorcerer. You're only prolonging the futility."

The captain's voice.

But Lord Aldric Jitan's words.

EIGHTEEN

✳

Salene had no difficulty seeing General Torion. The man in charge of returning her to Westmarch brought her right to his commander, bypassing several guard stations in the process.

No, Salene had no trouble seeing the veteran soldier . . . but convincing him of the veracity of her story was an entirely different matter.

"Lord Jitan?" muttered the general. He started to take her by the shoulder, then thought better of it. Instead, he sat down on the edge of his desk and frowned at the noblewoman. "Let me summon a priest, Salene! Clearly, the evil knave's still got you under a spell! The only threat to the security of Westmarch comes from him!"

"But Jitan—"

"While I dislike the arrogant bastard—and for more reasons than that he, too, seeks your hand—there's no proof to match your words, and the say-so of one noble against another isn't sufficient anymore. If it was, the cells would be full of the entire aristocracy!"

Stepping up to him, Salene put one slim hand on his chest. She gazed into his eyes. "Torion . . . at least make certain that the guards on the outer walls are doubled. Zayl said something about spiders—"

Again, he cut the noblewoman off. "First, I hardly think we've much to worry about *spiders*, Salene. Perhaps if this were Lut Gholein or the necromancer's own foul Kehjistan, a swarming of Poison Spinners might be concern for the farmlands, but what little we've got in the way of deadly spiders is hardly worth a panic—"

"A poison spider decided the heir to the throne, Torion."

"If so, it's proving a fortuitous decision, but that's not my point. Besides, even if I'd like to assuage you, I couldn't. It's not only the patrols searching for your damned sorcerer. With the grand exhibition of strength planned for the morrow, I've already drawn more than half the men from the walls who are generally assigned there. The king wants a fresh, strong force present when he displays himself to that mongrel bunch seeking his crown. If they—"

But now it was the Lady Nesardo who interrupted. Her expression aghast, Salene blurted, "The walls—the *outer* walls—they've been stripped?"

"Only for tomorrow's gathering. Mostly toward the forest, too, where there's not much to worry about save a few night howlers and maybe a band of brigands."

"The walls . . ." She tried to think. "*Justinian* asked for this?"

"An unorthodox decision, but a workable one. He's right about the need for a show of strength on his part, and this is the only way to gather enough trusted men in time." He exhaled. "Salene, in some ways it's like Cornelius reborn! He has his quirks, but the lad's coming into his own, truly."

The noblewoman could still not believe what she was hearing. "Justinian . . . ," she murmured. "*Justinian commanded it . . .*"

Torion suddenly stood up, his gaze looking past her. "And speaking of Justinian, here comes Edmun Fairweather now."

Turning, Salene all but collided with the chest of the king's aide. Edmun Fairweather took a step back and, with a courteous smile, bowed to the noblewoman. "The lovely Lady Nesardo! This is a golden opportunity! The king was just speaking of you!"

"And we were just speaking of Justinian," added Torion. "What can I do for you, Edmun?"

"Actually, general, the point of my visit stands between

us! His majesty, in order to best show the nobles the backing he has, wished to speak with the most prominent of them, the great lady here! I've been riding high and low throughout the city, looking for her!"

His declaration sounded so outrageous to Salene that she nearly called him on it, but at the last moment thought better. Besides, it suddenly occurred to her that Justinian might be more persuadable than the general when it came to reinforcing the walls, especially if he coveted her backing so much.

But she did not wish to travel alone with Edmun, whose virtue Salene did not trust. "I would be honored to speak with the king." She glanced coyly at Torion. "But I insist that the general join us."

"That I will," answered Torion before Edmun could protest.

Salene understood why the veteran officer agreed so quickly. Torion thought that he could keep her from defending Zayl and spreading her fearful stories about some spider demon. When the time came, though, the king *would* hear her warnings.

She only hoped that Justinian would also *listen.*

The Lady Nesardo had not been inside the palace since more than a year before good Cornelius's death. She had not spoken with Justinian for more than a year before that. Thus it was that her image of the young monarch—the timid, uncertain dreamer—was utterly shattered by the reality.

Justinian, alerted by messengers, met them in the throne room. Based on what Salene gathered from Torion, the great chamber that the heir had once abhorred now seemed a far more favored spot than his former haunts— the kitchens and his personal quarters. In fact, when the three were announced, it was to find the king relaxing on the throne, a parchment in one hand, a goblet in the other. To Salene, he looked so much the picture of confidence that she almost wondered if he was simply posing.

Justinian immediately set down his goblet on a small, elegant table next to the throne. Keeping the document in one hand, he shook the general's with the other.

"Always a pleasure to have your company, Torion!" His eyes all but lit up at the sight of his other visitor. "And the Lady Nesardo! Did I ever tell you what a crush I had on you?"

Considering that he was no older than her, that meant that there had lurked a possibility that Salene could have potentially become queen. Had her father been alive at the time, even keeping the family fortune together by marrying Riordan would have looked a poor second to gaining the throne.

That Salene had no desire to become queen would have meant nothing.

Despite not wearing a gown, she did as protocol demanded and curtsied. "Your majesty honors me."

"No, my dear Salene! You honor me." King Justinian glanced at Edmun. "You may go."

The retainer bowed low. "I am but a whisper away."

"Naturally." As Edmun left, the lord of Westmarch handed the parchment to Salene's companion. "I've looked it all over, Torion, and it's good, yes, but I want a bit more yet."

He started to go into details about the coming events marking his ascension. Salene tried to pay attention, yet at the same time Justinian talked, the noblewoman thought she heard whispering. Salene surreptitiously looked for Edmun or some guard lurking in the vicinity, but saw nothing.

Yet, the more she focused on the whispering, the more it grew distinct. In fact—

In fact, it repeated nearly word for word what Justinian was saying. No . . . *Justinian* was repeating what the unseen whisperer said.

Even as Salene realized that, the whispering abruptly halted. Salene had the uncomfortable sensation that she was being stared at, but not by either Torion or the king.

However, a moment later, Justinian *was* studying her. He briefly frowned, then, eyes still on her, said to the general, "Torion. Something's come to mind that needs immediate attending to. Lord Vermilion reported that his son's wandered off, likely to a brothel, but possibly to somewhere more dangerous. This is a delicate matter, and I need you to see to it that he's returned without incident to his father. You know how much we need Vermilion's backing . . ."

"I do indeed, your majesty. I'll deal with it now."

Salene had not expected Torion to be sent away, especially so quickly. She wanted him to stay, but could find no excuse. The general kissed the back of her hand, then, leaning close, muttered, "Please be cautious what you say . . ."

Justinian took his whispering for words between lovers. "I'll take good care of her, Torion. She'll be back in your arms before you know it."

From anyone else, the general would have taken umbrage over such a comment. To his king, the veteran commander simply bowed and replied, "Nothing would please me more. Good evening, your majesty."

The Lady Nesardo's gaze followed Torion out of the chamber. Then, realizing how she must look, Salene quickly returned her attention to the king . . . only to discover him staring at the empty air to his right.

Just as abruptly, he stared at her again. His smile had an artificial quality to it that made the noblewoman very uncomfortable.

"I hope you feel safe being alone with me, my lady," he said.

"You are the king."

He chuckled. "A cautious answer."

There was more whispering, but this time unintelligible. Salene's brow arched as she sought to understand what was being said.

Justinian noticed immediately. "You seem—distracted—Lady Nesardo. Are you ill? Do you feel uneasy on your feet? Are you hearing *voices*?"

Without meaning to, she took a step back. "Your majesty, if you'll excuse me—"

The king's expression grew ghastly, becoming a parody of cheerfulness. "Are you referring to me . . . or are you speaking to my *father*?"

"Your—your father?"

"Oh, but can't you see him? He's standing right next to me! I thought that if you could hear him, you could certainly see him!" He looked to the empty air again. "She can't see you, Father!"

Salene squinted. With concentration, she almost thought that she could make out a murky form that might pass for something human. *Might.*

"That—is that King Cornelius?"

Justinian IV clapped his hands together. "Yes, yes, it is! He came to me in my hour of need, Lady Salene! I was so fraught with anxiety and fear! I never planned to be ruler! That was my brother's position! I was simply supposed to live out my life, doing nothing and, therefore, doing no harm!"

"Then, your brother died—"

"You can be assured that I was the most tearful of all, even more than Father! Still, even at that terrible time, I thought Father would live forever! He'd always been the toughest of us all . . ." He shook his head mournfully. "But not tough enough, I discovered."

The whispering began again. Despite being unable to understand it, Salene suspected that it involved *her.*

"You're quite right, Father," the new monarch said with a boyish nod. "She should. Why, I think that she should be very, very honored!"

Honored? For some reason, she doubted very much that whatever he offered would be an "honor." Salene knew that she had made a terrible mistake coming here, but who would have dreamed that Justinian was haunted by something claiming to be his own sire? True, Torion's description of the king's transformation of character should have given her pause, but even with all else that had happened, never would Salene have expected *this.*

Justinian gave her a bow. "My Lady Nesardo, I hereby grant you the privilege of being my guest this evening . . . and perhaps the next, too, if necessary."

"Your guest? Your majesty, I don't think that I—"

"Can refuse? Oh, I agree!" He looked to the murky form. "That is right, isn't it, Father? I thought so! Am I learning well?"

There was more whispering. Salene concentrated harder, hoping that somehow she could better see and hear the shade of the late king, but to no avail. She doubted that it was accidental. Something was terribly wrong here. The advice Justinian was getting seemed not at all in character with the old king as she knew him.

Although she failed to hear it better, she did notice that the shade grew slightly more distinct. Salene frowned at what she saw. In all ways, it *seemed* to be Cornelius. She caught the outline of his beard, his nose, and other features. Just enough to make her believe that he *was* indeed Cornelius.

But as she continued to concentrate, Salene sensed something else. There was an aura around the specter, one that had a different feel to it, as if it had been placed around Cornelius against his will.

Was it a spell?

Salene wished that Zayl were here with her. He would have known what all this meant. He would have understood how to unravel the questions before her . . .

But Zayl had trusted in the noblewoman, and so she focused this time on the aura itself. There was a dread familiarity to it. How that could be, Salene did not understand, yet the more she studied the aura, the more she felt certain that she recognized the origin of it.

An image of Karybdus flashed in her mind.

The spell was his.

Justinian was being guided by a spirit forced to do the *bidding* of the necromancer.

"Justinian—" she began.

"Hush, my lady," the young king commanded, gesturing with one hand. "Not now.

Salene's voice ceased. She opened her mouth, but nothing came out.

With the possessed shade ever at his side, the lord of Westmarch looked past Salene and clapped his hands. She immediately glanced over her shoulder, there to find Edmun Fairweather already waiting.

"Your majesty."

"Time to seal the palace."

The lanky aide bowed deep, his expression bearing a carnivorous smile. "As you say, your majesty."

As he departed once more, Salene caught him glimpsing not at Justinian . . . but rather at *Cornelius*. She let out a silent gasp, wondering how it was that the servant could so readily sense the ghost.

Justinian caught her arm, turning her to face him again. He smiled. "As I thought, Father insists that you stay close! He believes that you might try something silly, and I wouldn't want to have to hurt you if you did." After observing her futilely trying to tell him something, he gestured with his free hand. "You may speak again."

"Your majesty! This is all wrong! Your father is not acting as he should! He's under the control of a necromancer named Karybdus!"

The king's good humor vanished. "Karybdus brought my father back to me! He came to me in the moment of my greatest need! You'll not speak ill of a good man!" He flung her toward the dais. "Sit there!"

His words were more than simply a demand; they were a command that Salene found she could not disobey. Her body placed itself on the dais against her will.

Salene had never heard of any trait for magic running through the royal line and had to assume that somehow Karybdus—perhaps through Aldric Jitan—was also the cause of this. Whatever the source, Justinian clearly reveled in it.

The king's rage vanished as quickly as it had appeared. He went to where his goblet sat and took another great gulp. Then, acting like an eager young boy with a secret, he sat down next to the Lady Nesardo.

"Tonight, it begins! They'll never question my right to reign! When this is all through, everyone will see that I am the true king! No one'll ever call me 'Justinian the Wide-Eyed' again!"

"What—what do you mean, your majesty?" Salene had the horrible idea that she knew.

"It was so very clever! The nobles are all in attendance in the capital! Most of the guards have been stripped away from the outer walls—Father's suggestion, that! When the city's under attack, I'll be waiting for the right moment to come to its rescue! I'll be commanding the forces that Torion's gathered for me—but only after it's clear that none of those would-be usurpers can do anything!" He grinned wide. "I'll be the one to save Westmarch from the *spiders*! Me!"

He *knew*. He knew everything, and yet Justinian was content to sit here and let it all play out. He was content to sit and drink while scores perished . . . or faced some worse fate.

And it seemed that there was nothing that Salene could do about it . . .

They set Zayl on the stone floor with surprising care. The necromancer slowly raised his head . . . only to see the boots that surely belonged to the legendary Karybdus.

But Karybdus was not yet looking at him. The other Rathmian gazed at the possessed soldiers with what only his counterpart could tell was a hint of frustration. He held out his hand, and one of them gave him Zayl's dagger and the much-damaged pouch containing the skull of Humbart Wessel.

Karybdus brought the pouch up to eye level. Without opening it, he sensed what was within. "Animated. Amusing but useless."

"You find me 'amusing'?" said the mercenary's hollow voice. "If I had jaws, I'd bite your nose off! See how amused you'd be then!"

Their captor's eyes narrowed. "Be silent."

The curse that Humbart had just begun cut off in mid-sentence.

Setting the pouch on the floor beside him, Karybdus inspected Zayl's blade. "Finely attuned," he complimented. "A particularly well-crafted piece, too."

The other necromancer said nothing.

Satisfied, Karybdus glanced at the soldiers. "Your task is done. You are dismissed. Go."

The soldiers stayed where they were.

"Allow me, sorcerer," boomed a voice both familiar and yet not. "Go! I will summon you when I need you."

Like marionettes, the men turned as one and left. Pushing himself up, Zayl beheld Lord Aldric Jitan, but as he had never seen him before. Jitan stood by the altar—and by the limp, pale corpse of Sardak Nesardo—one hand holding forth the Moon of the Spider, the other clutching the bloodied sacrificial dagger.

Aldric seemed twice as large as Zayl remembered him and his hair flew as if electrified. His eyes blazed crimson and his skin was the color of the ivory part of the artifact. Zayl's higher senses noted a black aura about the man, one with no human origin.

Smiling at the prisoner, Lord Jitan cavalierly thrust the dagger back into Sardak's ruined chest. Only then did Zayl see how terribly the body of Salene's brother had been butchered. In addition to drawing the blood, they had also cut out the heart. In the process, the noble and his companion had shoved aside the rest of Sardak's innards as if so much offal.

An unexpected urge to beat the noble into the floor filled Zayl, but he managed to smother most of the emotion. Yet, as *he* had noted Karybdus's earlier frustration, so too now did the older necromancer see what coursed through the younger.

"An unseemly display. You let attachment color your efforts and lead you away from the proper course of the Balance."

"At least I have not forgotten entirely to what I have devoted myself."

Karybdus sniffed. "Nor have I. I am more resolute than ever that the Balance be maintained. I have made sacrifice after sacrifice to ensure that."

The younger Rathmian dared sit up. He indicated the carnage and the insidious creatures that had once been men. "This is your notion of sacrifice, Karybdus? What has become of you? Surely, you have fallen prey to the life-tap—"

His words actually made Karybdus laugh. "Is *that* what you think, young one? That I, who strove against demons and dark spellcasters for so long, absorbed the life forces of too many evil ones and thus *became* them? Perhaps someone less so, but I *am* Karybdus, am I not?"

Zayl sought to rise, but an invisible force kept him in a kneeling position. He glanced at Aldric, who looked like a child with a new toy. A very *deadly* and powerful new toy . . . and one whose repercussions the noble surely did not comprehend.

"If not that, then what? What has changed?"

The gray-haired necromancer bent closer. "*Nothing* has changed, young Zayl. I still hold the same belief I held the day I accepted the mantle. There is nothing more important than the Balance, and I do what must be done to keep it even. You, of all, should be able to appreciate that." He straightened. "When first I sensed your presence and realized that it was you, I briefly thought of asking you to join me in this crusade. But almost immediately, I saw that you had become blinded, that you were swept up in the same terrible mistake so many of our brothers and sisters were."

"And that is?" asked Zayl, seeking some manner by which to escape the spell and stop this travesty before it was too late.

"That there are *two* sides to the Balance. There must

always be." Karybdus took on the aspect of a teacher. "How otherwise could it even be called so?"

"Good and Evil, yes. You preach nothing I do not know."

"Then let me tell you this—"

At that moment, Lord Jitan called, "Is this necessary? The next phase is—"

The armored spellcaster glanced at his partner. "The next phase is still minutes away, my lord, and I would have Zayl—who deserves it most—understand why I do what I must. After all, for the sake of the Balance, he let his own parents *perish*."

Lord Jitan let out an eager gasp. "Did he really?"

Zayl felt as if Karybdus had taken the sacrificial dagger and cut out his heart. Shaking his head vehemently, he cried, "I did no such thing!"

"You know it was otherwise. You know that all understood that." Karybdus forced his counterpart's face toward his. "I knew them both, you know. Fought beside them before you were born. I can say without hesitation that they were very proud of your decision . . . at least, after the pain stopped and they moved on to the next plane of existence."

"Stop it! Stop your lies!"

But the senior Rathmian went on, "If there is Good, there must be Evil to *balance* it out. Your act is an example. You had to do what resulted in their deaths because it was the *correct* thing to do. However, too often, all our kind does now is fight Hell's minions. Think very carefully, Zayl. All that for the side of Good! The imbalance is growing overwhelming! Something must be done to bring the world back to an even state!"

And, at last, Zayl did understand what Karybdus meant—understood it and abhorred it.

For centuries, the Rathmians had fought the servants and powers of the Prime Evils, who sought to sway the mortal plane completely to their will. In Zayl's mind, never could enough be done. A world dominated by the

Prime Evils was a world forever out of balance and, there-fore, lost.

Yet, Karybdus, whose triumphs over the Darkness were legion, now believed that he and the others had done *too* much. He obviously felt that the world had slipped too far toward the Light, which according to the principles of Rathma, could lead humanity to a stagnation and a loss of conscience as terrible in its own way as anything falling to the Darkness might.

Over the centuries, there had been much debate among the Rathmians as to the limits of their involvement in the affairs of the world, but never could Zayl recall anyone's suggesting anything as mad as what Karybdus proposed.

"What I did . . . ," he murmured. "What *happened* . . . is in no manner equivalent to what you are doing, Karybdus!"

"Your mother and father might beg to differ."

Without realizing what he did, Zayl leapt to his feet. "My parents perished because of my *mistake*! I am the one who destroyed the ship and all aboard! I take the blame for that, just as I always have!"

His skeletal hand caught a startled Karybdus by the throat. The other necromancer gasped and tried to pull the fleshless fingers free. "My lord!" he grated. "If you would . . ."

An oppressive force tore Zayl's fingers from his adver-sary's throat before slamming the younger necromancer to the floor again. Try as he might, Zayl could not so much as move a finger.

Karybdus rubbed his raw throat. "It is a pity you cannot see reason." He held Zayl's dagger ready. "I am truly sorry for what I must do. I have the highest respect for your capabilities, Zayl, even if they are misdirected."

"Yours—are—misdirected—" the prone figure man-aged.

"His will's impressive," remarked Lord Jitan.

"Yes. After he is dead, I won't bother summoning his shade. It would be too stubborn." Karybdus tsked. "I find my fellow Rathmians make terrible servants. His parents were much the same after I raised them up. I was forced to send them back quickly. Such a shame, truly."

Zayl let out an enraged gurgle at this newest revelation, the most he could muster under the relentless onslaught by the empowered noble.

Leaning over him, the armored necromancer said, "Fear not. You will soon be able to discuss your guilts and motives with them. Farewell."

Zayl braced himself. Slain by his own dagger, there would be no hope for resurrection, even should some trustworthy necromancer find him in time.

The chamber suddenly darkened. It was not, however, any simple shadow that fell upon the room, for instead of black, it was a deep but very obvious crimson.

From Aldric, there was a stunned oath; from Karybdus, a sharp intake of breath. Zayl sensed the other Rathmian withdraw the dagger.

"That's it, then! Isn't it?" called the noble. "The second phase of the moon!"

"Yes." Karybdus's footsteps marked his departure from his frozen adversary. "The cycle of the Moon of the Spider is at its apex. It is time for you to receive the full gifts of Astrogha!"

"Don't—" breathed Zayl, trying to warn Aldric. "Not— what it—seems!"

But Lord Jitan did not hear him. Still grinning, he positioned himself next to the altar. On the other side, Karybdus thrust Zayl's weapon into his belt, then pulled free the sacrificial blade. He proffered the dagger—its point covered with Sardak's cold, congealing life fluids— to the noble.

"Let me touch the center of the pattern with this," explained the Rathmian to Aldric. "Then, hold the artifact directly over your head. Make certain that it almost touches your skull."

Try as he might, Zayl could utter no more warnings. He watched helplessly as Jitan complied.

The moment the blood touched, the arachnid design

stirred as if alive. At the same time, a crackling sound like a mixture of thunder and lightning filled the chamber. Outside, the wind howled.

Yet, through a tiny crack in the ceiling, the light of the moon somehow shone down.

Shone down . . . and struck the artifact at the very same point that the blood had.

The electrifying aura around Aldric increased a hundredfold. He stood like a wild banshee, his expression monstrous in its delight. Everywhere, the transformed servants bowed their horrific heads low to the ground. Their hisses sounded almost like words—or rather, one word.

Astrogha.

"Unbelievable!" Lord Jitan shouted gleefully. "I can feel the power coursing through my system! I can sense where each of the spiders are! I can feel them emerging from the shadows to march upon the city! I can feel—"

His mouth suddenly went slack.

The sphere above his head had *cracked open.*

And in perfect imitation of the image on the outside, eight long, vile limbs ending in blood-red talons stretched down and caught the noble's head in a viselike grip.

"Sorcerer! Karybdus! What's the meaning of this? Something's gone dreadfully wrong! Help me!"

But Karybdus merely stepped back and watched. "Nothing has gone wrong. Everything is as it should be. I am very sorry that this must be done, but this *must* be done."

"But—" Lord Jitan got no further.

The spider's limbs thrust hard into his head.

He shrieked for several seconds, his cry dying off in a pitiful sob. Blood spurted from the wounds, and although it was clear that by the end he had to be dead, he did not fall, any more than the soldiers in the forest had.

The chamber continued to crackle with otherworldly energies. Zayl felt the pressure holding him to the ground lessen, but not enough to allow him to rise.

Karybdus came around the altar. Still holding the sacrificial dagger, he approached Aldric Jitan. The spider that continued to emerge from within the sphere was several times larger than the previous ones and had eight clusters of eight burning orbs atop its squat head. Sharp, tearing mandibles, not fangs, sprouted from its mouth.

From within Karybdus's cloak, his own spider crawled up upon the necromancer's shoulder. Zayl could not help notice the similarities, even if perhaps his rival did not.

"Zarakowa ilan tora Astroghath!" the gray-haired Rathmian intoned. He drew an eight-sided image with the dagger, then added, "Istarian dormu Astroghath!"

Myriad energies played around the noble. The huge spider set itself in place. Yet, unlike the smaller ones, it did not simply sit atop, but enveloped a good portion of Aldric's skull.

And from Aldric's twisted lips, there came a horrific sound, laughter such as no human had ever uttered.

"I am to this mortal plane returned!" hissed an awful voice not at all akin to the noble's. "I am from the foul prison freed!"

Karybdus knelt before the figure. "Welcome back, my Lord Astrogha . . . welcome back."

But the thing within the shell that had once been Lord Aldric Jitan did not even look at Karybdus. Both the man's and the spider's many eyes looked instead at Zayl.

Looked instead at Zayl, with hunger.

NINETEEN

Despite their numbers having been halved, the guards at the gates facing the greater forest were not so very concerned. There was little to fear from this direction save a few marauding wolves or other beasts of the forest. Of course, had they been on patrol like those who had ridden out with Captain Mattheus, they might have been more anxious. Since the return of the men with the Lady Nesardo, there had been no sign of the rest of the riders, including the adjutant himself.

Thus it was with some relief—and yet some trepidation—that a sentry up on the wall spotted a lone rider approaching. His plumed helm gave him away long before his face became visible in the torchlight.

"'Tis Captain Mattheus!" the man above shouted. "Open the gates! 'Tis the captain!"

Others scrambled to comply. With so few men left, it was necessary for two to climb down from the wall to aid in opening the huge wooden gates that were the first protection of the capital.

General Torion's aide silently rode inside. One of the soldiers ran up to take the reins of his steed.

"Sir," the man blurted, staring at the mount's head. "What ails the animal? Does he have an injury that his skull must be bound up like that?"

The officer's cloak covered most of the top of the horse's skull and neck. To the soldier who had asked, it was a wonder that the steed could even see from beneath such a bundle of cloth.

"An injury, yes," answered the rider. Still holding the

reins, Captain Mattheus glanced back at the gates. "Douse the torches and lamps."

Those nearest him stood perplexed. The man who had sought the reins finally asked, "'Scuse me, sir, but did you say to put out the torches and lamps?"

The brim of the officer's helmet hid the eyes as Captain Mattheus looked down at him. "Douse the torches and the lamps. Put out all fires."

"What's this about dousing everything?" asked an approaching figure. His armor was in better condition than that of the other soldiers and he bore insignias that marked him as commander of the watch. "Captain Mattheus, sir!" The newcomer quickly saluted. "It's you who orders this?"

"Douse the torches and the lamps," the rider repeated. "All fires."

"Are we at risk of an attack?"

There was a pause, then, "Yes. An attack. Douse all fires. Quickly."

The commander of the watch turned to the others. "You heard him! Stefan! Get those torches on the wall! You three! The lamps! Hurry!"

Throughout it all, Alec Mattheus watched from the saddle. Each time a flame was extinguished, he nodded.

As the last of the torches was being put out, the commander of the watch asked, "Any further orders, captain?"

The adjutant eyed the man's covered head. "Remove the helmets. Toss them aside."

"Beg pardon, sir? That really an order?"

The rider nodded once. "An order."

With a shrug, the other officer signaled the men to do as commanded. Only Captain Mattheus kept his helmet on.

When all the men were bareheaded, the captain abruptly urged his mount on. Completely confused, the soldiers at first simply watched him ride off.

"Any other orders, sir?" the commander finally shouted.

"Remain at your positions" was all the figure said before vanishing into the darkness.

Once Captain Mattheus was gone, the officer in charge

turned to his men. "Get those gates shut again! You heard! There's an attack coming!"

There was some fumbling in the dark, but they soon had the gates secured. The commander, who had served directly under General Torion during the first months of his career, went over the orders he had been given. He knew that Alec Mattheus was highly respected by the general— the captain would not have been made Torion's adjutant if he had not been—but, considered with a few moments' thought, none of the man's orders made any sense. It was only out of respect for who he was that the commander and the others had obeyed Mattheus to the letter.

But still . . .

"The hell with orders, even from one such as him," grumbled the officer. "Someone find me my helmet! Stefan! Get those torches lit again!"

"But Captain Mattheus said—"

"I'm takin' responsibility! You heard me! Gerard! You get over there and—what the devil makes you so jumpy?"

The other soldier peered into the shadows behind him. "I thought I heard something!"

"I'll not be having any man scared of shadows on the walls when there's an attack brewing! Boromir! You take his place right—"

Something the size of a cat moved past the boot of the man to whom the commander had been speaking. Before its shape could register, the commander noticed another moving toward Gerard.

"There's something on me back!" Stefan suddenly shouted.

With that, dozens upon dozens of black shapes poured out of the night—black shapes, the commander of the watch belatedly noted, that had evidently climbed up over the outer wall and into the city without any of them noticing.

Cries rose from other men. The officer drew his sword as three more shapes converged on him. As they neared, he skewered one, but the other two split ranks, coming at him from opposing sides. He knew that by the time he dealt with one, the other would be upon him.

His eyes adjusted enough to the gloom to finally see the creatures for what they were.

Spiders . . . a veritable sea of giant spiders . . .

The cries died almost as quickly as they rose. To that which controlled what had once been Alec Mattheus, they had been music. Perched atop his head and all but hidden by the plumed helmet, the spider caused his host's mouth to momentarily rise up at the ends in a parody of a smile.

The way was clear. The others had entrance into the city.

Soon, they would all have hosts. Soon, the Children of Astrogha would once more flourish . . .

"That one is of no concern to you, my lord," Karybdus remarked. "His death is overdue. I shall slay him in your honor."

"No." The voice now had a raspy quality to it, one that stirred every nerve in Zayl's body. The possessed Aldric tossed aside the shell that had been the Moon of the Spider like so much garbage and strode easily toward the captive necromancer. Unlike the other spiders, this one had complete control over his host. When the mouth of Lord Jitan moved, the mannerisms were not all that different from the living man's. "No. He is to be preserved."

Frowning, Karybdus replied, "As you desire, Lord Astrogha, as you desire."

"My children, to the city of men, go," Astrogha said to both. "They will of their hosts drink and become one. My power will again grow! A god I will be again!"

"A god—you never were!" Zayl finally managed to say. He glared at the macabre figure. "Only a lowly demon, Astrogha! That's all you'll ever be! A footstool for Diablo, the true Lord of Terror!"

The spider's body pulsated. A look of righteous fury swept over Jitan's contorted face and one hand went up, a dark ball of flame materializing above the palm.

But the flame was quickly snuffed out by the closing of the noble's fist. Through his host, Astrogha smiled again. "From my Lord Diablo, I would never that title take! His vassal I am, but ruling in his name, he will not mind! This kingdom of men will be made over in my image, but it will be to serve the ultimate desire of the great Diablo . . ."

Zayl looked to his counterpart. "Karybdus! Can you not see yet the insanity you unleash? Is this what you want?"

"It is exactly what I want. It is exactly what is needed for the world."

"This will send the Balance reeling to the side of darkness!"

The armored Rathmian shook his head. "No. It will not. The Balance will be preserved."

Zayl gaped at him, wondering how even at his maddest Karybdus could possibly believe that.

"Enough is the talk," rasped Astrogha. The demon turned back to the altar. "The hold is not yet true. There must more time be."

"The timing will be perfect," Karybdus, eyes lowered, smoothly assured the demon.

But in those eyes, Zayl saw what Astrogha did not. Karybdus did indeed intend to preserve the Balance. He planned some *betrayal* of the demon . . . but when would it happen? Surely not before countless lives were lost to the minions of this false god.

Zayl was tempted to tell Astrogha this, but he doubted that the demon would listen. Like so many of his hellish kind, the spider was vain to the point of utter self-denial. That someone would be able to outwit him would be beyond his comprehension.

But, if anyone was capable of doing it, it would be Karybdus.

The possessed noble returned to Sardak's ravaged body. Astrogha dipped a finger in the congealing life fluids and brought it to Aldric's mouth to taste. "So long ago, since such nectar I have tasted! So long ago, since trapped in that accursed bubble!" With a sudden rage, the noble shoved the corpse off the side. "An injustice, it was! A crime, it was!"

"They did not understand," Karybdus murmured, placating the creature.

"Understand, they did not!" agreed Astrogha. "Gave to some great power, much knowledge . . . and only asked a few souls and blood for such! Small, compared to mortal greed!" He turned to gaze at Zayl. "But others, jealous they were of me! Tricked my own into betraying me, then creating *that*"—the demon indicated the discarded casing— "here, where the planes are most close, where easiest it is to bind to my greatness."

And when Astrogha manifested next, the sorcerers were waiting for him. At the cost of their own lives, they sealed him inside.

But Astrogha's followers stole away what was soon called, because of its appearance, the Moon of the Spider. After much calculation, they determined that at certain times through the centuries, the planes of the mortal world and Hell touched just right so that the forces of the latter could be used to free their lord. However, they also needed something that already bound the demon in part to their own realm.

His children's blood.

It was possible for demons and mortals to mate, generally to the horror of the latter. Yet, few there were of such children that survived to adulthood. If they did not die in childbirth, they were generally slain soon after by those who knew them for what they were. But, despite his own appearance, Astrogha's get looked more human than most and many were even beautiful or handsome to behold. Thus, they survived where others did not. For the servants of the spider, this presented a bounty . . . at least for a few generations, when the intermingling of normal mortal blood with that of Astrogha's line reduced the ties to the demon until they were all but nonexistent.

Undaunted, the priests did the only thing that they

could. Whenever someone was discovered with even a hint of the heritage, they were secretly taken and slain upon an altar. By intricate spells, their living blood and heart were preserved indefinitely. Other spells refined the blood in the hopes that when the proper phase came, it could all be used as if pure.

But such butchery could not go unnoticed forever. There were those—the Sons of Rakkis in particular—who discovered the cultists living among them. With the questionable assistance of sorcerers such as the Vizjerei, the Sons of Rakkis located the hidden temple beneath what had then been a church. The location had served as a nexus of forces reaching even into Hell, perfect for the cultists' use. The soldiers and spellcasters put an end to that use, freeing the sacrifices and slaughtering all but a few of Astrogha's followers.

Those few fled across the sea, where they bided their time and awaited the moment of destiny. With them, they brought the preserved hearts and some of the purified blood. When at last the moon itself came into alignment, they cast the spell—and only too late discovered that they had planned insufficiently. The weaker blood did not serve its entire purpose; it freed Astrogha, yes, but made him only a ghost of himself, far too weak to battle the Vizjerei who discovered his return.

"Forced I was to flee back here in the hope of true blood of my children to bind me better to this world again," hissed the spider. "Smelled it even from across the Twin Seas . . ."

The Sons of Rakkis were no more—their fall a mystery even to the demon—but Westmarch as a kingdom now flourished. The surviving followers hid the weakened demon in the ruins of his old enemies' mountain stronghold, then sought out those of the blood.

But the Vizjerei followed more quickly than even Astrogha had imagined they could. Most of his human puppets were slain and the sorcerers used their last strength against the demon; they lacked the power to destroy him, but they did manage to seal him again in the orb. That done, they placed his guardianship in the hands of one of their own already slain, then came to this place where Zayl was now a prisoner with the intention of destroying it.

"It was built to best enhance the link between the planes," Karybdus kindly explained to his counterpart. "To destroy it would have weakened that link to the point where even pure blood would have no longer sufficed to free him. But, for some reason, they failed." The older necromancer tsked. "So, that is the reason for the corpses I found here."

"My vengeance works slow sometimes, but works nonetheless," mocked Astrogha, again tasting the life fluids. "They entered, only to be bitten by the smallest but deadliest of my children. Perished, they did. I felt it even in my accursed limbo . . . ."

Karybdus glanced up at the ceiling. "My lord, the time of the next phase is nearly upon us. You would do to make preparations."

"Yes, correct you are." Astrogha reached a gore-soaked hand toward Zayl. "Come to me, my *chosen* one . . . ."

Both Rathmians stared in utter confusion. Zayl it was who recovered first. He recalled both his horrific journey to the netherworld and his encounter with the undead priest in the underground temple.

"It *was* you," he blurted. "You who stole me from the prison cell, who guided the undead worshippers in the hidden temple . . . ."

Karybdus looked at him as if he had joined the demon in some special madness. "What are you speaking of? I am the one who raised the dead of Astrogha below House Nesardo . . . and what is this about the prison cell?"

The captive necromancer met his counterpart's gaze. "Are you not then privy to all that occurs? I would have thought otherwise. You raised the dead, but Astrogha guided their hand afterward. They *knelt* to me, Karybdus! Called *me* 'master'! I did not understand why until now."

"You are making fanciful tales! Astrogha was imprisoned in the orb! He could not affect this plane from in there!"

Zayl sneered. "But so close to the proper phase, when the planes are so in sync, he could do *some* things . . . and without realizing it, you helped him with your own efforts!"

"For which a reward you shall receive," the demon promised through Lord Jitan. "Once this finer vessel is mine and my *full* glorious self has taken over ъ . . ."

"But the vessel *I* provided you is perfect, my lord," insisted the gray-haired Rathmian. "He is of the blood. He has the latent ability for sorcery! He is—"

"He is not *this* one." Aldric's tongue licked his lips. "This one is so much better. Long have I studied him. Perfect, he is."

"But he is not of the *blood*."

"For this, necessary it is not." Astrogha beckoned to Zayl. "Come . . ."

Against his will, the captive spellcaster stood. Karbydus did his best to hide his emotions, but Zayl, adept at reading one of his own kind, saw the growing consternation. Whatever plan the other had in mind to rid the mortal plane of Astrogha was made all the more difficult by the demon's choice of Zayl as its ultimate host. A skilled necromancer, with all his arcane knowledge, would make the spider much more formidable. All that Zayl knew and could do would be at Astrogha's foul command.

For all his vaunted reputation, Karybdus had blundered terribly.

But the errors of his rival in no way assuaged Zayl. As he moved helplessly toward the macabre figure, he desperately tried to come up with some defense against Astrogha's possession. Once the spider's legs burrowed into his skull, the Rathmian would cease to exist as a separate entity.

Try as he might, Zayl could come up with nothing. Curiously, though, for all his fear for his soul, his greater concern was for the innocents of Westmarch . . . and, most of all, for Salene Nesardo.

The possessed Lord Jitan seized him by the shoulders, holding him in place.

With a horrific sucking sound, the monstrous arachnid atop the noble's head pulled free its limbs. Blood and other fluids dripped from both its legs and the terrible, gaping wounds lining Aldric's cranium.

The spider—Astrogha—crouched briefly, then leapt onto Zayl's hooded head.

The Rathmian tried to shake the fiend off, but the demon held tight. With one leg, it kicked off the hood, the only shield of any kind left to its prey.

At the same time, Aldric Jitan suddenly shook. His grip on Zayl failed. The mismatched eyes rolled inward . . . and the ambitious aristocrat's corpse tumbled to the floor in an awful heap.

Out of the corner of his eye, Zayl saw Karybdus shifting position, but otherwise the other necromancer did nothing but watch. If he intended to do anything to stop the demon from gaining all that Zayl offered, it seemed it would wait until the latter was already dead.

The frozen spellcaster felt the tips of the legs caress his skull. In his head, the voice of Astrogha resounded. *Yes, perfect you are . . . we will be one . . . and all will become my children . . .*

Pain coursed through Zayl's head . . .

The spiders came from everywhere.

At first, they flowed over the unprotected wall, but then the sentries—now hosts for the Children of Astrogha—reopened the gates, the better to let the swarm through.

The sea of arachnids poured into the nearest buildings, slipping through cracks much smaller than their bodies. Within moments, shrieks from inside those buildings filled the night—short-lived shrieks.

And as some of the children found their hosts, the rest moved on. This human city was vast. There would be enough for most of the swarm.

Besides, those that did not find them here . . . would simply move on to the next human habitation.

General Torion debated riding back to the palace and retrieving Salene from the company of the king, but thought better of it. In Justinian's care, at least there would be no doubt as to her safety. Besides, to return might have insulted the young king, something Torion did not want to do at this delicate juncture.

Having dealt with his lord's requests, the veteran commander had no other pressing duties, but found he did not wish to return to his quarters just yet. The day's affairs had wound him too tight.

At last, Torion decided to make his rounds. He really did not have to perform them anymore, for good men like Captain Mattheus and others generally did them for him, but the familiarity of the old routine would help him relax.

He considered riding to the western gates, but finally chose the ones on the northeastern edge. Those were the ones facing the vaster forest and the mountains, the ones most stripped of men. Now would be a good time to teach those left that, even though they had the quietest section, their smaller numbers demanded greater diligence.

Sentries on duty at points along the way saluted him sharply as he passed. Like them, Torion was wearing his helmet. He disliked the unwieldy thing, but the rain had started up again and the visor actually served better to keep the water out of his eyes than any hood.

However, as he neared the gates in question, Torion noticed several things amiss. The first was that the area ahead seemed far darker than it should have been. Even in the worst weather, there were always a few oil lamps lit, if nothing else. There was also a strange shifting of the shadows, as if they were alive.

Then, he heard the first scream.

"By Rakkis!" The general drew his sword and urged his mount forward. However, the well-trained steed, instead of obeying, balked. Try as he might, Torion could not get the animal to go more than a few steps . . . at which point it always retreated again.

Another cry reached him. Something moved in the shadows, something roughly the size of a cat . . . but with too many legs.

What had Salene told him? A tale about . . . spiders?

"Impossible . . . ," he muttered. "Impossible . . ."

But it was best not to take chances. Something was terribly wrong.

He looked back over his shoulder toward where he had seen the last sentries. "Alarm! Alarm! Possible intrusion at the gates! Intrusion at the—"

A heavy object fell upon the head of his mount. As the horse shrieked, another object dropped onto Torion's arm. Torion had a glimpse of several legs and multiple eyes.

He cut the creature through the back with the edge of his blade. It hissed, then fell from his body. But even as it did, two more dropped upon the general's shoulder.

Still shouting, Torion batted off one. "Alarm! Alarm!"

From down the street he heard the calls of other soldiers. However, the first to appear did so from the direction of the gates. The man, a subofficer Torion recognized, walked awkwardly toward the struggling rider.

Something warned the general that not all was as it seemed. "You there!" he cried, slaying the other creature. "What's going on? What's happened to the rest of your men?"

The soldier did not reply. He continued to close on his commander. Behind him, two others materialized from the dark. They moved in the same jerky manner.

Torion tried to turn his horse around, but now the animal stood as still as a statue. He saw that one of the spiders rested atop its head. Torion angrily slashed at the creature, tearing it free of the horse—

And leaving most of its eight legs still embedded in the unfortunate animal's skull.

Torion had only a moment to register the terrible image

before the horse collapsed. He tried to throw himself to the side, but did not quite make it.

He hit the street with a harsh thud. Pain coursed through his left leg. The veteran soldier tried to move it, only to find it pinned under the body of the horse.

Another spider leapt on his chest. He attempted to slap it off, but the beast held on to his glove with its fangs. Torion gave thanks that the spider had not managed to bite through, for he was certain that the fangs were highly poisoned.

More spiders crawled over him. Why none had bitten him yet, General Torion could not say, but he suspected the answer was not one he would have liked.

A figure loomed over him. The subofficer. With his free hand, the man reached for Torion's head.

No, not his head . . . but rather his helmet.

The general twisted away. As the soldier leaned forward for a second attempt, Torion saw that the man's helmet was slightly askew.

Underneath it, there was movement.

With all his might, the struggling commander thrust up at the soldier. The blade caught the man in the throat. The helmet tumbled off.

As with the horse, a spider perched atop the dead soldier's head. Torion did not have to guess what it was doing there.

He tried to pull back as the body fell, but still his leg was caught. Torion cursed, aware that his options were running out.

Then, light filled his gaze. There were shouts of consternation, but also of determination. The arachnids atop him suddenly scattered as a torch came near.

"We've got you, sir!" called a soldier, seizing his arms.

"Keep your helmets on tight!" he warned. "Watch the shadows! Don't let those spiders get close!"

Even as he said it, a cry alerted him that for one man, the warning had come too late.

There was also a clash of arms. As the general was lifted

to his feet, he saw two soldiers doing battle with a pair of the possessed men from the gates. The latter still moved oddly, but somehow they managed to not only parry every strike, but to counter with their own attacks.

Torion counted the men with him. Seven still trustworthy. A quick scan of the shadows warned him that they would soon not be near enough.

"Retreat! Retreat! Keep those torches and lamps toward them! Hurry!"

Most of them obeyed quickly enough, but the possessed soldier fighting one man suddenly reached up and batted the latter's helmet free. Immediately, a spider leapt atop the hapless fighter, sinking its limbs into his skull with an audible cracking sound. The soldier dropped to his knees for a moment, then, with the same glassy stare, stood up and followed his former opponent.

"Move back, damn you!" Torion continued. He eyed their surroundings. "Clear those buildings, quickly!"

But from within came cries that told the general he was too late for the occupants. Swearing, he started to back up farther, then came to a halt. He stared momentarily at a window next to him.

"You there!" Torion shouted at a frightened soldier. "Your lamp! Hurry, man!"

All but tearing the light out of the other's hands, General Torion threw the lamp at the window. The brass lamp smashed through, breaking in the process and spilling its oil everywhere.

Flames erupted inside, some of them quickly eating away at a curtain on the broken window.

The flames revealed several of the spiders clearly for the first time. Torion had never seen their like before, although they had some resemblance to the fabled Spinners. As far as he was concerned, though, they were nothing but grotesque demons, and if the flames drove them back, as they seemed to, then he wanted all the fire he could muster.

Even if it meant burning down all of Westmarch.

"That other lamp! Into that building!" He had no care about those within, for by now they were either dead or worse.

Flames rose on both sides of the street. A few of the foul arachnids caught fire. The rest pulled away.

Torion prayed that the incessant rain would not dampen both the fires and his hopes. His plan appeared to be working. The flow of monstrous spiders had ceased. They milled around as if not certain what next to do.

Then, one of his men grunted and fell over. Behind him stood what at first appeared to be just another soldier. Only when the figure looked up again did Torion see that the helmet did not quite fit, as if the man attempted to hide something underneath it.

Before anyone could stop him, the possessed soldier ripped off the helmet of the man he had stunned. From the standing figure's back leapt a spider. It landed on the prone sentry and immediately bore its limbs into his head.

Torion suddenly realized that the danger to the city was on a much greater scale than he had imagined. This soldier had not come from the gates. He had joined the party from farther *back.*

The general charged the pair, running the standing one through the throat before he could react, then burying his blade in both the head of the man on the ground and the parasite atop it. Another soldier finished off the spider trapped in the helmet of the first.

Freeing his blade, Torion stared at the tide that was again flowing toward them. "Retreat! Damn it, retreat! And I want every man to flatten his helmet to his skull! Any man not doing so risks execution! Understood?"

He did not wait to hear if they did. The rain was still light enough for the torches to have some effect, but the battle was lost here. Torion cursed, aware that the reinforcements he needed were much deeper into the center of the capital, sent there by his own order at the king's request.

The king! Torion seized a man. "Grab a horse! Ride to the

palace and warn his majesty! Tell him that the entire city is in danger! Tell him we need every man available, especially those he requested for the assembly tomorrow! We'll hold the way as best we can!"

As he sent the messenger off, screams arose from other parts of the city.

"They're everywhere," muttered the veteran campaigner. "They're everywhere . . ." But they seemed to especially come from the direction that Salene had said they would. Torion almost regretted not having told the messenger to bring her back so that he could question her more about this insidious invasion, but then imagined the noblewoman falling prey to a spider. No, he would *never* risk that happening. Best that she stay where she was. In the palace, she would be secure.

Besides, once Justinian received the message, surely help would soon be on the way . . .

TWENTY

The first, distant scream sent Salene leaping to her feet in horror. If she could hear it here in the castle, that did not bode well for the city.

Justinian seized her hand, and although a part of her tried to summon the power that she had used on Torion, nothing happened. The king pulled her back down onto the dais, forcing her next to him.

"You should really calm yourself! All we have to do is wait here until it's the right time! Then, everything will be all right. You'll see . . ."

"All right? But your majesty, what about the people? What about all those people who suffer? What about all those innocent deaths?"

For a moment, the uncertain Justinian that she recalled suddenly reappeared. His hand shook. He quickly glanced to the side, where the specter of Cornelius drifted. Cornelius, who spoke not his own words of wisdom, but the tainted words of Karybdus.

There was more whispering, again nothing that the Lady Nesardo could understand. The anxiety swiftly left Justinian's face. Exhaling, he looked to Salene. "Now, you see? You even had *me* worked up for a moment! Just as I told you, it'll be all right! Father said so, and he knows. He always knows."

Salene had tried to explain the truth about the late king's ghost, but Justinian had not believed her. Nevertheless, she tried a second time. "Your majesty, I believe you when you say that is your honored father, I do, but I tell you again that he is under a *spell*! He speaks the lies of the necromancer, Karybdus! Your father would never have allowed such carnage, for any reason! He loved the people! He protected them! Now, Cornelius is being forced to speak against his own will—"

"Really, am I going to have to silence you again, Lady Nesardo? You know how fond I am of you, but to speak against my *father* so? You accuse him of being nothing more than a puppet! And of the good Karybdus, too!"

She gave up. Justinian could not or would not believe that anyone could command his father, even in death. Worse yet, he saw the necromancer as a trusted adviser! How long had Karybdus planned this travesty?

More screams pierced the thick walls of the palace. The king took another sip of wine, then offered her some.

From another direction and far nearer came words of argument. Justinian cocked his head in curiosity. Salene leaned toward the voices, trying to hear. The frustration in one of them matched her own spent emotions. She hazarded a guess that someone was trying to warn the king, but could not gain entrance.

Moments later, Edmun Fairweather slithered inside. From an innocuous servant, he had become to the noblewoman a fiend as evil as Lord Jitan or Karybdus. She suspected that he willingly participated in the horror now taking place outside.

"What was that disturbance, Edmun?" asked the king.

"As expected, a soldier from the watch. Said he was sent by General Torion. I informed him that you were not to be interrupted at this time. He raised a fuss. I finally had the guards arrest him and throw him in a cell for the night. With your majesty's permission, of course."

Justinian considered. "Well, if it must be. Still, see that he's made comfortable and given food from our kitchen, Edmun. The man was only doing his duty, after all. He didn't know better."

"As you say, your majesty—"

The Lady Nesardo could not hold back. "Edmun Fairweather, I understand why the king acts so, but what about you? You must realize what is happening! Will you stand idly by while this horror takes place?"

His expression remained bland, but his eyes flickered dangerously. "I live only to serve my lord. He commands, I obey."

"And you are splendid in your loyalty, dear Edmun," Justinian said, beaming.

The servant bowed graciously, then departed.

Salene frowned. For some reason, when Edmun Fairweather talked of his loyalty to his lord, she had the feeling that he referred to someone other than the king.

Aldric Jitan? Perhaps. Karybdus? Unlikely. She could not see Edmun so devoted to a necromancer.

She grimaced. She was getting nowhere worrying about such things. Salene had to act.

But how? When she had wanted to leave, Justinian had prevented her with ease. He seemed to be able to wield magic, while her own powers—granted, often unpredictable anyway—now appeared to be failing her utterly. She was certain that it was something the king was doing . . . but what?

Ever aware that the shadow of Cornelius listened to all, Salene said, "I meant to ask before, your majesty: Is such skill with magic something that's run through your family? I've heard no legends . . ."

As the noblewoman had hoped, Justinian was quite willing to talk about himself to her. Perhaps he even thought that she had begun to have interest in him. She did not like toying with the king, but saw no other choice.

"No, no. Nothing of the sort. This is really something of my own! A special gift I received." His hand started to rise to his throat, where, for the first time, Salene noticed a black chain. Whatever the chain held lay atop his chest. "Would you care to—?"

Salene heard the sudden whisper that cut the king off and had no doubt what it concerned. Verifying her suspicions, Justinian quickly shifted his hand to his cheek. He pretended that it had always been his intention to merely scratch his face, as he continued, "I believe, that is, that I'm the first to display the talent. Perhaps on my mother's side. She was descended from royal blood from Lut Gholein, you know. All sorts of mystical things go on there, I'm told. That's where it traces from, yes."

Justinian looked quite pleased at what was to her a very unconvincing explanation. Salene nodded as if she believed him, but her thoughts stayed fixed on the chain and what hung from it. Whatever it was, the noblewoman believed it to be not only the source of the king's new abilities, but the loss of her own.

More cries arose. They were now nearly constant. Her hand trembling, she said, "Your majesty, I believe I would like some wine after all."

"But of course!" The king reached up to the table and took a second goblet. He filled it, then turned to her.

As he did, Salene reached for the goblet. Their hands collided, sending the cup and its contents spilling over the floor. Justinian instinctively grabbed for the fallen goblet.

Lunging, the Lady Nesardo seized the chain and tore it free.

"What—" was all the young monarch could manage before Salene tugged away the object under his shirt. The noblewoman immediately pulled out of his reach.

The object dangling from her hand was a triangular bronze medallion upon which had been engraved an eye surrounded by what appeared to be teeth. The medallion radiated the same kind of dark energies that Salene felt whenever she had to journey through the old dungeons of her home. Clearly, this artifact had not been created with good intentions in mind.

"Give me that!" snapped Justinian, grabbing for Salene. "I need it!"

His arms closed on her—

And suddenly Salene stood *behind* him.

How she had suddenly gotten there, even she did not understand. Justinian whirled, his face now frantic. More and more he resembled the son of Cornelius as she knew him—afraid and uncertain.

"You'll ruin everything! It was all planned so well!" He lunged for Salene a second time.

For a second time, she vanished from one location and appeared in another, this time near the doors. However, now Salene saw that the medallion had momentarily flashed when she had desired to be away from Justinian.

In fact, she also felt the magic flowing through her once again. The medallion, it seemed, was a complex creation. For Justinian, who truly had little or no inherent ability for magic, it gave him *just* enough to make him think himself invincible. Unfortunately against the powers unleashed by Karybdus and Aldric Jitan, Justinian's skills would prove quite laughable.

However, for one with latent power, such as herself, apparently the medallion could do much more. It enhanced her abilities to the point where she could focus her spells as never before.

Which meant that she might at last be able to do *something*— but only if she fled the palace.

Hands seized her from behind in a viselike grip. She felt hot breath upon her neck and heard Edmun Fairweather's foul voice say, "And *what* do you think you do, my lady?"

Justinian clapped his hands. "Praise be that you're here, Edmun! She took the medallion!"

"So I see, your majesty . . ." In whispered words for Salene alone, he added, "But my Lord Astrogha will not allow this!"

Pressing her against his chest with one hand, he pulled the other back.

The king looked panicked again. "Edmun! There's no need for that! Just take the piece from—"

Not waiting to find out what her assailant intended, Salene attempted to do what she accidentally had to Zayl. She touched Edmun's hand with her own and focused her fury into that touch.

But if the noblewoman expected to singe his hand

enough to free herself, what happened was far more startling. There was a rumble, as when a fire leaps to life . . . followed by a shriek from the man behind her.

As Salene tore away, a tremendous wave of heat washed over her. She stumbled a few steps, then turned and witnessed the results of her attack.

Edmun Fairweather was a living inferno. Flames entirely engulfed him, yet touched nothing else, not even the floor beneath him. The fire had spread so quickly that the king's aide was still very much alive . . . but not for long.

Continuing to scream, Edmun dropped something. To Salene's horror, it was a dagger very much akin to the one with which Lord Jitan had intended to sacrifice her.

My Lord Astrogha . . . Edmun had whispered. That the spider's influence reached this far stunned her. How long had Edmun served the demon?

Yet, what mattered was that he would serve no more. The treacherous aide took two steps toward her, then, with a feeble groan, fell. The eager flames continued to consume his twitching form, yet the carpet underneath was not even sooty.

With a choking sound, Justinian fell back onto the throne. He sat there, just shaking his head over and over.

"Father . . . Father . . . ," the ruler of Westmarch finally uttered. "What do I do?"

Hearing that, Salene quickly turned to confront the shade. She would not have Karybdus's foul words come filtering through the mouth of Cornelius's ghost.

But although the specter of the old king remained, the taint that reminded her of the necromancer did not. Cornelius suddenly seemed free of Karybdus's influence. Salene could only assume that whatever spell had been cast upon the old king, removing the medallion from his son had somehow severed it. Moreover, upon hearing the whispered words next spoken, Justinian's expression hardly hinted that Cornelius still followed Karybdus's instructions.

"I did *what*?" The son blanched. He shook his head in renewed horror. "But I never meant—I only did what I thought would make you proud—"

"Your majesty!" the Lady Nesardo interrupted, her use of the term meant for *both*. "Lord Torion sent a messenger! You need to speak with him as quickly as you can! The city will be overrun by creatures . . ." She went on, explaining everything she could in as little time as possible.

"Yes, of course!" Justinian responded once she had concluded. His fingers tapped nervously on the throne's arm. "The men for the demonstration, they should be of help! We must clear the affected areas . . . Guards! Guards!"

It took more shouting to summon the soldiers, Edmun Fairweather apparently having sent them far away. The king gave several anxious commands, more than once glancing at where the ghost of his father stood. Fortunately, only he and Salene could see the specter.

Finishing with the soldiers, Justinian again cocked his head toward his father. "Yes! Yes, he should be!"

"What is it, your majesty?"

"Torion! The general must know that help is on the way! He must understand that he has to hold on! Blazes! Where *is* that messenger?"

Salene fingered the medallion. A daring thought occurred to her. "There may be another, swifter method . . ."

To his credit, he understood immediately. Understood and rightly feared for her. "You can't be serious, Lady Salene! Best to dispose of that foul thing at once! You saw what a cursed fool I was with it—"

"I've no other choice, your majesty . . . *We've* no other choice."

"I forbid it!"

Salene ignored his protests. Shutting her eyes, she clutched the medallion tight to her breast, trying to ignore the chill she felt from it. In her mind, Salene pictured Torion. She had no idea how to actually transport herself to him, just hoped that whatever natural instinct had brought out the skill would enable her to—

It was raining on her.

Shouts filled her ears as she focused on her surroundings. There were fires burning, many of them halfheartedly because of the never-ceasing rain. A scream stirred her to the bone.

Then, she saw the general.

Torion stood outlined by one fire, shouting orders to archers whose bolts were being tipped with rags. Salene guessed that the rags would next be soaked in oil.

From behind her, she suddenly heard a low hiss.

Without hesitation, the noblewoman turned and thrust out her hand. A ball of fire burst from it—just in time catching a huge, black form leaping for her head.

Squealing, the giant arachnid dropped to the ground, its legs curling in as it burned.

"Salene!" Torion came rushing up to her. "It *is* you! Damn, woman! What in blazes are you doing in the middle of all this? You get back—"

"Torion, be quiet! You have to listen!" When he finally clamped his mouth shut, she quickly told him all that had happened.

"Damn it! I should've known! I should've! It was too good to be true about the boy!"

"It couldn't be helped!" Salene insisted. "Not with Edmun, Lord Jitan, and Karybdus all plotting it!"

"Well, good riddance to Master Fairweather, anyway—"

Their conversation was interrupted by more screams. A flow of spiders appeared out of the shadows to the left of the defenders. Two men were caught by the abrupt tide. The spiders swarmed over them. As per Torion's instructions, their helmets were bound tightly to their heads. Unfortunately, finding no manner by which to remove them, several of the spiders finally *bit* the pair.

The effects of the virulent poison were instantaneous. The men screamed and tore at their bites. Harsh spasms shook their bodies.

A breath later, they were dead.

General Torion swore. "Get those torches over there!

Bring another barrel of oil! We lose this section and we've got to back up nearly to the palace!"

It was a choice of burning the capital or falling victim to the spiders. Salene understood exactly the terrible decisions that Torion had to make.

Then, her eyes alighted on one of the barrels of oil. She glanced down at Karybdus's foul amulet, then back at the oil.

"Torion! Have them stand away from that barrel . . . and the one next to it!"

It was to his credit that he obeyed with only a glance at her. The veteran soldier quickly cleared his men away from the barrels, then nodded.

Not certain at all about what she hoped to do, Salene nonetheless concentrated on both containers. At the same time, she tightly clutched the medallion.

As if shot by a catapult, both barrels flew up into the air, then dropped unerringly toward the thickest concentration of the macabre arachnids.

Just before they landed, she pointed at each.

Bolts of flame shot from her hand. They darted toward the barrels with such swiftness that the noblewoman dared not even blink for fear she would not see the results.

The explosions came almost simultaneously. A fiery rain spilled down upon the area . . . and over the spiders. The creatures perished by the scores, roasted alive as quickly as the one that had earlier assaulted her. The shrill hisses they made as they burned made more than one person there cover their ears.

With a gasp, Salene bent over. Her last effort had spent her. There were limits to what she could do, even with the medallion.

Torion saw her collapse. "Salene! Are you ill?"

"I—I'm fine! I just—just have to rest—" She fell against him.

"Small wonder, after *that* display! How did you—"

She shook her head, indicating that she would not speak of it with him.

With an understanding nod, the commander looked over her head to one of his men. "You there! Water for the lady! Hurry!"

"Torion—" the scarlet-tressed woman managed murmured. "Did I—did I stop them?"

He turned her toward the inferno. A few of the spiders in that direction still lived, but they milled about in confusion. The rest were charred heaps. "You've bought us time, aye, Salene. You've done that."

"But only time."

"Unless they stop coming, yes," he admitted.

There was only one thing left for her to do, then, the very thing that she should have done in the first place.

"I've got to go to him."

"Hmm? Him?" General Torion pulled her straight. His eyes glowed in the light of the fires. "You don't mean that devil of a sorcerer—"

"His name is *Zayl*." Her voice softened. "Just Zayl."

"Salene, I forbid it!"

She raised her hand to him. He instinctively pulled back, then grimaced.

"You can forbid me nothing, Torion. I have to go to him. It's our only hope!"

"Then, I'm coming with you!"

The noblewoman stepped back. Her body still cried for rest, but she could not have that luxury. "You're needed here. Westmarch is counting on you, Torion . . ."

"Salene!" He started for her.

Gripping the medallion tight, the Lady Nesardo imagined Zayl. She saw his brave, pale face, his studious eyes, and the brief smile he had shown her. She even envisioned his right hand ungloved, no longer seeing it with revulsion, but with understanding.

There was a terrible wrenching in her gut. The air felt forced from her lungs—

Salene collided with hard, wet earth. The force with which she struck sent the medallion flying from her hand. Even as she rolled to her left, the dazed noblewoman heard a sound like someone dropping a rock into a lake.

Her momentum sent her tumbling along for several more seconds. She was finally able to grasp on to a bush rubbing against her face. Her legs flung forward, but her overall momentum finally stopped.

For a time, all Salene could do was try to get as much air as she could into her lungs. The cold ground, the chill rain . . . none of that mattered. Her head felt as if the hooves of a hundred horses—riders included—were running back and forth over it.

Then, a bright light somewhere ahead caught her attention. She blinked, trying to focus on it. As she did, the pounding in Salene's head subsided and her breathing regulated.

And with her return to something resembling normalcy, Salene recalled Zayl.

Fear for him gave her the strength to push herself up. Her wet hair clung to her head and shoulders. Wiping some away from her face, she looked around. Curiously, despite the rain and mist, there was light enough for her to see her immediate surroundings.

Unfortunately, what she did not see was the medallion. Where it might be was soon painfully obvious. Not far from her, a wide stream, swollen from the downpour, cut across the landscape. She recalled the sound that she had heard.

It was a choice of taking precious time to search the stream or reaching Zayl on her own. Salene did not even know where she was, and could only assume that she had reached the limits of her spell.

That brought another concern to the forefront. *Could* she reach him? If even with the power of the medallion all Salene had done was drop herself into the middle of the vast forest, then how could she trust that her next attempt would do any better? Before stealing away the artifact from Justinian, the noblewoman had never even *tried* such a spell.

Stop it! Salene demanded of herself. *Sardak is gone, Torion and the city are in danger, and Zayl may be moments away from death!* Oddly, Zayl concerned her most of all.

"One quick look," the bedraggled woman muttered. "If I can't find it right away, I'll try to do it myself!"

Her boots constantly slipping on the slick ground, Salene made her way to the stream. It looked to be twice as large as normal and the fury with which it rushed made her wonder if the medallion was even in the area anymore. The small, light piece might very well have been swept much farther down.

But she had to look. Cautiously putting first one foot and then the other into the stream, Salene peered into the water. At least the light from above allowed her to see a bit—

Suddenly wondering about that light, the Lady Nesardo looked up.

A shadowy spider all but covered the lunar orb.

"No . . . no . . ." For the horrific arachnid to be so prominent meant that there was no more time. Karybdus and Aldric had been waiting for just this moment.

Frantically, she leaned down to the stream and splashed away at the water. Here and there, she caught glimpses of the bottom, but saw nothing other than rocks and moss. Salene began to shake.

Then, another light—one that reminded her of the comforting one she had first noticed—appeared among the trees to her left. A subtle yet arresting tone—music?—also seemed to come from that direction. Salene looked at the light . . . and noticed that framed in it was what appeared to be a glorious figure with a long, shadowed hood and a robe of silver. For just a moment, the startled noblewoman also thought she made out wings of fire . . . but when she blinked, they were nowhere to be seen.

"Who is it?" she called, wary of any stranger in the forest.

The figure did not answer, but continued to walk toward her. She imagined it to be male and much taller than herself or even Zayl. The noblewoman cocked her head; the tone resonating from the direction of the stranger touched her as no song she had ever heard.

"Come no farther! Tell me who you are first!"

Still he did not answer. Salene tensed. She doubted that she could summon up so much as enough flame for a candle, much less a bolt to throw at this newcomer. Still, she had no intention of simply standing there while danger possibly threatened.

"Your last warning!" she cried. Salene raised a hand up in preparation. If she could at least summon enough to frighten him . . .

The light behind the figure faded away with such abruptness that Salene had to blink to adjust her eyes.

And when she opened them again, she saw that what approached her was in no manner human.

It was a night howler.

More to the point, by the fur, scars, and, especially, the eyes, she somehow knew it for the one that had carried her off from the temple.

TWENTY-ONE

Karybdus had not survived for more than a century by being unwilling or unable to adapt. He had clearly underestimated Astrogha's reach into the mortal plane from the demon's prison. A careless mistake, but one not insurmountable. The armored necromancer always considered other options in advance, and so he already knew what he had to do.

If Astrogha desired Zayl's body, Karybdus would grant him that . . . for a time. In truth, no one knew a Rathmian's strengths and weaknesses better than one of their own, and that fact worked to Karybdus's advantage. He had already laid a number of subtle spells upon the late Aldric Jitan that would have enabled him to cast out Astrogha when the world was in true Balance; variations of those could be cast upon Zayl. The younger necromancer's own protective spells and inherent power would mask them even better than the ones on Karybdus's aristocratic dupe.

But he had to act fast. Invisible to the mortal eye—with the exception of a skilled spellcaster such as himself—was the work that the demon now did in preparation to taking Zayl. However, the demon was finding Zayl's resistance much greater than expected. Karybdus applauded his counterpart's able, if ultimately futile, defense. It proved the strength of Rathmian training . . . and also bought *him* the time that he needed for his new spellwork.

The so-called Children of Astrogha were simple to fool, little more than weak manifestations of the master demon. Karybdus concentrated. Besides, he would not need long to finish his work.

He withdrew from his belt the ivory dagger taken from Zayl. It was now the key to his plans. Another variation of the life-tap would ensure that, when the time came, the spider demon would find his "superior" body even more fragile than the one for which he had abandoned it.

But as the necromancer surreptitiously began his spells, he failed to notice the black pouch lying to the side. Had he noticed it, he might have seen how what seemed eyeholes lay pressed against it—eyeholes focused in *his* direction.

The legs pressed against Zayl's skull with such force that at any moment he expected them to crush his head. Yet, he knew that what *would* happen would be far more horrifying. Each of the appendages would bore through the bone until they buried deep inside the brain itself. There, they would meld with his mind. Once that happened, there would be only Astrogha, no more Zayl.

But it would not end there. Astrogha would use the necromancer's learning, his abilities, to enhance his own demonic powers. The secrets of the Rathmians would be added to the spider's vast knowledge . . . and surely that would mean a far greater danger to the mortal plane.

How could Karybdus let this happen? Zayl no longer believed that his counterpart had become a victim of his many battles against the Darkness. No, the legendary necromancer was simply mad . . . not that knowing that was any comfort to Zayl.

The insidious voice of Astrogha filled his mind again. *Give in to my will, mortal Zayl, and you will become a god . . .*

I will become nothing! the necromancer returned. *Take what you must, but I will not give it to you!*

He could not understand why the demon did not just possess him as he had Lord Jitan. Surely, Zayl's skull was no thicker than the noble's.

Was there more to it? Could it be that what Zayl knew, what gifts he had, the necromancer had to *surrender* to the demon? Perhaps Astrogha risked losing what he sought if he simply made Zayl an empty host such as Jitan.

So, perhaps there *was* one card still left to play. Now he understood why the spider had worked around Karybdus to draw Zayl to him even before he was freed. After having fought and lost more than once against sorcerers like the Vizjerei, Astrogha sought to ensure that he would never be defeated again.

Zayl knew that he would rather become like Aldric Jitan than grant the demon's monstrous desire. He strengthened his will and felt Astrogha's anger when the latter realized that the Rathmian would not fall prey so readily.

But Zayl hoped that Astrogha did not also realize that there was a limit to the human will. The necromancer wanted his fiendish adversary to lose patience and slay him before he started to falter again. If Zayl's will began to fail and Astrogha noticed, then the demon would surely triumph.

All that you dream, you can have, the spider murmured. *Riches, power . . . an empire . . .*

You mean you will have them . . .

I will not do to you what I did the fool! Astrogha sought to reassure him. *Do you not recall how my followers of old called you their master? Share with me what secrets you hold and I will share mine . . .*

It was not the words themselves that were beguiling, for they were basic and blunt. However, woven into each syllable was another form of magic, a subtle one that burrowed into the unsuspecting mind the way a worm burrowed through a rotting corpse. Merely listening to Astrogha allowed that magic to penetrate one's thoughts . . . unless that one was skilled in deflecting such tricks, as Zayl was.

Yet, again, even he had his limits . . . and they were approaching faster than the Rathmian desired.

But, other than continue to pray for death rather than possession, Zayl could think of *nothing* to do. There was no one there who could help him, either, for there was only Humbart, who lacked even a full skeleton, much less mobility.

If he was to perish, though, Zayl took comfort in one thing. He had sent Salene back to the city. She would escape from there. At least, if he had failed in everything else, he had not failed in that.

Surely, she was safe . . .

He had fought many battles over the span of his career and, at the moment, General Torion would have traded this monstrous struggle for the very worst of them. The best he could say of the situation was that his men were temporarily holding their own. Some reinforcements had arrived to back up those with him, but reports from the rest of the capital indicated that, even when those sent by Justinian arrived, their numbers would not be great. Most of the soldiers Torion had originally expected were now needed elsewhere. It seemed that at this point the spiders were pouring over *every* wall.

But that was not the worst of it. Reports also filtered in concerning many defenders and even innocent civilians who now walked the capital as the living dead, their bodies mounts for the hideous arachnids. Several initial positions had fallen because of soldiers' ignorance of the terrible fate besetting those whose heads were not covered sufficiently. Fortunately, thanks to Torion himself, word had quickly spread as to the danger.

But the spiders kept *coming*. For every one that was skewered on the end of a sword or burnt by oil and fire, there seemed a dozen more—maybe even a hundred.

Where do they all come from? the veteran commander wondered as he helped roll another barrel of oil forward. At least a fifth of the capital was either ablaze or had already been burnt. Even more of it would have been if not for the fact that the rain was growing stronger. It was necessary to fuel every blaze with oil or some other flammable liquid, but finding stockpiles was becoming more and more difficult. Several places where oil and such should have been stored had been emptied out previously. From what little he had gleaned, the orders to do so had been signed by Edmun Fairweather. Torion cursed the dead man constantly and hoped that his fiery demise had been long and painful . . . and even then it would have been too kind for the general's taste.

Passing the barrel on to another soldier, Torion paused for a breath. Justinian, now back to his senses, had turned much of the coordination of the struggle over to his far more skilled and experienced commander. It was not vanity for General Torion to think that, without him, the efforts to save everyone from this nightmare would not be nearly so organized. Of course, he was fortunate in that several of his top officers had so far managed to survive. Wherever possible, Torion had put one of them in charge. His one regret was that no one had seen Alec Mattheus. There had been a message sent much earlier—when capturing Zayl had been the only concern of the evening—that had said the captain intended to take a patrol and follow up a hunch beyond the city walls.

Torion had resigned himself to the fact that the man he had once assumed would be his successor had likely perished out there, fighting to the last against the eight-legged fiends.

Taking another deep breath, the general surveyed the vicinity. A line of archers worked steadily to send oil-soaked fire arrows wherever needed. They were defended by soldiers armed with swords, pikes, and, naturally, torches. To the north . . .

To the north, and heading toward Torion, was a helmed figure that looked much like the missing Alec Mattheus.

The weary commander grinned. He started toward the captain. Alec, his expression dour, slowly saluted the older fighter. In his other hand, the adjutant held a well-used blade.

"Alec, lad!" called Torion, forgoing military protocol. He was too happy to see his aide. With no sons of his own, he secretly considered the captain the equivalent of one. "Where the blazes have you been? Are you all right?"

There was a silence, then, the approaching figure responded, "Yes. I am all right."

His voice had a monotone quality to it that did not surprise Torion. All the soldiers were exhausted, and Alec looked as if he had been dragged through the streets.

"Well, glad I am to see you, lad!" The general glanced back at where the men were moving the barrels. "Maybe you can take over while I see how the others are—"

Out of the corner of his eye, Torion noticed the adjutant reaching toward him in an attempt to wrest away his helmet.

Reflexes honed on the battlefield still barely enabled the older officer to prevent the helmet from being torn free. Torion stared aghast at the captain, refusing at first to believe the obvious.

But all he had to do was look closer at the way Alec's own helmet hung to see that it sat just a little too high. Perhaps he would have noticed it sooner on anyone else than on Captain Mattheus, denial a powerful force.

But soon there was no denying that what stood before him was no longer his trusted aide.

As General Torion drew his sword, the captain thrust. Torion let out a grunt of pain as the tip of the blade cut across the side of his neck, just missing the vein.

He deflected the next attack, noting with concern that the figure before him fought more and more with a style he recognized as akin to Alec's. Well aware of how skilled his adjutant was, Torion pressed harder.

Finding an opening, the veteran commander lunged. His aim was true; the sword cut right through the captain's unprotected throat.

A thick, half-congealed mass that had to be blood dripped out of the horrific wound . . . but Torion's adversary did not even slow.

Swearing, the general stumbled back just in time to avoid a swing to his head. One part of him registered the fact that his opponent was still seeking to strike off his helmet, while another part wondered just how to defeat something already dead. The spider atop Alec Mattheus's body clearly had more control than most . . .

Gritting his teeth, Torion lunged again, and this time, like Alec, he attacked not the body, but the helmet.

Even alive, Captain Mattheus had not quite been the general's equal, and Torion succeeded where his possessed adjutant had not. The edge of his blade caught the helmet's edge. With one twist, it tumbled off, clattering onto the street.

"By Rakkis!" growled Torion as he stared at his true foe. The spider hissed, and Alec's body reacted with a furious series of cuts and slashes against the commander. For a moment, Torion was put on the defensive. His strength began to flag.

No! I will not let this happen! He stared into the face of the man he had considered both his successor and his son and, with a prayer for Alec's soul, thrust.

His blade cut the spider in half. A foul, greenish goo spilled out of the monster.

The captain's expression contorted. His body went through a series of grotesque spasms.

Then, at last, Alec Mattheus dropped limply to the street. His sword still lay tightly gripped in his hand.

Struggling for air, General Torion gazed at the corpse. This one, more than any other, affected him personally. He looked over his shoulder to where other soldiers—and several able civilians—were valiantly struggling to hold back the tide of evil.

And although he had won his own battle, the commander of Westmarch saw that, unless some miracle happened, the defenders would be able to do no more than hold. They were merely mortal, while the spiders kept coming and coming and coming.

It was all up to Zayl, then, General Torion realized. All up to the man he had tried to hunt down.

All up to the necromancer . . . and, Torion suddenly thought, *Salene.*

You delay the inevitable . . . , hissed Astrogha in his mind. *We will be one . . . one . . .*

Zayl felt his will weakening. He knew the demon felt it, too.

And when we are one, I will give you the pleasure of slowly slaying the gray one who thinks me so foolish . . .

He meant Karybdus. So, Astrogha was not so blind. He knew that Karybdus was still a Rathmian and, therefore, a threat.

But did the demon realize just *how* cunning Karybdus was? Zayl was not so certain. Either way, the mortal plane would suffer.

Then, the spider did something that shook Zayl. Even though it still fought a mental duel with the Rathmian, it also began spitting from its mouth a horrific, sticky substance . . . a *webbing* of sorts. True spiders did not spin their webs so, but Astrogha's form was a resemblance, nothing more. The demon continued spitting, the magical webbing wrapping itself around Zayl's feet, his legs, then the rest of him.

Astrogha was preparing for the moment when his host would finally give in to him. The demon desired his true, hellish form, and from Zayl's body he would re-create it.

And there was nothing that the captive necromancer could do about it.

Karybdus watched the spinning with detachment. The full cycle of this rare lunar convergence had little time left to it, but Astrogha clearly would complete his transformation before then. The armored necromancer secreted Zayl's blade in his belt again. Everything was prepared. Astrogha would be permitted his brief return to the mortal plane, accomplish what was necessary for the Balance . . . and then Karybdus would send the arachnid back to Hell forever. There was a fine line; each event, such as unleashing the demon in Westmarch, could be allowed to proceed only so far. One could not let matters get out of hand . . . not that *he* ever let them.

After that, it would be time to move on elsewhere to determine what next had to be done. Karybdus suspected that he had much work ahead of him before the Balance would truly be even. There had been too many generations of Rathmians simply fighting evil. Likely, it would take him another hundred years to set things straight.

But he was *Karybdus,* and so he knew that he would accomplish it . . . no matter what sacrifices—such as Zayl, Lord Jitan, and the innocents in Westmarch—had to be made along the way.

The night howler had carried Salene through the forest at a dizzying pace, the furred giant able to avoid tree limbs and ravines with utter ease even with the human cradled in his arms. When the forest had given way to the high hills, he had proven just as capable, scurrying up rock and avoiding several of Aldric's monstrous servants, whose locations the beast seemed to know in advance.

Salene could still make no sense of the vision that she had experienced prior to the night howler's startling return. The noblewoman could only imagine that her exhaustion, coupled with her risky use of magic, had combined to addle her senses for a moment. Besides, of a far more important concern was finding Zayl before it was too late.

Which seemed exactly what the forest dweller wanted, too. Unable to make sense of his grunts, Salene finally assumed that somehow the necromancer had communicated with the night howler and showed the beast how to find her. That was the only explanation for his being in the right place at the right time.

It gave her hope . . . not much, but some.

But now, as they neared the place where she had almost been sacrificed, Salene's fears magnified. In addition to sighting several of Lord Jitan's mutated servants, there were also about half a dozen men . . . if one could call them that anymore. They strode around as if sleepwalking and each wore some odd headpiece. Their expressions, to the extent that she could make them out in the light emanating from within, seemed slack, lifeless.

Worst of all, she recognized them as some of Alec

Mattheus's men, the ones who had followed the captain in pursuit of the necromancer.

And the fact that they were here and clearly under the control of Zayl's adversaries could only make her assume that Zayl himself was now a prisoner. Even Salene could sense the ghastly forces emanating from the ancient ruins, forces which, had he been free, the Rathmian would have surely put an end to by now.

"He's in there, isn't he?" she whispered to the night howler. "They have him, don't they?"

The creature's low grunt was unintelligible, but somehow his tone made the noblewoman think that she had guessed correctly.

Nothing good could come of Zayl's being a prisoner of Jitan and the other necromancer. Salene determined to rescue him, if nothing else. Somehow, if she managed to free Zayl, surely he would come up with a way to defeat the madmen.

But the only thing Salene could think to do was to go charging in the front. The night howler had shown her where a tunnel led in through the back, but it was well-guarded by the man-spiders and seemed a path less likely to success than the main opening.

She would have liked to have gotten a better look at the front entryway, but for some unknown reason, her gargantuan companion would not let her stray any closer. It was as if he sensed something that she did not.

Thinking of all she had done with and without the medallion, Salene chose her best options. What she would do upon entering was clear; reaching that point was another matter.

"If we could only draw them away . . ." But there were far more guards than ever and, when she squinted, Salene thought that she even saw *spiders* crawling over the hill. So many spiders that she could not believe it.

That made her think of what was happening in Westmarch. She suddenly glanced at the night howler again, wondering how the two of them had managed to avoid the vast swarm. The vision of the robed, winged figure once more came to mind, but it hardly seemed compatible with what stood next to her.

She shook off such mysteries. The Moon of the Spider hung high overhead. Salene sensed that soon it would vanish and that when it did, all would be lost.

Staring at the terrifying guardians, she whispered, "I think I know how I might be able to get some of them to move, but—"

Only then did Salene discover that she suddenly spoke only to empty air. How had such a giant left her side without her noticing? She looked around, fearful that something had befallen the forest dweller . . .

But in the next breath, there was a powerful roar and a crashing sound—then a muffled hiss that Salene recognized as one of the monstrous sentries dying violently.

Immediately, most of Aldric's servants surged forward as a single pack. The soldiers and the spiders followed suit. A few stayed where they were, but now Salene had hope. If she could repeat what she had done in the throne room . . .

"Please . . . ," she prayed, not quite knowing to whom. "Let this work."

Salene focused on an area near the entrance, one momentarily devoid of guards.

Suddenly, she stood at the very spot.

One of the remaining monsters started to turn in her direction. Salene focused on what she could recall of the interior, choosing a location near the inner entrance. She hoped that choosing such an out-of-the-way place would keep her from being immediately discovered.

She vanished from the first location, just missed by the sentinel.

And materialized a second later into a nightmare.

Zayl, it appeared, was about to be *eaten.*

His will was failing. Zayl knew that he had but seconds left before his defenses crumbled and Astrogha was able to take *everything*. After that, it would require only a few short minutes for the demon to finally fully manifest.

If he still had his dagger, it would have been different. So closely bound already to the spider, Zayl could have used the dagger to better effect against Astrogha's powers.

But he did not have his dagger.

Karybdus did.

Karybdus heard the howl. He focused, seeking the cause. At the very edge of his perception, he sensed the night howler. The Rathmian found it curious that the beast would be just there, where he was *barely* noticeable. Karybdus did not believe in coincidence. Something was wrong.

A moment later, he sensed the presence of another . . . one familiar to him.

The woman. The Lady Salene Nesardo.

His bland expression hiding his surprise, Karybdus whirled in the direction he knew the woman had to be. Yet, when he looked, she was not there. Instead, the necromancer sensed her to his right.

Yet, the noblewoman was not there, either.

Karybdus's brow furrowed as he suddenly realized what was happening.

But understanding came too late, as a bolt of fire struck him in the chest, sending the armored spellcaster hurtling into the wall behind.

Shaking, Salene stared at the black-clad villain, praying that he would not immediately rise. When Karybdus did indeed stay prone, she turned back to the terrifying spectacle.

Sardak's mutilated body lay nearby, the horrible things done to it nearly causing his sister to vomit. She immediately understood that they had used his blood—even poisoned—as they would have hers.

But even worse to her than that was what was happening to Zayl. He still lived, but now lay all but totally bundled up in a large sac, out of the top of which his head and skeletal hand partially thrust.

And atop his head, a monstrous spider so hideous that it could not have been born in the mortal world continued to spit webbing from its mouth as its legs held the necromancer's skull pinned.

The spider's eyes glittered, and she was certain that it registered her presence. Nevertheless, it did nothing but continue to confidently spin its webbing over its victim. It acted as if it had no worry concerning the newcomer.

The noblewoman quickly found out why. Movement above barely warned Salene of attack. She pointed up and just managed to catch one of Aldric's servants as it attempted to drop on her.

As it landed in a fiery heap near her, the Lady Nesardo wondered just where the treacherous noble was. Her answer came a moment later as she looked past Zayl. One glance at what remained of Aldric was all that Salene needed to understand that she could hesitate no longer.

Worse, from within and without, more of the mutated servants began converging on her location. Now she understood why the beast atop Zayl had not been concerned—it had apparently summoned them. The others were wary of her, especially having seen how she had dealt with Karybdus, but their numbers would soon give them the courage they needed to attack. In the meantime, they bought the larger spider the time it required for its insidious work.

Salene eyed Zayl. All her most successful spells so far had had to do with either teleporting her or unleashing fire, neither of which helped the necromancer. She doubted that she could destroy the spider without killing Zayl as well, but if she did nothing—

"Lass!" called a welcome, familiar voice. "My lady!" shouted Humbart from somewhere. "Over to the side here!"

Hissing, two of the servants leapt at her. Instead of throwing fire at them, Salene instinctively shifted position. She ended up near Humbart's torn pouch while the two monstrosities tumbled in a confused heap. The others hesitated, not certain how to adjust to this new challenge.

"Good lass!" the skull commended. "Neat trick, that!"

"Never mind! Is there anything I can do for Zayl?"

"Only one thing! Give him his dagger back! It'll help him! I promise!"

She quickly looked around. "But where is it?"

"That damned Karybdus has it! In his belt! I saw it!"

Eyeing the still form, Salene hesitated. "His belt?"

"'Tis the best, possibly only chance!"

That was all Salene needed to hear. She took one last glance at Karybdus, assuring herself that if he was not dead, he was certainly unconscious.

A moment's thought and she stood next to the deadly necromancer. With a glimpse around her to make certain that none of the creatures was near, she bent to Karybdus's side and pushed away his cloak.

There! Salene drew the ivory dagger from his belt—

And, at that moment, Karybdus opened his eyes.

"No," he murmured. "I think not."

His gloved hand seized her wrist. Salene tried to transport away . . . but nothing happened. She attempted a bolt of flame, with a similar lack of results.

"I have sized up both your abilities," Karybdus explained, as if speaking to an apprentice being tested. "And have compensated for them. There is nothing you can do."

Salene took a desperate swing at him with Zayl's dagger. He deftly caught her other wrist.

"Nothing," he repeated. "Absolutely nothing."

TWENTY-TWO ⊕

Salene struggled to free herself, but the necromancer's grip proved unbreakable. She avoided his direct gaze, aware what it could do. Even then, Salene knew that, sooner or later, Karybdus would either drain her strength from her as he had done once before or use some other diabolical spell to put an end to her.

She eyed Zayl's dagger. If she had at least been able to give it to him, her sacrifice would have been worth something. Humbart had said that, with it, Zayl would have had a fighting chance.

If somehow she could achieve *that*—

An invisible force tore the dagger from her hand. At first, she thought it the work of Karybdus, but an angry grunt from her foe told her that it was not so.

The dagger fluttered above, as if waiting. Salene stared at it, wishing that it would somehow return to Zayl.

No sooner had she thought this than the ivory blade darted toward the younger necromancer.

It was her *will* that guided it, Salene realized. *She* was the one making it fly to Zayl.

"No!" Karybdus tried to shift her so that the Lady Nesardo would be forced to look into his eyes. Salene struggled to maintain a general view of where Zayl lay.

Without warning, a huge form burst into the chamber. The night howler, bleeding everywhere and with one arm hanging uselessly, dragged in with him seven servants clinging to his body. Each step clearly took extreme effort, but the forest dweller did not stop. When one of those atop him moved too near his good hand, he quickly grabbed it by the head and simply crushed its skull.

His presence drew the other servants from Salene. Seeing the giant as the most immediate danger to their master, they fell upon the night howler with abandon.

Karybdus's attention was also momentarily caught by the night howler's stunning arrival, and that proved all that Salene needed. Pulling up slightly, she fixed on Zayl's protruding hand.

The dagger slid down between the webbing, fitting perfectly into the skeletal grip.

Salene felt Karybdus's hand release her wrist. But before she could react, his fingers tightened around her throat.

"You are endangering the Balance," he told her, only a slight inflection in his words indicating his tremendous anger. "There is no greater crime. You *will* be punished . . ."

Zayl felt numb all over. His mind could barely focus, yet his will still struggled to keep from allowing Astrogha inside.

Then, a wonderful and familiar warmth touched the hand that could feel it least. The necromancer's bony fingers tightened around something lying in the fleshless palm.

And, instantly, Zayl's hopes revived.

The words came instinctively, words in the special tongue taught by Trag'Oul to Rathma centuries before.

Words which caused the ivory dagger he now held to flare bright and powerful.

Zayl felt the spider's sudden revulsion. As best he could, the trapped spellcaster twisted the dagger to wherever he sensed Astrogha to be.

One leg pulled away from his skull. The pressure on the Rathmian's mind decreased accordingly. Encouraged, Zayl turned the blade back and forth. More legs withdrew and strands of webbing fell away as if air.

Better able to move his head and arm, Zayl struggled to free himself from the hideous sac. His head suddenly pounded and he realized that Astrogha was desperately trying to overwhelm him.

I deny you! he told the demon. *Slay me, but you will never have me!*

The pressure vanished. Zayl hesitated, strongly suspecting that it was a trick.

The spider dropped from his head.

Even as he silently rejoiced at his harrowing escape, the necromancer grew concerned over what Astrogha now planned. Time was rapidly running out for the demon to achieve his rebirth. Astrogha had to have something else in mind to give up on Zayl.

Bearing that in mind, Zayl furiously cut away at the thick webbing. Each moment, he expected Astrogha or one of Astrogha's servants to attack, but none did. And where was Karybdus in all this? Surely his rival would not permit him to so easily escape.

As he cleared away the webbing, though, Zayl at last noticed other sounds, unnerving sounds. He heard a pained roar that could have only come from the night howler, who had somehow returned. There were the manic hisses of the transformed servants, the man-spiders obviously flinging themselves on the forest dweller. The necromancer even heard *Humbart's* frantic voice... calling to him.

"Zayl! Zayl, lad! He's got her, that bastard has! Karybdus! And he's—sweet mother! Get away from there quick, lad! It's swelling!"

The last referred to something near Zayl, something he was just noticing himself. He sensed Astrogha using the weakened boundaries between the planes to draw the power he needed to re-create his true self.

But what did the demon use for a body?

Zayl had only to look up to see. Astrogha had returned to Lord Jitan's remains, seizing them before they could grow too cold to use. The spider had covered much of the body with his webbing and already some horrific transformation had begun, for within, the noble's corpse had grown more massive than any mortal human's could ever be. Already it rivaled even the night howler, and it continued to swell.

Zayl muttered a spell and cast the dagger. It flew unerringly at the huge white sac—only to bounce off as if it had hit steel.

As the blade returned, a mournful cry snared his attention from the seemingly invulnerable demon. With a full score of attackers upon him, the powerful night howler had finally been overwhelmed. The brave creature dropped to his knees. He managed to batter another of his adversaries into pulp, then, with a defiant groan, fell facedown onto the stone floor.

Zayl gestured. The Teeth of Trag'Oul materialized in force and, driven by his masked rage, pincushioned the creatures atop the furred giant. The Children of Astrogha per-ished as one, living only but a breath or two longer than their valiant opponent.

But there were still others, and worse, he saw Karybdus and Salene struggling near the far wall. There were forces gathering around the other Rathmian. They were forces which Zayl recognized as the formation of a most terrible spell . . . a spell which Karybdus planned to focus upon the Lady Nesardo.

Gritting his teeth, Zayl looked to the dead night howler and began muttering the words. He would not let Karybdus harm Salene or anyone else ever again.

The words were simply spoken, but the effort drained Zayl as even his struggle against Astrogha had not. Yet, as he watched the mists swirl above the giant's corpse, he felt darkly satisfied.

"Karybdus!" Zayl roared. "Karybdus! As you seem to no longer make use of your soul, I see no reason why you should even carry it with you anymore!"

As he hoped, his counterpart could not help but look his way, disrupting Karybdus's own spell at the same time.

Above the night howler, a skeletal form—a bone spirit —with a vague resemblance to the furred giant rose high up in the air on wings of ether. In many ways, it resembled the crypt fiend that had attacked Zayl, but it was so much more.

With a vengeful howl, it flew toward Karybdus.

The other Rathmian's reflexes were swift, but even Karybdus could not move out of the way in time. Instead, he forced Salene in front of him just as the bone spirit reached the pair.

But, unlike the crypt fiend, the thing that Zayl had called up did not attack so indiscriminately. Those Zayl desired protected had nothing to fear from it. Salene was perfectly safe, even used in so base a manner as her captor just had.

Karybdus, however, was not protected. In less than the blink of an eye, the revenant darted around the Lady Nesardo. The armored necromancer did not even have time to gape as the bone spirit thrust its skeletal claws through his chest—

And pulled them free a moment later bearing a silver glow in their grip. The shrieking specter immediately returned to the night howler's body, then dropped through it into the realm of the dead.

Along with it, it took Karybdus's soul.

Or had it? Even as Salene ran to Zayl, the gray-haired spellcaster—who had appeared ready to collapse—straightened again. Ashen-faced but still menacing, Karybdus rasped, "A bit . . . of soul . . . lost . . . is not so burdensome as you . . . might think, young Zayl. . . . Over the years, I have lost some before, but I have . . . always replaced it . . ." He raised a hand toward the running Salene. "From those who truly no longer need it . . ."

"Salene!" Zayl shouted. "Watch out!"

His own reactions too slow, Zayl feared the worst for her. Yet, as Karybdus gestured and the Talon of Trag'Oul formed, Salene suddenly *vanished*. The bone spear instead struck the wall beyond, with such intensity that the entire chamber shook and chunks of ancient mortar came crashing down. A chain reaction started, huge cracks quickly running all the way back to where Karybdus stood.

As for Salene, she now stood next to a distracted Karybdus, in her hand a weapon of which Zayl was all too familiar.

The sacrificial dagger used on Sardak.

"For my brother!" the Lady Nesardo cried.

She started to plunge the heinous blade into the back of Karybdus's neck, only to have his monstrous familiar leap out from the confines of the cape. As the spider tried to bite her, Salene defended herself and slew it.

But from Karybdus's reaction, she might have indeed plunged the dagger into him. He let out an uncharacteristic cry and shoved her back. As his familiar tumbled into his arms, the stricken necromancer knelt to the floor and began frantically trying to heal the gaping wound.

A shaken Salene materialized by Zayl. Helping him to his feet, she stared at the necromancer with red eyes.

"Zayl, I—"

"Never mind!" He pulled her back just as another servant leapt at them. Zayl held high his dagger, its light blinding the creature in mid-leap. It collided with the stone altar and before it could recover, the necromancer stabbed it through the parasite atop the head. That done, Zayl held the dagger to his lips, then muttered. Around them suddenly formed a large barrier of bone, against which the other servants battered themselves to no avail.

Taking a deep breath, the Rathmian continued, "We must deal with Astrogha! Before time runs out for all of us!"

She looked at the monstrous transformation and shook her head, unable to utter any answer. Zayl understood exactly how she felt, for the demon's work was nearly done. The sac had swollen to twice the height of the night howler and more than that in width. Within it and partially silhouetted by the sourceless glow, something that was no longer Aldric Jitan stretched and shaped. It had some semblance to the mutated servants, yet was clearly more foul. There were eight limbs and an overall appearance akin to an arachnid, but with some touches in the shape that were more human. A huge, bulbous head sat atop, one with large clusters of eyes evident. Movement at the front of the head marked what was surely a pair of mandibles. Through the webbing, coarse black hair—the demon's coat—thrust out in many places.

Zayl eyed the ceiling. He sensed that the Moon of the Spider had nearly reached its conclusion and that the shadow would soon vanish. If that happened and nothing had been done to stop Astrogha, then the demon would complete his transformation and walk the world in his true form, with all his powers at their peak.

If that happened, there would surely be no hope for Westmarch, and perhaps for the rest of the Western Kingdoms.

But what could Zayl do? He had failed at every turn to outwit Karybdus and the demon, and in rescuing Salene had only given them Sardak to use as a sacrifice instead—

Of course! the Rathmian abruptly thought. *It is all in the blood!*

He spun toward Salene. "Listen to me and forgive me for what I ask, my lady! There is but one hope to cast Astrogha out before he is completely a part of this plane! Your blood—"

"My *what?*"

"Be at ease! We need not much! Not even that what we took in your house to summon Riordan! Only enough to tip red the point of the dagger you took! You are of the line of Astrogha! Your blood is that of two realms—"

Salene did not want to hear his words. "I am descended from *that* thing?"

"Only by the blood!" the Rathmian insisted. "There is no other link! Your heritage is human, of this plane, but the fact that you have that one link to the demon is not only his blessing, but his doom! What allows him to bind himself here can also *sever* that connection!"

A horrific, ripping sound filled the chamber. From within the sac, a frightful limb that ended in five clawed but human hands reached out, feeling the air.

The Lady Nesardo's expression hardened. "What must I do?"

"Give me the dagger . . . and your wrist."

She offered both freely. Zayl, with an apologetic expression, wiped clean the blade, then pricked her wrist.

Defying gravity, the blood flowed *up* the point. Zayl watched patiently, despite the constant assault by the monstrosities beyond the bone wall and Astrogha's emergence.

"Done!" he finally announced. Whispering over the dagger's edge, he watched in satisfaction as a dim, green glow covered both weapon and blood. He then handed the dagger back to Salene.

"Only you can do this. His bloodline, your blood, your hand. I apologize that it must be so—"

Wielding the dagger like a fearsome warrior, Salene replied, "Just tell me how to strike! I've lost too much because of that *fiend*!"

"The head. It must be the head. Between the eyes. There is little time."

"Then, I should go, shouldn't I?"

And even as Salene said it, she disappeared.

Zayl almost reached out to her, but knew he could change nothing. They were both very much aware that it was possible that, even assuming she succeeded, Salene would perish.

But the necromancer was determined to do what he could to prevent such from happening. His own blade held ready, he turned to Astrogha. Two more of the macabre limbs had freed themselves and now they tore off the webbing covering the demon's face.

"*Yesssss!*" Astrogha hissed. "*To my glory am I returned! The world shall my children devour!*"

Salene materialized on his back. She thrust the blade in exactly where Zayl had said.

The demon howled in agony as the dagger readily slid in. He shook vehemently, and only because she held on to the hilt did Salene keep from falling to her death.

But, despite the necromancer's calculations, Astrogha

did not die. The Moon of the Spider had progressed too far for even this method to destroy the demon. He felt torment, certainly, but no more.

Clawed hands sought after the Lady Nesardo, tearing at her garments with fiendish abandon. Zayl realized that she was so distraught, she could not concentrate enough to teleport herself away.

"To me, Salene!" he shouted. "With the dagger! Hurry!"

The wall of bone suddenly shook, but not due to the efforts of Astrogha's children.

Karybdus, his face white and contorted, stretched forth his hand toward his rival. The barrier shook again, this time pieces crumbling off. "I will . . . not permit you . . . to undo my years of effort! Poisoning the heir to the throne, manipulating that buffoon of a noble, and working on the weak mind of the new king . . . I will not permit it!"

The rest of the wall finally shattered . . . just as Salene appeared, falling into Zayl's arms.

"It—it didn't work, Zayl!"

"I know, but there is one more chance! You have the dagger?"

In response, she held up the weapon. In addition to her own blood, there was now on the tip a dark ichor that Zayl recognized as what passed for some demons' life fluids. Despite the intensity with which Salene had buried the blade into Astrogha, there were only a few drops.

They would have to do. But there was still the danger of the other necromancer.

"Salene! Whatever power you can throw at Karybdus, do it now! Hurry!"

He spoke none too soon, for the armored Rathmian was already casting. Salene unleashed a raw burst of fire in his direction.

Better prepared this time, Karybdus easily turned it away, ignoring the Children of Astrogha who perished in the flames simply because they stood in its new path. Still, it forced him to begin anew his spell, which was all Zayl asked.

As for the demon, all but one of his grotesque limbs was free. Shreds of Lord Jitan's garments hung here and there and in the monstrous countenance of the arachnid Zayl could just make out vague features once belonging to the noble. The spider might not have gained Zayl's learning and powers, but Aldric's certainly augmented Astrogha's own. The arachnid was now far more formidable than when he had faced the Vizjerei.

With two limbs, the demon clutched the wound in its head. Black fire coursed from the area as Astrogha healed himself.

Yes, it was obviously too late to destroy the fiend, but Zayl no longer had that in mind.

Whispering his spell and drawing an oval shape with three crosses upon it, the necromancer touched the sacrificial dagger's tip to his own and pointed both, not at Astrogha, but rather at the discarded remains of the demon's former prison.

This is the place where the two realms are closest, where the boundaries are weakest, Zayl reminded himself as he concentrated. *This is why the Vizjerei created the sphere here and why they attempted to destroy this temple afterward!*

He heard a cry from Salene, but dared not break his concentration. It was now or never . . .

The shell that had been the Moon of the Spider opened like a flower . . . or perhaps a hungering mouth. The sphere swelled and as it did, Zayl felt a great wind arise. A wind rushing *into* the artifact.

"*Whole I am again!*" hissed the giant arachnid, not yet noticing what happened behind him. He eyed the necromancer. "*Yours the first blood upon which I will sup!*"

Four of the limbs darted toward the necromancer, and even then, Zayl did nothing but focus.

The clawing, grasping hands came within inches of his body—and could reach no farther. They struggled against an invisible but irresistible force.

"*What is this?*" demanded Astrogha.

"I am returning you to the only world you will ever rule,

demon!" yelled the necromancer. "The only one you deserve!"

The gargantuan spider peered behind it . . . and for the first time, Zayl heard fear in the demon's voice. "*No! Not there! In there I will not go! Never again!*"

"But you must! You have no choice!"

Within the swollen shell, a vast emptiness beckoned. The wind grew stronger. Zayl's cloak flowed madly toward the artifact, but the Rathmian was able to stand his ground.

One of Jitan's transformed servants was ripped from the wall to which it clung and went flying past both Zayl and the demon, vanishing into the shell. Another followed, then another. As the Children of Astrogha, they were cursed as the demon was and so had to share his fate.

However, then something else happened for which the Rathmian had not planned. On the ground near the altar, Sardak's body shook as if suddenly alive. It slid slightly toward the direction of the shell, only to become caught between several large chunks of stone that had fallen from the ceiling.

The Nesardos, too, were bound to Astrogha, which meant that they were also in danger of being sucked into the orb.

Fearing for Salene, Zayl momentarily dared take his focus off his spell. Only then did he discover that, to his horror, she lay unmoving on the floor. Her body also sought to slide toward the sphere, but, like her brother's, had momentarily become wedged.

The necromancer tried to reach her, only to be suddenly pulled toward the struggling Astrogha. The demon had managed to snag his leg. The small but vicious clawed hands tore at his garments, ripping through the skin in some places.

Leg nearly buckling, Zayl tore his dagger from the spell-work and slashed at the clutching hands.

Hissing, the demon released his hold. Astrogha now clung to the edges of the gigantic shell, desperately seeking purchase. He spat webbing Zayl's way, but it landed short, draping over the altar. If the demon thought the heavy stone piece would save him, he was horribly mistaken. Instead, as the tension increased, the altar came loose. The demon's efforts to pull himself toward it instead sent the altar flying at him like a catapult missile.

It struck the spider full in the torso. Astrogha's grip failed. With a frantic hiss, the gigantic arachnid went spiraling into the blackness. "Nooo!" he cried. "Noooo . . ."

Astrogha vanished, but the orb continued to suck in all things bound to the arachnid. Behind him came the rest of his horrific children, each of the creatures scrambling for purchase they could not find.

Zayl felt even the sacrificial dagger seek to follow Astrogha into the shell, but the Rathmian needed it a few moments more. He had to be absolutely certain that the sphere would seal . . .

An armored forearm wrapped around his throat. In his ear, he heard Karybdus snarl, "You have ruined everything! The Balance may never be put even now! You blind fool!"

"The only one—blind—" Zayl managed, twisting around so that the two faced one another, "—is *you*, Karybdus! Blind, to your madness, to your evil!"

The older necromancer paid his words no mind. "Give me the dagger! There is still time to remedy this!"

Few moments had there had been in his life when Zayl had felt true rage. The greatest was that day when his spell, needed to cast out the evil against which he and his parents fought, also destroyed by cleansing fire everyone but Zayl. That Zayl had survived—almost completely unscathed—had ignited an anger at himself with which he had fought for years afterward. He had even dared the unthinkable, trying to fully resurrect his parents and, in their place, give his soul to the realm of the dead. Only the work of his mentors had kept him from creating an even worse disaster and finally forced him to come to grips with the fact that he could not have changed what had happened to the only ones for whom he had ever deeply cared.

But if there was an anger approaching that, it was what Zayl now felt for Karybdus, whom he had once admired so greatly. Karybdus had made an abomination out of everything Zayl believed in. He had become what all outsiders feared the Rathmians were. Worse, at their feet lay a woman who had come to Zayl for help, a woman who had affected him in a manner unaccustomed. The thought that Salene was dead, dead at Karybdus's hand, was the final impetus the younger necromancer needed.

"The dagger is yours, Karybdus!" he cried into the other's face. "May the Dragon take you both!"

He thrust Astrogha's blade into his adversary's chest. Where nothing else had penetrated the enchanted armor, the demonic dagger—fueled by every last iota of Zayl's magic and, even more, by his will—bore through the metal as if it were soft mud.

Karybdus gaped as the blade cut through his black, soul-lost heart.

Zayl spun him around, so that the gray-haired spellcaster's back was to the closing shell.

"The Balance shall be maintained," he whispered to Karybdus.

Zayl shoved his foe as hard as he could, releasing his grip on the dagger. Karybdus made a desperate but feeble grab at Zayl's cloak . . . and failed.

With a wordless cry, the armored necromancer went hurtling after the spider demon and his fiendish get. Karybdus struck the gap just before it would have been too small to take him. He grasped at the edges, but with no more success than Astrogha. Karybdus was sucked inside.

His scream ended only when the Moon of the Spider at last sealed itself shut.

Spent, Zayl dropped to one knee. Around him, the temple, stressed far too much by the powerful forces in play, began collapsing. The necromancer paid it little mind, caught between his regret for Salene and the sinister orb.

As the insidious lunar phase finally passed, the sphere suddenly began to shrink, rapidly returning to its former state.

Zayl knew that he had to do one last thing. Even if the temple was falling apart, the Moon of the Spider could not remain here. It was too close to the weakness between the planes. Even the slightest risk that Astrogha might somehow free himself again could not be taken. And then there was Karybdus . . .

Zayl tried to rise and when that failed, forced himself to crawl. The orb, now no larger than when Aldric Jitan had wielded it, taunted him with its closeness, but more and more Zayl suspected that it would remain out of his reach. He could go no farther.

Then, a pair of powerful hands gripped him at the shoulders, lifting him as if he were a baby. Zayl could only imagine that the night howler had somehow survived and now sought to aid him. He tried to thank the unseen forest dweller, but words proved past him.

At last, Zayl could touch the Moon. Clinging to it for support, he pressed his dagger against the side and uttered one last spell.

They came as shadows, all three. He had felt their distant presence since the first time he had come here. Little more than shadows, they were still clearly to him Vizjerei. Karybdus had done something upon entering this place to eradicate their threat, but even as only memories of men, they would do for Zayl.

Swallowing, he managed to say, "The . . . the Moon . . . take it! I command you to bury it at the bottom of the deepest point in the most obscure body of water possible, there never to be found by man, demon, or angel ever again!"

The middle of the three reached down and, with hands of smoke, took the Moon of the Spider into his vaporous arms.

It will be done, came a whisper in the necromancer's ear. *And gladly . . .*

And with that, specters and orb disappeared.

Rolling onto his back, Zayl prepared to order the night howler to take Salene's body back to the gates of the city, so that she could at least have a proper burial. To his surprise, however, nothing stood above him. When he twisted his head to the side, it was to discover that the night howler lay where last he had seen the furred giant. The creature had done nothing to help him; in fact, Zayl finally recalled that he had even summoned the brave creature's spirit against Karybdus.

Then . . . what?

Before he could answer that question, a groan from his side made him tense. A feminine groan with only one possible source.

Turning back on his stomach, Zayl attempted to crawl again. A second groan reached his ears.

"Salene . . . ," he whispered. "Salene . . ."

And suddenly, the Rathmian heard, "Z-Zayl? Zayl?"

He permitted himself a brief smile . . . and then promptly passed out.

Throughout the city, and especially where General Torion fought, the situation had grown beyond hope. There seemed more spiders than leaves on the trees of the entire forest, and they moved with a relentlessness unmatched by even the most dedicated defender.

In the general's mind, it was the end of Westmarch.

But then . . . but then a strange and glorious thing happened. As one, the sea of arachnids came to an abrupt halt. They simply ceased moving. Certain that it was some horrific trick, the humans hesitated.

And then, before their eyes, the spiders began decaying. By the hundreds, they simply crumbled to ash. It was as if something had drained all life from them in one astonishing instant. Some were caught in mid-stride, others atop their hosts. Wherever they were seen, they perished there and then without the least warning.

Now covered in ash and bereft of any control, their victims collapsed like rag dolls. The falling bodies scattered the dust that had been the terror of the kingdom, and the rain, now pouring harder, quickly began washing away the nightmare.

Someone let out a nervous laugh. It proved contagious, spreading from one survivor to the other in the space of a few seconds. The laughter, more of a release than anything else, soon encompassed the capital.

And General Torion, commander of the king's forces, laughed the loudest, for he knew better than any other what sort of escape had been granted to not only his people, but to the rest of the Western Kingdoms as well.

TWENTY-THREE

Voices reached his ears, both of which Zayl recognized even through the door. His gloved fingers hesitated on the handle as he listened.

"Justinian still insists on meeting him, Salene. I actually believe that he wants to give the man a medal."

"Now what would the Church say about *that*, Torion? The king of Westmarch honoring a necromancer in the heart of their domain? The Zakarum elders would have fits!"

There came a chuckle from the general. "Might be worth it just to see what they'd do!"

"Well, I can tell you that Justinian will have to be disappointed. Zayl would never accept such glories."

"And what *would* he accept as a reward . . . or should I say *who* would he accept?"

The Rathmian deemed this the moment to open the door before the conversation turned very uncomfortable for all.

General Torion and Salene stood just inside the sitting room entrance. Both turned in surprise toward the Rathmian. The officer was clad as he had been the first time he and Zayl had met, save that this time he wore his helmet even in the presence of the Lady Nesardo. Zayl could hardly blame him; he suspected that many of the capital's citizenry were keeping their heads covered after the horror of the week before.

Salene's expression blossomed when she saw the Rathmian, and he felt an unfamiliar lightness fill him. Maintaining a look of indifference despite his inner emotions, he bowed his head to her. She was clad in a wide, flowing gown of forest green and silver, with ruffled trim around the shoulders and the bound bodice. Her hair tumbled down over both shoulders and a string of pearls decorated her throat. Although Zayl had refused three invitations by Justinian IV to come to the palace, Salene had finally granted the king his request to see her. In this manner, she was able to explain matters to the satisfaction of Westmarch's young ruler.

She was also able to promise that what she knew of his part in the night of terror would never be spoken of by her to anyone. Justinian's guilt was great, but he had been manipulated in the most cruel fashion possible, and even Zayl saw no good coming from letting the truth be known. General Torion had the right of it when he had told them that Justinian's downfall would only mean more bloodshed and havoc than had already occurred.

"Sorcerer," greeted Torion.

"General," Zayl returned, matching the other's brevity. To Salene, however, he said, "I am pleased that you arrived back so soon, my lady."

"Are you really?" Her eyes sought to ensnare him.

Steeling himself, the Rathmian added, "I would have hated to depart without a farewell."

Behind her, Torion let a smile briefly escape. Burying it, he nodded to the Lady Nesardo. "I have to return to my headquarters, Salene. There's still much to clear up and many good men to replace . . ."

"Yes . . . Alec Mattheus among them."

"Indeed. And now that the bodies of the dead have all been given their final rest, we've got to get to work on rebuilding the city." He kissed her hand. "I will be around soon. There's much we need to discuss." To Zayl, he bid good-bye with, "Fare you well, sorcerer . . . and thank you."

The Rathmian bowed his head slightly. Only when he heard the general depart the house did he start to explain. "My work is done. It is time I moved on. There are other emanations I sense. The Balance is still threatened . . ."

Her eyes hardened. A look of determination filled her expression. "Then, I'm coming with you—"

"Your part is done, my lady. It was enough that you managed to use your gifts to bring us—*and* Sardak—back here before the last of the temple collapsed, and then insisted on taking care of my injuries. But enough is enough. It is time you lived life as most should. Your brother is but three days buried and—"

"And so my life *here* has concluded! There is nothing left for me but this building, which I care very little for now! Do you think that I can return to what I was after all that happened to—all that happened?"

The necromancer shook his head. "You *must* remain— for the good of the kingdom, if nothing else. Justinian needs guidance, and not merely from a loyal soldier like the general. He will need someone like you."

She opened her mouth to argue more, but could not. Yet, Salene did not entirely surrender. "He's a quick learner. He won't need such guidance long . . . and his father still watches over him . . . thanks to you."

Zayl said nothing, merely nodding his head. The shadow of Cornelius would guide his son for a time more before returning to his rest. Westmarch needed such stability, even if none would know the truth save Salene and Torion.

Determined to leave before matters got more compli-cated, the necromancer suddenly strode past Salene, mov-ing so swiftly that the Lady Nesardo had to give chase. She caught him just as he opened one of the great doors lead-ing out. Barnaby, whose duty it usually was to stand by for such a task, had not so curiously vanished just before the hooded spellcaster had come downstairs. Despite every-thing, the servants were still wary of the reputation of Zayl's kind.

"One more thing before you go," said the noblewoman, catching his *right* hand without any sign of aversion for what lay hidden in the glove.

He started to ask her what that one thing could be—and Salene kissed him lightly on the mouth.

When she pulled back, there was a hint of mischievousness in her smile. "A little color serves you well, 'Just Zayl.' "

The hooded figure bowed his head, then quickly stepped out into the security of the night. At the last moment, he blurted, "Farewell . . . Salene."

Tethered at the base of the outside steps was a fully laden horse, a horse once belonging to Sardak. Salene had insisted that Zayl accept the animal and what it carried, if nothing else. He had not argued with the gift. The animal and supplies would be needed where he was going.

The wind was strong, but the night was clear, for the first time since his arrival. Zayl worked at the bound reins, finding them for some reason more knotted than they should have been.

From the pouch at his side, a voice quietly said, "I'd wager my life—and afterlife—that she's still watchin' from the doorway, lad."

"It is no concern of ours, Humbart."

The skull let out a snort. "Oh, aye, I believe that as much as *you* do."

The knot finally loosened. Undoing the reins, Zayl leapt up into the saddle. As he did, he could not help but catch a glimpse of the doorway.

Humbart would have won his wager.

Pretending he had not seen her, Zayl urged the horse down the pathway to the gates. Not at all to his surprise, they already stood open, likely at General Torion's suggestion. The guard pointedly found some other direction to look as Zayl approached. The necromancer quickened his mount's pace.

But as he neared, Humbart muttered, "Look behind you, Zayl, lad. One last time."

He did . . . and saw that she still stood watching.

Although Zayl gave no hint of this to his companion, the skull chuckled. "Thought so."

The next moment, they rode past the anxious guard and through the gates. The darkness beckoned Zayl on, as ever, both companion and adversary to the necromancer.

And from across the estate of House Nesardo, a figure who resembled a mercenary with many faces but was so much more watched the necromancer and the woman he had just left.

They had been tested and had risen to that test. The watcher nodded. A pair with potential. True, he had aided a bit by guiding the Rathmian's night howler to where the creature could be the most help to the duo, but it had been through their efforts most of all that the evil had been vanquished.

It would be interesting to see how they fared when next brought together.

With that thought, he spread his fiery wings and, unseen by all, took to the sky.

ABOUT THE AUTHOR

Richard A. Knaak is the *New York Times* bestselling fantasy author of 29 novels and over a dozen short pieces, including *The Legend of Huma* and *Empire of Blood* for *Dragonlance* and *The Sundering* for *WarCraft*. He has also written the popular *Dragonrealm* series and several independent pieces. His works have been published in several languages, most recently Russian, Turkish, Bulgarian, Chinese, Czech, German, Hungarian, and Spanish. He has also adapted the Korean manga *Ragnarok*, published by Tokyopop.

Future works include *The God in the Moon*, first in the *Aquilonia Trilogy*, based on the worlds of Robert E. Howard. *Diablo* fans will be happy to know that Knaak has also agreed to write *The Sin War*—an epic trilogy that will explain much about the conflict. He has also contracted to do the three-volume *Ogre Titans* saga for *Dragonlance*—a sequel to his popular *Minotaur Wars*—and will be concluding *WarCraft: The Sunwell Trilogy* with *Ghostlands* for Tokyopop. In addition, he plans other works with the leading manga publisher.

Those wishing to find out more about his projects or who would like to join his e-mail list for announcements should visit his website at www.sff.net/people/knaak.